To Shatter the Night

MORE FROM KATHERINE QUINN

MISTLANDS

To Kill a Shadow

To Shatter the Night

KATHERINE QUINN

NEW YORK TIMES BESTSELLING AUTHOR

Entangled Publishing, LLC
644 Shrewsbury Commons Ave., STE 181
Shrewsbury, PA 17361
rights@entangledpublishing.com

Entangled Teen is an imprint of Entangled Publishing, LLC.

Visit our website at www.entangledpublishing.com.

Edited by Jen Bouvier and Justine Bylo
Cover design by LJ Anderson, Mayhem Cover Creations
Stock art by Polina Bottalova/Gettyimages, kathygold/Depositphotos,
EnvantoElements
Interior map art by Andrés Aguirre Jurado
Interior design by Toni Kerr
Interior formatting by Britt Marczak

Deluxe Hardcover ISBN: 978-1-64937-679-4
Ebook ISBN: 978-1-64937-489-9

Printed in China

First Edition December 2024

10 9 8 7 6 5 4 3 2 1

entangled teen
an imprint of Entangled Publishing LLC

Never stop climbing your way out of the darkness. Dawn is inevitable, and you are stronger than you believe.

And to Daniel, who reminds me every day there is joy to be found in each precious moment

To Shatter the Night is an epic romantic adventure about finding love in the darkness and bringing the light back to a dying realm. However, the story includes elements that may not be suitable for all readers, such as animal mauling, animal death, blood, death of a loved one, torture, whipping, near-drowning, breaking bones, and limb loss. Readers who may be sensitive to these elements, please take note.

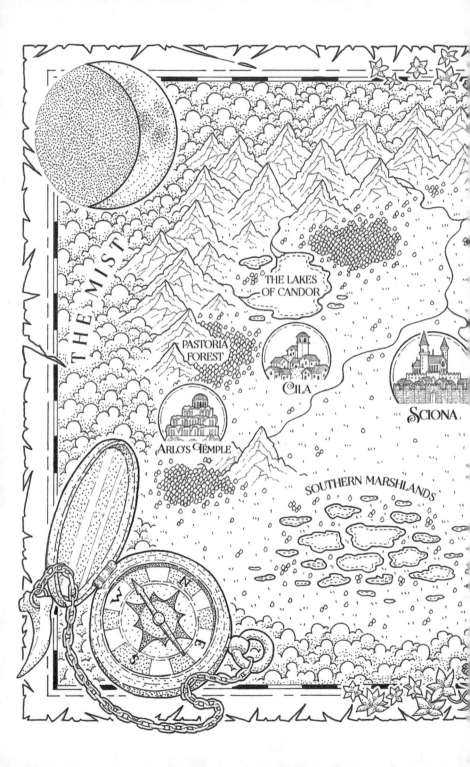

The day will be restored when the darkness falls for the light.

…

Or it's a bunch of rubbish and we'll all end up killing each other and the world will end.

There's a prophecy for you.

FOUND IN THE DIARY OF AURORA ADAIR, SUN PRIESTESS

Chapter One

Kiara

A woman came to us today. There was something about her that sent fire into my veins, and her eyes…bright amber eyes that reminded me of the sun we had just lost. She offered me her hand and told me her name was Rae, though I couldn't help but think it had been a lie.

Found in the diary of Juniper Marchant, Sun Priestess, year 1 of the curse

Jude Maddox, Commander of the Knights of the Eternal Star, thought he could play the sacrificing hero and abandon me in the Mist. Thought he could run from me.

As if I didn't enjoy the chase.

Jake and I followed Jude's trail until it vanished entirely, his tracks swept away by the wind.

It was quiet here. Eerily so. No masked men jumped out and attacked, none of Lorian's monstrous wolves lunged for our throats, and not a single living soul—winged or earthbound—dared approach.

We pressed on, the haze lessening the closer we drew to the border of Asidia. That didn't mean the danger had passed.

Our confidence was dwindling, but I was never one to quit

in the face of poor odds. Not when my broken heart ached and fury drove me. I'd been shunned before. Looked at like discarded rubbish. A cursed deviant to stay away from.

But that had been *before* him.

Jude's absence made the hollow pit in my chest expand, even if I knew he left because he believed I'd use the Godslayer blade on myself and give him the final piece of a goddess. It didn't matter; he should've known me better. *Trusted* me.

Now, all I ached to do was yell at him face to face.

Too bad he'd gotten a head start. I wasn't a patient person.

Something had changed since we left the clearing where I killed Patrick. The Mist was not as...docile. Perhaps Jake perceived the unnatural shift as well. We often traveled in uneasy silence through the thicker haze, barely able to breathe properly.

Days ago, we stumbled upon hoofprints leading northeast, and a flimsy hope bubbled to the surface; they could belong to Jude. He could've happened upon one of our lost mares and found his way out of this wretched place.

Knowing time wasn't on our side, we only stopped to rest or eat. I'd stumbled across a rare patch of edible shade berries. While not poisonous, they certainly tasted that way.

Any day now, maybe in mere hours, we'd reach the border and return to the realm Cirian ruled over with a heavy hand. I wasn't sure which was worse—being back under Cirian's thumb, or being stranded in the cursed lands where nightmares lived.

"He better not have lost the Godslayer," Jake grumbled at my side, his shoulders drooping from exhaustion. I'd done my best not to look too closely at him—every time I did, guilt churned in my stomach and I would hastily turn away. I was the reason he was in this mess. "With our luck, the king already captured him."

"So optimistic," I said, feigning a playfulness I knew would soothe Jake's nerves. "If Jude got captured that easily, then he's not the man I thought he was."

Jude was too damned stubborn to get caught so quickly. Besides, it would deflate his ego terribly. He was, after all, the formidable and dastardly assassin of the king.

I squinted at the skies, making out the barest hint of the northern star resting beside the blue-tinged moon. Out here, miles beyond the border, the moon was twice its size, battling to be seen amidst all the melancholy gray and spindly trees.

I hated how beautiful I found it. Whenever Jake settled down to rest, I'd take first watch, staring up at the moon's milky surface. In those moments, I wondered if Jude was looking at it, too. If he regretted abandoning us. *Me.*

My newest scar throbbed. The memory of the day it had been inflicted often caused my chest to warm with the oddest prickling sensation. Inches from where my heart thudded, the wound Jude had healed was raised and raw, a reminder of what we endured.

I ran gloved fingers across the jagged skin, a weak smile tugging at my lips. While I despised what Patrick had done, my scar connected to the commander in a way I couldn't decipher. I'd left my mark on him as well. Thin, twisting black vines covered his chest where I'd placed my power.

It was my brand, matching the scars on my hands left by the shadow beast.

"If Jude *were* smart, he would've killed you and reunited all three of Raina's keys when he had the chance," Jake said after a while. "*But…* I suppose you're much too charming to die. Such a shame."

Jake chased me out of that ill-fated clearing where I killed Patrick, the immortal who'd cursed Asidia with his greed. He'd once been a friend, but friends didn't stab one another in the chest.

Jake stood beside me since, dedicated to the cause, never hesitating to follow my lead. He didn't complain, nor did he stop.

Although, his devotion hardly meant I didn't *occasionally* have the urge to smack him.

"As much as I don't want to die, that *would* have been the easy choice," I admitted softly, trudging ahead. All the commander had to do was drive a dagger into my heart with a special god-crafted blade and release Raina's missing divinity from my chest.

"But simple choices are rarely the right ones," Jake said quietly, avoiding my gaze.

My brows scrunched. "When did you become so poetic?"

"Near-death experiences will change a man, Ki," he replied. "And I was always gifted with words."

"Only when you want to lure someone to your bed."

He shrugged. "It doesn't hurt—"

I stopped short, holding out a hand as the hairs on my nape rose. "Shhh," I warned.

Wisps of fog curled around me like a lover, traveling up from my boots to my thighs. I ground my teeth as a sudden spark of white light flashed across my vision. I blinked, willing it away— willing away my new *power*. It was terrifying and exhilarating all at the same time, that rush—and I feared its unknown strength more than anything else.

It was happening again.

The gloomy world sharpened. Became illuminated as if I'd dragged a gleaming fire just above the tops of the trees. One of Raina's gifts—her sight in the dark.

Her powers made a few appearances over the last couple of days. I didn't think I'd ever grow accustomed to it. To the peculiar sensation of the accompanying heat in my chest. Or how my shadows seemed to wither inside when her magic appeared. Almost like my darkness battled my light inside the confines of my own body.

It wasn't pleasant.

Dipping into a crouch, I snuck to the nearest tree, needle-like reeds poking through my trousers. Phantom fingers traced down my spine, and I shivered.

The Mist was hauntingly quiet, making it easy to hear...

Voices.

The hair on the back of my neck raised. Something was close. Or *someone.* My shadows seeped out of my pores without my notice, curling around me like they wished to shield.

"Now I'm frightened." Jake noted the shadows with a scowl. "They always appear when we're about to be attacked or killed."

He wasn't wrong.

Looking ahead, I glimpsed a flicker of movement. A shift of a cloak. Long, curly black hair.

"See that?" I tilted my chin. It appeared to be two figures standing close together, but the thicket made everything difficult to see. I led the way forward, hoping for a better vantage point. The farther I went, the more my shadows tightened around my chest.

A woman with brown skin and tight leathers came into view. On instinct, I grabbed Jake, pushing him beside me and behind a tree. The wide trunk shielded us.

"Cirian is nothing!" the woman said. "It's the Moon God we must worry about. He's out of control. If he's not stopped, he'll destroy the day. If he kills those two, then all will be lost."

Destroy the day. I stifled my gasp. If the Moon God actually wished to rule over the world, he obliterated the hope of the sun ever returning.

"He will try to find Maddox first," a deep growl of a man's voice answered. "He's in Fortuna now."

"But he *should* be trying to break into the Moon God's temple, not wandering aimlessly around Fortuna like a fool," the woman added under her breath.

"Before Kiara killed that little weasel, he told me the moonstone does exist. That it cannot only summon the ancient bastard, but *trap* him. Then Jude can use the blade to turn him mortal."

If that were true...it changed everything.

I grimaced before peeking around the tree. The man wore a furred hood that covered most of his features, but he had a strong chin, and his build was that of a bear's.

"Listen, Lorian," the woman said with a sigh. "I don't want to be involved any more than you do, but he's stealing our damned powers, and I can barely manage to travel, let alone control a single godsdamn soldier. We have to warn the chosen ones that Cirian isn't the only one out for them."

Lorian. God of Beasts and Prey.

I turned to Jake, and he mouthed, "*Holy fucking shit.*"

Lorian grumbled a curse. "Then you do it," he said. "I got involved already and nearly killed Raina's grandson. I say let them figure it out."

"Can you just be agreeable for once, you stubborn man?" the woman snipped, a hand going to her hip. I narrowed my eyes, picking up on her lithe physique. She appeared a warrior, through and through, covered in fighting leathers, and the glinting of metal shined in the dim light.

"I'm usually agreeable. You just make it difficult."

"I swear, if I could kill you, I would," she threatened, shaking her head. "I—"

Behind me, a twig snapped. The sound seemed to echo throughout the woods, and the pair arguing glanced up. I glared at Jake, who merely averted his eyes in reply.

"Someone's here." The woman unsheathed a sword at her belt. Slowly, she glanced around.

Fuck. Whoever she was, she spoke with a god. And probably

was one…

Lorian sniffed the air like a beast before his shoulders drooped, losing some of their tension. "It's just them, Maliah. Kiara and the loud one."

"Rude," Jake whisper-hissed beneath his breath.

Maliah. Goddess of Revenge and Redemption. My idol since I was a child. Instantly, unwelcomed butterflies stormed my stomach.

"Come out!" she called, sheathing her sword. "We know you're here, and I really don't feel like chasing you at the moment."

Jake and I exchanged glances. "We're already knocking on death's door. Why not chat with a couple of angry gods for a minute?" he said, sarcasm lacing every syllable.

I rolled my eyes but stepped out from behind the tree, my hands raised.

Maliah and Lorian froze as I approached, my knees trembling from the thought of standing before two powerful immortals.

"Eavesdropping is rude, you know." Maliah crossed her arms.

This close, her beauty was beyond anything belonging to this plane, her brown skin practically glowing in the moonlight, her hair a lustrous crown of shimmering curls. Covered in head-to-toe leather, a various assortment of gleaming weapons strapped to her toned body, the woman was nothing if not a threat. Beneath her clothing, I could make out every ripple of her toned muscles. She quirked a brow, drawing attention to dazzling green irises that gleamed with mischief. Gods, even the moon seemed to shine solely on her.

Shit, I was focusing entirely on the wrong things.

Jake's footsteps sounded behind me. I secretly hoped he would stay hidden.

"I didn't mean to eavesdrop," I protested. "We happened to

hear voices, and—"

"Decided to listen in?" Maliah dropped her hand from her hip. "Of course, it's *you*." She shot a pointed look to Lorian, who still refused to lower his hood. All I could make out was that stubbled chin.

Inside, a voice screamed at me to run. Any sensible person would. But my beast clawed at my insides, aching to be freed. Tingles shot through my gloved hands, drawing my focus down to where wisps of black smoke danced shyly at my fingertips, pulsing in time with my enraged heartbeat.

The dark was so much easier to succumb to than the light.

It felt safer.

Destroy her, the night whispered in my head, the voice both my own and that of a stranger.

I tensed. I'd always believed the night to speak, but never so clearly.

The goddess cocked her head, appraising me in a way that left me feeling lacking. When she eased closer, moving like a serpent in the grass, I instinctively raising my dagger in warning. The act earned me a rumbling laugh.

"You realize that pathetic knife won't hurt me, right? Only Arlo's Godslayer can." Darkness stormed in her green eyes at the mention of the God of Earth and Soil—a man I once presumed to be my uncle.

Arlo hadn't been much help in the Mist, and certainly not after Jude's abandonment. If I ever saw him again, we'd have words. Or, more accurately, we'd speak with our blades.

"My apologies." I bit my tongue and hurriedly shoved my knife into its sheath before frowning. "Why are you in these woods?"

It all felt too...coincidental for my liking. After so much betrayal, it would be hard to trust again.

"We're near Fortuna," Lorian replied for them both. "Raina's descendant is there."

Maliah shoved at his chest, though he didn't budge an inch. "Don't tell her that! Then she'll go there. If they're in the same place, it'll be easier for Cirian and his master to catch them. And that blade *cannot* fall into their hands."

"We're going for Jude regardless." I spoke before thinking. As usual. A trait I seriously needed to work on. But I refused to abandon Jude like he'd done me. Because that's what it felt like: abandonment. I wanted to both pull him close and smack him at the same time.

Maliah pointed an accusatory finger at me. "Told you she would do something rash, Lorian. *She's* the wild card." She faced me, her gaze taut with frustration. "You need to go to the Moon God's temple, not find the boy. That can come after."

"No. I won't wait." What the hells was wrong with my mouth?

"Let her try," Lorian offered on our behalf. "She might get there in time before Cirian sends his men."

My pulse thudded at my throat. Guards were going to search Fortuna, and Lorian insinuated it would be soon. I had to get to Jude first. He couldn't be captured. Tortured. He'd been through enough. I might be furious with him, but I'd do everything in my power to prevent him from enduring more pain.

"Fine." Maliah waved her hands in the air. "But after you get your commander, go to the temple. Lorian over here learned something that might interest you."

He sighed in blatant exasperation. "There's a moonstone there that can trap the god. If you find it, then you must turn the Godslayer on him to turn him mortal. I have it on good authority that the moonstone will not only lure him, but trap his divinity as well. All that needs to happen after is someone to claim the pieces of divinity and take his position." I couldn't see his eyes, but I *felt* them sear into my skin.

I turned to see the shocked look on Jake's face. We both

knew this was bigger than we imagined—to confine his power and keep the kingdom from succumbing to eternal day. "Care to lend a hand?" I quipped, the shadows rolling up my frame at my command, the frail branches of the trees shuddering. The goddess' attention drifted to the trembling leaves above my head, her brows scrunching. Then her stare took in my magic, her lips twisting in reply.

"I just did," she said, jaw tense as if I'd insulted her. "Do you truly think us that indifferent?"

Yes, I'd *often* thought them to be indifferent. It felt unfair that all of this lay upon our shoulders. Hells, I hadn't even known our true enemy until Jude's note warned me that others besides Patrick sought us. Sought *me*.

"Lorian cannot shift, just as I do not retain the same influence over warriors that I once held. I can't command armies with a single thought or guide the minds of the vengeful and ruthless." She glanced to the many polished blades at her belt, avoiding my stare. I had the suspicion it was shame she tried to hide, and a wave of pity struck me—she was so unlike the notorious goddess I'd placed on a pedestal. "If you find a way to free our powers from whatever spell the Moon God is casting, then myself and the other deities will be free to help you bring back the sun. *Preferably* without killing you."

Oh, I'd like that very much.

Lorian lifted his chin, releasing a piercing whistle. The noise sliced at my eardrums, forcing me to cover my head. When his call ended, I lowered my arms, looking at him curiously. He merely stared back.

A minute later, a spotted jaguar strode into the clearing.

"Seeing as you're risking everything, I'm assigning protection until you reach the city," he said in that deep tone of his. "Brax, here, will be an excellent guard on your travels."

The giant beast prowled closer, and it took everything

within me not to bolt. His claws alone could rip the flesh from my bones. Behind me, Jake made a whimpering sound. I was surprised he'd been so quiet this entire time.

"Thank you?" I said it like a question, unsure of what else to say.

"We must go," Lorian said, nodding to Maliah. "If we stay in one place for too long, he'll find us."

I opened my mouth to ask more, but a brilliant haze of cobalt blue and fiery red whirled together, the colors dancing. They encircled the immortals, winding up their bodies and covering the tops of their heads.

Jake grabbed my hand, squeezing tight as we watched two of the strongest gods, even with diminished powers, vanish before our eyes.

Leaving us with...Brax.

"Hells. Now we're stuck with the damned jaguar," Jake groused. The creature's tongue poked out as he eyed Jake. "And he better stop gawking at me like that."

"He won't hurt you," I said at the same time my shadows coiled out, at the ready, should my flimsy promise fail. A rush of energy surged, and I all but floated in place, my skin itching once more, pulled taut.

"We weren't meant to hear that conversation, but we did." I looked to my friend. "We're close to Fortuna. Close to Jude. Once we tell him what we've learned, he better get ahold of his damned senses and come with us."

"That man has never had senses. Especially when it comes to you," Jake supplied, and I couldn't help but agree.

My hurt from earlier returned.

Both my light and shadow magic reacted to my emotions— the shadows so easily riled when distraught. It had become so deeply embedded in my core that I feared it would respond with the barest hint of anger before I could wrangle it back. I shut my eyes and exhaled slowly, evenly. I had to be calm, find my center, and learn how to command both forces before they eventually destroyed me. Thinking of Jude didn't help matters.

"I pray this talisman does what Lorian claims. We alone won't be able to kill a god, not when it took Jude and me both to end Patrick's life." I shook my head, needing to move in order to release some of my pent-up frustration. "And he wasn't nearly as great of a threat."

A part of me wished to run and find Jude and never look back, to leave this plague of a mission behind. We could have a good life, maybe, tucked away in some small town, become new people without the burden of saving Asidia on our shoulders.

I wished I could be selfish. I *wanted* to be so badly.

Jake met my stare, a silent conversation passing between us. Slowly, the uncertainty left his eyes, and the confidence he typically wore like a shield fell back into place.

We were doing this. Together.

"Never in my life did I expect this," he said, motioning to where the gods once stood. "But I'm glad I'm experiencing it all with you."

I looked away. "Stop. You're making me want to hug you," I said, the urge strong.

Jake laughed. "*Oh, no*. Not a *hug*. Although I *have* earned one…"

"So dramatic," I teased, shoving playfully at his chest. He grinned and ruffled my already tangled hair.

"Well, come on, then. Let's go get your commander," Jake said. "Once we have Jude, we'll arm ourselves the best we can. We may not be the ideal band of heroes, but you, me, and Jude are all this sorry kingdom has."

"Eloquent," I said with a snort. But the vision of me fighting alongside them flashed across my mind.

Shadows curled at my fingertips, but within my chest, a

small spark of warmth flared at the thought of Jude. It tended to do that, Raina's gift, whenever Jude's face flitted across my mind. Her power was made of fire and hope and passion. I wondered which magic of mine would show itself when I found him. Jude shouldn't fear the jaguar at my back or the god set on our destruction.

He should fear me. Because I was coming to Fortuna, and I was coming for him.

CHAPTER TWO

JUDE

It is a mystery as to why the gods hid after the disappearance of the sun goddess. Some say they are cursed, just like our lands, while others believe they are afraid. Though of what is not certain.

EXCERPT FROM ASIDIAN LORE: A TALE OF THE GODS

The Sly Fox was as rowdy as ever.

A band struck up a merry tune on the center stage, and drinkers swayed while clutching their full mugs of ale. The place reeked of sweat and drink and bad decisions.

"Oh, no, not today!" Finn groaned when he saw me approach.

I'd been forced to come here every day since I'd arrived in the city, and every day, I was turned away. Seeing *that woman* was the only solution I had at the moment. She had knowledge, and she refused to see me.

It was risky showing up in such a crowded establishment when my face was plastered on wanted posters throughout Fortuna. I'd lived in relative anonymity as King Cirian's assassin, but now, my likeness was everywhere. I loathed it.

How the king even knew I was alive and not dead in the Mist remained a mystery.

The hulking bodyguard stood before a red door leading to the Fox's study, where she was no doubt hiding from me. The woman hadn't shown her face in her own tavern since I'd come seeking aid. If I didn't know any better, I'd say she found me a threat.

"As I've told you the last five times, the Mistress will not see you, and she certainly doesn't have what you claim." Finn crossed both arms, his forearms like tree trunks. "As an upstanding citizen of Fortuna, she—"

I waved a hand to stop him before he embarrassed himself. He'd given that same speech many times over, but everyone in the entire realm knew just how *upstanding* the infamous thief truly was.

"We both know what she keeps behind that locked and heavily guarded door, and if anyone has what I need, it's her."

She had robbed every city in Asidia, selling secrets, ancient texts, and classified information as easily as jewels. She left a single claw mark after each heist, which wasn't exactly subtle. But I was here for information…and there was also the little conversation we'd yet to have. One that was nineteen years in the making.

I glowered at Finn, the seven-foot-tall, three-hundred-pound bodyguard smirking before me like a king ruling over a kingdom of thieves and cutthroats.

"Regardless of what you believe"—Finn leaned closer, his voice a throaty rasp—"you won't get help from her. She's been through enough, and you are a complication she doesn't need. One I won't allow to hurt her further."

Hurt *her*?

We were inches apart. His heated breath was fanning across my cheeks, his lips pulled up in a snarl. I recognized that look on his face, the defensiveness. How quickly his mask had slipped.

He might care for her, but I still wouldn't bow. I had

someone I, too, cared for.

"Tell the Fox I'm not leaving Fortuna," I warned, lowering my voice to a menacing rumble. One didn't need to raise their voice to deliver a threat. Isiah taught me that. "She either sees me or…" I stepped closer, allowing Finn time to inspect the now-infamous scars marking my face. "I will be forced to share some things the Fox would rather be kept secret."

Me.

Finn's eyes flickered to the blade strapped to my belt as I pulled away.

It wasn't the Godslayer. I wasn't careless enough to keep it on my person, and as the good commander I'd been trained to be, I had prepared a backup plan…however flimsy it was. Still, a sheen of sweat lined his deep brown skin. Maybe he wasn't as immune to me as I believed.

Finn's nostrils flared. "I'll relay the message, *again*, but if you step out of line and make any attempts to harm my mistress, know you'll have to face me first." He was loyal to a fault, a rarity in this place. I wondered how the Fox had garnered such devotion.

I stared a beat longer, watching as another bead of perspiration slid down his temple, gliding over a tattoo of a detached claw inking the right side of his face.

The mark of the Fox. Of my mother.

I dipped my chin in understanding, though we both knew this was far from over. Spinning on a heel, I crept deeper into the tavern and to the end of the bar. When Finn's attention was averted, captured by a man wearing an obnoxious orange coat, I slipped out my blade. The counter was riddled with cuts and stains, so when I carved my initials onto the side of the bar—along with an uneven crescent moon—I doubted anyone would pay it heed.

Kiara would know. If I ever got caught, she'd know I was

here, and maybe by that time, I would have convinced the Fox to help.

Slipping my dagger back into its sheath, I stood before the bartender could shuffle my way. Shoving open the doors, I braced myself for the blast of cold. It stung my cheeks after being inside the tavern's warmth.

With a grimace, I tugged my hood low over my eyes and strolled through the corrupt underbelly of Fortuna. I hated this city, which reeked of all the things I detested about humankind.

Not that I particularly liked many people to begin with.

The thunderous shouts of lively peddlers advertising their wares echoed from every direction of the main square. Some promoted fake cures for incurable ailments, while others offered illegal drugs or drinks that could transport you to a new world where reality couldn't touch you.

For once, I was tempted, but I needed to stay alert.

I was grateful that the scowling patrons ignored me, scurrying by in their thick, woolen cloaks, their necks protected by heavy, patterned scarves that concealed the lower halves of their faces.

Unlike most cities in Asidia, once they shed their layers, I'd find dresses and tailored suits of lively colors and designs. Rich brocade and velvet. Elaborate top hats of satin. Plunging necklines and shorter hemlines. People exposed copious amounts of skin, reveling in the sin of the flesh. Their kohl-lined eyes and painted lips were brazen and seductive.

While this was a place I had no desire to stay, I couldn't deny there was an exciting freedom here that was absent from any other region in the realm. Perhaps because Cirian had yet to stake his claim on it.

The stable I rented for Starlight came into view on my left, and before I thought better of it, my feet were moving in her direction.

Orion, the young stable hand manning the entrance, tipped his red checkered cap to me upon arrival. I kept my hood low, not trusting the lad to keep his mouth shut and collect a reward for turning us in.

"She's been cranky all day," he complained, scrubbing a muddied hand across his face, grimy streaks left in his wake. "None of the boys can settle her."

She probably missed Kiara.

So do you, you fool. My pulse hammered at my throat at the very thought of her. But now wasn't the time to wallow.

Orion directed me inside and unlocked the largest stable.

He waved an impatient hand to the last stall. I flipped him a stolen coin in thanks. I hadn't wanted to rob men of their coin purses, but I'd been desperate, and some of the bastards deserved it; I didn't take too kindly to those who treated others they deemed below them poorly.

An agitated neigh sounded from her pen, and I peered inside, finding Starlight rearing on her hind legs, clearly not pleased with the cramped quarters.

"Shhh, girl," I cooed, holding out placating hands. "It's just me, old broad." I used Kiara's nickname for the beast, and at the sound of it, Starlight settled on all four legs. Though her eyes narrowed as if she were glowering.

This was no ordinary horse. My suspicions had grown since she'd found me in the Mist, no wound on her belly from when the masked men—or the *undead* men—first struck her with an arrow. She *should* have been dead.

Bringing my hand to her nose, I let her sniff me before I brushed my palm across her side. "It won't be long," I whispered. "As soon as I get the answers we need, we'll find her."

Starlight nickered.

"You don't believe me?" I asked, drawing back to peer into her eyes. "You know I miss her, too." I said that last part softly.

Admitting it out loud cracked the mask I compelled myself to wear.

With a huff, the mare pushed forward, resting her head on top of my shoulder. I continued to shush her, rubbing at her coat.

The connection between us grew with every touch. It felt natural to be astride her, familiar in an impossible way. Then again, nothing was impossible; I was Raina's *descendant*, for fuck's sake.

"I hate to leave you, but I can't stay too long," I murmured after fifteen minutes had passed. "Hopefully the next time I see you, we'll be leaving this place."

Starlight grunted once more when I broke eye contact. At the door to her pen, I stopped.

Before I thought better of it, I tossed a red matchbook to the side of her enclosure. A claw and ale symbol was embossed in gold on the sides, the sigil for The Sly Fox Tavern. This wasn't the first time I'd left a clue for Kiara to find should I be captured and she needed help. Help the Fox better offer soon.

My initials were now carved into the bar at The Sly Fox, as I suspected she'd scour all the taverns for word of my presence. At the gambling den, The Rolling Dice, a portrait of a blossoming green field hung in the main room, its flowers reminiscent of the ones found in our glen. If you looked closely enough, you'd see where the parchment folded up, leaving just enough space to slip a note between the art and the frame. A note that simply read, *Sly Fox Tavern*.

I hadn't signed it, but Kiara would recognize my handwriting.

I whispered my goodbyes to Starlight, my stomach tying itself into knots as I left the stables.

If anyone had told me a couple of months ago that I would be feeling guilty for leaving a horse, I'd have laughed in their face. Then again, I would've laughed had they said I'd meet a vulgar, sarcastic, violent, and stunning woman who'd steal my heart.

Isiah was probably chuckling from the realm of the dead. My fingers traced my old knight's pin. It wasn't the one that Kiara took from his dead body, but it symbolized our brotherhood. The cold metal was a comforting weight in my pocket. I never realized he was my closest friend until I lost him.

Back in the frenzy of the main boulevard, I stole past a few beggars and a flurry of children playing with a tattered deck of cards. A group had gathered to watch, some onlookers placing bets.

As if the people sensed who walked among them, the crowd parted, permitting me room to slip through the tangling bodies and down a vacant avenue lit up by muted sunfires.

A bookshop and a curtained-off tea house had their signs set to *open*, though the latter sold anything *but* tea. I had a decent idea what wares were sold inside, judging by the man who'd just left it, the top buttons of his trousers undone, and a dazed yet exuberant expression on his ruddy face.

The bells jingled as I opened the door to the bookshop. The only acknowledgment from the burly proprietor sitting at his desk was a single indignant grunt. He'd been paid handsomely to keep his mouth shut. As far as he was concerned, I was a ghost.

I crept through the stacks of books and dusty shelves, making my way to the back of the store, where a wooden staircase led up to the owner's suites.

There wasn't a sunfire in sight, but I'd grown up in the darkness, and it was as much a friend to me as my blade. Still, being alone now, cloaked in night's eternal shade somehow felt... heavier than before.

Past the dingy bathing chamber with its chipped porcelain tub were my humble quarters. I slid the long copper key into the lock and eased inside, bolting and securing it behind me.

While I hadn't lived in the lap of luxury at the palace, at least

I'd been afforded a decent bed. Here, a cot had been shoved into a corner on the floor, the cotton blankets moth-eaten and stained with gods knew what. Aside from the mattress, the space could only accommodate a modest armoire, one door barely hanging on.

No one had discovered me yet, but safety was an illusion— no matter where I went, Cirian would search for me. The wanted posters were proof of that.

Our original group of recruits and knights should've returned to Sciona by now, and if Cirian didn't believe I'd died in the Mist, he'd suspect I'd defected...which I had. The penance for deserting was death, but I imagined he had other plans for me, ones that were far, far worse than a sliced throat. Somehow, some way, he *knew* I lived.

He'd never get the Godslayer, and that gave me hope.

Dropping onto the mattress with a groan, I shrugged out of my cloak and jacket before bringing my hands to rest on my knees. The silence taunted me more than the screams echoing in my nightmares. Whenever I shut my eyes, I heard her voice and glimpsed her face contorting in agony as Patrick's blade pierced her skin.

Kiara. She was both a gift and a curse, and the thoughts not devoted to my plan were dedicated to her ethereal image. I couldn't help it, and I'd long ago ceased to try. Instantly, heat curled within me.

A headache formed between my brows, and I let my head fall onto the stained mattress. Outside, soft rain pattered against the thin plane of the window, its steady melody coaxing me into a much-needed sleep. It had been days since I'd truly shut my eyes and rested.

Before exhaustion finally won, I allowed myself to envision luscious red hair and amber eyes filled with fire. In this waking dream, I wound my arms around her body and tugged her close, inhaling the scent that was distinctly hers.

But the thing about pretending was that it never lived up to the real thing.

. . .

I woke to the sound of furious knocking.

Instantly, I was on my feet, my blade poised. The shopkeeper knew not to come anywhere near my room, so it couldn't be him, which meant—

Shit. I snagged my jacket and cloak and raced to the window facing the back alley. A heartbeat later and the pounding ceased.

Just as I leapt onto the metal ledge outside my room, the door flung open, the wood shattering and splintering. I caught sight of three armed men wearing the crimson of the King's Guard, silver helmets covering their heads.

Cirian's men.

"Stop!" one of them shouted, but I was already dropping from the second story and onto the street below. My boots barely made a sound when I landed in a crouch.

I peeked over my shoulder before taking off into a run, finding one of them waving wildly out the window. His oafish comrades were likely sprinting down the steps to give chase.

All traces of sleep were gone, replaced with welcomed adrenaline.

Failure wasn't an option.

If my life was the only one on the line, I would've faced them all and hopefully left a slaughter in my wake. But there were people relying on me now. People who cared if I lived or died. Such a burden their love had become, and yet I carried it tightly.

Not to mention the lives of an *entire* realm.

I snagged the timepiece from my jacket pocket, noting it to be three in the morning. Even now, the city thrived with drunken revelers, and it wasn't hard to slip into the masses, secure my hood in place, and blend in.

Slowing, I attempted an easy gait, my pulse hammering and sweat slicking my brow. I'd been found sooner than I expected, and without a clue as to how to save Kiara from an untimely end, we were both screwed.

The truth was, I should've known better than to linger here. My pride had gotten in the way, my need to show my mother I wasn't some child she could toss aside again. Not that it mattered to her in the end. People didn't change, no matter how much their actions could tear at the scraps of your heart.

Seeing as I couldn't return to The Sly Fox, I continued down one of the larger streets, passing by a couple of the more modest gambling dens teeming with patrons.

Shouts rose at my back, but I didn't run.

Instead, I ventured into The Rolling Dice, moving through the packed red velvet-lined tables and through the throngs of warm bodies surrounding them.

My shoulder collided with a woman wearing a crimson overcoat, the impact causing her to lose her grip on her tray. Full drinks went soaring in the air before landing on patrons, who cursed as they furiously wiped at their drenched clothing. I was already at the kitchen's entrance by the time the waitress scanned the room for the offender.

Cooks waved their hands in irritation as I rushed by their prep stations, and a few of the servers spared me curious glances—though none stopped me as I sprinted toward the door leading to the alley.

The brisk northern air struck my face with surprising force, the wind shoving my hood down and exposing my easily identifiable face. I yanked it back in place, thankful that not many people milled about. Most were hidden away inside the tents that lined the alley. I craned my neck, homing in on a green tent I had recently purchased. I'd bought it after the lad had agreed to my terms. Maybe I just hadn't liked the sight of a young child shivering in the cold while others indulged in petty excess.

It was time to employ my backup plan.

Kiara would be clever enough to locate my whereabouts. She wouldn't stop until she cornered me and had the pleasure of telling me off to my face. I had to hope she was on her way here if she wasn't in the city already.

I pulled open the flap and dropped to a crouch.

As I expected, the little bastard instantly shot up from his restless sleep, a crooked knife held in his small hand, his green eyes bleary.

Good lad. He had decent survival skills.

"It's time," I barked. I tossed him the pouch at my waist. "When she comes, deliver the package."

Before the child could argue, I was shooting halfway across the alley and slipping into the crowd. Not one precious second could be wasted.

The street urchin I found on my third day in Fortuna held my future in his hands—*all* of our futures. Along with the rest of my coin. I prayed I'd been right about him and that he'd come through instead of simply stealing my money.

I *had* to believe he would.

While his clothes were torn and threadbare, he possessed one thing of value: a shiny pendant of Raina. When I spotted him in the crowd, he tilted his chin and boldly met my stare. The unnatural heat I was becoming more familiar with had flowed through my veins in those precious moments we locked eyes. That was when I'd placed my life in the slippery hands of fate. It felt…right. Like the very heavens guided me.

With the boy in my thoughts, I headed toward the wagons preparing to leave the city. I had to get out of Fortuna and into the safety of the surrounding wood.

Merchants loaded up their wares, barking orders at their apprentices to hurry before the new day came. I eyed an open wagon transporting barrels of ale, a thick flap of blue linen tied over the sides to conceal the merchandise. *There.* That would be my way out, and once through the gates, I'd slip into the night.

While the owner was busy tending to his horse, I crawled below the tarp and beyond the containers of ale, careful not to rest my weight in one place. Any sound would give me away.

Shoving behind a barrel, I focused on keeping my breathing even.

The wagon took off five minutes later, and the tension tightening my shoulders lessened.

It was working; I was escaping Fortuna and on my way out of the city. My next plan would be to locate one of the sun priestesses of the past. Maybe they had information.

The cart jostled, the wooden wheels striking every nook in the cobblestone street. I leaned back, cramped and uncomfortable.

"Halt!"

I froze, every muscle rigid. We should've made it to the gates by now.

Boots struck the ground, and my throat constricted as they grew louder. They headed my way.

Rustling sounded. The tarp was whipped off.

"Well, look what we have here."

Hands encircled my ankles, and I was dragged through the barrels, a cry trapped in my throat. Those same hands held me down, and before I could even lift my blade or see the face of my attackers, a steel-toed boot raised over my head.

CHAPTER THREE

KIARA

I know you were sent into the Mist weeks ago, but I haven't heard a single word of your return. If anyone could go into the cursed lands and live to tell the tale, it would be you. Meaning, you're alive and hiding out somewhere for deserting. I'm not foolish enough to wait for you to contact me, but I also won't just sit around.

AN UNMAILED LETTER FROM LIAM FREY TO HIS SISTER, KIARA FREY, YEAR 50 OF THE CURSE

We breached the outskirts of Fortuna a few hours later. Slipping past the Patrol had been easy, as most of them had been face-deep in a glass of ale. I couldn't blame them. If I had been sentenced to their lowly ranks, I'd be drunk off my ass, too.

Brax stalked us like a shadow through the trees, prompting Jake to steal nervous peeks over his shoulder, the muscles in his neck straining.

"You're gonna hurt yourself if you keep doing that," I warned.

Jake shot me an incredulous look. "You're telling me you're totally fine turning your back on *that*?"

He had a point.

"I'm not. But Maliah and Lorian seemed to be speaking the truth. As much as I hate to admit it"—I pushed confidence into my tone—"I'd say the gods need us more than we need them."

Jake grumbled. "I will say, when I was recruited for the Knights, mingling with the divine wasn't what I pictured. I blame you."

"Fair enough," I said, shooting him a wry grin. "But we're lucky that Fortuna isn't well-guarded, so we have that going for us." A small mercy.

I motioned for Jake to stop as the towering wooden gates to the city came into view. Fortuna flickered like an erratic candle in a storm, resting at the foot of the hill we'd just ascended.

"Hey, since we're here, I wouldn't suppose you'd be fine with me taking a turn at the tables?" Jake cocked a questioning brow, an impish gleam igniting in his eyes. I'd missed that spark. "I'm rather exceptional at dice if I do say so myself, and we have traveled far…"

He wanted to gamble. While we had a price on our heads. Of course he did.

"You've never mentioned that skill, which is surprising since you brag about everything else you're mildly accomplished at." I shuddered, recalling all the many, many *private* details he'd shared.

Jake shrugged, but pride puffed out his chest. "I have loads of skills you don't know about. And not *all* of them are related to bedding handsome men."

Yep. There it was.

"So humble. I pity the poor boys you've lured with those crystal-blue eyes of yours," I teased. "Maybe one day you'll find someone that makes you give up your playboy ways."

Jake's features wrinkled into a look of disgust. "Doubtful, Ki, but keep on dreaming. That boy would have to check off every damn item on my list."

"I'm sure it's long," I said, although from what I'd learned, Jake didn't appear to have a type other than "breathing."

"You'd be surprised," Jake said, not blinking an eye at my sarcasm. "Cute but intelligent. Bold but gentle. And he can't be funnier than me."

"So, no sense of humor, then?"

Jake nudged me. Hard. "Pettiness isn't a good look on you, Ki."

"I'm just being honest." I tapped his nose, and he scowled. "At least you're handsome."

That seemed to ease him, and his lips twitched as he suppressed a smile. Flattery was the surest way to his heart.

Jake and I fell into a comfortable silence as we scouted the gates.

We'd grown attuned to each other, able to sense when one of us required a distraction from the thoughts running wild in our heads. He took care not to mention Jude and instead supplied me with stories—too many—of his life back in his village of Tulia.

My favorite being the one where he and Nic dressed the town's statue of Arlo in ridiculously large hats for a month straight, much to the officials' annoyance. Apparently, Arlo had looked rather dashing in a violet ensemble with tulle and dyed yellow feathers.

"I say we just wing it and enter," Jake said.

Images of Arlo dressed in—gods forbid—bright *colors* vanished from my head.

Jake crossed his arms. "I mean, if Cirian and his guards haven't come this way, then—"

"Wait, what's that?" I pointed to the woods, the sound of hoofbeats growing louder by the second. Flames illuminated the leaves as a horde of men emerged from the woods, torches carried in their black leather gloves. They were all carefully concealed beneath thick hoods, but I glimpsed a flash of red below one untied cloak. I grimaced as their leader shouted orders, riders hastening to comply.

The King's Guard.

"I'm counting two dozen," Jake supplied in a rush, crouching in a gathering of reeds. I copied his pose. There wasn't much cover, and if any of the soldiers looked hard enough, they'd probably spot us.

"We need to find him *now*. Before they do. I know he's there." As though to confirm, my scar warmed. It ached now and again, the Godslayer Blade having forever left its mark. "If the king abducts Jude, and Cirian is the Moon God's pawn, we'll lose before we even begin."

"As if we aren't already at a disadvantage."

"Screwed or not, we've got to hurry," I encouraged, already bursting into action and racing down the far end of the hill and away from the main gate tower. I prayed the guards wouldn't turn their heads, but I was covered in enough filth that they might not spot me. I spared a peek over my shoulder, finding two blue eyes glinting in the night. Brax remained on the outskirts, standing watch.

I shivered as I flung my hood over my head and quickly tucked my red hair out of sight. Jake sprinted to keep up as we reached the wooden walls, out of breath and panting.

To our left, the King's Guard soared through the gates, receiving only withering looks from the half-awake watchers stationed atop the walls.

Cirian didn't have many friends in the north. Fortuna and the cities surrounding it acted like kingdoms of their own, able to take care of themselves without the king's aid.

I grabbed Jake and wrapped my arm around his waist, tugging him closer to the entrance. We could be two lovers in search of rest or some gambling for the night. The guards wouldn't know unless they'd been instructed to find us and given our descriptions. I relied on the chance they hadn't.

Jake stiffened when we came into view of the gates, but when I made a theatrical show of nuzzling into his chest, the watchers we approached paid us little note.

Like I'd prayed, they saw us as nothing but a harmless pair in search of a little drink and fun. No one looked twice. They were too busy focusing on the guards, who were parting the crowded streets like a crimson plague.

Through the gates, we came into the main square of the city, which was ten times the size of Cila's. Packed with colorful vendor carts and exuberantly dressed magicians and contortionists, it would have been a splendid scene of enchantment, if not for the fear washed across the faces of the masses as they took in the storming soldiers.

People—who'd been playfully roaming the avenue before—now ran, trampling over others in their haste to get away. In a blink, Fortuna became a place of horrifying chaos.

The guards shouted, some hopping off their horses and immediately snatching citizens, pulling them close to their faces and screaming. I couldn't make out the words, but I bet it had to do with Jude, especially when I looked to my right.

I nudged Jake, pointing at a wanted poster tacked to a lamppost. It was a crude drawing of Jude, the artist turning his full lips into a scowl. Below, it read, *Reward for capture. Alive.*

"At least Cirian wants him alive," Jake said with a grimace.

Regardless, his face was now known, and anyone who spotted him here might very well give him up for the right price.

Someone bumped into Jake's shoulder, causing him to stumble. He managed to right himself and, still holding on to my arm, pulled me into the closest alley as pandemonium unfolded.

A man shrieked as the crowd knocked him to his knees,

barely rolling over before a steed trampled him, the blows from its hooves killing him instantly. The guard atop the horse snickered, spitting at a stunned stranger before jerking the reins and aiming deeper into the city.

Another soldier whistled at a woman passing by, shouting crude words that made her scurry away in more than fear for her life. When she vanished, he resumed his assault on other victims, cursing at their backs when they ignored his vile language.

"Disgusting," Jake spat, restraining me from racing into the streets and tearing the offending guard from his horse.

My nails bit into my palms hard enough to draw blood.

Rage simmered within me as painted doors were kicked open, the intricate carvings etched onto the frames ruined by steel-toed boots. The King's Guard rushed into dwellings and shops, tearing apart homes and livelihoods as if they had every right.

Men and women and children shuffled into the streets wearing nothing but their underthings, sleep wiped from their wide eyes. One of the crimson bastards even struck a young boy no older than ten when he went to reach for his mother, who was protesting loudly, tears tracking down her ruddy cheeks.

Jake's grip on me tightened. I hadn't realized I'd been struggling in his arms, too focused on trying to reach these criminals wearing the colors of the realm's supposed protectors.

"One day," Jake promised in my ear. "You'll get your chance to end those bastards, and when you do, I hope you aren't merciful."

I nodded, my eyes prickling. If we survived this journey, I'd make it my life's mission to unseat such cowardly men of unearned power. I'd raise my blade and slice off the hand of any who struck a fearful child, who cornered terrified women, and who beat the defenseless.

I may not be the most skilled fighter, nor the most selfless, but I never had it in me to sit back and *watch* when I could do something about it. Looking at such abuse now made bile rise in my throat. I hated that the only thing I could do was swallow it down. The realm was at stake.

Drowning out the screams, the panicked cries, the injustice occurring all around us, I motioned to where the guards moved into groups, each setting off in a different direction.

"They're splitting up," I murmured, my voice raspy with anger. "They're trying to find the commander, which means we have to find him first."

I *felt* him. My *magic* felt him. My scar throbbed in tune with my heart, and my shadows mingled with the sliver of Raina's warm light, my body abuzz with more than trepidation and wrath.

Where would Jude hide in this place?

Without the luxury of time to scour the city, I'd have to take a guess, which felt all but impossible given I'd never set foot here before.

"He wouldn't stay at one of the gambling dens, as his face would be far too recognizable," I said. "I'd say he chose an old inn off the beaten path, in a quieter part of town. Or he'd bargain with someone for a private room in their home." That's what I would do, at least. Better to stay off the books entirely.

"Then this area wouldn't be the place to look. It's *all* shady dens and taverns." Jake subtly scanned the narrow avenues before setting his jaw. "Wait. Come with me."

I didn't argue as he steered us from the congested square, guiding us toward a grimy side street brimming with run-down townhomes.

The sunfires barely glimmered here, and we stumbled over the uneven stones. I wished we had a torch, but that would've bought us even more scrutiny. No one here carried them, seeming to have adapted to the dim. We'd be obvious outsiders.

"I came here once with...with Nic, when his parents sold their famous gin," Jake said, his voice laced with grief.

My heart skipped several beats at the way he spoke his name like a familiar prayer. Nic had been a beautiful blur of smiles and lilting words, and while I hadn't known him long before he was killed in the Mist, an ache took residence in my chest.

"I remember that this part of town offered a few inns. The section over here had some shops as well, but it's definitely not... savory." He peered over his shoulder, and I tracked his gaze to a rushing river, a tarnished bridge reaching across. "That's where the wealthy live. The lucky few who got out of the slums. He wouldn't go there. He'd stick out too much."

"I'd venture to say that those across the river would rat him out in a heartbeat." I peered across the water, finding the silver homes and their neat rows too orderly for my tastes. There were no sounds of life emanating from its banks, and even the guards crossed to its side with hushed voices and soft feet as if in respect.

I preferred the chaos of the northern side of the city, where the streets curved without reason, and the shops and taverns were all bright colors and uneven lines.

Jake shook his head. "Everything has a price here, Ki."

Of that, I knew all too well.

We hurried down the sprawling boulevard, mindful to keep our heads down.

We'd made it a decent way away from the initial onslaught of the soldiers, and I took stock of the city and its many eccentricities as we hurried through.

We passed a wood-paneled tavern entitled *Death's Door*, the walls painted all black, and the patrons inside hunched over the bar, their faces practically in their drinks.

Many more taverns blurred together, but the fourth

captured my fleeting attention.

Bright red doors were sprung wide open. Copper fixtures carrying fresh sunfires highlighted its name, The Sly Fox, and raucous laughter reached my ears, floating out beyond its doors as singing voices mingled with rowdy music.

Jake tugged me forward, but something about that particular tavern tempted me. It might've been the swaying bodies swerving about the dance floor, or the way every inch of the space was covered in bright tapestries.

Surely they'd heard the screams by now? And yet they all drank and danced and smiled as if the outside world couldn't touch them.

On a closer inspection, I realized it was one of the few taverns the guards *hadn't* assaulted, no broken windows or towering guards questioning patrons. I wondered why. Perhaps the owner had already paid them off.

"Almost there," Jake whispered into my ear, and I swiftly glanced away from The Sly Fox. He brought us down a few more quiet streets, the shutters of the shops and homes all closed tight.

We'd just rounded another corner closer to the outskirts when we happened upon several merchants loading up their wares.

Wagons of Fortuna's renowned ale were lined up, tarps tied down over the merchandise. The drivers grumbled, clearly irritated more by the possible delay than the threat to people's lives.

I flinched as invisible fire slid down my back, my magic awakening. Something told me we were in the right place...that Jude was close. Raina's magic was calling to him.

I shoved Jake behind a row of stacked crates and placed a gloved finger against his mouth. His lips parted, but I shook my head, mouthing, *"Wait."*

Both light and dark battled once more, one turning my body

hot and then the other cold with each breath. I clutched my chest, teeth grinding together, the ache throbbing and painful.

A shout sounded, succeeded by the pounding of boots. My heart skipped as I peered around the crates, careful to remain hidden in the dim.

Three King's Guards lugged an unmoving body behind them, the prisoner's legs dragging in the dirt.

The longer I stared, the more potent my fear became, swarming into my chest like a hive of insects, nipping and stinging my insides.

The prisoner... I squinted, icy-hot chills accompanying the buzzing of my skin.

The edges of my vision shifted as black clouds curled around my periphery. They danced before skittering away, a pale-yellow light replacing the darkness and heightening my sight.

It reminded me of what had happened in the Pastoria Forest with the two patrolmen, and then back in the Knights' sanctum when I'd led our group through the underground tunnels. I'd been able to see better than the other recruits, though the shapes in front of me had been tinged in that same pale-yellow glow.

Warmth overpowered the ice in my blood, and Raina's magic ignited my every pore. Narrowing my gaze further, I willed everything to clear. My desire drove my power, commanding it with thought alone. As easy as breathing.

The body they lugged was carelessly shaken as one man clearly struggled to uphold his end. But the pause allowed me to see the captive's face.

I'd already suspected whom they'd captured, but witnessing his slackened features broke me in ways I hadn't anticipated.

Jude.

His head lolled to the side as the men hauled him to an incoming surge of their brethren.

There was no mistaking it. They had Jude, *my* Jude.

The raven hair, the twin scars across his left eye. The fresh wound across his right, inflicted by Patrick. It wasn't nearly as deep and would eventually heal, but the sight of it made me want to murder the man all over again. I really should've taken my time destroying him.

Even after spending a week imagining all the things I'd tell Jude—or more likely, all the things I'd *scream* at him—I only desired to rush to his side.

I wanted to hold him, to protect him from the bastards harming him. The commander had been through enough torture in his lifetime, and the guards were touching what I now considered *mine*.

Jude's legs skidded across an uneven patch of stone as one of the men lost his balance, but they were merciless and tugged at his arms.

A hiss slipped through my lips, and Jake gently nudged me, forcing me quiet.

Inside, I was a furnace of pure, searing fire, willing to set the whole city aflame in order to get to Jude.

The divinity that connected me and Jude grew stronger the closer I got to him.

When the guards carried Jude below a fluttering sunfire gem, its golden glow highlighting the commander's face, Jake sucked in a stunned breath.

"Shit. What do we do?" he asked, barely above a whisper.

I was about to say screw it and run out and attack without a plan—when a pack of soldiers scurried from the shadows. More than a dozen surrounded Jude, each man holding the hilts of their daggers.

"We have to get to him. Before they take him back to the capital." Sciona wasn't too far, maybe three days if you rode quickly and through the night, but that was precious time we might not have.

"Ki, we're outnumbered. *Beyond* outnumbered."

I heard his words, and I understood them. But that didn't stop me from allowing the all-consuming frustration and yearning to overflow. My scar grew hot, too hot, and I clutched at it, placing my gloved palm over the jagged wound.

Curls of darkness sailed into my eyes, the hand above my heart engulfed in shadows. They didn't fight for supremacy. Rather, they burned along with the fire of a god as they swirled from my body like extensions of myself, itching to move. To go further than the confines I'd placed them in.

Both night and day working together, both furious, each powerful in their own right.

Deadly.

"You need to calm down," Jake warned, but his voice was muffled. Far away. Unimportant.

What I craved to do was *move*.

Driven by recklessness and the magic living in my blood, I grabbed the corner of a crate. I was about to slip beyond the refuge it provided and go hurtling toward the guards, dagger raised, when the smell of burning wood assaulted my nose.

"Ki!" Jake screamed, and I wrenched my hand back from the crate.

A sparking golden flare ignited in the palm of my hand where the shadows spun about my fingers. A flare that set fire to the crate I'd gripped.

The flames licked at the wood, spreading. Quickly.

Cursing, Jake snatched me around my middle. "We've got to get out of here before they find you, too," he insisted, shouts of alarm already renting the air.

I fought him, but Jake held on, dragging me back and away from my target.

I should've been capable of bucking him off, but my limbs didn't quite feel like they belonged to me, and my head grew unbearably foggy. Whether my weakness was due to shock at seeing Jude captured, or the fact I'd just set a fire using my fucking hand, I was rendered useless.

Jake all but carried me through a back alley.

The pungent haze of smoke reached us, and I wondered if the flames had spread to the other wares and carts.

In a fit of rage, I lost the chance to save him. My brooding commander. My Jude.

The heat emanating from my scar was my entire world, the ice shooting down my spine and along my arms becoming an afterthought.

"We need to get somewhere safe," Jake mumbled. He swerved to the left, helping me down a side street. A run-down inn loomed before us, its chipped sign — *The Two of Spades* — hanging off one hook.

"Wait here." Jake propped me against the wall as he ventured inside.

I sucked in air as my vision cleared and the black spots began to disperse.

A part of me wanted to cry, to break down and succumb to the guilt. But another, larger part of me wanted to scour the earth and shatter the skulls of all the guards who placed a hand on my Jude.

In the end, I stood tall, trapping my tears…because if I allowed them to fall, there'd be no stopping.

For Jude, I could be strong just a little while longer.

CHAPTER FOUR

JUDE

Our boy does not belong in my world. He's meant for greater things. I may not be able to be a mother to him, but I will protect him by staying away. You're not a good man, but this is your chance to become one.

LETTER FROM UNKNOWN SENDER TO JACK MADDOX, YEAR 32 OF THE CURSE

"Wake up, Commander."

A whooshing sounded a second before leather struck my bare back, the stinging radiating down to my toes. The clanging of metal rang overhead as I arched, trying to escape the sensation of a thousand little cuts searing into my skin.

I was on fire, burning from the inside out, hardly able to move.

Peeling open my eyes, I craned my neck, taking in my hands imprisoned in metal cuffs, a chain running through them and attaching to a hook in the ceiling. Whirling black etchings marked the deep steel, a single blue gem affixed at the center of each cuff.

They'd stolen my boots and shirt, but thankfully, I retained my trousers, though they were muddied and stained in red splotches.

I groaned, unable to help myself. The agony of the strike had settled, but the pounding ache across my back was somehow worse than the initial blow.

"There he is!" The too-cheerful voice belonged to a hooded figure in the far corner of the cell. I'd heard that voice somewhere before...

My temples pounded viciously, but I forced myself to straighten, to tilt my head and find the muscled King's Guard behind me, a whip resting idly in his hands.

The man who'd called out—the one clearly in charge—remained in the corner, his identity concealed. *Coward.*

I knew this game. I'd played it countless times in the past. First they'd deliver pain, then, after I was well and truly wrecked, they'd demand whatever answers they sought. If that didn't work, they might try again, using a different, more *unpleasant* method. I'd pass out, and the cycle would continue.

"J-just kill me," I rasped. My parched throat felt like sandpaper. If he killed me now, I wouldn't have to suffer from dehydration.

Water deprivation was one way to break me, and I was all too aware of the other ways to inflict suffering. Perhaps it was only fitting that I took my turn experiencing what I'd once dealt.

The hooded man stepped closer, a distant sunfire casting a ghoulish light across the planes of his silver mask. Instantly I recoiled, the cuffs chafing my raw skin. The pain became an afterthought.

The hood fell to the man's back and every muscle in my body tensed.

Cirian.

I wanted to both hide away and lunge for his throat.

Memories washed over me—of the day he'd made me kill my father to save myself. The creature before me was no man. He was my captor, my tormentor, and the demon that would forever haunt my nightmares.

"Be careful about moving too much. Those chains are special. Like you." His tone was sharper than a blade's edge. "Should you try to use your…gifts, you will sadly find them useless. Though it may hurt, and I'd hate for you to experience any unnecessary discomfort."

He almost sounded genuine.

I glowered in reply, instinctively jerking on the chain. A stinging shock jolted through my body, all the way to my bare feet.

Cirian sighed heavily. "How many men have you tortured in these very cells, Maddox?" he mused, grasping his chin between his thumb and forefinger. "Probably too many to count, eh?" He circled me, pausing briefly at my exposed back.

A second ticked by, and then, "You got this tattoo without knowing what it represented. I always thought that was interesting."

"What are you talking about?" I asked, my aching arms trembling. "It means nothing." Just a silly design I'd drawn from time to time.

"Three circles, entwined together, united. Come on, Maddox, I know you understand where I'm going with this. And those vines? Look familiar?"

Shit. I *did* understand.

Three keys, and three missing orbs of Raina's divinity. And the delicate pattern of vines was reminiscent of…of Kiara's scars. Prickly and unrefined, yet evocatively stunning.

"I can't blame you," Cirian said, languidly moving to stand a foot from my face. My reflection glimmered in the cool silver of his mask, my hair matted with blood and red staining the side of my cheek. Whoever knocked me out had done a suitable job. "You've had much on your mind lately. Namely, a young recruit. Kiara, right?"

I bared my teeth. Her name coming from his lips stoked the flames of my rage.

My entire body heated, and beads of sweat formed on my brow. He was provoking my power, proving that it couldn't save me.

It merely raged within the confines of my skin, coming to life in a way it hadn't since I'd fought Patrick. The very day it had awakened.

If I continued on in this way, I'd burn myself alive before he had the chance to kill me.

"So angry. And it took so very little." Cirian shook his head. "Ever since the square, when she protected her weakling of a brother, you've been besotted. But you should've listened to your old friend and kept her at a distance."

Isiah, he was talking about Isiah.

I wished my hands were freed so I could wipe the self-satisfied look off his face. He knew what buttons to press, and I wasn't in the right frame of mind to fight him. Besides, what did it matter if he knew of my fury? I *wanted* him to see — it would make his eventual death all that much sweeter, and I wouldn't even deign to use magic on him.

No, I'd make do with a simple, dulled blade. Prolong his death as I sawed through his thin skin and into bone.

If only he knew of the ending I envisioned for him, perhaps he wouldn't be standing there, sneering like he'd won.

Every good general knew a single battle didn't determine a war.

"It's a shame you didn't heed his warning." Cirian *tsk*ed. "You had to go and fall in love with the one person you'd never be able to have. It would be even more heartbreaking if you weren't already scheduled to die yourself."

I ignored the comment about my death, focusing on the smaller details.

The king hadn't been present during the Calling. I wondered what spy had whispered in his ear. Carter? Harlow?

Cirian cocked his head. "It seems that the prophecy might've held some truth to it after all," he mused.

As if summoned, the words rang in my mind, clear as a bell. *The day will be restored when the darkness falls for the light.*

My mother's book of lore contained a passage about the sun priestesses and their desperate prophecy. I had never taken it seriously before.

"Ah, I see you know it," Cirian remarked drily as the connection dawned on me.

If Kiara—a creature of the night—fell for *me*, Raina's descendant, the *light*...

Could the cure truly be something so simple? Could we fix the world together?

As if reading my mind, Cirian drawled on, "It's not as simple as you think, boy. Besides, I promise you, it would've only ended in heartbreak at the end. Love is utterly useless in our world."

Love was such a simple word for an emotion that held more power than any magic in the realm. It could start wars. End them. Love was the single thing I'd convinced myself I'd never experience...but was the tangible pressure in my chest love? Was it love I felt whenever I envisioned her in my arms, her lips forming a crooked smile when she came up with some cunning plan or devious retort?

The chains clanked together as I lifted my head, which might as well have been weighed with stones. Sharp tingles raced down my spine, but I kept my chin raised. Proud.

"She won't let you catch her," I said. "Kiara is far too smart for that."

"No. She's desperate, and she wants *you*," Cirian snapped. "She'll come out of hiding to save you from me." The invisible noose around my neck tightened. "Once she's captured, I'll have all three pieces, and I'll destroy them forever."

Destroy them. Not take them. Not use them for himself.

Destroy.

"What does it matter to you?" I placed a strained smile on my lips. Warm blood slicked my teeth. "Why are you fighting to destroy the day?"

"I fight for Asidia and its people," he muttered. "They may *think* they want the sun to return, but think of the peace our realm has experienced. The night soothes and calms their tempers. It has united the mortals and brought them together as one."

He spoke of *mortals* as if he weren't one.

I squinted in the low light, taking in the smoothness of his exposed skin.

He'd ruled on the throne for decades, and yet he had the appearance of youth. Not one wrinkle showed around his lips, his neck too taut for a man supposedly well into his fifties.

Something about him wasn't *right*. Never had been.

"Who are you truly?" Perhaps he was working with a powerful entity, maybe a god. Cirian wasn't clever enough to gain such power by himself. He may be cruel, but cruelty didn't equate to cunning.

"I serve a much bigger purpose than you could ever comprehend." The gray of his eyes suddenly swam with swirls of charcoal, and I jolted back at the unnatural sight.

What in the hells?

He blinked, and they reverted to normal, but I knew what I'd seen. The shimmer of twisted deviance.

Cirian was finally showing me a glimpse of the monster beneath his mask.

He stepped as close as he dared. Another inch and I'd be able to give him a nasty bruise in exchange for a headache. "You're going to be my bait," he said simply.

"I'd die first."

"You know nothing, Maddox, and your ignorance will be your end." Cirian's vindictive grin dropped, and he resumed his travel around me, the thud of his boots beating in my skull like a death drum.

"You won't win," I panted, knowing the true torture was set to commence. The whip cracked as it hit the floor, the king's guard all too keen to deliver punishment.

"You've always been so focused on the details rather than the bigger picture," Cirian added, slamming the cell door closed. "In the meantime, please enjoy the entertainment. I'm hoping it will bring you around to being cooperative. In the end, you'll see that all of this was necessary."

The whip struck me before he got out the final word. Though I could've sworn I heard the king take in a labored breath before his footsteps pounded the stones and left me to my demise.

I bit into my bottom lip, the coppery tang of blood filling my mouth. Warmth trickled down my spine, slipping into open wounds, making me hiss.

Another strike landed, but I didn't allow the guard the satisfaction of a flinch.

The king and his men had hurt me long enough, and my voice belonged only to me. Instead of focusing on the bite of the whip, I pictured my hands around the king's throat, squeezing the life from his soulless eyes.

I envisioned slicing the throat of the very guard who tortured me now, and then I imagined raising my weapon to the men who'd captured me in Fortuna, delivering them the same gruesome fate. Thinking of their demise emboldened me, allowed me to take each assault with renewed purpose.

Whether fantasy or the future yet to come, my darker side reigned, and this time, I let it.

Give me your best, I thought, closing my eyes as more blows landed and split my skin.

I'd either die in this cell or, somehow, I'd find freedom. But whatever happened, I refused to allow the king to break my spirit.

Not when I had something to fight for.

For Asidia, for Kiara, and for *myself*, I'd live to fight another day.

And I planned on spilling blood.

Chapter Five

Kiara

I haven't heard anything in days, but I know you're alive.
Mother and Father may be pissed at me, but for once in my
life, I'm taking a risk. I'm going to steal a page from your
book.

An unmailed letter from Liam Frey to his sister, Kiara
Frey, year 50 of the curse

I woke to Jake's bright blue eyes.

"Morning," he said, an anxious smile playing on his lips.

The single lamp lit on the inn's bedside table cast the dingy
space in shadows. I must've passed out as soon as we'd stumbled
inside; I still wore my boots.

"Tell me yesterday was a dream."

Jake solemnly shook his head. "I'm sorry, Ki. I wish it had
been."

I cursed as I eased onto my elbows, scanning the small room
and its chipped green walls.

"We've missed our chance now. Cirian will be in a position to
either kill Jude and keep the Godslayer or lure us to him, using
him as bait." That's what I'd do if I were a malevolent asshole
with a crown. And if Maliah was correct, and he was ruled by

the Moon God, Cirian wasn't Jude's only foe.

Jake shifted to the side table and returned with a pair of worn black gloves.

"You burned the other pair," he said with a shrug. As if his offering didn't mean the world to me. "I snagged these from the innkeeper's office, so try not to make a show of flashing 'em around. The bastard certainly overcharged us enough."

"One day in Fortuna, and you're already a thief?" I tried to smile, but it hurt. I clutched the gloves affectionately to my chest.

Jake scooted against the headboard, and I did the same, allowing myself to lean against his shoulder and revel in his solid comfort. He reached for my bare hand and held it in his, uncaring of my scars.

We sat there for many long minutes until Jake spoke.

"We'll find him, Ki, but not before we get a plan in order. Gods, I'm surprised they caught him to begin with. It's rather disappointing."

I shoved up from the bed, ignoring a wave of dizziness. Something nagged at the frayed edges of my thoughts, but I couldn't quite piece it all together.

"Ki..." Jake warned, rising with me.

"You're right. Jude shouldn't have been captured so easily." Granted, there *had* been a decent number of soldiers storming the city, and Jude had likely been taken by surprise. Cirian wanted him in his clutches, and he'd sent out an entire army.

"Now what?" Jake asked, his lips twitching as he fought to keep them from slipping into a frown. Gods, he was trying so damned hard to be brave. It made me try just as hard.

Steeling my spine, I held his stare. "We're going to need some horses."

• • •

Half of the people meandering about the streets of Fortuna still appeared drunk from the evening before, and the other half rushed through the masses, likely on their way to work.

More than one door hung off its hinges, and plenty had been removed entirely. The crimson soldiers had done a number on the city, and homes were boarded up with plywood and tin.

I ground my teeth when my boots sloshed into what appeared to be a pool of blood.

Those men *enjoyed* their assault. They decorated the city in red and left it in shambles without a glance back. Yet the citizens carried on without pause.

"There."

I grabbed Jake's hand and forced us to a halt. There was a stable across the boulevard, and as our luck just so happened, the only person standing guard at such an early hour was asleep, a worn checkered cap pulled low over his eyes.

My pulse hammered in my throat as we rounded the softly snoring man, a set of iron keys clutched in his hands. I motioned silently to Jake.

"No," Jake whispered, but I'd already reached for the keys. He didn't have a tight grip, and if I could just—

The snores ceased. As did my hand. I held my breath and waited, sweat slicking my brow. A moment later, the wheezing snores continued. I sighed in relief.

Wrapping my fingers around the main ring, I gently pried the keys from his grip. When one of the keys clanged against another, he flinched, those snores once again coming to a halt. I could sense Jake's eyes on me, could feel my muscles tensing, readying to bolt.

But the man just adjusted in his chair and slumped backward, fast asleep.

Thank the gods.

Waving Jake ahead, I slipped into the stables and assessed the locked pens.

A distinct prickling sensation slithered down my spine. I frowned as an odd sense of familiarity accompanied the feeling. Like I'd been here before—which was impossible.

"Check the stalls," I whispered to Jake. The first two I came across were empty, though the third had a mare that appeared suitable. I kept going, inexplicably drawn to the last stall.

Heat simmered beneath my skin at what I found—

"*Starlight*," I croaked, peering through the iron bars of her locked stable.

She *should* be dead. But...

I reached through the bars, my hands trembling, my eyes prickling with relief. Her human-like black eyes peered back at me, sparked with knowing. She dipped her head in a slight bow, always regal.

Gods, I wanted to rush inside and run my hands through her forever-tangled mane and kiss her nose while she snorted in affront. My heart, for just a moment, felt lighter.

"She's alive," Jake muttered from behind me, as stunned as I. "Impossible."

"Apparently not," I said, blinking back the threat of tears. Before the Mist and all of its illusions, I would've made myself believe that my mind was playing tricks on me. I knew that wasn't the case.

Starlight was another mystery I'd yet to solve.

I clutched the iron lock with a grimace as Jake went to work trying out the different keys. "Did she find Jude and bring him here? We saw hoofprints in the Mist." I swore the mare smiled in reply.

"That's a stretch," Jake replied, finally finding the right key. He twisted the lock. "But then again, she's not dead like she's supposed to be, so it's a possibility. She always creeped me out."

I swore Starlight glowered at him in return.

"We're getting you out of here," I told her, opening the pen. I tried to run my hand down her shank, but she pulled back, her front hooves rising a few feet from the ground.

"Whoa, we're leaving," I tried to soothe. "It's all right, girl."

Again, she reared back, coming down hard and rustling the hay in her pen.

I stepped closer, her movements having shifted the straw.

A flash of red caught my eye.

"What is that, old broad?" The sunfires illuminating the stables flickered, their glow weak, but I saw the symbol clear enough.

A square matchbook...with what looked to be a claw mark decorating a pint of ale.

I picked it up, twisting it this way and that. It was just a matchbook.

Starlight thumped her hooves as if in frustration.

"What is it?" I asked, feeling foolish for speaking to a horse.

Starlight inched closer, hot puffs of air escaping her nostrils. She touched the matchbook with her nose before lifting her head and centering those unusual eyes on me.

"Does this mean something?" I held it up, frowning.

Starlight nickered, whipping her head. Her agitation was well known.

"You don't think..." Jake trailed off, scoffing. "It can't be a clue."

Starlight pierced him with her signature scowl. I don't believe I'd ever seen another horse make such a face.

I pursed my lips, thinking. "If Jude *did* find her in the Mist and rode her here, then there's a *chance* he left this here. Like you said, a clue."

It was a small chance, but a memory flickered to the front of my mind.

"Oh, gods. What's that face?" Jake grumbled.

"I recognize the name," I murmured. "That symbol... It's a tavern by the main boulevard. The one with all the bright tapestries."

"I wasn't paying that much attention. Though, in my defense, there *was* an attack happening," Jake said, gnawing at the inside of his cheek. "Should we check it out before we head to the capital? Just to be safe?"

Starlight seemed to calm, even trotting back to my side. She bumped her muzzle against my chest, and I ran my hand along her neck.

"I say we go. If it *is* a clue, then we'll kick ourselves later for not paying it attention."

"She better be right." Jake shook his head, his hair flopping in his eyes. He scowled at Starlight, his stare narrowed.

"We'll be back really soon," I promised the mare, who pushed into my chest with vigor. I hated to leave her here a second longer, but we couldn't ignore the possible gift that had fallen in our laps.

Stepping away, I quickly gave her my back before I hesitated any longer. Jake locked the pen but slipped off the key before we placed them back before the stablehand.

"The Sly Fox," I said to Jake once I'd ushered us beyond the main boulevard and down a side street. "It had a claw mark on its sign. It could be a long shot, but—"

Pain devoured my torso, my scar ablaze. Through the thin linen of my shirt, it shined—only dimmed when Jake dragged my cloak across me in an attempt to shield its unnatural glow. I stumbled, half tripping into the nearest alleyway.

"What's happening?" Jake asked, holding me upright, a deep crease running through his brow. "Your skin is burning up like the other night."

The pain was too much all at once, like a thousand bee

stings prickling my flesh.

I brought my hand to rest on the scar, praying for the agony to cease, to allow me a chance to suck in the air I desperately needed.

Jake pestered me for answers, but I was physically unable to talk. I was suffocating, drowning in magic I had no idea how to stop. How to command.

Both light and dark were working together, but this time, it felt different. Like I had no control over my actions.

I slumped against the stone wall behind me, landing on my bottom, gasping as warmth trailed down my cheeks. Salt slipped between my lips. Tears.

Jake's face faded in and out as black dots danced across my vision, the heat in my chest warming to an excruciating degree. Was this what it felt like to die?

That's when I heard it—

My name.

"*Kiara.*"

Everything went still. I'd recognize that voice anywhere, and its deep timbre chased away some of the panic. Just enough for me to take in a deep gulp of air.

My fingers clutched at the raised and jagged wound running wildly below my heart, my connection to the commander. Our matching marks of death.

"*Kiara,*" Jude's voice called out again, tinny and stifled.

I couldn't hear anything else but him, and the black spots from earlier swelled until they eclipsed the alley and Jake entirely. I sensed the shadow beast within me rear its head, battling to overpower Raina's light. It surged to the forefront, my body tingling before growing numb.

A figure wavered into view, a lone man curled into a ball, unmoving.

Winding clouds of ash enveloped him on all sides, but

the smell... I could *smell* something rotten and coppery and mildewed.

"Jude?"

The man shifted, groaning.

In this in-between place where a film of black coated my eyes, I couldn't make out much.

Still, my heart rate doubled and a twisted relief coursed through my veins. It *was* him.

Jude moved again, and this time, I was awarded a better view of his face. His deep onyx hair fell across his right eye, his stormy pale blue one almost incandescent in the dim. I noticed that his hand rested on his chest—right above his scar.

"Jude, where are you?" I tried and failed to advance.

My limbs wouldn't work, frozen in place like I was stuck in mud.

I didn't understand how I'd gotten here, or if this was all a dream, but it felt too damned real for me to do anything but claw my way to him.

"Now I'm hearing your voice," Jude whispered, a grumbling noise of anguish slipping free from his throat. He rolled onto his side, exposing his back—

I swore the walls trembled at the enraged growl that reverberated in my throat.

His back was covered in vicious red that had crusted at the seams of a dozen or more gashes. Each of his exhales caused them to split, beads of fresh blood bubbling to the surface. I'd never seen such cruelty.

"What the fuck did they do to you?" I thundered. My teeth ground together as I fought against the invisible barrier. "Who whipped you?"

I'd kill them. I would draw out their death for hours. Days. Take my time with it.

A chilled breeze swept across my brow, shadows curling

around my shoulders. My beast demanded blood.

Slowly, sensation came back to my hands, though every particle of air stung.

"I used to be able to withstand hours of his *play*, and now look at me. Hearing voices." He laughed, though it was brittle.

"It's me!" I shouted, pounding on the barrier, gritting my teeth as I attempted to move. "Turn around and look!"

My demand must've broken through his daze, because Jude turned over, though he hissed in pain. A deep furrow took up residence between his eyes. "Kiara?"

"Yes, you fool!" I yelled, elated given the circumstances. He could hear me, too. See me. "Now where are you so I can wring your neck for leaving me?"

I inspected the rocky walls as the darkness crept away, but they offered no clue as to his location. The common stones could belong to any of the fortresses near Fortuna that Cirian had gifted his lords. If he was already imprisoned, then he couldn't be in Sciona. Which meant we had a chance to catch up to him.

Jude awkwardly pushed to his elbows, his hands manacled in thick silver. "Gods, it *is* you," he said, shock widening his eyes. "Only you would threaten me in the state I'm in."

"I'll wait until you're healed before I make good on my threats, but tell me, before whatever this is goes away. We saw them take you from the city, but we lost track…"

Because I'd set a damned fire and ruined our chance to fight back. Nope. I wasn't going to say that.

Jude opened his mouth but shut it. Instead, he peered down at his chest. The mark I'd left on him shone in stark contrast with his pale skin, the veiny blue-and-black lines sprouting like twisted vines. "It warmed right before you came," he said, almost to himself. I tapped my chest, focusing on its heat. His head popped up. "How is this possible?"

I definitely was going to strangle him. "Tell me where you are."

Jude went stiff but shook his head. "Cirian. I...I don't know where I am."

I understood his features well enough to know when he lied.

"I'm going to find you," I promised, my eyes prickling. "You better not give up until I do—"

"It's a trap," Jude quickly interrupted. "Cirian wants to use me to get to you." He groaned, trying to push to his feet. His voice turned firm. "Don't come, Kiara. Don't let him get you. If there was ever a time you listened to me, please let this be it."

Maliah had warned us that Cirian was under the Moon God's control. And if Cirian had Jude in his possession, our faceless enemy had him as well.

Jude stumbled, righting himself a moment later. He took a step closer, toward me, and all I wanted to do was reach out and hold him. He lifted his hand, wonder brightening his brown eye. When he moved to touch me, to cup my cheek, his hand struck a barrier of impenetrable nothingness.

He cursed. "Of course. That would be too easy."

I brought my hand to where he hovered, our palms an inch apart, separated by magic and defeat. "We weren't made for easy, Commander," I said, my voice a rasp. The burning in my eyes increased. It was a sensation I wasn't accustomed to.

Jude's throat bobbed. "I never should've chosen you," he said, his lips thinning.

"Enough with all that," I grumbled. "I'm your reflection, Jude, remember? Our destinies were always entangled." I just so happened to fall for him. And fall hard I did.

The room gave a violent tilt. We didn't have much time.

"Listen," he started, urgency replacing the adoration he'd radiated seconds before. "The boy in the green tent..." His words were breaking up, his voice muffled. "...in the alley at

The Rolling Dice. He has…"

Then I couldn't hear him at all.

He mouthed my name, but the fire within me was dissipating, and the in-between world was gradually disintegrating piece by piece like grains of sand blown away in a storm.

"Jude!" I cried, wisps of onyx shadows winding about his frame, devouring him.

My shadows.

I screamed his name until my voice grew hoarse and I couldn't see a damned thing. I screamed until a jerk caused my body to *fall, fall, fall—*

Hands gripped my shoulders, solid and firm.

The grimy stones of the alleyway came back into focus, as did a notably concerned Jake.

I gasped, inhaling the putrid air of Fortuna. "Jude," I panted, meeting Jake's bewildered gaze. "I saw him."

"What are you talking about?" Jake rasped, helping me rise. He ran a flustered hand through his hair, his body visibly trembling. "What just happened? One moment you were fine, and then you went into this creepy, catatonic state. You were practically gray. At one point I swore you flickered out of existence entirely, and I thought—"

I noticed his cheeks were wet, his eyes rimmed in red.

Shit.

"I'm fine," I promised, though it was a lie. The lingering effects made me dizzy, but I swallowed down the panic to hug him close. I wound my arms around his waist and pressed my head against his rapidly rising and falling chest. "I'm all right, Jake. I'm here."

He'd thought he lost me. Like he lost Nic.

Jake's grip on me tightened to the point where I couldn't suck in a full breath, but I didn't mind. It was a reminder that we were still here, still fighting, and still together.

I drew back to look him in the eyes. Another tear fell, sliding down his cheek and to his stubbled chin. Catching it with my finger, I proceeded to wipe away the rest of the wetness, rubbing soothing circles on his skin with my thumb.

"I'll explain," I promised. "But we have a real lead now, Jake." Another treacherous seed of hope planted.

We just had to follow the trail of clues Jude left behind before Cirian murdered him.

Which meant we could already be too late.

CHAPTER SIX

JUDE

To fear the darkness is to fear one's own mind.

ASIDIAN PROVERB

My cell reeked of decay and mold, and every lungful of air took effort.

My ribs were surely broken or at the very least bruised. A sharp stinging ran down my spine, and whenever I moved so much as an inch, the fragile skin of my back split. Blood gushed from the lacerations, warming my punished flesh.

And yet, even doubled over, my eyes prickling from the agony, I focused not on my back, but on *her*.

I saw Kiara. She'd been hazy at best, barely a flicker of a form, but I'd seen her.

Or I had been easily broken, I thought, though the sound of that didn't ring true.

Magic *had* to have been involved, even with the peculiar manacles encircling my wrists. I didn't recognize the blue-tinged metal, but the center gem reminded me of how the moon looked in the Mist when it had been ringed in blue.

Thankfully, they weren't tied together at the moment. Not that it did me any good.

No matter how hard I tried to pry them off, they remained firmly in place. Whatever they were made of seemed to smother most of the divinity floating in my soul, making it impossible to escape. I rotated my hand, inspecting one of the cuffs.

There. Faint marks, like they'd been etched as an afterthought. They formed a crescent moon so miniscule, I'd overlooked it before. If I peered hard enough, I could even make out a triangle surrounding it.

Every god and goddess had their individual symbols and marks, much like signatures. This was the Moon God's. Undoubtedly, enchanted.

And yet Kiara had been able to reach me.

Why? If the manacles dampened magic, how had she…

It hit me then—

Our scars. They bound us together, each of us touched by a blade crafted by a god or the magic of one. I'd healed her using a divine force, and she'd done the same for me.

Whatever the reason, her appearance had me thinking about what Cirian had said.

The prophecy.

I squeezed my eyes shut and brought my hands to my face. Maybe it *was* more than silly words uttered by sun priests. Raina had been killed by love, and maybe that was the tool we'd need to mend this mess.

Right now, my only hope rested in the hands of the young boy from Fortuna who hadn't the faintest idea of the treasure in his possession.

If I had the energy to do so, I could've kicked myself thinking of how I trusted a child with the most dangerous weapon known to man.

It had been the riskiest thing I'd ever done, which wasn't at all like me. But I'd grown more hopeful since meeting Kiara, even if I continued to fight such a foreign emotion.

Gods, I missed the days when I felt nothing. I felt *too* much now, and it was suffocating.

Lying on my side, I shut my eyes, my hand instinctively moving to rest above the raised wound beside my heart. In the consuming quiet, with only my mind as bittersweet company, I realized exactly how I felt about the woman who'd turned my world upside down.

The realization was more frightening than any curse or cure—

Because it had the power to both save and destroy the world.

Chapter Seven

Kiara

The Moon God was lonely in the heavens, overlooked by the sleeping humans he watched over. One gloomy winter night, he decided to create faithful companions. These were the first shadow beasts, entities initially fashioned to chase away nightmares, rather than cause them. When he failed, and his wicked creations ravaged the world, Raina was forced to hunt them down.

Excerpt from Asidian Lore: a Tale of the Gods

The Rolling Dice was your typical Fortuna gambling den, full of drunkards, loose coin purses, and overflowing cups of ale. Women and men wearing next to nothing paraded about the room, trays perched on their bare shoulders, the long, beaded belts at their hips dangling as they swayed to the beat of the live music playing onstage.

A gorgeous woman with deep golden skin and bright green eyes sang a lively tune that sounded both impossibly hopeful and melancholy. Coins were tossed onstage, and she blew the patrons a sly kiss, flicking her glittering dress as she moved expertly about the stage.

You'd have never suspected there'd been a brutal assault on

the city early that morning.

Jake had taken my vision of Jude in stride. He'd listened to my every word, his face an emotionless mask. I supposed after everything we'd endured, it wasn't the most bizarre thing to have happened. All he'd said after I finished was, "Give me a heads-up next time." He'd yanked me into a half-hug, grumbling about my antics giving him an early heart attack.

We huddled close now as I surveyed the many exit points, should we need a quick escape. Beside one door across the room, a painting caught my eye. It depicted a clearing of vibrant green leaves and soft flowers.

"Ki?" Jake asked, turning my focus back to the mission. The painting reminded me of the glen in the Mist—one of the happiest moments of my young life. I'd get another day like that again, if it killed me. But still I frowned, noting that it hung slightly askew.

"Jude told us to find a boy in a green tent. He mentioned an alley and then this place." I surveyed the bustling den with narrowed eyes. We hadn't found an alley on either side of the building. Perhaps it was out back?

Beside me, Jake eyed the tables with a tangible hunger. I recalled his mention of luck with dice. Maybe he *should* play a round, seeing as our bellies were filled only with a burned loaf we'd unearthed in a trash pile behind a baker's shop.

"Focus," I said instead. "Want to try to see if there's another exit?"

"Ki, I could earn *so* much here." His eyes glowed. "Money for food. Lots of fucking food. Gods, I'd kill for a sandwich. I think better on a full stomach."

"Obviously," I teased. "But you need to focus. No more talk of sandwiches." My own mind conjured melted cheese and fresh bread and meat. As if to prove a point, my stomach growled loudly.

Jake raised a brow. "Fine. We try the back. But I need food at some point."

I nodded, agreeing. Satisfied, Jake willingly followed me past the round tables and cheering men and women. Servers sauntered by, their eyes all lined in heavy kohl, their smiles brilliant and inviting.

"Let's go through the kitchens." Jake nodded to a swinging door, a server having just left it with a platter of something divinely deep fried. "Usually the kitchens have a back door where the cooks take their breaks."

When I shot him a questioning look, he added, "I worked in a kitchen for years back home. Nic, too." He marched ahead, his shoulders tenser than before.

We had to wait a few minutes next to the door for it to clear. The second the opportunity presented itself, we slipped through the swinging door and into the kitchen.

Cooks shouted profanities as we passed, but none blocked our approach, too busy with the stacks of orders pinned above their heads.

"Through there," Jake hissed, directing my attention to the back door. It was slightly ajar, frigid air seeping into the sweltering heat of the kitchens.

We shoved it open, and I grimaced when it immediately slammed shut behind us.

He'd been right. There was another alley behind the den. "Good thinking," I told Jake, and he gave me a quick smile.

The narrow alley boasted a few tents, the unfortunate of Fortuna seeking relief from the chill any way they could. My heart ached, but I pressed on, peeking into each one as Jake dutifully scanned the area for signs of danger.

There was a family of four huddled inside one, the mother rocking her child to sleep, dried tear tracks marring her cheeks. Another tent contained three older children, an array of stolen food shoved into a pile between them.

My stomach churned. They deserved so much more than this.

Sometimes a simple offering of kindness was all it took to change a life. But kindness, like the sun, appeared absent in Asidia.

Begrudgingly, I tore away from the shelters we'd already checked and homed in on the smallest tent tucked away in the corner. As I grew close, I noted it to be a shade of pale green.

"The boy in the green tent…in the alley at The Rolling Dice," Jude had said before the vision broke away.

This had to be it.

I crouched before the flaps. "Hello?"

When no reply came, I twisted to Jake, who simply shrugged and waved his hands before him as if to say, "*You go in first.*" He was chivalrous in that way.

Undoing the ties, I ripped open the flaps, meeting a pair of vibrant hazel eyes.

A frail boy peered up at me from the back of the tent, a dulled kitchen knife clutched tightly in his hand. A meager fire burned in a chipped porcelain basin, bits of rubbish stacked beside it to keep it ablaze. It provided enough light to glimpse the fear he emanated.

Holding up placating hands, I said, "We're not here to hurt you."

His thick brows furrowed as if he hardly believed that. Good lad.

"A friend of ours told us where to find you." I gave him my best attempt at a lighthearted smile, hoping it came across as friendly.

"Let me see your hair," the boy demanded, swallowing thickly. He motioned for my hood with the crooked blade, slanting his chin defiantly.

I bit back my smile and heeded his request, allowing the cloak to fall. He was right to be distrustful. When my red hair swept across my shoulders, the boy visibly relaxed, an audible exhale whooshing from his mouth.

"He said your hair was the color of the warmest flame." A feeble smile lifted his lips. "He didn't lie."

Jude. Always the poet. My heart panged in my chest, his name transporting me back to that putrid cell trapping him. No matter how furious I was, I couldn't fight my own heart.

As much as I sometimes wanted to.

"Do you have something for us?" I asked through gritted teeth, my pulse hammering in anticipation.

My vision had been true, then.

Somehow, I'd found Jude, and I couldn't wait to attempt it again, even if I hadn't a clue how to summon such power—all I gathered was that our scars were involved. But the vision hadn't revealed his location. Trap or not, uncovering this mysterious talisman below the Moon God's temple could wait.

The child scrambled to reach behind him, tossing aside two thick blankets and retrieving a bundled package tied with a tattered leather string.

"He gave me this tent," the boy said, nodding to his humble surroundings. "No one had ever given me anything." His eyes fell to the package in his hands. "I didn't open it. I wanted to, but...I couldn't. The man had been too nice to deceive. And h-he told me the kingdom was at stake. That I would be its protector." For the first time, innocence shone in his stare, and my chest squeezed, knowing this boy had been robbed of a true childhood.

Jude had shown this child a small kindness, and in return, he'd been gifted with his loyalty.

"Here," he said, handing it over with trembling hands. "I protected it, just as he asked." The proud tilt of his chin loosened some of the grief weighing in my stomach.

I took the package and gently undid the strings. Peeling back the rough paper, I caught a hint of shining onyx metal.

Jake sucked in an audible breath behind me. The Godslayer.

Jude had been smart enough to keep the Godslayer somewhere safe and off his person should he be captured. He'd taken a huge risk leaving it with this child, but I admired his faith.

"Thank you for guarding it." I smiled, dipping my head in gratitude. "You have no clue what you've done to help us…"

"Grey," he finished for me. "My name is Grey."

"Well, Grey, if I had coin, I'd surely give it to you. But I can only offer this right now." Digging into my pocket, I retrieved the pin Jude had left me back in the Mist. The emblem of the Knights of the Eternal Star.

The gold of the sun gleamed in the weak light of the boy's fire, and his mouth fell open when he took in the blade piercing the shimmering orb.

"Kiara, are you sure?" Jake inquired at my side, kneeling into a crouch.

I nodded. Jude had given me this pin as a goodbye. A goodbye I had never accepted. Besides, his heart didn't lie with the Knights. It never had.

"This belongs to a man who will one day save our kingdom," I said, brushing my thumb over the metal. "He'd want you to have it, Grey." I held out the offering.

Grey slowly reached for it, his chest rising rapidly, his hazel eyes aglow with wonder. "Was it him? The man who asked for my help?"

"It was."

He closed his dirt-streaked fingers around the token before clutching it to his chest as though it were the greatest gift he'd been given.

"And he chose you to guard Asidia's hope for a reason." Grey lifted his eyes from the emblem, meeting mine. "When the day finally returns, remember that you had a part in that."

Before I let the flap close, I saw Grey bring the pin to his face, and for the first time since laying eyes on him, a genuine smile danced on his lips. With all the care in the world, he tucked his new treasure into his breast pocket, right above his heart.

But that wasn't all I saw.

Sitting beside him, right next to a pile of papers to be used for kindling, was a matchbook. A *red* matchbook with a claw and ale symbol embossed in gold.

I didn't believe in coincidences.

Reaching into my own pocket, I retrieved the matchbook I'd found in Starlight's stable and held it before me.

I turned to my friend. "Are you in the mood for an ale, Jake?"

· · ·

The Sly Fox wasn't nearly as thriving as the other day, which worked well for us.

Vibrant red-and-orange tapestries woven in intricate designs were hung haphazardly about the space. Paintings and sculptures of the bar's namesake were displayed with pride, and metal foxes jutted out from the walls, their silver claws supporting several torches.

"I would've sold the dagger if I were Grey's age," Jake murmured as we entered the tavern. A young, dark-haired man strummed a blue guitar in the corner, singing some old folk song while a couple danced clumsily in each other's arms on the floor.

"Good thing it wasn't you, then," I remarked shrewdly. "You'd have sold the Godslayer for a sandwich."

He groaned. "Why the hells did you have to bring up a

sandwich? You're killing me, Ki."

Again, my stomach decided to growl like a beast.

Ignoring the hunger pains, I marched over to the counter and popped into an empty seat, Jake filling the one beside me.

"Two ales and whatever your cook is serving," I ordered the barkeep, a burly man who appeared as if he hadn't smiled a day in his life. He grunted before ambling off.

"Hopefully the owner we're likely looking for doesn't mind that we don't have coin to pay for those ales," Jake whispered, resting both elbows on the wooden bar. He grimaced when the fabric of his shirt met the stickiness, and he returned his arms to his sides, subtly wiping at the cloth. It was fruitless, seeing as his shirt was already beyond repair.

"You need to work on your whispering." I sighed. "And yes, if anyone knows of Jude's presence, it would be the owner. This place…it was the only bar that wasn't hit during the attack. I think whoever owns it holds some power."

I did a quick scan of the room. A steely-faced man with a shaved head stood before a red door off to the side of the bar, his eyes aimed our way. One thick brow raised when our eyes locked. I hastily looked away.

Not more than a minute inside, and already we'd failed at stealth.

I tried to convince myself that his interest was simply because of my enchanting and alluring presence, but I knew I resembled weeks-old waste. I desperately required a bath, and I couldn't even feign confidence in my present state.

"What? If anything, they're looking at you." Jake poked at the tip of my drawn hood. "You're practically screaming, 'I'm here on a secret mission.'"

I grumbled as I lowered my hood. Maybe it was for the best.

My fingers danced nervously across the bar's surface, my nails catching every now and again on the jagged carvings patrons had left behind. Some were crude in nature, others a pair of initials surrounded by off-centered hearts.

My fingers stilled as a thought flitted through my mind.

I stood from my seat, ignoring Jake whisper-hissing my name. People had carved their marks into the wood. There had to be hundreds.

"What are you doing?" Jake tried his best to grab my arm, but I slipped farther down the bar.

If Jude had been here, if he left that matchbook as a clue, then something told me I'd find another surprise. Maybe it was wishful thinking, but—

At the end of the bar, nearly hidden by shadows, I saw the hint of a crescent moon. Moving closer, my eyes widened as I took in the crude "J" and "M" carved right below the moon.

Wandering back to Jake, I took a seat. "He was here," I said. "I saw his initials. And a moon." Jake curved his body to where I'd been, but he was too far away. "Believe me. I'd recognize his handwriting anywhere."

I knew it was his because I'd kept his letter of warning from the Mist. The same long *J*, the same curving *M*.

Before he could say anything, the guitarist from earlier finished his piece. The tavern was suddenly too quiet.

Ambling to the bar, the scrawny musician took a seat and held up a finger for the bartender, dark curls falling into his even darker eyes.

His clothes were colorful, like most in the city, though he'd paired his patterned yellow shirt with a red silk cravat that had to be worth a large sum. That, and his right index finger flashed with a brilliant ruby ring.

Based on his profession, I had the sneaking suspicion he hadn't obtained the cravat or the ring through legal means.

"Better not skimp out on me, old man!" he yelled, and the bartender extended his middle finger in reply.

"Cheapskates," the musician grumbled.

Another idea popped up, and I nudged Jake in the ribs, staring pointedly at the musician.

"Gods, Ki," Jake groused. "Why'd you do that?"

"I bet a musician would know an outsider if he saw one."

"So…?" Jake's brows pinched together.

I motioned with my eyes to his left, to where the musician sat, and shot Jake a seething look. *Come on, Jake. Use that annoying charm for good.*

"Wha— *Ah*." Jake's entire face lit up. He cleared his throat, and a wicked smile slowly curled his lips. Jake swiveled in his chair.

He transformed into a different man before my eyes; his posture relaxed, his chest puffing out ever so slightly. Jake raked a hand through his tangled hair, his attention homing in on his target.

"Excuse me, so sorry to bother you." The musician stilled, eyeing Jake with a hint of interest, his eyes brightening.

"Yes?" he asked.

"I couldn't keep my eyes off of you when you played," Jake cooed, and I watched in wonder as the musician mirrored his grin. "You're too handsome to be playing here…"

The man's cheeks pinked. "Cam," he answered Jake's unspoken question. "And is that so?"

"Oh, yes." Jake sat forward. "Talented *and* handsome? You're every person's dream. I'm Jakob, by the way. One of the people who couldn't resist you."

Jake's given name sounded off when he spoke it aloud.

The man waved his hand in the air, his blush growing a deeper shade. "I'm far from decent. You're being too kind."

"Oh, I'm hardly ever kind." Jake smirked, and even I felt the effect of its potency. "You just brought it out in me."

I slanted back in my seat, shaking my head. I let Jake work

his magic on Cam, the pair exchanging heated looks whenever I peered over.

When the bartender came back with our order—ale and some sort of soup; again, items we couldn't pay for—I enjoyed the show of Jake charming the artist within an inch of his life.

Five minutes later, he let out a boisterous laugh, and they knocked shoulders like they'd known each other all their lives. And through it all, the man's cheeks held that deep red hue, obviously enchanted by whatever Jake murmured into his ear.

By the time I finished my soup, my belly full and warm, Jake brought up the tavern, starting by asking about the owner and how he'd come to play here. A decent place to start. Cam shot a quick glance at the red door before returning to Jake.

"The owner likes me," Cam replied with a sly wink.

"And how could he not?" Jake beamed, light reaching his eyes in a way that stole even my breath. Not that I'd admit it to him. Gods damn him and his charm. If I'd have known he was this good, we might've used his skills earlier.

"*She*," the musician corrected. "And she's not easy to please, although you'd certainly *want* to."

Was she the one Jude had visited? First, the matchbook, and then Jude's initials…

"I do love some gossip," Jake said in a whisper, leaning in conspiratorially. "Who is this mysterious owner?"

The musician glanced around the room before answering. "The Fox is Asidia's greatest thief. She can steal *anything*. You have enough coin, and she can get it done." Cam snapped his fingers. "The woman is legendary in these parts. No one messes with her."

Hmm. I'd heard of a few famous criminals in Asidia.

There was Tommy "Two Face"—the infamous master of disguise who robbed half the south. The Crimson Blade, a northern warrior turned mercenary who killed for coin. And the always entertaining Annibel "Sweetheart" Fields, a woman who killed off every man who had the misfortune to call her sweetheart. Their wanted posters had been plastered in the town square of Cila, but my focus had been on weapons and training. Besides, I'd never imagined I'd *seek* one of them out.

"Damn." Jake took a sip from his "borrowed" ale. "The Fox sounds incredible. I'd like to meet her."

"Oh, you will."

The voice didn't belong to Cam, whose face turned a sickly shade of white, his eyes peering over Jake's head.

Jake and I turned at the same moment.

The man who'd guarded the red door stood before us, his brawny arms crossed. Tattoos swirled up and down his impressive forearms, creatures and monsters and celestial symbols alike. I noted that a fox mid-pounce took up the most room on his right arm.

Slowly, I brought my attention to warm brown eyes that were at odds with his intimidating veneer.

"Looks like you'll get your wish," he said with a cruel smile. "Mistress wants to see you. Now."

Chapter Eight

Jude

You better have spent the money I sent on the boy. If I find
out it all went to ale, you'll be hearing from my men. And they
aren't nearly as nice as I am.

Letter from The Sly Fox Tavern, sent to Jake Maddox, year
32 of the curse

"How long has he been asleep?"

"Five hours, sir."

"Tell the king I'm here and I'll report shortly."

I groaned, opening my eyes. Boots thudded against the
stones. I counted only one pair.

They'd unhooked my shackles from the wall, allowing me to
move around—not that I got far. My hands were still encircled
by the cuffs, that peculiar metal digging into my wrists painfully.

Climbing to my feet, off the soiled pallet, I forced myself to
stand tall. Stabbing aches fired down my back, the dizzying rush
nearly causing my vision to turn black. If I didn't clean my new
wounds soon, they'd become infected.

The foreboding footsteps came to a halt.

I squinted. A cloaked figure loomed behind the bars, but it
wasn't Cirian. This man had to be around six and a half feet, and

tufts of auburn hair poked out—

My heartbeat thudded in my ears, louder than any of the man's steps.

I went rigid. "Harlow?"

A key turned in the lock, and a second later, it swung open with a groan, revealing the lieutenant's scowling face.

We'd never been friends, not like Isiah and me, and talking to the man was akin to having a conversation with a brick wall. But if he was here now...

He'd been sent to interrogate me.

The ache of betrayal settled in my gut.

"You've fallen far, Maddox," Harlow said, his voice rougher than stones and just as cutting. He sauntered into the dimly lit cell, lowering his hood. His gaze flicked behind him, and then he began to circle me, the whites of his eyes flashing. "I see you didn't retrieve the *cure*, then?"

When I didn't deign to speak, he continued. "Most people with any sense wouldn't hold out on Cirian. He's hounding for the blade and very disappointed you didn't kill the girl." Harlow heaved a sigh, assessing me like I was a puzzle with a missing piece. "You know he'll instruct me to search the entire kingdom for her. She's still out there, running. Alive."

A wave of pure, animalistic fury wrestled through me.

"Touch Kiara and I'll flay you. Slowly," I threatened through gritted teeth. My magic burned my chest as an image of her flickered across my thoughts, her body broken and in a matching cell.

Harlow or any of Cirian's sadistic men wouldn't get to her. Not while air still filled my lungs. At least they hadn't caught her trail.

I limped over to where Harlow stood, my upper lip curled as I added, "I'm disappointed in *you*. All this time, I thought you were one of the rare good ones in the palace. Not one of Cirian's mindless minions. You certainly proved me wrong."

Perhaps I couldn't trust my gut as I'd thought.

Harlow shook his head, a weary expression contorting his angular features.

"You know nothing, Jude," he whispered. "And you have no idea what I'd be willing to do to defend my kingdom." He chanced a look over his shoulder before turning back to me. "You have to listen to me. Nothing is what it appears, but I think you already knew that."

My brows scrunched at his words.

"Your destiny doesn't have you dying here," Harlow said, his voice firm. "You've trusted all the wrong people for so long, and now it's time for you to trust me."

He was simply trying to gain my confidence. I knew this trick well.

I spat in his face, and the thick globules dripped sluggishly down to his chin. He swiped the insult with his sleeve, sneering.

Gods, that had felt good.

"Clean yourself up, Commander," he ordered a little too loudly, his hand diving into his pocket to retrieve something. He tossed it at me. I caught it with a grunt, my back stretching painfully, my lacerations pulled taut.

A jar of healing ointment. The same kind I'd once given Kiara.

Harlow bestowed me a lingering look reeking of sympathy.

I bit my cheek until I tasted blood.

I wanted absolutely nothing from him, especially not his pity.

The note the king had given me before I'd left for the Mist danced across my mind. Cirian had wanted Kiara dead—to destroy the power she held trapped inside her mortal frame.

As a leader of the Knights, I couldn't picture Harlow following through on the plan, but…the king did hold him in exceptionally high regard. Harlow heeded the king without thought, perhaps even knowing his true ambitions.

Harlow turned when I snatched his cloak, halting him. I had to make one final appeal.

"Harlow."

He flinched, craning his neck until his eyes bored into mine. I thought I glimpsed a hint of remorse, however small.

"You claim all you wish to do is defend our realm, but if you capture Kiara, you will be its ruin. If Cirian has told you the truth at all."

If she was killed with any mortal weapon, Raina's power would die with her. Not that I'd allow anyone near her with the Godslayer. I'd kill any who tried.

I wanted Harlow to deny my claim, for his face to scrunch in confusion. It didn't.

Harlow shook me off, his expression once again turning unreadable. "Stay alive, Maddox, and when we meet again, maybe things will be clearer for you. I'm not your enemy. I never was."

Then why didn't he speak of what he knew? He claimed he didn't plot against me, but he still marched from the cell and bolted it, locking me in. A prisoner.

Harlow wasn't my friend or ally. The ointment had to be a trick.

With him at the helm, it would be a matter of time before he found Kiara. That ache in my chest grew, becoming painful. I barely noticed the way the cuts on my back split open as I paced.

I had to get out of here. Had to warn her.

I'd been in worse situations before, and while exhausted and beaten, I wouldn't stop until I broke out of this prison. I grasped the jar of healing ointment, nearly crushing it in my hold.

Unscrewing the lid, I scooped some salve on my fingers, wincing as I reached around and brushed it on the smarting lacerations.

Cirian and his men had caught me off guard in Fortuna, but in a day or two, I would be ready to fight my way out of here. If they didn't kill me before I healed.

My hand fell across the scar bonding me to Kiara. Against the impossible, I still sought her in the darkness, a lost ship seeking a beacon of light to guide its way home. Magic had saved us both, and it wouldn't be easily dismissed.

Chapter Nine

Kiara

Not much is known about the Fox, but her ability to steal the rarest artifacts has grown legendary. She once snuck into the palace itself, robbing the king of his treasured texts, all supposedly ancient tomes carrying spells and secrets belonging to the gods. The Fox is rumored to maintain more knowledge than any mortal in the realm.

Excerpt from Asidian Lore: Legends and Myths of the Realm

"I hear you've been looking for me."

The Fox propped her boots onto her mahogany desk and crossed her reedy arms. She was small in stature, and I reckoned a gust of wind could knock her straight onto her back. I shifted in my seat, Jake beside me in a matching leather chair.

The study was more like a museum—covered in trinkets and statues and art, it was an eclectic and oddly warm space that went at odds with the rumors of the cutthroat thief.

In fact, I could hardly believe the woman before me was the famed outlaw the musician spoke so highly of. If not for all the beefy-looking bodyguards in the hallway, I'd have imagined this was some mistake.

"Well?" the woman pressed, her features stone. "Did you come to gawk at me or merely waste my time?"

Gritting my teeth, I swallowed down the temptation for violence. I'd have to wait until *after* I got the answers I came here for.

Shame.

"Jude Maddox," I said, his name echoing in the study. Her eye twitched, her jaw clenching tightly before she righted herself.

She *did* recognize the name.

My pulse kicked up as I studied her with renewed interest. "He came to see you."

"Anyone ever tell you that your manners could use some work?" she asked, cocking her head. Her chin-length black hair shifted, the ends cut in a razor-sharp line. All of her features were like that—sharp and severe, like she'd lived a life free of peace. Only her brown eyes flickered with hints of gold, the irises warm and enticing.

"Countless times. Though I'm sure you're not qualified to offer lessons." I scowled at the lingering brute who'd been extra rough when delivering us to her office. He perched against a side table in the corner covered in loose papers, his nostrils flaring.

"Want me to *politely* escort them out?" he asked, making a point to glower my way.

"Leave, Finn."

"But—"

"Leave," she said again, waving an idle hand.

The hulking guard grumbled something that sounded like *should've listened to the boy.*

When he shut the door much harder than necessary, the dusty bookshelves lining the room rattled.

"Don't mind Finn," she said, sighing dramatically. "He's just overprotective. Like your guard dog." Her gaze flickered to Jake, and he growled, which didn't help his case. "The least we can do is talk about this like civilized adults. I like cutting to the chase. No need to go asking my patrons about me, though I'm flattered."

"It's not flattery," I argued. "You recognized the name. I saw it on your face." Her entire posture had shifted at the mention of Jude. I'd been right about the matchbook after all.

Her tranquil facade vanished, replaced by something sinister. She threw her legs off the desk and leaned forward in her seat, her palms slamming down hard against the wood. "What the fuck do you want with Jude Maddox?"

"What did Jude want with *you*?" I volleyed back, eyeing the contents of her desk from the corner of my eye. As the Fox seethed, I spotted a sheathed dagger made from the Rine Mountains, a worn map of Sciona, and a—

A silver compass.

One that appeared remarkably similar to the compass Jude had used in the Mist.

"It's a nice piece," she remarked drily. I lifted my head, finding her eyes glued to the object in question. "It would fetch a few coppers."

"Then why did Jude Maddox give it to you?"

The Fox straightened. Jake's hand went to his dagger.

"I'm going to ask again, and it'll be the last time," she began, her tone turning whisper soft. "How do you know Jude? The truth, if you'll indulge me...*Kiara*."

She knew my name. Likely knew Jake's as well. If she really was an infamous criminal, she'd be smart to have spies all over the city watching for newcomers.

I considered her, our eyes battling for dominance as we glared at each other. She had the ability to unsettle me while at the same time stoking the flames of my temper. And gods knew she shouldn't do that. Not after I'd set fire to those crates with only a touch.

"I— Jude is..." What? My commander? My friend? Yes, he was both of those things, and yet— "I care about him."

The words hung heavily in the air, suffocating me long after they left my lips. We'd been drawn together because of Raina's magic...but the moment I'd looked into his smoldering gaze and just a hint of my own fire mirrored back, a different sort of spell had taken hold. And it had nothing to do with a goddess.

The Fox studied me intently, so still, I was sure she didn't breathe.

Moments passed before she nodded, satisfied by whatever she saw on my face. "Jude came to me for help," she said softly. "For information, to be precise."

"Which was?" Jake pressed, finally lowering his hand from his hilt.

The Fox eyed him, her nose wrinkling. Jake instantly sat up straighter like he'd been reprimanded by a superior. I bit down my smile.

"It doesn't matter. I told him I wouldn't help. Besides, while he might've been after a few of Cirian's ancient texts—which I may or may *not* possess—he'd still be out of luck. It would've been pointless to tell him that the books only point to a specific location, and entering that place without getting caught—or killed—would require my expert services. Which I can't provide."

Ancient texts? What could he need with—

Oh. The only feasible explanation was that the commander thought our answers lay in some dusty old book. And the location the thief spoke of... It had to be the Moon God's temple, right?

"Why did you turn him down?" I asked.

"He didn't have enough coin," she said simply. "I can't send my men out into danger with nothing to gain from it. It breaks every code I live by."

A thief with moral codes. Still, her excuse didn't sit right with me. She was putting on a show for me this very minute, trying her best to appear unaffected.

That, right there, was a red flag.

"You're lying." The accusation flew out of my mouth in a breathless rush. I was exhausted by games. Exhausted by obstacles keeping me from the truth of *my* life. And Jude had become a large part of it.

In a flash, she reached into her jacket and retrieved a dagger, slamming its tip into the polished wood. The hilt trembled, a ringing echoing.

"Never accuse me of lying. Not unless you wish to lose your tongue."

Her threat sent my pulse hammering, and my magic responded, the need to lash out clawing at my chest. A violent chill worked from my arms and to my gloved hands, the sensation like jabbing needles. My eyes slid down, my frustration literally seeping out of my pores—

Gray wisps coiled out, leaving the barest trace of smoke in their wake. I silently cursed, shoving my hands into my lap and out of sight.

I needed to get my shit together or the Fox would kill me right now. Exhaling slowly, I tried to reel back my emotions, thinking instead of happier things—like sword throwing with Micah, or, rather, Arlo. The red covering my vision eased away, and the small trace of shadows mercifully eased back inside, though they did so begrudgingly.

Bold. I needed to be calm and bold and play her game. Taunt her.

I reached for the dagger splintering her desk and toyed with its hilt, grateful my hands didn't shake.

Without looking up from the blade, I said, "Jude's been captured. The king's men took him early this morning, and I fear what they'll do if I wait any longer. You *are* connected to him, and I would gamble to say you don't like the idea of him imprisoned."

I lifted my chin to find the Fox's eyes alight with fire. All pretenses were gone, her fury a palpable thing. That rage thrummed my power and spoke to me in a way that was all too familiar.

"Captured?" she asked so quietly, I could barely make out the word. She'd shown her hand, and we both knew it—Jude was the key.

"He's probably being tortured as we speak." This time I ground my teeth, trying to keep my voice even. Thoughts of him in that cell haunted me. With every blink, I saw him, curled up on the stone floor and covered in blood.

Across from me, the Fox had gone pale, even as her eyes sharpened.

"You obviously care about him, too, or you wouldn't be so bothered," Jake muttered, voicing my own thoughts. "You're practically humming with anger." He glanced at the door and back. "It's just us now. No need to pretend in front of your hired muscle."

The Fox shook her head, her lips thinning into a straight line.

"We need to save Jude before the king kills him." I stood, my hands clenched into fists. "He's only alive because they want to draw me out of hiding. While I'd prefer not to fall for that trap, it doesn't mean I'll just stay here and allow him to die." If the thief wouldn't help, we were wasting time here.

"You don't know how to break someone out of a cell, recruit. I'd bet you'd be caught in five minutes."

"Then help us," I returned.

She ground her teeth but didn't avert her gaze. "He'll want to go to the temple if we manage to get him out."

"Look at that. She knows about the temple, Jake," I smugly replied, keeping my eyes firmly on the Fox. Jake sat up in his chair and played along.

"Sure looks that way, Ki."

"And?" I gestured for the Fox to continue.

"And it's not just *any* temple. It's where many a treasure hunter has gone to die. It has traps and beasts and all manner of things waiting for you." She looked to her bookcase, where a row of leather-bound tomes sat, some coated in dust. "Only the clever ones sought the talisman." Her eyes shot to me knowingly. The Fox knew about the talisman, meaning Jude had been right to search for her. "Their bones will rest beneath the earth forever."

Well, Maliah didn't tell us *that*.

"We're asking you to help Jude, not to break into the temple. That's up to you," I said carefully.

"You couldn't find the real entrance to the temple if you tried. I've studied the damned place for years."

"So you won't do it?" I cocked a brow. "Help Jude or help us get to the temple?"

At some point in the conversation, we must've inadvertently drawn closer together. Her, on the other side of her desk, leaning forward. Me, mirroring her actions.

"The gods are devils," she spat. "Just like the damned king." She rubbed at her forehead. "If Jude's…alive, then…"

"Then?" I pressed, knowing I had her. The Fox was breathing hard, sweat trickling down from her brow.

At her reluctance, wisps of my shadows traversed across the wood, slithering toward the thief. She watched them move, her lips parting as they encircled her wrists and played with the tips of her fingers. She shivered, but she did not retreat.

If anything, they softened her prickly exterior. I made no effort to call them back.

"I see," she said, calm, unfazed. "I suspected you were the same Kiara from the stories. Attacked by a shadow beast and lived to tell the tale." She cocked her head. "I just never expected for you to come waltzing into my study. What a fun surprise."

"You're not frightened?" I asked, the words slipping out before I could catch them. They sounded so small I wished I could reel them back.

The Fox flashed her white teeth. "Oh, on the contrary. I've experienced more of the divine than one would think." I frowned at the cryptic words, taken aback by her apathy. I'd expected a better reaction than *that*.

"As long as you don't use that shit on me, I won't have to kill you," she added somberly.

Hmm. I may have liked her.

"Since you stand no chance on your own, I'll offer my services. For a *price*," she enunciated. "But if he...if Jude is dead, the deal's off."

"He's not," I said adamantly. I'd know. I didn't know *how*, but my shadows would feel his absence—*I* would feel it.

"You'll help us get the commander back and navigate this temple?" I clarified, already knowing her answer. I resisted the urge to smile.

The Fox clenched her fists before bringing them to her sides, hiding them from sight. "As long as I get to claim whatever treasures we find. I need to pay my men, after all. Since the boy went and got himself captured, it appears he's forced my hand."

She was trying so very hard not to appear affected by him, yet she couldn't fool me; I recognized that look in the mirror.

I held her stare once more, pretending to consider. "Deal," I affirmed. "You can have everything besides the talisman we require."

"Return here tomorrow at dawn," the thief said, her attention solely on me. "And don't make me regret this."

• • •

I couldn't sleep that evening.

Jake snored loudly beside me, the two of us sharing the single bed the inn offered. On top of the snoring, he shifted in his sleep.

I was about to give in to temptation and elbow him in the ribs, when my scar gave an unpleasant throb. I jolted up in bed as nausea churned in my stomach and the dimly lit room blurred. I slipped from the bed, stumbling on my feet as stone walls and rusted chains flashed across my eyes.

With each second, the scene before me changed—from the cell to the grimy inn's room and back.

I felt in between worlds, stuck in a place that was neither here nor there. Drifting without a life raft. Fear slithered into my veins and cold sweat slid down my back.

I didn't recall doing so, but I must've brought my gloved fingers to the scar. The wound pulsated under my touch.

Jude.

The last time I'd envisioned him hadn't been nearly as intense, but I recognized the bond we shared tightening, pulling taut. Demanding I find him.

I don't know how, I wanted to scream, but no words came from my lips. Jake's snores were replaced by the roaring of my blood in my ears as I staggered for the door, needing fresh air.

A thousand needles pricked my hands as I opened the door and crept down the hall and past the empty front desk. I all but floated down the steps until I faced a narrow side street.

Barely anyone lingered. Though I doubted people would come to my aid should they see me fumbling down the boulevard, now gasping for air as my lungs constricted.

It was getting worse, and I couldn't see well enough to find my way back to the room.

My hands sought out the solidness of a nearby wall, my fingers trailing over coarse brick until a slip of space opened between buildings. It was a tight squeeze, barely large enough for me to move through.

Safely hidden away, I pressed my back against the wall before crumbling to my knees, the dust from the ground kicking up to reach my nostrils.

I panted, staring down at my arms, noticing that they were flickering in and out of focus. The dungeon shone clearer than the alley now, but shadows clung to my frame, winding up to my face, making the world hazy.

I might've let out a scream, but my ears started ringing, and the black spots that had threatened earlier now swelled. And all the while, my scar throbbed.

My magic reached for Jude, luring me further away from Fortuna. I gave in easily as delicious tingles raced up and down my arms, my legs, my torso. It was a sensation of free-falling, and my stomach lurched into my chest.

And then everything went still.

I opened my eyes.

Fortuna was gone. The alley a memory. I now stood in the same prison I'd first seen Jude, yet this time, my commander hovered before me—

Shackled to a wall, his back exposed.

Red dripped freely from gaping wounds, his tattoo destroyed, only traces of black ink visible.

For a second, I was too stunned to react, to move, to do much of anything. It had to be a nightmare, a sick, twisted dream.

A whip sliced through the air, carving up his back, blood spilling out. Jude screamed, and the sound of it was my undoing.

"This all will stop if you tell me," the surly guard holding the whip promised. He rubbed at his sweat-slickened forehead with a frustrated grunt. "Just say the words, and save yourself the pain."

Jude said nothing.

Fire licked at my insides, and for once, I couldn't tell if it was magic or merely my fury. I clenched my fists and moved a foot forward, sensation returning to my body.

I wanted to lunge at Jude, to shield his body with mine, to erase that haunting scream he'd released from my memory. But I wasn't entirely in control, and each step was met with resistance.

I didn't care. Nothing would stop me. No otherworldly magic or in-between realms.

I didn't understand how any of this worked, but seeing him tortured made the impossible trivial. I *was* getting to him.

The guard didn't notice me. No one came barreling my way, no shouts ensued. I was invisible, and I hated it, because I wanted so badly to wrap my hands around the stout man's neck and have him look into my eyes as I snuffed out the last ember of his life.

Only Jude kept me moving toward him, the smell of copper heavy in the air.

I was a foot away, close enough that I could see the wet blood ooze in rivulets from his injuries. I reached out with tentative hands. They shook. *Everything* shook.

The whip hissed before slashing *through* my body, shadows skittering off my form like rippling water. Invisible and incorporeal, a phantom that could do nothing but watch this horror.

Still, I aimed for Jude's cheek, needing to touch him, my only thoughts ones of protection.

An inch from his pallid face, I met a horrid wall of resistance. One that drove desperation into my body, the feel of it wild and unhinged.

I pounded on the barrier of packed air, tears welling in my eyes with each futile blow. After minutes of my useless fighting, the remnants of my armor cracked, reality surging forth to devour me. Anger morphed into sorrow, and that sorrow consumed everything that I was and ever had been. I lowered my arms, barely able to stand upright.

"Jude," I croaked, tears burning down my cheeks. Without the will to keep them in check, they silently fell, one by one down my cheek and to my lips. "I'm here, Jude. Please look at me."

My voice was the only weapon I possessed, and I despised how weak it made me feel. This time I couldn't use my hands or a weapon—just...*me*. And sometimes I didn't feel nearly good enough. Yet the longer I took Jude in—focusing on his gruesome cuts—the clearer the cell became, and the more my limbs weighed heavy with sensation. It started to feel as if I truly stood there, in that cell, and still no one heard my screams, until—

"Kiara?" Jude murmured, no louder than a whisper. He blinked away the sweat dripping from his forehead and into his eyes. He looked as if he was about to lose consciousness. "You're back."

The guard paused his assault, but a second later, he struck Jude again. I screamed as Jude remained silent, my roar of rage shaking my bones, seeming to rattle the walls of the cell.

Bile rose, threatening to spill. It seared my throat when I swallowed it back down. His wounds were too much, his agony too clear. I shifted away from his back like a coward.

"Jude, listen to my voice," I begged, my tears unrestrained, knowing I could do *nothing*. How useless I felt. How worthless.

I didn't care that I cried. Tears were nothing more than pieces of our souls escaping, and I sobbed as if my own back was being whipped, as if my skin was being torn apart.

In a way, watching this was worse.

"I'm here. I'm right beside you. And I'm coming for you." Shadows curled at my fingertips when another unforgiving lash met his skin. My shadows flared a vicious silver before sparking, reminding me of lightning during a storm. My grief grew stronger, my will to fight against the impossible blossoming like a weed through stone.

His entire life, people had given up on him. I never would.

"Jude?" I half sobbed, half choked out. "Are you with me?"

His body shivered as though I had caressed him. "I miss you," he murmured, his head sagging between his shoulders. He couldn't even manage to lift it and meet my eyes. "I never thought I'd miss anyone. It makes this so much worse."

My heart broke in two—I felt the same way, and he was right—it made everything worse, that much harder.

"Don't you dare give up," I snapped, wishing I could grab his chin and force his head up. "Because when I save your ass, and when I finish burning every person alive who dared to hurt you, you're going to let me finally take care of you, you stubborn, stubborn man."

I couldn't breathe properly with how hard the tears were escaping. "Jude, I— What I feel for you... Watching this is killing me." Truly, parts of myself I didn't know existed ached, and a great emptiness yawned in my center, the void it birthed hungrily consuming rational thought. I'd never felt such a thing, being so hollow, empty in a way that hurt.

Jude moaned as he raised his head, tilting his chin. I caught sight of his right eye, which no longer held the same warmth I'd come to know.

The sight sent a surge of enraged fire down my spine.

"Kiara, I may be hallucinating, and I don't care. I just need you to know..." He coughed, sputtering as a jolt racked his frame. I hissed, clenching my hands into tight fists. Jude continued, his voice nothing but a whisper. "I know you don't like emotional speeches, but if I die, then I need to say this."

Screw that. "You're not dying—"

"I think I started falling for you the moment I laid eyes on you in Cila. And I think I fell completely when you kissed my scars in that glen and let me see all of you. I saw a woman who'd fought death and risen from the ashes. I s-saw...I saw *you* as clearly as you saw me, and for the f-first time, my reflection didn't frighten me."

That day when I kissed his scars, and he'd kissed mine, I'd plummeted, diving into a place of no return. And gods above, I didn't want to ever leave. That was when Jude had begun to feel like *home*.

And my home was slowly being torn apart, piece by piece.

"Don't you d-dare," I stuttered, choking on my tears. "You are not giving me a goodbye speech. I won't allow it." Jude made a sound of protest, but I cut him off. "No. I won't stop until you're fighting at my side. Whole and *mine*," I promised, and the gold in his brown eye blazed. Then I said the words I'd felt for some time now, words that would have frightened me before but came so easily now. "I'm falling, too, Jude Maddox."

The instant the confession fell from my lips, the gray film clouding my vision slid away.

I stumbled back in surprise, and Jude twisted, forcing me to take in the macabre lashes marring his back.

Light filtered through the high window of the cell, gilded rays streaming across the grimy stones and dancing along the plane of Jude's brutalized skin. It was as if someone had ignited a thousand torches and held them overhead, casting the world in brilliant golden clarity.

It couldn't be... I had to be seeing things, because that light—there could only be one explanation.

I gasped, as did the guard, who dropped his whip and released a shrill cry of alarm.

The man's mouth opened comically, his stare landing on me for the first time. He blinked, wiping at his eyes furiously.

I ignored him, focusing on the light, which was soft yet shimmering. It reminded me more of the gentle glow of the glen, but its presence weighed heavily, and it only strengthened…

"Jude, look!" I was motioning toward the window, which was barely a foot in height.

I dove for him, about to force his chin up, when I remembered I couldn't touch him here, not in this impossible place. Something still held me back. A wall I hadn't yet torn down.

The commander groaned, his eyes shuttering. Crimson dripped from his back, splattering to the stones, and each inhale became more and more ragged.

"Wake up!" I demanded, delirious, shaking so hard, my teeth rattled. "Jude, please." He had to see, had to notice what shone clearly across the cell. He had to be given this small ounce of hope. Somewhere, just outside this cell, a change was happening all across the realm. Not all was lost.

But Jude only whispered my name once more before his eyes shut completely.

"No!" I roared. "Don't leave me. *Please*. Don't you dare go…"

He didn't move, his chest so painfully still.

Jude couldn't be dead. He had merely passed out. He would wake, and I would find him, and then we'd save our realm. And then…then who knows what may happen? Whatever it was, I envisioned him beside me. He would get to live. No, *we* would.

Because we had fucking earned it.

I was still crying his name when I was thrust from the vision, torn away from Jude and the cell where we both just exposed our hearts.

A collection of alarmed screams pierced my ears all at once.

When I opened my eyes, I was no longer in that cell, no longer with Jude. Wetness coated my face, an abundance of tears staining my skin. They kept on coming, making it hard to see, blurring the dingy alley of Fortuna.

I was back.

People cried out in alarm, but I made out the distinct sound of Raina's name. Swiping away the tears, I scrambled to my feet, hobbling out onto the boulevard, drawn by the shouts.

A few people rested on their knees, heads bent toward the sky. It was dark, not a trace of light to be seen, but still they swore and prayed and murmured Raina's name like a prayer.

"She came!" one woman exclaimed, rising from her position on the ground. "She's coming back!"

I snatched the nearest man's cloak and yanked him to my side. "What happened?" I asked, my voice hoarse, tears drying on my heated cheeks, exhaustion causing me to sway.

Twice my size, the weathered man could likely snap someone in half with a flick of his wrist, and yet, when he turned to me, his eyes twinkled like those of a child.

"Light," he murmured. "For just a moment, there was light."

Chapter Ten

Jude

Lorian and Maliah have never been known to get along. Rumors argue that they are too much alike. Both are strong-willed, though Maliah has often taken their challenges past fairness.

Excerpt from Asidian Lore: Legends and Myths of the Realm

"Holy gods, you did it."

I woke to a soft, feminine voice whispering in my ear.

I could have sworn something wet and scratchy lapped at my back, but I was too drained to accomplish the simple feat of opening my eyes.

"Wake up. Before that insipid guard returns. I would hate to stain my hands with his death." A pause. "Well, actually, he might deserve it. Take your time."

Every muscle went taut. The voice sounded *real*. Not like the ethereal sound of Kiara's voice when she came to me in a dream or hallucination. The last time she'd visited, finding me in the tangled web of my own mind, she had told me she was falling for me —

I was too pessimistic to believe that was real.

"Wake up," the voice demanded once more, no longer patient.

I forced my eyes open, the room a blur as I searched for the newcomer. "W-who are you?"

The chains imprisoning me clinked together as a lock turned. Gravity was my newest foe, and I collapsed to the floor in a messy heap, stinging pain slicing across my body.

I peered up at my supposed savior, blinking away the black spots.

"Hello, Commander." A woman no more than five feet tall waved. She was dressed in all leather, and knives and additional weapons decorated her full belt.

"Who are you?" I repeated, shoving to my feet. I rolled my shoulders back with a grimace, my back a mess of agony and reopened cuts. I'd never seen this woman before in my life.

If she chose to fight me now, she might just win. I simply didn't have the strength. Lack of food and water did that to a person.

Her eyes flickered down... My wrists. The manacles that bound my power lay on the floor. They held the imprint of fingerprints, as if the metal had been pried off by hands fashioned of flames.

She'd *freed* me.

As if I'd called it forth, heat churned in my chest, my magic bubbling to the surface now that the cuffs were off. I felt whole once again, the steadying presence of my power seeming to press affectionately against my insides.

The woman smiled, a wicked thing that hinted at cunning and deceit. "I'll tell you who I am when we're safely outside these walls. Time is of the essence, Commander. Oh, and you're welcome," she added, glancing at the manacles. "Those bastards were *not* easy to remove."

"Why would I trust—"

Movement caught my eye, and I instinctively reached for my

nonexistent blade. My breath caught as a *fucking* jaguar slid out from the shadowy corner of the room, its slick, speckled coat glistening beneath the fluttering light of the sunfire.

"Is that—"

"Yes, it is," she replied as if bored. "Which I'm sure is a shock, but do hurry and control your excitement. You can pet him when we get out."

I wouldn't touch that thing in a thousand lifetimes. I'd never seen one in the flesh, only heard the legends of how sharp their teeth were and how easily their claws sliced through bone.

Suddenly, the woman's presence felt less like a gift.

"Well, come on," she insisted, giving me her back as she waited for me to follow.

I hesitated. She may or may not be here to help me, but she *had* unlocked my cuffs. This opportunity couldn't be wasted, and if she wished to stab me in the back later, then she wouldn't be pleased by my reaction.

The scar beside my heart pulsed as I pursued the woman and the predator at her side. My body was humming with a divine power that grew stronger, even as my injuries pulled open with every step.

It was a sentient thing, this magic. It required air to breathe, same as me, and now that the cuffs were off, it might as well have been hyperventilating.

"Hurry!" the woman hissed. She opened the unlocked door to the cell, the hinges squeaking in protest. I winced, waiting for a surge of guards. No one came.

Marching through the cell, she waved me down the torchlit hallway, bringing me to a circular staircase.

There wasn't time for indecision now. If guards came, we'd be trapped in the stairwell, and my chance of finding Kiara and warning her would be lost. I rushed up the steps.

At the top was a door, and like the one leading to the

dungeon, it was unlocked.

"What did you do with all the guards?" I asked between my teeth.

"I didn't kill them, if that's what you're asking. Not that you should care." The sparse sunfires cast ghoulish circles below her narrowed eyes.

Get out first, then interrogate her, I reminded myself. And she was right. I *didn't* much care about the guards who'd taken turns whipping me.

Sliding out into the hall, I kept close to the wall, avoiding the brighter sunfires.

All of these fortresses appeared the same—cold and fashioned with dull stone. They belonged to generals the king favored, men who had risen up in the ranks by showcasing their unwavering loyalty. I'd visited a few during my time with the king, often when I was on an errand to deliver a threat.

Hanging on the wall was a single blue banner embellished with an ochre starwing. The sigil belonged to General Devonshire, a man who was currently sweeping the southern marshlands for rebels.

Meaning security wouldn't be as stringent with so many of his men by his side.

By the looks of it, we were in the servants' quarters now, and judging by the clatter of pots and pans ringing down a winding corridor, it was dinnertime. These halls should be all but empty. The timing was perfect.

"Through there," the woman commanded, pointing to a chipped blue door.

It had been left ajar, brisk air sweeping across my bare skin. With one final glance at my unexpected hero, I poked my head through the gap and immediately cursed.

A soldier paced in front of the woods, a hint of auburn hair poking through his hood. Harlow.

"Someone's out there," I hissed.

"And? Kill them. I don't see the problem." She shrugged. "He's wearing the king's colors. Therefore, he's marked himself as a target. It's *his* fault, really."

I was torn between lunging at the lieutenant and sparing his life. Why I felt so merciful, I couldn't discern. But that hesitation was answer enough.

I didn't want to kill him. Not today, at least.

"I *know* him." I spoke through a clenched jaw, not about to argue with this woman about the moralities of killing a brother. Even if he was a traitor. I'd slayed enough of my own men to never want to lay a hand on them again, regardless of us being on opposing sides.

Before I could say another word, the woman kicked at the door with a booted heel, her pet lunging into the night. I fought to grasp her arm, but she moved too swiftly, slinking out of my reach as if her body was made of smoke.

"Wait," I called, but she'd already extracted one of the blades at her hip, a cruel smile on her lips as she faced Harlow's back.

He'd left me in the dungeons, all but dead. I shouldn't feel bad about his impending demise, and yet—

I sprinted after, and this time when I grabbed for her, I made contact.

My fingers curled around her wrist, and the woman hissed, dropping the knife. She stumbled and clutched at her hand, her wrist encircled with a painful-looking burn.

I backed away. *Had I done that?*

Her cry alerted Harlow, who whipped around from where he'd been gazing off into the distance. Considering the thick black trees encasing the fortress and the mountains peeking through the leaves, we appeared to still be in the North.

"Maddox," Harlow spoke, his tone relaying nothing. "How did you get out here?" His eyes flickered to the woman and her jaguar before returning to mine. "You need to get back before the others notice," Harlow ordered, taking a cautious step closer.

He inched for his weapon. If he thought he was going to put me back in that cell, he was wrong.

"Believe it or not, I'm trying to help you," he argued. "And Kiara."

I snarled. "Do not say her name."

Harlow held up placating hands. Ironic, as one of them now gripped a blade. "I swear to you, Jude. You must trust me. Timing is everything." He peered around us, then let out a weighted sigh and said, "We're ten miles from Fortuna—"

His words were cut off by the hilt of a sword.

The stranger had advanced on him before I could react, pulling a longsword from her sheath and jamming the hilt against Harlow's temple. His body struck the hard earth with a resounding thud. Stunned, I whirled on her.

"What?" She shrugged. "He was talking too much, and we have to get out of here."

"He was likely going to let us go," I said, turning to make sure Harlow lived. His chest rose and fell steadily, and I let out a relieved exhale. It hadn't been a lethal blow.

She sheathed her weapon. "We don't have the time for idle pleasantries."

I decided that I didn't care for this woman at all.

Still, I ran with her into the trees, allowing the obsidian woods to devour us.

Soon, the usual dim blocked out the flickering lights of the fortress at our backs, and I could barely see my feet flying across the uneven earth. Reeds nicked my bare feet, branches slicing my torso. I was half-dressed and fleeing imprisonment, and I had never felt so out of control in my life.

My eyes ached, starting to burn. Yet the farther we ran, the less they bothered me, and the brighter the woods became. As if my sight had adjusted and the moon had doubled its size.

"Almost there!"

Her beast growled as he scurried by me, on the heels of his mistress. The oddity of it all finally caught up.

I stopped running.

"Why are you helping me?" I called out, forcing her to slow. She let out a dramatic sigh before turning and walking back.

"Because this is the first time Cirian has stepped away, leaving me the perfect chance to sneak in. And believe me, I want to stop that masked puppet as badly as you do." She cocked her head, delivering a look reeking of malice. A person could choke on that look alone.

"Some call me Maliah," she continued, seeming to enjoy the way my lips parted at the revelation. "And now you're going to owe me a favor when you're not being hunted like prey." She drifted backward, her boots crunching the thick underbrush. "When that day comes, I expect you to fulfill your end. I've learned it's always a good idea to befriend those *before* they rise to power."

A fucking goddess. And one of the more ruthless ones at that.

I never believed I would prefer for Arlo to show up, but desperate times and all that.

"Maliah. Goddess of Revenge and Redemption," I murmured, needing to say it out loud. It was rumored the main gods and deities like her used to roam the earth, mingling with the humans. But that had been decades ago, and after Raina had vanished, so did the rest of the divine.

"The one and only," she said, continuing to slink away and into the woods. "I would've visited you earlier, but I had enemies to shake. You're not the only one being hunted."

Who was she running from? Her enemies could very well be my own.

Maliah peered overhead, to where a starwing fluttered down and landed on a branch. She scowled at it, shooing it away with a hiss. "But this is where I leave you. Can't stay too long in one place."

I had so many questions.

Instead, I asked the only question that mattered to me.

"Kiara," I yelled, compelling the goddess to stop once again. She groaned as if my very voice brought her pain. "Do you know if she's all right? Have you heard any news?"

"I've seen her," Maliah admitted, and my heart thudded wildly in relief. "She's doing her part, same as you."

I was tempted to ask if she'd been furious, even if she'd appeared nothing short of desperate when she visited my dreams—but that likely had to do with my bloodied state. I didn't care if she held on to her anger for me leaving; I deserved it. But seeing her again would be worth her wrath. Especially after…after what we'd said in that cell. It felt cemented then, our bond, and as if agreeing, my scar twinged in reply, a flood of warmth blazing along the vine-like scars she'd gifted me.

It truly hadn't been a dream.

"My sources have reported that she's engaging with the Fox. They're planning on heading to Mena first before engaging in your rescue." She smiled broadly, clearly proud she made it here first. "You might be able to intercept them if you hurry. Apparently she was able to convince your mother to help her better than you could."

Kiara was with my *mother*?

Fuck. The combination would be disastrous.

Maliah waved her hand in farewell, her body blurring as the darkness swept her up. "Don't let me down, Commander. I have a lot riding on you."

A growl echoed, and both beast and goddess vanished into thin air.

Leaving me alone and defenseless in the woods.

Gods, I should've at least asked for a blade. Or a shirt.

Thinking of blades, I surmised that if Kiara had tracked me to Fortuna and located my mother, she *should* have the Godslayer in her possession by now, especially if my intuition about Grey had been correct. Or the kid had become the richest nine-year-old in the city.

My mother chose to aid Kiara after denying me. It stung. Perhaps she had a change of heart after the king's men had stormed Fortuna and stolen me in the night.

The remaining question, however, was why my mother journeyed with Kiara at all. The texts she'd stolen throughout her life were rumored to contain ancient spells…spells that *might* allow us to unite Raina's divinity without one of us dying. It had been my only hope.

Yet the Fox's involvement told me the tomes didn't hold all of the answers we required.

And her risking her life to aid a fugitive—who *wasn't* her own son—had my heart beating faster with an emotion I wasn't familiar with.

Without a choice but to do as Maliah instructed, I headed east.

The pain that had radiated from my back eased as I strode through the underbrush. That divine warmth contained between my ribs stirred, sliding around to my torn skin and washing over the fresh lashes. I halted, squeezing my eyes shut as the burning turned into a soothing numbness. I pictured a healed back, unmarred by Cirian's vicious whip. He didn't deserve to mark me. He'd never had that right.

My pulse thundered, a full-body shudder working its way up and down my form. Reaching behind me, I prepared to assess the damage done by the guards.

I frowned. My fingers connected with dry, smooth skin.

No pain. No open wounds. No cuts.

I cursed, dropping my arm and feeling around. My back...it was healed. Just as I'd pictured.

I shut my eyes and imagined the cut on my cheek gone as well. Patrick was just as vile as Cirian, and while his mark was shallow, I preferred his mark to be a distant memory.

My hand trembled as I guided my hand to my face.

Smooth skin. It was gone. Same as the lashes on my back.

All healed with a *thought*.

Moving to my left side, I sucked in a wavering inhale. The twin scars crossing my left side remained, still as deep and angry as before. Attempting to wish them away led to nothing. After three tries, those *gifts* from my father endured.

Regardless, my wonder couldn't be diminished.

In the Mist, I'd unwittingly healed Kiara, saving her from the maw of death. I shouldn't be surprised I'd now mended a few fresh lacerations.

This development was a reminder I was no longer just Jude Maddox, Commander of the Knights of the Eternal Star. Within my chest, I harbored two of the three missing keys of divinity from a fallen goddess—

Which meant I wasn't entirely human. Not anymore.

CHAPTER ELEVEN

KIARA

*Originally brushed aside as nightmares, some speculate that
shadow beasts had more power than they were given credit
for. It makes sense that they were strongest at night when the
moon—their creator—brightened the sky.*

EXCERPT FROM ASIDIAN LORE: A TALE OF THE GODS

I sprinted back to the inn as frail, gray shadows trailed from
my gloved hands.

Shoving open the door, I rushed toward a still-snoring Jake
and shook him until he cracked open his bleary eyes.

"Ki? What's wrong?" He groaned as he shifted in bed, lifting
onto his elbows. Leaning over, he reached for a pack of matches
on the bedside table and lit the oil lamp.

My cheeks were still sticky from shedding so many tears,
and my eyes were likely bloodshot. I didn't think I'd ever cried
as much as I had in the last twenty-four hours. Perhaps it was a
lifetime of suppressing tears that now caused them to flow.

As if to confirm, Jake peered into my eyes with a deep frown.

"I saw Jude again," I said, lowering my voice to barely above
a whisper. "But this time, something…happened."

I felt like I'd disconnected from my body. Been forced

into that cell to witness the most horrific scene imaginable. My damned eyes prickled, and just when I thought there was nothing left, a single droplet slipped free.

I'd left him there. Abandoned him like everyone else. And he didn't look like he'd been breathing when I'd been thrust out of the vision.

He's not dead, I repeated in my head. I couldn't believe anything else.

"Gods." Jake swallowed visibly. "Ki…"

"It was bad, Jake. I was feeling dizzy, and I went outside for fresh air. My body felt like it was in two places at once, like I was slowly flickering out of existence, and then…" I paused, sucking in air, realizing I was rambling a mile a minute.

"When I opened my eyes, I wasn't in Fortuna, but back in that cell, and Jude was being tortured. His back was so bloody… so torn from the whip. They're killing him there, and I could do *nothing*." Jake rested a hand on my shoulder before tugging me in for a tight hug. I nestled into his embrace, resting my cheek on his chest while he ran a comforting hand through my hair. "I wasn't sure when I'd see him again. I wasn't sure if he'd make it through another round of torture, and when he confessed something, I did, too."

"What did you say?" Jake asked, holding me tight, tethering me to this plane.

"I said…"

That I was falling for the commander in a way my cynical heart never thought possible.

Jake must've read the truth in my silence because he let out a knowing sigh.

"I think I understand," he said slowly. "I see the way you two look at each other. The way you've *always* looked at each other."

Why couldn't I say it aloud? Maybe because the moment I did, it would be real, and then if I lost him, it would hurt even more.

No, that wasn't right.

It would kill me even now, even if I was too cowardly to say what my heart clearly felt.

Swords, arrows, blood? Easy. But an emotion as dangerous as love? Hells, that was an opponent I wasn't sure I could fight.

"After Jude told me how he felt…I saw the light in his cell for just a second, but the world *glowed*."

Jake released me, keeping me at arm's length. "I don't understand how that would be possible without you carving out your piece of divinity."

I laughed, but it was brittle. "I don't understand *anything.*"

"Good thing we're on a mission to find answers," Jake supplied, trying to smile for me. He eased back on to the bed to study me. "I swear there has to be a way out of this without you dying. I would *kind of* miss you, Ki."

"You'll never have to miss me," I vowed, even if I was uncertain I could promise such a thing.

Jake sucked in a sharp breath as his eyes sparkled with thought.

"Out with it," I demanded, scooting even closer to him until I was practically in his face.

"I'm thinking that you might have just shown yourself a way out of this mess." My brows furrowed. "As sappy as it sounds, Ki, when you and Jude…'opened up,' it might've allowed the keys access to each other. Reuniting them, if only briefly. And then there's that whole 'darkness falling for the light' prophecy I never put much stock in." He waved his hands around before dropping them at his sides.

"You're right. That does sound extraordinarily sappy," I agreed, my scar throbbing even as I deflected. It didn't burn as it had before, and I wondered if that meant Jude was asleep or if he'd closed himself off to me. Maybe once I figured out how to use this power, I'd be able to call upon him at will.

Shadow beasts hadn't earned their name without reason. Made of the night and its shadows, they could alternate between their phantom and corporeal forms with ease, able to move through space without hindrance. Meaning visiting Jude, in whatever form I had taken, *was* entirely possible.

But what else could I do? Could I *travel*? Did I vanish entirely when I accessed these gifts? I held too many questions, and I practically crumbled beneath the weight of them.

"Sometimes the answer is both the simplest…and the hardest. Destiny brought you and Jude together, but it didn't demand that you fall for the guy." He gave me a knowing look, and I hid my eyes with my hand. "Obviously, you did," he continued. "Don't even try to deny it." He raised a brow when I opened my mouth. I shut it. "It's up to you whether or not to heed its wishes."

"It's real, right?" I asked, more softly than I'd ever spoken.

Real that he loved *me*, not the woman I presented to the world. That strong, cocky facade. The me that felt fear and hope in equal measure. The me who wanted a partner, an equal, to stand by my side and fight with me.

Jake sighed in frustration. "We can't control who we care for. So maybe get out of your own way and let someone in. *Truly* in. I know that love scares the shit out of you, and I know you're afraid, but you can't fight your feelings, Ki."

He'd never been so serious, and the intensity in his stare shut down any retorts I had. Jake was right.

"You were touched by darkness. And him? Born from light. Two halves of the same whole," Jake said. "I don't care if I sound like an absolute sucker for saying this, but if any two people could rewrite the rules, it would be you and Jude. All you have to do is let him in."

Chapter Twelve

Jude

I miss him sometimes. Especially at night. Especially when the silence allows my thoughts to wander to dangerous places. I thought it would've gotten easier, that I was strong enough to do the right thing. But as time passes and his face becomes a memory, regret seeps into my soul and squeezes. I have to remind myself he's better off away from me. Right?

Unmailed letter from The Sly Fox Tavern to Jack Maddox

A day passed.

Maliah's encounter made every dark corner of the forest a threat, and I knew I'd have to steal a weapon sometime soon. My magic, the restless entity inside of me, wasn't yet controllable, and I'd feel better with a blade in hand.

After I left the fortress, I snuck into the city of Eldwin, stealing a muddied pair of boots from the back room of a butcher's shop. That evening, I crept to the outskirts of the city, snagging fresh trousers, a cloak, and a shirt from a clothesline.

Fully clothed, my feet finally protected from the harsh bramble of the woods, I pressed on to Lis, a humble town about two days' walk to Mena.

Like most cities in Asidia, statues of the gods were

everywhere. Lis favored Arlo, likely due to its past as a booming agricultural town. His image had been erected in the town square, the god rising from a patch of flowing vines and bulbous black weeds.

The tavern was the only place alive at this late hour, lights pouring out onto the bricks, welcoming the weary inside.

One thing I'd learned about people while traveling across Asidia, performing all the king's *business*, was that they tended to overshare when ale flowed and a band struck a merry tune. I'd go to fill my belly as well as my ears with gossip about the king.

Fixing the hood of my stolen cloak in place, I headed inside.

The warmth emanating from the hearth washed across my skin, the smell of cinnamon and something sweet mingling with the potent scent of ale. I chose a seat in an unlit corner where the sunfire had gone dim.

When the waitress approached, I rattled off my order, careful to turn my cheek and hide my face. She hardly spared me a glance before rushing away to retrieve my drink and meal.

I could almost imagine what Kiara would say if she were beside me, observing the lively bar and all of its odd patrons. More than likely, she'd command me to "stop brooding " and force me to my feet for a dance, even though no couples swirled around the floor.

Yet the more I thought of Kiara dancing, the more absurd it sounded. She would probably grumble about the lack of violence.

"Oy! This lad isn't paying!"

I lifted my head, wrenching free of my daydream.

A lad with curly brown hair and bright blue eyes gripped the bar with both hands behind him, his expression one of confusion.

I'd seen him before. *Where*, I wasn't certain.

His features weren't particularly unique, but...I never forgot a face. Rising from my seat, I inched closer for a better look.

He trembled but kept his head up, his chin raised in defiance. I cursed the second all the pieces clicked together.

The boy who'd run after Kiara when I recruited her. He screamed her name until his parents held him back.

This close, I noticed he had her slightly upturned nose and the same pointed chin, and while his eyes were blue rather than a fiery amber, they retained a similar shape, almost too large for his face.

Liam.

Kiara's brother was in Lis. Here.

I ground my teeth when the barkeep snapped his greasy fingers, motioning for the muscle of the tavern to approach.

"If you can't pay the full amount, then you know what we do to thieves." The barkeep said it all with a smile.

Liam shook his head back and forth, his curls sticking to the thick sweat on his brow. "I didn't know, sir! I swear, I left the rest of my coin at the inn. I told you I can retrieve it!"

I grimaced. One should *never* leave their coin at an inn. It practically begged thieves to take it from you.

He would be dead in seconds.

I groaned as I stood. This was going to be a long night.

"If he says he has the coin, he has the coin." Everyone stopped at the sound of my voice. Dropping my hood, I allowed the sunfires to highlight my milky eye and scars.

There was no going back now.

Liam, who had to be around my age, shot me a wary glance. Slowly, the uncertainty creasing his brow shifted into a look of recognition. His stare aimed at my scars, my mismatched eyes. He must've seen the wanted posters.

"I—" The barkeep halted, his hands still outraised before him. "Our policy…"

"We'll get your coin and deliver it to you by dawn tomorrow,"

I said firmly.

The brute the barkeep had signaled pushed up the sleeves of his shirt.

"I know who you are, *Commander*," he sneered, "and there's a hefty reward for your capture. Seems like we've found ourselves a much bigger prize, boys."

Startled gasps echoed around the room. My eyes were glued to the bastard who had the audacity to believe he was about to get rich.

"My friend and I are leaving," I reiterated, striding into the fray. The man shook his head leisurely, a vicious grin curving his thin lips. "Last chance," I warned, making a grab for Liam's hand. The wily bastard scrambled out of reach. I sighed in annoyance, but after the stories he'd likely heard, I couldn't fault him for his lack of trust.

"I think the odds are in my favor," the man said, quickly glancing around the tavern. He cracked his knuckles, scars and bruises from previous fights decorating his skin. A few other drunken patrons stood, rolling up their sleeves and assuming positions around the obvious ringleader.

How ready these men were to brawl. It would be a shame it wouldn't end the way they believed.

"Stay back," I ground out, hastily making contact with Liam. "I...I'm Kiara's commander, and I'm looking for her, too. I'm on your side. *Her* side."

Liam let loose a tame curse, a slight rasp lining the word. If a fight broke out, he wouldn't last. His condition had been the entire reason Kiara had been chosen to replace him during the Calling, and I couldn't allow him to get caught in the crosshairs.

"Trust me, Liam. Please," I implored as his stare widened. He hadn't expected me to know his name.

It was a gamble, seeing as the lad probably hated my guts, but even if he despised me for picking Kiara on that fateful day, he needed me to get him out of there first. *Then* he could plot my murder. He remained silent, but he gave me a slight nod. It was all I needed.

"Well." I faced my first opponent. Warmth infiltrated my chest as I fashioned my hands into fists and assessed my opponents. "Shall we get this over with? I have places to be."

A woman to kiss.

"Cocky shit, aren't we?" a raven-haired newcomer snapped, his upper lip curling into a sneer.

I had two options. Either I fought every last one of them, using energy I didn't care to waste or I could simply cause a distraction.

Fight smarter, not harder, Isiah had always said.

Just as the first brute came barreling toward me from across the room, his fist cocked and ready to plow into my face, I grasped the wooden bar behind me. Tightly.

I had to *try*. To see if I could wield my magic.

I'd healed myself with a single thought in the woods, desperate to rid myself of the newest wounds Cirian had gifted. Now, I was desperate for another reason—Liam.

Doubts clouded my mind—that I wasn't skilled enough, that I didn't have a clue how to handle such power—but I focused on Kiara's brother, reminding myself over and over again that I'd done it before, and I could very well do it again.

I chanted a single word, *burn*, repeating it in time with my heartbeat.

Burn, burn, burn, burn.

The heat trapped inside of me seared before it shot out in a deluge of fiery release. It felt divine, like I'd finally come up for air after nearly drowning.

Pure relief swept through me, and I nearly smiled.

No one seemed to notice what I'd done at first. Using that to my advantage, I dropped to my knees, spinning away a split second before the man's punch would've connected with my ribs.

Little did he know, the damage was already done.

The brawny giant rushed me again, and I blocked his assault with minimal effort. On the other hand, I might have *enjoyed* fighting these men. It was almost too easy, and I needed a little bit of fun.

Alas, the smell of smoke began to waft to my nostrils.

The remaining drunkards, who'd been all too thrilled to join in on the fight, froze, bewilderment causing them to still, mouths agape.

A couple of shouts sounded, calling for water, the barkeep frantically moving to smother the flames behind the bar. But they grew fast, much faster than I thought possible. Glasses of liquor shattered, sending fragments of glass flying through the air, a large piece striking one of the would-be attackers in the shoulder. Blood poured out of the wound, his white shirt stained in a pool of flooding red.

That was all the opportunity I needed. Liam squeaked as I grabbed his arm, hauling him in the direction of the doors.

"Let go!" Liam griped, fruitlessly yanking his arm. I didn't relent. He repeated his request several more times as we stumbled out onto the street. I ignored his pleas entirely.

Half-awake villagers left their homes—likely hearing the commotion—and gathered around the burning tavern. Smoke billowed from the open doors, men and women coughing as they rushed toward safety.

There was no time to feel shame.

Down the next street, I yanked Liam to a halt. "You may not believe a word I say, but I know your sister well," I said, my fingers digging into his shoulders. He narrowed his eyes, but at least he wasn't fighting me anymore. "I'm the one who chose her that day instead of you. And if we don't find her soon, the king and his men will. I'm trying to make sure that doesn't happen.

There is much you don't know."

Liam opened his mouth to ask more, but I was already pulling him in the direction of the woods.

All I'd wanted out of tonight was a decent meal.

When his breaths became ragged, I slowed with a foul curse on my lips. Kiara would murder me if anything happened to him.

"Are you all right?" I asked once we reached the hill's summit. I hadn't wanted to stop sooner lest the townspeople spot us.

Liam tumbled to his knees when I let go of his arm, his chest heaving. Hovering overhead, I looked down as he struggled, feeling utterly useless. I lifted my hand, about to pat his head like a fool, but thankfully, I snatched it away at the last second.

"Can I do anything?" I asked instead, sinking beside him. Liam clutched at his chest as he wheezed, beginning to hyperventilate.

I'd pushed him too far.

Taking his shoulders again gently, I angled my head, catching his wide eyes. "You need to breathe with me. Slowly, Liam. Can you do that?"

Fuck. I was outside my comfort zone. Isiah would've known exactly what to do and how.

"Hey." I snatched his chin and kept him in place. "Breathe with me, nice and slow." I inhaled deeply, maintaining eye contact.

Liam struggled, but eventually, he managed a mouthful of air. I counted to five and released my exhale. He imitated me, tracking my every movement, and minutes passed as we rested before the woods, both of us on our knees.

His wheezing remained, but it didn't sound as loud, and his exhales grew less frantic, his panic abating. It took another five minutes—minutes we likely didn't have—before he regained control, and even then, it was tenuous at best.

"Better?" I asked sometime later, leaning away to study him. My nerves were frayed, and sweat pooled at my lower back.

Liam swiped at his forehead, brushing aside some loose curls. He nodded. "I—I'm not a fan of cardio," he managed with a weak laugh.

"Your sister said the exact same thing once." I smiled, a genuine one. "Which reminds me. What were you thinking, leaving your village to come search for her? You are searching for her, right?"

I could already tell Liam maintained the Frey stubborn streak. Lovely.

He jerked his chin. "I heard rumors that some of the Knights had returned but that they'd deserted. Of course, I imagined Ki would be among the claimed traitors." His smile dipped slightly. "She was always the rebellious one of the family."

I grinned with him. Liam held an air of innocence that I couldn't help but covet.

"The king sacked Fortuna and the North," he continued, and now, confidence emboldened his words. "Meaning, there was a chance he'd missed some of the eastern villages. I had to start the search somewhere, and I've already combed through four towns before I came here."

"That was entirely thoughtless," I remarked drily. "A complete and utter guess. A foolish one at that."

"So what? I'm supposed to stay in Cila and *wait* for Ki to be arrested? Or wait until I hear she's dead, for that matter?" He sighed, and his entire body trembled as if an icy breeze chilled him. "She's saved me my whole life, and it's about time I return the favor."

"You also know she'll stab me if I let anything happen to you, right?"

Liam's lips curled. "Looks like someone got to you before her." He tilted his head toward my twin scars. I almost reached for the one Patrick had inflicted, forgetting I'd removed all traces of it a day before.

Using *magic*. Gods, it still felt weird to think about.

Liam smirked, but it wasn't in a cruel way. His sharp tongue and dry humor were Frey traits.

"Very funny," I said, trying to sound stern. I failed miserably, and my lips quirked.

"Are all the rumors of you true, then?" he asked. "I mean, I heard whisperings about your badass scars"—he waved a hand in front of my face, a slight blush painting his cheeks—"and they definitely add to the allure." He froze after the words had tumbled out of his mouth. "Shit, I didn't mean—"

"I know what you meant," I said, saving him from rambling. Not that it stopped him.

"But quick question before I begin my more serious round of interrogation. How did you start that fire? I didn't even see a torch nearby." Hesitantly, he rose to his feet. I joined him.

"Saw that, eh?" I walked into the brush, giving him my back. I heard light footfalls behind me. I reminded myself to keep my pace slow and easy.

"Kind of hard to miss, *Commander*," Liam mocked, his voice lilting.

"We have a lot to discuss." I sighed.

CHAPTER THIRTEEN

KIARA

You haven't written me for many months, and I worry something awful has happened to you. Please write and let me know he hasn't discovered our true mission. He's always within reach of the king, and I fear news might've already spread.

LETTER FROM AURORA ADAIR TO UNKNOWN RECIPIENT, YEAR 49 OF THE CURSE

The Fox insisted we head southeast.

She knew the locations of several fortresses belonging to the king where Jude might be held. There were over a dozen, but the thief had narrowed it down to three, all thankfully not too far from the temple.

Since we planned on traveling by horse, I insisted I free Starlight from those dank stables. She seemed pleased enough to see me again, though I couldn't help but sense she'd expected Jude to walk into the pen and was slightly disappointed it had been me.

Finn and another of the Fox's comrades, Dimitri, accompanied us.

Dimitri was the quieter of the two men, although his pale

brown eyes held a twinkle in them that hinted at more than mischief. Lithe and tall, and flaunting an obnoxious orange coat, he came across as a man not belonging to the criminal world.

Whenever he caught me staring, he'd smile and wave, and I'd scowl, too skeptical of his exuberance to return the gesture. My poor manners didn't stop him from trying, and when we fell into line beside each other on the path, he'd whistle this tune that reminded me of a lullaby. It was oddly calming.

A full day and a half passed, and no one pursued us.

Except for the bright blue eyes trailing us.

Lorian's little pet tracked us from Fortuna, the jaguar keeping a far enough distance away so the others didn't notice. But I did. In fact, I noticed more than I ever had before.

The night seemed to be alive. It *moved*, sentient wisps of darkness curling about the trees and laying atop the leaves like fluffy clouds. Whenever my anxiety reared its ugly head and I thought of the worst, it was there, reacting to my magic, to *me*. Phantom shadows wrapping around my frame like an embrace.

Sometimes I swore I heard the night speak, a quiet thing meant to soothe my fraying nerves. Nerves that caused a constant ache in my chest. Its voice was muffled, though it held a steady rhythm, beating in time with my own anxious heart. I hated to admit that it relaxed me.

On the third morning, the air had shifted.

For the first time in days, my scar ached and throbbed with warmth. My shadows, which hadn't made an appearance since Fortuna, whispered at my fingertips, seeming to stretch and yawn after a long nap. A fluttering of wings sounded as they slithered out, the rustling of the spindly limbs and brittle leaves causing me to flinch.

"Something wrong?" Jake asked at my side. He rode one of the Fox's steeds, a mighty onyx beast that towered well over Starlight. Not that she hadn't immediately asserted dominance by stomping none too gently on its hoof.

I shook my head. "No. Just an odd feeling." I spared a glance behind me, spotting the raven-haired thief and her two comrades whispering among themselves, a decent distance away from where we led. I'd yet to uncover her true name, and I doubted she'd tell me if I asked. Names were sacred; sometimes a name was the only real thing you owned.

"I hate your *feelings*," Jake said with a sigh. "They typically end up with an arrow being shot at us or someone trying to stab you."

He wasn't wrong.

I scanned the trees hugging the sides of the uneven road we traveled. It all looked the same, the stone path we ventured down made of nonsensical turns and narrow trails nearly hidden by the thick brush.

We'd come across a few merchants and other weary nomads, but so far, we hadn't faced any trouble. According to the Fox, this route was only taken by the desperate or the foolish. The more popular roads boasted fewer criminals and cutthroats outrunning the law. I supposed it fit—we *were* wanted for desertion.

The Fox had been quiet since we'd left the city, though I occasionally caught her staring. Like now. The second she realized she'd been caught, she hastily jerked her chin and whispered something to Dimitri, who glanced at me with another one of his too-wide grins.

I was tempted to open my mouth and prod her, to ask what her fixation was, when Starlight wrenched her head back and whinnied, the muscles of her back tensing.

"Shhh," I soothed, rubbing the side of her head. Her ears flicked back, a clear sign she was on edge. She wasn't the only one.

Gripping the reins, I closed my eyes, shivering as ice trickled across my torso and slid down my spine. I'd felt *off* for quite some time. No matter how hard I tried to shove aside my worry that something was amiss, my body wouldn't allow me.

My hands shook, and suddenly the sensation of falling sent my heart stuttering in my chest.

The world felt too large at that moment and our task too impossible. The magic inside of me was tied to my emotions. And my emotions were all over the place.

I became lighter as I embraced the feeling of falling and accepted the numbness that stole me from reality.

In utter darkness, with only the sound of the horses' hoofbeats, I let go. It was like shoving off from the side of a cliff, not sure if you'll hit the rocks.

The free fall felt divine.

Deeper and deeper I plunged into my magic, as easy as breathing. The real world slipped through my fingers, and I floated, moving with the breeze, a wayward starwing with my wings outstretched.

So free, so weightless, I soared above the tops of the trees, the entire realm below. On the horizon, a speck of orange burned, and my sharpened senses picked up the scent of fire. My invisible wings tilted, and I plummeted, sailing toward the source of light. Toward dying flames not yet smothered by heavy boots.

There were no bodies moving around the smoldering pit, but there had been recently. The abandoned camp rested about a mile away, right off the path we traveled.

There were footprints. Far too many of them.

"Ki."

Jake was calling my name from far away, but I hovered above that fire, studying the cracked branches and twigs where boots had walked. Those prints guided me to the telltale marks of wheels denting the earth.

"Ki!" Jake tried again.

I gasped when I opened my eyes, my body jerking forward in the saddle.

My gloved hands were nearly transparent, and my forearms shone an unnatural gray. I brought one to my face, inspecting the shimmering skin. It didn't look solid. Didn't look *real*.

"What just happened—"

"You were flashing in and out of existence. I swore I saw *through* you at one point." Jake's voice shook, and he snuck a hasty look backward. "Good thing our new companions didn't see. They seemed to have slowed, likely plotting our murder. If they'd seen you…" While his words held sarcasm, I understood him too well.

"I'm all right," I said, regaining my sense of balance.

The corners of his eyes were creased, and he held one hand out toward me as though reaching to grasp my arm. Still, he didn't touch me. Like he was *frightened*.

I held up a hand, needing a moment. Jake eased back in his saddle, running his hand anxiously down his steed's neck.

Taking in deep breaths, I used the same techniques I performed with Liam back at home when an attack struck him. Minutes passed, and slowly, the wave of lightheadedness lessened into something manageable.

The steady pounding of hooves reached my ears as the Fox and her men picked up the pace, their forms now indistinguishable on the curving trail.

I thanked the heavens they hadn't seen.

"Ki, you were *pulsating*," Jake began once color had returned to my skin and my exhales were no longer ragged. "Shadows were swarming you and I—" He stopped abruptly, the pulse point at his throat thumping wildly.

When Jake didn't know how to solve a problem, he panicked, especially when it came to the people he cared for. As this was all new to me, I couldn't comfort him. But I could tell him the truth.

"I was…flying," I whispered, meeting his somber expression. "I couldn't feel my body. Up there"—I craned my neck—"I saw an abandoned campsite not too far from here. There'd been a lot of boot prints, more people than the average traveling party." I suspected the King's Guard. Starlight whipped her head around and nuzzled my leg as best she could, and I reached for her mane, running my hands through the tangles.

Jake massaged his temples. "Well, we should stay off the main road for a while just in case. Though I want to make it clear, we are certainly returning to the whole *flying* aspect later. And if you could *not* have a new ability every damned day, that would be great as well. You're making my head spin."

"Sorry, Jake, I—"

I turned at the roar of thundering hooves coming from up ahead in the distance, yanking on Starlight's reins.

"What's the matter?" the Fox called out as she angled her steed my way, suspicion gleaming in her eyes. "You're paler than snow, child."

As if she cared.

"I think we're about to have some company," I said when she halted five feet away, Finn and Dimitri at her back. Dimitri's focus lowered to my gloved hands, a brow raising.

"And how could you know this?" Finn questioned, sharing a look with the thief that I couldn't decipher. "More of that dark magic?"

He'd made it clear he wasn't an admirer of mine.

"If my *dark magic* will save us, then I wouldn't question it." We locked eyes, Finn being the first to glance away. "I may not understand my power, but I sure as shit listen to it when it's telling me an enemy is approaching. It's yet to be wrong."

"Believe me, you *should* listen," Jake said. "I'd say we get off the road. They could be Cirian's men."

The Fox's brown irises were cold as she studied me longer than was comfortable. I exhaled in relief when she finally jerked her head to the side, her men obeying her unspoken command. All three aimed their horses for the tangled woods, the thick underbrush a mess of twisting vines and spiky shrubs. Jake and I tailed them, delving safely into the cover of the forest.

A minute later, my vision was confirmed when I peered over my shoulder.

Horses…and a lot of them. Their hooves thudded upon the earthen path, heading our direction.

Squinting into the dim, I noted the blurred shapes of approaching figures. Fog swirled around their feet and stretched up their torsos, those on horseback nearly lost entirely to the dark.

The Fox slid the loose sunfire she carried inside the deep pocket of her cloak, delivering us into near darkness. The moon was surrounded by clouds today, and barely any of its serene glow penetrated the gray.

"Hurry," she hissed, yanking her steed deeper into the woods.

Jake and I persisted, but Starlight flung her head from side to side as if protesting. I patted her mane, trying to calm her, but she let out a loud whinny.

Whoever neared would've heard that.

She resisted the entire way into the cover of the trees, and I couldn't ease her. Starlight was spooked. Or pissed.

It was likely both.

Dismounting, I ushered Starlight deeper into the forest and away from the threat. The road was just visible enough that we glimpsed a caravan of the King's Guard, their troop a blur of red.

Their bright tunics could be seen, even in the murky night, and the steel carriage that rolled front and center squeaked with every rotation of its wheels.

They weren't even trying to be stealthy.

I seized my dagger and positioned it before me. The Godslayer remained tucked away in my sheath. Safe until I could bloody it with our true enemy.

Jake nudged me with his elbow, directing my attention down the line of soldiers. One of the men stood out from the others, wearing all black, his broad shoulders outfitted in a fine linen cloak of matching color. I homed in on the lone figure.

I needed to see his face. Something about his posture was eerily familiar.

As though answering my unspoken prayer, everything came into agonizing focus. Heat burned my eyes as flashes of pale yellow flared out from where we hid, painting the trees, the path, the road. I blinked, taking in the now-illuminated faces of the Guard and their clanking weapons. A wave of nausea rose at the suddenness of my gifted sight.

Ever since Jude and I had spoken in the dungeon, my other senses had begun to flourish.

The yellow glow increased, eventually stretching to expose the features of the group's leader atop his steed. His cutting jaw and narrowed eyes immediately gave him away.

Harlow.

Before he passed the section of the woods where we hid, he slowed, holding up a single hand. The carriage screamed to a jerky stop. His horse whinnied as it pranced in place, restless. He craned his neck toward the dense trees, to the thick underbrush.

Jake squeezed my arm, nearly cutting off circulation.

Minutes passed, and Harlow had yet to react, his features like stone. When he swiveled his head in our direction, gazing *right* where we crouched, it was my turn to squeeze Jake.

If he found us...

I made out the hint of a smile, a knowing one, and my heart plummeted into my stomach.

He was going to give us away. Going to—

Harlow waved his men forward.

An audible rush of air left my lungs as I watched him. That knowing grin remained, and it haunted me long after he and his soldiers vanished from view.

He'd *known* someone was there among the dark trees, and yet he alerted no one.

I didn't understand.

The Fox and her men didn't move from their hiding spots until ten minutes had come and gone. My vision returned to normal, the glow having gradually dissipated. But I didn't need heightened sight to see her withering look that said what she didn't: that she regretted taking us up on our offer. She might be able to escape notice, but not Jake and me, not when the king was so desperate to get his hands on us.

"We should settle in the woods," the Fox whispered once she'd sidled up to me. "We need to steer clear of the road. Wouldn't want your *friends* to find us." The thief studied me from boots to crown, her nostrils flaring.

"Agreed," I said, bestowing her a stiff nod. Seeing Harlow shook me, and I wasn't in the right frame of mind to craft a half-hearted lie.

The Fox returned to her horse and proceeded to lead us deeper into the forest. Jake and I held back.

"So you *flew* this time?" Jake asked. An astounded smile curled his mouth.

"I think so? One second I was riding Starlight, and the next, I was flying like a damned bird." It sounded absurd to my own ears, even after all we'd been through. "Oh, and I also believe I can see in the dark, so there's that. When the Guard approached, I wished I could see them clearly, and then, I *could*. They were flooded in a soft yellow light, nothing too bright, but I made out their features well enough."

Gods, it felt good to confide in someone.

Jake snorted. "Of course you can see in the dark." He was obviously growing more and more exhausted each time I opened my mouth. "That little skill would've been useful in the Mist."

As if I had any clue then what I would become.

We caught up with the others, who had settled among the trees. The Fox lay back, both hands behind her head, her stare trained on me. Finn and Dimitri worked to make a fire, their sunfires beginning to sputter. Finn grumbled a curse before tossing his drained gem to the side, the muscled giant easily irritated.

The Fox occasionally glanced his way, but more often than not, she smiled at his frustrations. And Dimitri...he watched everything with his bright smile, his brown eyes constantly alternating between gleaming and clouded, the effect like torchlight peeking out from behind a dense wood. Naturally, he was still whistling that tune.

Meanwhile, I stood in stunned silence. Which was a rarity.

The searing of Jake's gaze finally prompted me to turn his way.

"You're in your head," he whispered.

"Yeah, it's a dangerous place," I murmured, head bowed. I was becoming something new and powerful, and I feared what other so-called gifts might assault me now that I'd let the beast come out to play.

Jake grasped my chin and forced me to face him. "Ki. You may not like that part of you, but it just saved our lives. If you can hone these skills, we might be able to make it out of this mess alive. You're bigger than the magic inside of you. You just need to tame it."

I shook my head in disbelief, dislodging his hold. His words were exactly what I craved to bolster my waning confidence. "*You* might regret choosing my group that day in the sanctum, but I'm selfishly thankful."

"Family, remember?" he said, nudging my shoulder.

I groaned playfully. "Just don't get too cocky about it, all right?"

I could practically feel him rolling his eyes as I took a seat beside the building fire. Jake had been right. Practice was what I needed to save Jude and protect us all, no matter how risky it felt.

Or maybe I was frightened by what *honing* those skills would mean—

What it would make *me*.

• • •

I woke later that evening to the sound of footsteps. A hand covered my mouth before I could scream, and a strong body shoved me deeper into the earth. Instantly, I flailed, struggling to toss my assailant off.

"Stop fighting," a deep voice hissed. "I'm here to help."

My thoughts swam as panic reigned. I would know that gruff voice anywhere.

Harlow. The bastard had come back.

I went limp, prompting his grip to loosen, if only a fraction. Ice coursed down my throat, torso, and my spine, awakening my shadows. They thrashed in preparation.

Harlow might've bested me once before, but he wouldn't be able to now.

He never should've come back and challenged me.

"You've been a difficult person to find," he whispered, releasing my mouth.

I didn't scream. I didn't need to. In a moment, he'd be nothing but a pile of ash. My dark magic seemed to scream *yes* in response.

"Where is he?" I demanded, my body prickling. I could hardly keep the force of my shadows contained, but I gritted my teeth and reined them in—for now. "You have to know his location. With Jude gone, you'd be the leader of the Knights."

Harlow sat up, a crease forming between his brow. "I didn't hurt him, Kiara, I—"

"Make another move and it will be your last."

The warning came from my left, the Fox's raspy voice filled with steel.

My eyes flickered to her and the blade clutched tightly in her hand. She smiled, wide and full.

The others roused, and Jake lumbered to his feet. His upper lip curled back at the view of his former lieutenant pinning me down.

Harlow let out a rumble of annoyance before stepping off of me. He turned toward the Fox stiffly, his hands raised in a show of peace.

"You of all people have no part in this. You gave up that right a long time ago," he snapped, eyeing the Fox with distaste. "Leave us and there won't be any consequences for you or your men."

I frowned, but my attention swiveled to Jake, who inched closer, his hand on the hilt of his weapon. I lurched to my feet and took cautious steps toward him. My shadows coiled from my fingertips as I fumbled for my dagger. I'd strike with them first.

"See, that's where you're wrong," the Fox argued, nostrils flaring. While nearly a whole two feet shorter than Harlow, she somehow managed to look down on him. "Anything to do with my *son* would be my concern."

My heart stopped entirely. The *world* stopped.

Son.

The word repeated until it was the only one I knew.

The Fox was the mother who'd abandoned Jude. The mother who owned the book of lore he'd given me. She was also the woman who had delivered him into the clutches of sadistic men.

I wasn't the only one stunned into silence.

Finn's mouth fell open, and Dimitri's usual smirk dropped. The Fox had kept that secret from her most loyal men. It took me a moment to realize Jude had kept that secret from *me* as well.

He must've known who she was back in the Mist when we talked about his childhood. The first place he went had been Fortuna and to the Fox, and—

That's when I recalled the symbol on his compass. He'd used that thing so many times, his thumb rubbing nonsensical patterns on its surface when he held it. I'd also noted the details etching the device—a claw with a droplet of blood pouring from its pointed tip. The mark of the greatest thief in Asidia. His mother.

How in the living hells had I not put the pieces together sooner?

Tearing my gaze from her, I homed in on Harlow, observing him keenly as his jaw clenched in fury. "You don't deserve to call him by that title, Emelia. You have no claim to him at all." His tone was laced with pure venom as he said, "You're nothing but a traitor to our realm. A coward who ran with her tail stuck between her legs because you didn't want to accept your mother's truth. I bet you always knew what had been passed down to him. What your mother gave him. Or maybe Raina's power skipped you entirely, seeing as you're hardly worthy."

The Fox—Emelia—didn't so much as flinch.

Her *mother*. Raina.

Now that I knew the truth, I looked, *truly* looked at her.

High cheekbones, sharp, assessing eyes, hair the color of pure night. Lorian's words from the clearing came back to me.

"You have her nose," he'd said to Jude.

My chest warmed, Raina's divinity shoving to the forefront.

Emelia. Her name sounded soft compared to her deadly reputation. Though all notions of softness vanished a second later.

Emelia charged, her dagger a blaze of silver aimed for Harlow's chest.

Finn roared as Harlow deflected her blow, his dagger in his hands, meeting Emelia's with a reverberating clash. I moved toward them—preparing to liberate my shadows and turn Harlow to ash like I'd envisioned—when a whirl of brown-and-black spotted fur soared across my vision.

There was a snap of a jaw, the pounding of clawed feet, and the unmistakable sound of teeth piercing flesh.

Chapter Fourteen

Jude

I never wanted your son, and I don't want him now. I've done my best to toughen him up, but I think it's no use. If you're so worried, come raise him yourself.

Letter from Jack Maddox to The Sly Fox Tavern, year 34 of the curse

I heard screams from the distance.

At my side, Liam froze, his mouth agape as he whirled on me, a question burning in his eyes.

Another round of shouts was carried on an angry western wind. Screams of pain and fear.

An ambush, by the sounds of it. I surmised they were about a mile away.

"Do we…do we do something?" Liam asked, his hand moving hesitantly to his belt. He kept a thin blade there, but I doubted he knew how to properly wield it. Every time he so much as touched the weapon, he grimaced.

"No," I murmured, considering. "We continue."

My scar pulsated angrily, the muscles of my chest spasming.

It didn't matter what my body or my instincts were urging me to do—whoever it was out there, they were on their own.

I had to find Kiara, and Mena was still a ways away, given the casual pace we traveled. I wouldn't dare push Liam to go faster, and I was thinking of ways to secure horses.

Liam opened his mouth, but an ear-shattering screech cut him off. The unholy noise resonated, seeming to shake the tiny grains of soil under my boots.

"You can just sit there and ignore that?" He clenched his hands and scowled. An expression that was far too similar to his sister's. Gods, the longer I spent in Liam's company, the more he reminded me of her. Although, he tended to speak of books rather than weapons to fill the silence.

It made me miss Kiara even more.

"If we help them, we risk getting caught." Or worse.

"Kiara would help," Liam protested, crossing his arms.

"And she would likely get herself killed," I volleyed back, crossing my arms in return. "What if we walk into a fight, and the king's men are the cause? What good will we be to Kiara if we're in shackles?"

A spark of white flashed across both of my eyes, sending me a step forward.

"You all right?" Liam asked when I groaned, rubbing at my eyes like it would take away the stinging.

"Fine," I grated, but I was far from fine. When I managed to peel open both lids, the forest around us had changed. *Everything* had changed.

Rather than shadowy outlines, my left eye took in all the many curves and shapes of the world. They were covered in a blanket of gold, slightly blurry, glittering like gems. It was bright and clear and stunning in a way that reminded me of a dream.

Raina's divinity.

"Commander?" Liam prodded.

"I told you, I'm fine." I didn't mean to snap at him. I was merely on unsteady ground, lost to my power. This new sight would've sent me to my knees weeks ago, but I'd grown used to the peculiar, and instead of falling to the ground in fear, I merely dug my nails into the flesh of my palms. Pain was good. Pain steadied.

"It could be *her* down there." Liam threaded his fingers through his mop of curls, his indecision evident. "I want to at least check it out. We don't have to show ourselves." His stare morphed to steel, hardened further by stubborn determination. "I'm going with or without you."

So brave. So reckless. Such a Frey.

I massaged my pounding temples, considering.

Logically, the odds of it being her were next to none. But Liam had been right about one thing...*she* would have dived into the chaos headfirst, and while a month ago I would've scoffed and resumed my journey, I couldn't do so now.

And my magic...it had flared to life so suddenly, seconds after the screams.

I used to not believe in the absurdity of coincidences, but many things had occurred in such a short time, unimaginable things, and I couldn't turn my back on the impossible any longer.

"We'll check it out," I conceded, and instantly, my vision settled, the flashes of white calming until only the gold remained. They were satisfied by my answer. "*But* we stay hidden, and the *second* I say we turn back, you listen."

The Freys would be the death of me.

Chapter Fifteen

Kiara

Before Raina wiped away the Moon God's shadow beasts,
they roamed the world, devouring everything in sight. Their
method of attack was to surround their prey, their incorporeal
bodies wrapping around the victim while turning them to ash.
Yet even after the Moon God learned of their wickedness, he
protected them as one would their own kin.

Excerpt from Asidian Lore: a Tale of the Gods

The sickening crunch of flesh and bone filled the air.
Lorian's pet dug its jagged teeth into Harlow's arm, those
blue eyes glowing with hunger.

Our silent but deadly protector hadn't let us down.

I glanced to the heavens and delivered a quick thanks to
Lorian just as Harlow roared. He struggled to thrust up with
his dagger, but the beast clamped down harder.

The Fox wasted no time crawling away from the predator.
She sprang to her feet and raced to my side. "What in the living
hells… Is that a damned *jaguar*?"

Harlow screamed in agony as he placed both hands on the
creature and shoved it off. His right arm hung limply as he rose,
his black shirt damp with blood. The beast bared its teeth and

circled his new prey, seeming to almost smile. Brax was playing with his food; the lieutenant would've been dead already if the jaguar wished it.

My hand flexed around my weapon as I watched Harlow's face twist in pain. I didn't particularly like the man, but watching him being ripped apart had my heart dropping into my stomach.

The jaguar lunged again, growling with intent, but the lieutenant evaded him, nimbly angling to the side. I was surprised he was still on his feet.

"I'm here to *help* you, Kiara! Call off your guard dog!" he begged, just as the jaguar struck, this time clawing at his leg. The frayed rips of his trouser bared flashes of pale skin.

I lingered, caught between wanting to run and wanting to *help*.

Harlow wasn't my friend. He hadn't helped Jude escape his cell. But the fact that he let his men go gnawed at my insides. I couldn't help feeling like I was failing a test.

The Fox was scrambling to the horses, her men on her heels. Jake was motioning me toward Starlight when Harlow spoke again.

"Aurora," he called out when the jaguar clawed at his other leg. His clothes were nothing but shreds of ruined linen. He lashed out with his blade, slicing through the thick fur of the beast. It whimpered but didn't flee. "I knew her as a sun priest. We have the same g-goal!"

I jolted in place, stunned by the sound of my grandmother's name coming from his mouth.

"Kiara!" Jake frantically waved my direction, his wide eyes pleading with me to join him and run.

I stared at Harlow, even though his attention remained on his circling opponent. I could see the desperation there, the panic. He shot a brief look my way, and in that second of connection, I hesitated, rocking back and forth on my heels.

Who knew if he spoke the truth? It could be another lie. My

life was filled with them.

And…that was my answer; he had to be lying. If he had the same goal, then he'd have released Jude when he'd had the chance. They were supposed to be brothers, family—and yet he'd left him locked inside that rank cell to be tortured.

I wasn't like him.

"Brax, stop," I commanded the jaguar, whose taut body froze. Slowly, he unclenched his teeth from Harlow's muscle, easing back from his prey. He looked unpleased.

"You don't even deserve that mercy," I said over my shoulder as I took off in a sprint, suspecting that Harlow hadn't come alone. There could be a horde of men awaiting us.

Jake let out a sigh of relief when I pulled myself atop Starlight. The Fox, Dimitri, and Finn were already out of sight.

Harlow called out, sending my heart battling against the confines of my rib cage. His voice alone grated on my fraying nerves, his betrayal cemented in my mind.

"I've been protecting Jude for years. Doing what was always best for him. And *you*, Kiara!" I heard a body meet the ground, followed by a choked groan. "A-Aurora trusted me. It w-will be too late soon!"

I tensed, wishing to go back and question him, but Jake called my name, reminding me there could be others giving chase at this very moment.

We'd reached the top of a grassy hill, the Fox and her men near its peak. Starlight's muscled back tensed beneath me, and I clutched her mane in place of the reins, leaning across her lithe body. I hadn't the time to saddle her.

Two figures approached on foot, the clouds stretching across the moon making it impossible to see if they wore the Guard's red tunics. I simply knew they weren't part of our group of misfits. Meaning they must've tailed Harlow.

I urged Starlight on with a gentle kick to her belly, sending us barreling toward our newest enemy with ice in my veins. When I got near enough, my shadows lashed from my body in a burst of raw energy, the darkness climbing up my arms and rising above my head until I was cocooned in their soothing chill. My power flowed forth and curled around the two men, squeezing tightly. Gasps echoed and their hooded forms crumpled.

Some depraved part of myself smiled, and I exhaled in relief.

Truth or lies. Friend or foe. Right or wrong. All of it blurred to form one macabre painting of blood and loss. None of it mattered. I wouldn't allow one more person to hurt me. To hurt those I loved.

I tightened my shadows as they slithered up the men's necks. Choking and gurgling noises met my ears.

The buzz in my veins intensified, and I became drunk off the high of the power at my fingertips. It was so damned *right*. Nothing else had felt this wondrous, this easy. I wasn't Kiara anymore, not a girl with the weight of the kingdom on her shoulders.

I was the night itself, and how I reveled in all of its darkness.

Curling my fingers, I tightened my hold on the intruders. Anger and frustration mingled together and became my driving force, pushing me to explore the deepest corners of my soul. My emotions commanded my magic, and I didn't even attempt to restrain them.

That was when Starlight lifted onto her hind legs—

And bucked me off.

I toppled to the ground with a cry, my head colliding against stone. Black spots fizzled across my vision, and the ice I'd embraced receded to its prison.

A figure stalked toward me, their form fuzzy, a hood pulled down over their eyes. My head lolled to the side as a man crouched above me.

He whispered one word, one name. *Mine.*

I shut my eyes and let the night come.

CHAPTER SIXTEEN

JUDE

No path is straightforward. You learn nothing without getting
a little lost.

ASIDIAN PROVERB

L ife ceased to flow when Starlight bucked Kiara off, sending
her flying through the air and plummeting to the ground.
Her lithe body had gone limp, and her face—which had been
contorted with rage—was now slack.

Kiara.

The woman whose face haunted me, whose very voice had
become a song I played inside my head on painfully quiet nights,
lay before me, whole and *real*.

But she wasn't moving.

There were frantic cries, someone calling out her name. The
voice sounded familiar, yet even if it belonged to an enemy, I
couldn't find the willpower to care.

I had to get to her. Press my fingers into her soft skin and
inhale the sweet floral scent that was distinctly *her*. Assure
myself that I hadn't conjured the woman who was a living flame,
her light illuminating my demons and limning them in gold.

I ran. I ran until I was right there, beside her. I barely felt the impact when I dropped to the soil, my hands reaching for her like a star that had ventured too close to the earth. The pads of my fingers traced her form, my arms shaking as I searched for injuries.

Flaming red hair fanned across the coarse earth, her skin smudged with dirt from her fall. Her shadows slithered back beneath her torso, the wispy tendrils hauntingly beautiful under the moonlight.

Her chest rose and fell beneath my hands, and my eyes burned with a relief so consuming, it drowned out every sound and sensation. Slowly, cautiously, I brought my trembling hand to her cheek, curving my palm, shuddering when I felt her ice-cold skin.

Somehow, we'd found each other...even if she'd nearly killed me. As if in reminder, my throat burned, and I recalled how her phantom fingers had dug into my windpipe. It hurt to breathe, but she could've stabbed me at this point, and I'd have shrugged it off.

"Is she all right?"

I tilted my chin, not surprised when I found a pair of brown eyes speckled with gold staring back. My air turned to frost in my lungs when the Fox sauntered closer before dipping into a crouch a few feet from where I clutched Kiara. Her tone had been cutting, and my eye twitched at the way she stared daggers at the woman in my arms.

I didn't look at her as I replied, "She will be." It had been a nasty fall, but she just needed to rest.

A pained groan came from my left.

Liam.

I whirled in place. Twenty feet away, her brother lay sprawled upon the ground. When he attempted to lift himself, his lips twisted into an agonized grimace, his arms shaking from the effort. He toppled back to the dirt with a frustrated cry.

The Fox shot to her feet and ran to him as I tenderly released Kiara, who frowned in her sleep. I didn't want to leave her, but I had to check on Liam—if he perished due to her actions...that would be a blow she wouldn't survive.

"Commander."

Relief flooded me as Jake sprinted into view. He sank to his knees and grasped Kiara's shoulders before gently running his hands up and down her arms.

We locked eyes, and Jake jerked his head to where my mother examined Liam. "I got her for now," he promised, seeming to read my mind. "Go, check on him."

The recruit's face was a welcomed one, and something warm filled my chest as I shot him an appreciative nod and stood. I had the strangest urge to *hug* the boy, but I forced myself to turn. Every nerve in my body protested as I walked away.

The thief had her pack out, various medical supplies littering the ground around her and Liam. Her bodyguard handed her a glass jar that had rolled by his boot, and she snapped open the lid before rubbing it onto Liam's chest.

His distressed wheezes caused my heart to race.

"She's out of control," the Fox said over her shoulder, her fingers smoothing out the ointment. Liam gasped, his eyes wide. I swore he tried to shake his head as if saying, "*No.*"

Even with her brother splayed across the earth, I felt the need to defend her. "She just doesn't know how to use her powers yet," I said, my nails digging into the flesh of my palms. How could the Fox even begin to think Kiara would hurt Liam on purpose? She knew *nothing* about her.

My mother scoffed, though she avoided my eyes. "She's a danger to us all, and I won't let her—"

"You won't let her *what*, Mother? Kill me? You're the one who turned me down when I needed your assistance. You're the reason I was captured to begin with."

She went deathly still. Slowly, her stare lifted to meet mine, and a chill raced down my spine. The gall. The thief couldn't come flying back into my life and suddenly give a shit if I lived or died. She gave up that right nineteen years ago.

"If she hurts you, then I will do *whatever* I need to do to stop her." Her brown eyes glinted ominously in the moon's light. "Even if I have to kill her myself."

I all but growled. "Get close to her, and it'll be *your* life you have to worry about."

The Fox's shocked features went slack. I could tell she planned to spew more venom, but Jake called out my name.

"Jude!" Jake compelled my gaze to abandon my mother and her threats. "I'd come here if I were you! Kiara's awake."

Chapter Seventeen

Kiara

It isn't the enemy you should fear when you go into battle, but yourself. You never know what you're capable of until death hands you a weapon.

Maliah, Goddess of Revenge and Redemption

I peeled open my eyes at the same time I patted for my dagger. My body was bruised and ached with every breath, and my feeble attempt to retrieve my weapon failed. I dropped my arm to my side with a weak sigh. I was lying on my back, staring at the cloudy, black sky above, the moon all but invisible. Everything hurt.

Familiar hands stroked my cheeks, my hair, my shoulders. "Jake?" I rasped, his blurry face coming into focus. "What happened?"

I had willingly given myself over to the beast within, and while I remembered the initial rush of its shadows, the rest… wasn't quite as clear.

A strangled gasping noise filled the too-quiet air. I got to my feet just as movement caught my eye. Someone lay on the ground behind Jake, the Fox hovering over them as she rubbed some sort of salve onto their chest, a half-empty jar in her hand.

"Who is that?"

Fear became hands that snaked around my throat and squeezed. I wasn't sure I wanted the answer.

"Kiara, listen…" Jake began, but I was already rushing to the injured man's side, moving around the Fox as she worked.

There'd been *two* hooded figures on that hill, and I'd thrust my power out at them without thought, allowing my shadows to encircle their necks before I even saw their faces. But now, standing above the injured man, there was no doubt as to his identity.

"Liam?" My knees gave out, and I slumped to the ground. He couldn't be *here*, on the run from the king. I had to be hallucinating. But then my gloved hands went to his face and cupped his rosy cheeks, and I knew this was all too real.

His wide-eyed stare held mine, and a knowing look passed between us as he uttered my name. The skin around his neck held a darker color to it, even in the dim. I gently grazed the sensitive area, and he hissed through his teeth.

I thought I understood what regret was, but this was a whole new wave of fresh torture. He'd only venture from home for one reason: *me*. We were each other's rock, our bond a steadfast constant that refused to bend even under the most extreme pressure.

I owed him my life—my sanity—in all the ways that counted.

Salt exploded on my tongue as tears glided down my face and to my lips. Suddenly, the magic I'd coveted minutes ago turned into a cursed plague.

My body shook as the Fox worked, her lean fingers massaging clear salve onto his chest. My brother's breathing was ragged, but he fought to inhale the medicine.

"Breathe in deep, boy," she instructed. "This better work. It certainly cost me enough." She raised her brow at me. "You'll be reimbursing me, obviously."

"I'm so sorry," I murmured to Liam, ignoring the thief's quip. Gripping his limp hand in mine, I pressed it to my chest, to where my scar ached. Or maybe it was my heart. That felt like it ached, too.

"You d-didn't know." Liam managed a weak smile. "I'll be fine. I a-always am."

It didn't matter if he would be fine. The act I committed couldn't be erased.

Why is he even here? I screamed inside my head, furious at him. More furious at myself.

The Fox commanded him to breathe in deeply, and I mimicked the action, smelling mint and salt and some other scent in the air. My brother wheezed as he obeyed her instructions, and I froze, watching every rise and fall of his chest.

"And drink this." The Fox uncorked a crystal vial filled with an opaque blue liquid. She shoved it into his face, pressing it to his lips and forcing it down. He sputtered but swallowed it all.

"Come on, Liam," I coaxed, not sure what I was even asking of him.

Liam had come for me. My brother who couldn't fight or defend himself. My sweet brother whose heart was worth a million of mine. I couldn't bear it. I didn't feel worthy.

"Wait," the Fox whispered. "Look."

To my relief, Liam's wheezing eased, the hoarseness of his exhales growing quieter. I waited for anxious minutes, those ticking seconds feeling like hours as I studied his chest.

Liam, ever the stubborn boy I knew him to be, immediately tried to haul himself up into a sitting position. When he swayed, I grasped his bicep, making sure he didn't fall back to the earth and smack his head open.

"Not how I expected my b-beloved sister to greet me," Liam mumbled. "Though I can't say I'm surprised. You always did act f-first and think later."

I let out a noise somewhere between a sob and a strangled laugh and embraced him, making sure I didn't squeeze him to death all over again.

"You really have changed, Ki, haven't you?" he whispered into my hair.

I snorted and drew back to study him. His breathing *had* improved. I'd have to buy a thousand of those vials. Whatever had been contained inside just saved his life.

After I had nearly taken it.

"Gods, why did you have to come find me? I could've killed you!" I wiped at my eyes—I couldn't seem to stop crying these days.

"I couldn't let you have all the fun." Liam grinned, gradually hoisting himself to his feet. I lifted with him while he studied me, shaking his head at whatever he found. "I almost didn't believe Jude when he told me of what happened out there in the Mist, but damn. You're terrifying."

Jude.

"What do you mean?" I asked, voice quaking. He couldn't possibly have said—

A throat cleared from behind me, and the hairs on the nape of my neck rose.

I felt him before I saw him.

The air became charged like it did right before a storm. My heart skipped several beats as my chest warmed, chasing away the debilitating fear that had annihilated me seconds before. Only one person could ever coax such a reaction, and even with my back turned, my body knew his as well as it knew itself.

"Jude's talked about nothing but you during the last two days. Really, it's been a nightmare." Liam rolled his eyes, but they twinkled.

Those words affected me more than I let on—that Jude ached for me as much as I had him. It was time to turn, time to face him, and while every inch of me desired nothing more, I couldn't forget how he'd left me in the Mist. Afraid I'd use the Godslayer on myself.

He'd had a right to worry, but now that I'd been without him, now that I'd seen him broken and alone, I was too selfish to leave. Even if I doomed my realm.

The moment I both yearned for and dreaded had arrived, and it felt as if fate itself slowed down to watch.

Chapter Eighteen

Jude

It is often what we love most
that kills us in the end
But to die with a smile
isn't a terrible way to go

LORIAN, GOD OF BEASTS AND PREY

Gods above, she was more radiant than I remembered. When her eyes fluttered open, I forgot how to breathe, but who needed air when she looked at me like *that*?

It took everything in me to stand back once she rushed to Liam. Her brother needed her attention, and while I wasn't socially adept, I had an inkling that kissing her while he struggled to survive wasn't morally sound.

I observed the three of them now, my mother, Jake, and Kiara, all huddled around Liam. My girl stiffened beneath my gaze as if she felt it. Felt me. So why wasn't she turning? Was she that angry with me for leaving her in the Mist? It was for her own protection, but I doubt she'd see it that way.

"T-thank you," Liam said to my mother, staring at her in pure awe. When she gave him a half smile in reply, a foreign emotion burned in my veins. It felt like poison.

They shared a few words I couldn't make out, but Liam nodded at his sister once, his eyes flicking my way. Then Liam all but shoved her around.

Our eyes locked immediately, and it was like a punch to the gut.

I'd forgotten my armor, my shields, every weapon I'd fashioned over the years. They were reduced to dust, destroyed not by daggers or arrows but by something as simple and as devastating as those brilliant golden eyes.

I was about to damn the consequences and go to her, when a man I recognized from The Sly Fox approached.

"That bastard they call Harlow attacked," he said. *The screams*. Liam was right. Kiara had been attacked, and I hesitated. I'd wanted to *ignore* them.

"Harlow? He was out here?" I clenched my fists, furious with myself. I had given him the benefit of the doubt. But it seemed like my former brother was lying when he professed his desire to aid me. So much for loyalty.

"That jaguar got him good. Took a few chunks out, so I doubt we have to worry about him for now." The man lifted his dirtied hand before him. "Name's Dimitri, by the way." He shoved out his dirtied hand in greeting as if he hadn't just told me a jaguar attacked my old lieutenant.

I instinctively accepted, finding his grip surprisingly strong. The second he let go, I backed away. Thoughts of Harlow could wait. *Everything* could wait.

While I drank Kiara in like a man who'd wandered the desert for days and she was my only source of life, her surprised face morphed into one of shame. I knew her well enough to see the spark of fear cloud her face, that desperation to run causing her hands to twitch at her sides.

She blamed herself.

"Can we speak?" I asked, approaching. She backed up a

step. "Kiara?"

Her attention strayed to her brother, to her hands. As though blood marred them. "I-I can't. I—"

The wind whipped at her cloak, exposing the onyx blade strapped to her hip. The Godslayer. The boy from Fortuna had followed through, after all. The muscles in my neck loosened. That was one less thing to worry about.

Now, I just had to get her to speak with me. Yet she inched backward, moving away from everyone, including me. That hurt the most.

I sensed her hesitation. Her shame. It shone from her eyes, her trapped tears like liquid silver.

"I'm so sorry, Jude—" She spun around and darted into the forest, running from the aftermath of her power. Running from *us*.

Too bad for her, I would always follow. I took off, chasing her into the skeletal woods.

I called her name, squinting into the dim. A flash of her bright hair lured me deeper, branches snagging at my clothes, my skin. I chased her down until she reached a small clearing surrounded by stinging black reeds. There, she froze, her back to me.

"Kiara, turn around. Please."

"You should stay away," she warned, the wind stifling her words and carrying them away. "I-I need some time. I *choked* you for gods' sake!"

"What happened wasn't your fault." I ran a frustrated hand through my hair. "How were you to know we weren't King's Guards? Harlow could've very well brought reinforcements."

Kiara's breathing turned labored, her body shaking with either rage or fear. Both would be understandable.

I dared to venture closer, stopping when she whirled on me, eyes narrowed.

"I told you to leave," she grated out. "Besides, I thought you wanted to escape me in the Mist. Here's your chance!" She pointed to the trees. "Go!"

How the roles had reversed. She aimed to push me away because she feared she'd harm me. I wasn't easily frightened.

Boldly, I grasped her wrist and pulled her to me. Her hands went to my chest, and while she didn't pull back, I sensed she considered it.

"*Stop*. Stop blaming yourself," I ordered in my most authoritative voice. I wanted my words to sink into her stubborn head. "I left you because you'd have carved the final piece out of your chest and gifted it to me. We both know that."

"I still could."

"Don't threaten me with your life," I practically growled, a fierce protectiveness causing me to tighten my hold on her waist, my hands fisting her cloak. "I do not make decisions lightly, Kiara, but in that clearing, when Patrick nearly killed you, I made a vow, and I intend to keep it."

"What vow?" she asked, tensing.

Still, she held on to me, and I took that as a good sign. She was vulnerable, an open book of love and pain and everything in between.

"I grew selfish in the Mist. *You* made me selfish." I cupped her cheek, one hand remaining firmly on her waist. "I decided then that I'd do everything in my power to make sure you survived this mess, to find a way to save us both. Because for the first time in my life, I *know* I deserve happiness, and I want to be a man who deserves *you*."

Was she going to ignore everything we'd said in that dungeon? For a second, I wondered if I'd imagined the whole thing, but then my scar throbbed and Kiara went still. Slowly, she peered down at her own chest with wide eyes.

No, it had all been real. The proof of our magic was carved

into our skin.

When she pressed her body deeper against mine—returning my affections—my eyes fluttered closed. She fit me perfectly, her softness molding against every hard edge. It made my pulse soar.

"You feel it, too," she finally whispered, her hand moving to her matching wound. "It wasn't a dream, was it? I...I actually found you."

"It was real," I confirmed. I'd been half delirious then, and what I'd told her without hesitation echoed in my head. "I'm damn well thankful it was."

Her cheeks darkened, and she glanced down.

"Are you...are you hurt?" she asked, a hand moving to my back, barely a whisper of a touch.

"I'm all right. I promise." As if she didn't believe me, she slipped her hand below my shirt, her gloved fingers moving along the length of my spine.

I sucked in a sharp breath when she gently ran them up and down, from my upper back to just above where my trousers sat on my hips. Gods, she had no idea what she was doing to me, how she tortured me with a simple touch.

"There are no wounds..." Her face pinched in confusion, oblivious to my inner struggle. "And Patrick's cut...it's missing."

"I told you I'm fine," I said, attempting a light tone. It came out coarse and deeper than usual. "I—I think *I* healed it. Along with the injuries I sustained at the fortress."

"*Injuries*," she snapped incredulously. "What they did to you goes beyond cruelty. Beyond mere injuries. You were *torn* apart. How did you even escape?"

"Hey, I'm here. I'm alive," I said, needing her to calm. I worried her shadow beast would rise at the promise of retribution. Even as the fear crossed my mind, her eyes darkened.

"I'm going to kill them all. Slowly. First, I'll—"

"Kiara. I will gladly help you kill them when the time comes, but there are more pressing matters we should deal with first."

"You never answered my question," she pressed. Her roaming hands stilled, and I mourned the loss of their easy exploration. "How did you get free of that cell?"

I sighed. "There was a woman who helped me escape. She claimed to be Maliah herself." If we hadn't undergone the trials of the Mist, I might not have believed my own ears.

Kiara flinched, but her stare turned fierce, her gaze locked on me. A tremor worked its way through my body, her eyes seeming to see right through me to where my heart battered the confines of my ribs.

"We came across both her and Lorian in the woods before reaching Fortuna," she said with a frown. "They weren't pleased we were trying to save you with the Moon God at our backs."

The gods were banding together. While Lorian had aided Patrick with his wolves, he'd vanished when he learned of my true identity. I wanted to hold on to the notion that the immortals were on our side.

"Maybe that's why Maliah helped me," I mused. "She knew you'd be stubborn and disregard your own safety."

"As if you wouldn't have done the same," she countered, her hip angling into me. Heat flared as her movements stole any and all arguments I could've formed. If I didn't know any better, I'd say she was tormenting me on purpose.

"She also told us the God of the Moon is at the center of this," Kiara added, quickly dousing the flames that had been working their way to my core. "Cirian's his puppet, and they want to kill us so Raina's magic doesn't return." I immediately thought of Cirian, of what he'd taunted in that cell, how he'd threatened Kiara's life. My head was spinning, both anger and fear mixing together to form the most potent of poisons. "Maliah and Lorian said there's this object that can summon and *trap* the Moon God at his temple, and I confirmed this when I went to see the Fox."

She paused, raising an accusatory brow. "Your *mother*..."

She shifted away, the lies and truths I'd concealed creating distance. I shook my head at the action, my palms splaying across the entire expanse of her back.

"I didn't tell you about her because up until recently, I vowed I'd never see her again," I rushed to say. "She was all but dead to me."

The words rang hollow even to my own ears.

"I still wish you would have trusted me with that information," she began, slowly melting back into me. I swallowed down my sigh of relief. "But I understand why you didn't. It was your secret, and I can respect that."

"I have no more secrets left," I whispered, the tip of my nose grazing hers. "That, I promise."

"Good. Because I'm sick of them," she grumbled. "Every day there's a new one. It's getting rather old."

"I'm still surprised my mother helped." The Fox had made it abundantly clear she wanted no part in my endeavors. "Did she give you the texts she'd stolen from Cirian's palace years ago?"

"No. But she explained that all signs to save us led to the temple. Our plan was to rescue you first and then locate the talisman to imprison the Moon God. After insisting she was the only one who could navigate the inner temple, she all but demanded to come along for the ride."

I would've thought she'd send them on their way like she had me. Had me being captured affected her choice? Perhaps it was her pride at play.

"I probably shouldn't get so close to you," Kiara admitted, the clouds in her eyes swirling with fear. "I might hurt you again." Her hands dropped to her sides, but I grabbed her wrists, her pulse point thudding wildly against my fingers. The touch was like lightning.

"I made the mistake of running away. Don't you dare do the

same." Her mouth parted as she took in my words, forcing my gaze to lower. I nearly groaned when she bit her bottom lip in thought, her eyes hooded. "I'm far from done with you, Kiara Frey. And I don't know if I ever will be."

She hesitated for only a second, but it was the longest second of my existence.

Kiara pushed onto her toes, grabbed my neck, and then we collided.

My lips fused to hers, and suddenly, the world didn't feel so big, our trials not nearly as impossible. I wasn't that same boy who'd been scarred by his father. The man who slept with blood coating his hands. I wasn't anyone or anything. And there was a freedom to that, like the shackles of my past transformed to ash that floated away into nothingness.

I'd been given a gift I initially spurned, my fear holding me back. But no longer.

Standing on her tiptoes, Kiara arched into me, sliding her hands under my shirt, her gloved hands cool on my bare back. I wanted those gloves gone. I wanted to feel her, skin to skin. I wanted no more barriers between us.

"Take them off," I ordered, drawing back enough to speak. "*Please.*"

"I could hurt you," she murmured, going rigid.

"You're hurting me by *not* touching me." I took one gloved hand. "I want them gone. I want you."

"So bossy, Commander," she whispered, her movements slow as she pulled off the leather and jammed them into her back pocket. The slight tremble of her fingers wasn't lost to me.

"No. *Desperate,*" I corrected, kissing along her jaw. "I want to feel your hands on me."

So, so many *wants*.

And then her hands roamed, her gloves discarded, nothing but hands, lips, and shared eagerness between us. Everywhere her heat wandered, I burned. It was like she couldn't touch me enough, *feel* me enough, and her soft whimpers of desperation had me losing any semblance of control I possessed.

Not that I ever had much when it came to her.

Kiara was the air in my lungs, and for the first time in days, I *breathed*.

I whispered her name as her hands traveled to my face, cupping my cheeks and keeping me in place like she never planned on letting go.

The last few days became nothing but a horrid nightmare, each of her kisses erasing the cruel lash of the whip, each touch washing away my fear, my pain. My fingers tightened at the nape of her neck, and I wound my other hand around her waist, tugging and pulling until I wasn't sure where she ended and I began.

While I lost myself in her, I rediscovered the person I desired to be. The Hand of Death died when she murmured my name.

I traced the seam of her lips with my tongue, and when she opened, meeting me with equal hunger, I explored her mouth, wrenching another sweet sound from her.

"I'm supposed to be angry at you, make you beg for forgiveness," she murmured between kisses. She sighed when I tugged on her bottom lip, releasing it only to nip at her jaw. "I can't seem to remember *why*, though. I was angry about something, right? I wanted to yell at you and—"

She squealed when I grasped her legs and hoisted her up, forcing her to wind herself around my hips.

"Never mind," she rasped. "I'll be angry at you in a second."

Smiling against her skin, I walked forward, not stopping until her back was pressed flush to a broad trunk. I used its support to brush her cheeks, to touch her softness, to slip my fingers through her silken hair.

I would happily take her anger. I'd take anything she wished to give me like the beggar I'd become.

"Gods, you're killing me," I murmured, already struggling for air. She'd stolen all of mine. "I've dreamed of you every night, Kiara. Fantasized about the moment I'd hold you again. Kiss you." I pressed my lips to the corner of her mouth. "I should never have left."

She stiffened at my words. I drew back, my heart rattling my rib cage.

"No," Kiara snapped. "You shouldn't have. You didn't trust me. And you not only risked *my* life because of that, but you risked yours as well." She cast me a spine-tingling glower. Kiara may be petite, but her size didn't fool me. If she wanted, she could have a grown man flat on his back in less than a minute. I'd be a liar if I said it didn't turn me the hells on.

She snatched my hand and thrust it to her healed wound, over her beating heart. Her other hand rested above mine.

"You will never, *never* do something like that again," she warned. The hand on her chest warmed, matching the heat of my skin. "If you meant what you said in those dungeons, if you meant what you said tonight, then we do this together or not at all."

A hazy shimmer illuminated her body, radiating from her scar. Her eyes widened, but her attention wasn't on *her* chest. I glanced down, finding a similar glow emanating from *me*.

Kiara's anger slipped from her face entirely as my light evolved, the gold morphing into a shade of steel. Back and forth it flickered, from day to night and back again. She peered up through her lashes, astonishment clear on her face.

I felt it. The tether binding us.

It had been there from the beginning, but now, I could *feel* it as if it was a solid thing expanding between us. I'd questioned how she'd been able to visit me, but we were connected in a way that couldn't be logically explained.

Shadows unfurled from her like a cloak billowing in the wind, and for a heartbeat, her body wavered like an ashen cloud. A searing bolt charged down and across my chest, and I squeezed my eyes shut.

When I opened them, Kiara was...gone.

I spun, searching for her, but no one stood in the woods—

"Jude!"

Whirling around, I came face to face with the woman who'd been but a ghost a second before. While she no longer fluttered in place, her body once again solid, I noticed how she swayed.

What just happened?

"I—" She scanned the woods, a dazed look painting her features. "One second I was beside you, and the next I was so angry with you for leaving, and I thought of the cell and what you'd been through, and I..." She hissed through her teeth, trying to regain her composure, her hands visibly shaking in the dark. "I *moved*, Jude. I felt myself move. I heard a rush of wind, and I was being pushed somewhere else. I had to hold on to your voice to return."

"Your shadows," I whispered, stepping closer. She let me hug her, allowed me to push her head onto my chest as I embraced her. "Your emotions control them. It has to be how you found me. How you were able to visit me." When she'd healed me in that clearing, she'd left her mark on me, the same as I'd done to her. But the mark she'd gifted contained a piece of herself, her darkness.

"Before, when I visited you, my body didn't..." She waved her hands before herself. "It didn't *move* like that. But in the woods, on the way here, I swore I left my body and *flew*. I looked down on the earth, able to spot an abandoned camp once occupied by soldiers. Jake told me I was all but a phantom when this happened."

"Maybe you're growing stronger?" It was entirely possible.

She'd only recently discovered that side of herself. Who knew what she was capable of, especially with a sliver of Raina's magic inside of her? The shadow beasts of legend had been rumored to travel, freeing themselves of their physical bodies and evaporating into thin air. Some historians even argued they could access the spaces in between the worlds where no mortal could venture.

"Are you afraid of me?" she voiced hesitantly after moments of silence, of us simply holding on to each other.

I went rigid, aghast she'd say such a thing. Leaning back, I grasped her chin.

"If your darkness was the reason you found me, then it saved my life, Kiara." I shook my head. What didn't she get? I adored every part of her, especially the darkness. It was *her*, and I wouldn't want her any other way.

"I meant every damned word I said in that dungeon," I intoned, my voice coming out firm, unyielding. I needed her to understand. "I began to fall in love with you the very second you spoke my name." I kissed her gently. "And I don't ever wish to land. I love you, Kiara Frey."

My heart thudded in my ears as I waited for her to speak, to say anything. But she simply lifted onto her toes and pressed her mouth against my scarred cheeks, taking her time, savoring me.

She didn't say the words back.

I wish it didn't sting as much.

"I don't forgive you for leaving, but I'm not spending this time being angry at you," she said when she came up for air, and while not what I wished to hear, a tentative hope swept through me.

I lowered my lips back to hers, and when we touched, bursts of gold exploded behind my eyes. They were dazzling and overwhelming, and I never wished to stop kissing her.

So I didn't.

My fingers were once again tangled in her hair, my other hand pressing into the small of her back. I couldn't get enough of her taste, how delectable her lips were when I pulled them between my teeth, feasting on her. Consuming her. Devouring.

It wasn't until Jake screamed in alarm that we both drew back.

The glow…it was everywhere now. Just like that day in my cell.

In the heavens, surrounded by clouds of dense gray, shone an orb of pure, devastating light. I stumbled in place, consumed by its brilliance, shocked by its mere presence. The sun. It was fighting to return.

I turned to Kiara with a wide smile and drank her in— memorizing how the rays bestowed her skin with a rosy sheen, her hair the most vivid shade of copper.

Gorgeous. Every inch of her. And she was mine.

She met my heated stare. "Only you would look at me when there's a sun in the sky."

But she was looking at me, too.

I went to embrace her once again when the world dimmed, the effulgent light fading faster than it had appeared.

It didn't matter. For a few heartbeats, I experienced hope. Maybe Kiara didn't need to die after all. Maybe I could love her and save my kingdom without carving the missing piece from her heart. The whispered prophecy of the sun priestesses came back to me, and I gripped it tightly.

"Kiara, I think we can save Asidia without—"

Her mouth fell open, and blood dripped from her lips.

She murmured my name as she collapsed in my arms, and before I could manage to scream for help, she vanished entirely.

CHAPTER NINETEEN

KIARA

Today my granddaughter was attacked. When her parents rushed to retrieve supplies to heal her wounds, it was I who held her. I swore she wavered in and out of existence for the briefest moment, her body turning a pale gray. There is only one God I can seek, and I must swallow my pride to save Kiara's soul.

ENTRY IN AURORA ADAIR'S DIARY, YEAR 40 OF THE CURSE

I dreamed I was flying.

On wings the color of night, I soared, weightless and free. A small village rested below, though there weren't any children laughing or playing in the streets. The few people scurrying about kept their heads down, their too-thin bodies frail and weak.

Asidia was dying a slow and miserable death.

A select few crops had continued to grow after the curse, but over the last decade, the little they managed to cultivate wasn't enough. Even the air sometimes felt too thick, and Liam—and people with breathing problems like him—were struggling.

I angled higher. I didn't want to bear witness to such heartache. I'd known misery most of my life, the struggle that came with being trapped inside the confines of a cursed kingdom.

The winds shifted, and I allowed them to guide me, luxuriating in how the breeze ruffled my imaginary feathers.

Far in the distance, encircled by Midnight Blooms, stood a temple rising from the sea of lilac and blue. Marble columns climbed high into the inky sky, limestone fountains and stern-faced statues decorating a neatly manicured patch of flowers. At the apex of the temple, a crescent moon had been carved, three perfectly pointed stars surrounding it.

I dipped lower, drawn by the beauty of the shrine. While I'd never been to any of the gods' temples before, it was apparent who this one belonged to.

The Moon God, whose true name had been a mystery since the dawning of time. No one could remember it but the people continued to pray, gifting him with their most sacred wishes.

Prayers held power. They were more valuable than gold and material riches. Each wish was tethered to a soul, and when given to the skies, a part of that person would forever live in the heavens.

Swerving downward on a wintry breeze, I landed upon a trickling fountain at the temple's base, splashes of water sinking through my airy wings. A shiver racked my frame, and I shuddered in delight, stretching out my body and relishing in the gentle spray of water. In this form, there was a spreading numbness that prevented me from feeling pain or the burden of reality.

I never wished to leave.

"Kiara," a voice rumbled behind me. I craned my neck, finding the last person I ever would've expected. The last person I would have *wanted* to see.

My mind may have been clouded, but he wasn't a god one easily forgot.

What are you doing here, Arlo? I thought, suddenly angry.

So much for feeling numb.

The man I'd once known as my uncle drifted closer, his simple but luxurious blue robes swishing at his feet. He eyed me warily, stroking his graying beard. It was more unkempt than normal, and there were dark circles below each gray blue eye, making the angular planes of his face more ominous than usual.

"You're losing yourself, Kiara," he warned, his voice shaking the ground he stood upon. "The more you dip into the night's power, the more it uses you."

I'm fine, I insisted. *We've got the Godslayer* and *Jude. All we need now is the talisman Maliah and Lorian spoke of.*

We wouldn't be so easily defeated.

Arlo groaned, annoyance painting his features and twisting them. "I wish time had been on our side so you wouldn't need to go there." He looked away. "Once, a long, long time before you were born, there were whisperings among the sun priests and priestesses. They claimed that since a broken heart had caused the curse, only love could mend it. And perhaps such folly might've been true...*before.*"

Before what?

"Your accident changed you, my child. The moment that creature got its claws into you, you became a part of the night. An accident of the Moon God, one of his failed experiments, the shadow beasts were meant to be protectors. But intention is everything, and the god's intentions were not pure.

"You may hold the final piece of the sun in your soul, but you can't wield it as you might have. You gave into the night. You *Traveled,* and that in itself shows me you cannot control the balance."

I don't understand, I said, feeling lightheaded. The temple behind Arlo shook, bits of loose stone tumbling from the crevices.

"I must be quick," he said, impatient as always. "You and

Jude *could have* shared a different destiny. But right now, his love, his touch, is killing you. Your little confession set everything in motion…even if your heart is holding you back from giving all of yourself to him." I thought of Jude telling me how he loved me, and me professing how far I'd fallen. But Arlo was right—some small part of me held back.

I couldn't return the words that he'd given me with such care. Three little words that frightened me more than any curse.

"He's stronger in the mortal realm, more so than he should be," Arlo added tightly. "His power is only growing, and it's battling with your darkness, even if you have a piece of Raina. The beast's magic is just too overpowering. It's why he hurt you, why you collapsed."

We're going to fix that. Once we find a way to break the curse, without me dying, Jude and I—

"You have a merciless god after you, but you'd rather think of *love*," Arlo thundered. "Do you even know if it's love? Or are you and the commander drawn to each other because of the goddess's divinity inside of you both, the pieces yearning to be reunited?"

I wanted to deny his words. *But*…was there some truth to what Arlo insinuated? The pieces, the keys of immortality were begging to come together. Was I merely falling prey to their pull?

No.

I glanced at his face, surprised when I saw genuine concern contorting his face—the God of Earth and Soil was *worried* about me.

Regardless of what I feel for the commander, I began, my voice quivering with duplicitous doubt, *we're going to the temple, and we'll succeed, regardless of what you believe possible. You were the one who told me rules could be broken.*

He had to be wrong. He *had* to be.

A pillar plummeted, shattered pieces of marble crashing across the blackened earth. The temple behind us crumbled, a second pillar falling, the roof creaking as it, too, prepared to topple.

"Your enemy has ventured much closer than you could imagine, Kiara," Arlo said, forcing my attention away from the destruction. "I thought you would've learned your lesson with Patrick, but—"

I never heard his final words. The night twisted and blurred, and then my body sank into the vacuum of night, drowning in greedy nothingness.

Chapter Twenty

Jude

Love is no longer the answer. Only death.

Letter from Aurora Adair to unknown recipient, year 42 of the curse

K iara disappeared before my eyes.

Before I could assess the damage, to stem the blood pouring from her lips, she'd flickered out of the world like a weak flame.

I screamed her name, again and again, until the others surrounded me, begging to know what happened. I didn't have an answer.

Minutes passed, each ticking second an alarm bell ringing painfully in my head.

A flash of movement to my left caught my eye, a body slowly taking shape, quivering in and out of existence. I ran to the wavering form, wanting, *hoping*, it was her.

Through a patch of prickly reeds, situated on her back, eyes fluttering, was Kiara.

My knees dug into the dirt as I sank to my knees and pulled her into my hold, panic flooding my insides like a disease. She was limp, sickly pale, and oh so cold. She stared into nothing, unseeing, barely breathing.

Gently, I laid her back down, her brother shouting, Jake cursing and pacing. I shook her and frantically felt for her pulse. It was weak. Barely there. No matter what I did, she didn't stir, and the sight of the blood trickling from her parted lips had my powers bursting free.

I brought my palms to her chest, over her heart, and poured all my pent-up energy—every fear and doubt and shred of frustration—into her supine body. "Wake up!" I ordered, blazing light radiating from my hands. It illuminated the gloomy woods, gold touching the tips of the brittle leaves and making them glimmer like broken glass.

I sensed the others circle me, heard their voices, but I blocked them from existence. There was only the sensation of being torn in half, of an invisible blade cutting through my flesh and bone and deep into my heart.

Shoving against her once more, I roared, golden magic streaming into her with a sickening snap. It flowed above me, the brightest of light igniting the woods, the field, and the bewildered faces of my companions.

A thousand twinkling stars cascaded from me in a torrent of never-ending power, and I gave it all to her.

Nothing happened.

I was brought back to the field of Midnight Blooms when she lay bloodied and pale in my hold. That invisible dagger twisted, and I choked on memories of her anguish.

I didn't understand. I'd healed her before, and there wasn't a wound in sight. Her eyes were open, her chest moving rhythmically, and yet...

A gush of crimson sputtered from her lips, red seeping from her ears as she convulsed, shaking so violently, I feared she'd hurt herself by the action alone. In my panic, I yanked my hands from her, fearing my touch harmed rather than helped. When the tremors lessened, nausea churned in my gut.

Realization struck. My touch…it was *hurting* her.

Jake crashed to his knees, followed by Liam, both of them cradling her, trying their best to rouse her from her spell. Liam bellowed her name, but I barely heard his scream.

Everything was muffled, the only sound the hissing of the untamed magic in my blood.

We'd brought back the sun *twice* after revealing our hearts. It hadn't lasted, but I thought—

I thought we'd uncovered a way to end this nightmare. I thought I could be happy and that the light we'd delivered to the sky—albeit briefly—signified a chance at happiness.

I should've known nothing was ever that easy.

That inane prophecy wasn't real, just another fairy tale I'd latched on to, praying it would be our salvation. It was a lie, because as soon as we admitted our truths face to face, touch to touch—Kiara had been struck down.

The hand on my shoulder squeezed hard, forcing my gaze up.

My mother's dark irises were dulled. It almost looked like she was worried, but I wouldn't know—the woman was, in all truth, a stranger. The only people who'd given me that look before had been Isiah and Kiara. Isiah was gone, Kiara now unconscious.

And I couldn't save her.

"Get up, Jude," my mother commanded, her hands digging into my arms. With surprising strength, she hauled me to my feet, her grip firm on my waist.

I couldn't stop looking at Kiara, couldn't stop picturing her among all the other lifeless bodies that haunted me. Those I'd killed with my own hand, their throats severed, dripping blood, frozen screams on their chapped lips—

"Jude." The Fox grasped my chin and tilted my head her way. "I was afraid this would happen," she murmured softly.

I tracked her stare as it moved to Kiara. "I recognized her... otherworldliness back in Fortuna. It was the opposite of warm. I smelled rust and felt the harsh chill of winter when she entered my study, and I knew why. Her gloves couldn't hide it from me. I'd heard the story of the girl with hair of fire who survived the shadow beast attack in Cila all those years ago, and I just... I knew."

She guided me farther into the trees, Kiara growing smaller.

I wanted to fight my mother, and realistically, I could have, but my body retaliated against me. Hurting Kiara was worse than hurting myself, and I would surely do more damage if I gave in to temptation.

The Fox situated me far enough away that I could only make out the others' outlines. She placed both hands on my cheeks and said, "You need to stop believing in fairy tales, my boy. I thought you understood that there's no room for them in this world." Her thumb brushed the bottom of my twin scars, and an indecipherable look twisted her features. "I would've assumed it to be a lesson you'd learned long ago."

That pulled me out of my daze.

I went rigid, drawing away from her foreign caresses. She had no right to touch me in such a tender way. "You didn't stick around long enough to find out," I seethed, my frustration refocusing, selecting a worthy target. "You dumped me on the steps of a sadist, while you went off to live your life. Excuse me if I'm hesitant to take advice from a thief and a coward."

Something akin to hurt widened her eyes, and her lower lip quivered.

Gods, I looked so much like her. Why then couldn't I turn away?

"I didn't know what was inside of you until the day my mother passed," she whispered, her voice broken. "She carried her secret all her life. Gods, she didn't even tell me her real name." She scoffed bitterly. "Only when you were born did she ever show an ounce of love."

"Raina?" I needed to hear her say it. To confirm everything that I was incapable of wrapping my head around.

"She went by Rae after...after her fall," the Fox said, glancing at her boots. "The stories say she found a great love and lived a long mortal life, but those were fairy tales as well. People holding on to wishful thinking." Her head lifted to where the fog shrouded Kiara, something icy deadening her gaze.

I didn't trust myself not to go running in her direction, and I bit my cheek. The slight sting centered me.

"My mother was a cold woman. She didn't marry, but she had me at some point during her travels. I spent my entire life trying to gain her affection, her approval, her *anything*, but Raina had shut down after her lover's betrayal. She protected me, of course, yet she couldn't seem to love me. It was when she was on the edge of death that she gazed upon your tiny face with complete adoration. I hated her for it. I hated *you*." The admission was said quietly, like a secret, and it was a secret I suspected she'd never shared before.

The Fox wasn't the cocky thief I'd found in Fortuna. Her shoulders curved in on themselves in a way that made her appear smaller, her rage and grief nearly palpable enough to choke on.

All of it disoriented me.

"The past is the past," I forced out, my world spinning. How many times had I envisioned my mother apologizing? Speaking to me about her regrets, her guilt? But this wasn't an apology, merely a poor explanation that held no weight. "But I don't need to hear your excuses," I said. "You abandoned me. End of story."

The Fox let out a whimper, grasping my hand when a hoarse shout rang out. Jake.

"I think she's coming to!" he screamed.

My nails dug into the flesh of my palm, every inch of me battling against itself.

My magic was too hot right now, too out of control, to go near her. If that's what had hurt her—this unwanted power of mine—then I couldn't risk it.

We had become oil and flame, a deadly combination.

I grasped the nearest tree, my fingers curling against the coarse bark as I heard Kiara's voice. She said my name. Her first word was a shout for *me*. The man who'd hurt her.

The smell of burning saturated the air, and I turned, finding my palm aglow. The tree I leaned against was charred, dark smoke rising from the wood. With a curse, I wrenched away.

I ruined everything I touched.

The Fox dared to reach out for me again, but I ran.

I ran until I made my way to the clearing where our horses were kept, and I faced the sprawling field below, the moon exposed and bright against the vacant night sky.

With a roar, I held out my arms, screaming as fire and gold erupted from me.

I became a living flame, my rage kindling the blaze. Wings of burnt russet rose on either side, stretching from my shoulders, becoming looming threats of promised devastation.

Smoke clogged my nostrils as the grass at my feet began to char and wither.

I didn't care. I was on fire from the inside out, and I was so fucking angry.

How could I have ever imagined I could have her? She would never be mine. Never be able to love me, even if she wanted to.

My flames strengthened, carving a fiery path across the field, snaking up trees and tearing apart their thick branches like brittle twigs. When the entire clearing reeked of destruction and ruin, my power simmered, the intensity of its influence lessening.

I'd been born to destroy.

Born to kill.

Born to never love.

I swiveled around, mentally incapable of witnessing my handiwork.

My gaze lifted, and there she was, twenty feet away and surrounded by the others, her brother hovering beside her protectively. Even Jake shot me a wary glance, his hand instinctively going to his dagger's hilt. Finn and Dimitri merely stared.

The final ember of my magic faded, but I didn't move closer.

I promised I wouldn't leave again, and I wouldn't, but I couldn't allow myself to get near. I watched as her head turned to the burning field and then back to me. I could feel the outpouring of love radiating from that dark stare, and that's what killed me the most.

How cruel fate was—

My love could kill the one woman who owned my heart.

Chapter Twenty-One

Kiara

Rae was more than she seemed, more than we could've imagined. I'm sorry I never told you the truth. Hopefully, you'll forgive us both.

Letter from Aurora Adair to Juniper Marchant, year 32 of the curse

Jude stared back at me with a look I'd never seen before.

Utter and complete ruin.

He'd kissed my lips and professed his love, and the sun entered the sky. Those seconds after, my blood had begun to boil so fiercely, I felt dipped in flames. My shadows recoiled, hissing in my ears as they skittered back to their hiding place, escaping Jude's power.

His touch scorched the darkness thriving inside, sending me to my knees.

Unlike last time, we weren't in some dream world.

Our bodies were connected, and skin to skin, our magics fought. I didn't know if it was our words or our powers that battled, or if our declaration had somehow set a misguided prophecy into motion.

"Kiara..." Jude took a step closer, anguish creasing the

corners of his eyes. I wanted to rush to him and tell him it wasn't his fault, but after Arlo's warning in the void of darkness, I was hesitant to endure his caress.

Our love made our magic sing—but only the pieces of Raina. Not my shadows. And they were as much a part of me as the light. If not more so now that I'd embraced them fully.

What Arlo had insinuated…that I only loved him because of our shared power. That thought was a plague. It did its best to poison the affection swimming in my soul, and for once, I hesitated to shove it aside. Old fears reared their heads, arguing that I didn't deserve to be happy, that our connection was too good to be true. But I *did* shove it aside. At least, I tried to.

"What was that, Emelia?" Finn asked, running a nervous hand over his shaved head. "That was—he was—"

"He's carrying Raina's magic," she said coldly. "Or most of it, from what I'm assuming." She glanced in my direction. "That's why this mission is so hazardous."

"Gods, woman. You should've told me!" he argued back, but she silenced him with a withering look. "I knew about your mother, but your son carrying her power… How could you not share that? After all we've been through together?"

The thief's lips thinned. "I've kept my past a secret for a reason."

As Emelia continued to argue with Finn, I took stock of the commander. He stood frozen, his fists clenched, the muscles in his neck taut.

"It's all right, Jude," I promised, raising my voice so he could hear. "I'm fine." He merely gave me his back, unwilling or unable to look at my face.

I couldn't bear the thought of him blaming himself. He'd carried an abundance of shame and guilt, and finally, *finally*, when he let it all go and did something for himself, he was rewarded with more suffering.

Liam snatched my hand in his, hissing at the warmth I exuded, yet he didn't let go.

My body burned even as I shivered from the cold. I wouldn't last long in this state. Jude must've told him of our time in the Mist because he hardly appeared surprised. I was grateful I wouldn't be forced to explain.

"We need to get going." Emelia leapt in front of Jude as if protecting him from *me*. "The quicker we retrieve this talisman, the better. If the Moon God is truly after you both, then we won't have much time. Especially if the king is hot on our trails, too." To Finn, she added, "I'll explain everything. I only hid my past to protect you."

Finn's hands were balled tight, the muscles in his jaw feathering. He was hurt, and I couldn't blame him.

Before the Fox made for the horses, Arlo's unexpected appearance returned to my thoughts.

"When I was…unconscious, I was visited by Arlo," I said, knowing I needed to share, but having to force the words out regardless. "He claimed I *Traveled*. And maybe I did. I was soaring, flying in the form of a starwing over a ruined temple."

Dimitri, who'd been a silent observer this entire time, sprang to life. He sighed, giving his disorderly bright orange hair a tug as he paced. "Traveled, you say?" he asked, whipping my way. I nodded, and he resumed his relentless pace. "I've heard that word before…something about shadow beasts. My village was closer to the border, and the elders claimed they'd seen the beasts before. A few of our young even went missing, vanishing in the night. No one could catch the beasts in the act, though. They moved without detection. I've always wondered how they did it…"

Meaning I'd been correct. I *could* shift, change my form, and push the natural order of things. I glanced away, finding Emelia's eyes locked on me. No fear or anger radiated from her, and I was swept away by an odd sort of acceptance when she bit her tongue and faced a seething Finn. He had yet to come to terms with our situation.

I grimaced, hating to add to my companions' fears. "He also said our enemy was near."

Dimitri's nerves were wearing on my own, and I wished he'd stand still. He didn't. He huffed in annoyance and waved his hands around as if to say, *Of course.*

"Then you have to use that cursed blade on him." Emelia's attention landed on my sheath.

Protectiveness had me squaring my shoulders. "What are you talking—"

"Oh, as if I didn't suspect what that dagger was immediately," she cut me off and shrugged a shoulder, earning another groan of annoyance from Finn. "I've heard far too many tales of its strength against immortals. You were hardly stealthy concealing it. Besides, what's the use of this talisman if we can't release the god's powers?"

"What did you get us into, Mistress?" Dimitri groaned, blessedly coming to a halt.

She knew. I wasn't fooling anyone with wide eyes and weak deceptions.

"I have the blade that was used to steal Raina's power," I admitted for all to hear. "And Maliah and Lorian warned me that the Moon God wants to claim what lies within Jude and me. He's set on destroying the possibility of bringing back the sun, which is why we need to use this blade on him first."

It was a risk, divulging our secrets to the most famous thieves of the realm, but they had the right to know. Emelia took it all in without an ounce of emotion. I envied her for that.

"It has to be done, then," she said to Jude. "My mother didn't speak highly of the Moon God. I doubt much love was lost. But if he's after you, he's gonna try to catch you unawares. Meaning, we stick to the plan."

"I agree," Jake said, squaring his shoulders. "It's time to gain the upper hand. For once."

Emelia's gaze never strayed from Jude. "Until then, we can't have any repeats of…whatever *this* was."

I looked out to the smoldering fields, to the still-burning trees. Jude was capable of unimaginable destruction. In the span of a minute, he'd demolished over half a dozen acres of woods.

"Jude," I called out, demanding his attention.

Reluctantly, he turned, grimacing as though it physically pained him to do so. I doubted he'd been listening all that intently, his eyes glazed, his thoughts lost to the turmoil of his fears.

I wished I'd said the damned words back to him. That I admitted what grew inside of me every second I spent in his presence. But I hadn't, and the time had passed, and Arlo's words were a tumor growing inside of me, planting the seeds of doubt.

"We're going to figure this out. And we *aren't* separating. Not again." I held his stare until he was forced to nod.

He didn't like it, but he didn't have to.

Jude might believe we were already doomed, but I maintained hope—however small—and I had to believe it would be stronger than the uncertainties I battled in my head.

The commander wasn't my poison—

He was my cure.

$$\cdots$$

We stayed off the main roads, which made the journey twice as long.

Throughout, my scar ached, but it didn't warm as it once had. I attributed it to Jude keeping his distance.

Whenever I sought him, I'd find his head bowed, the hood of his cloak shielding his face.

On the rare times he did speak, it was with the Fox or her men. Dimitri whistled while he rode beside the commander. On any other occasion, Jude would've slapped the man off his horse.

Dimitri had stuck to his side shortly after we left the razed woods. His smiles were as genuine as before, if not brighter.

I realized why Emelia had brought him—he was the much-needed calm in their trio. That was, aside from his momentary panic in the clearing, which, to be fair, was expected.

Liam had briefly filled me in on all the chaos happening back home. I was stunned to hear how worried my parents were about my well-being. Maybe my shock was due to the assumption that they'd rather be free of me and my curse. They hadn't exactly been...warm.

Once this was all over, I knew I'd seek them out. Maybe our relationship wasn't beyond repair. The possibility added to the weak flames of my hope, its warmth just enough to keep me pressing onward.

I wasn't afforded the time to ruminate over my parents for long. Finn kept me company, probably due to Emelia wanting to keep a close eye on us. Or he was still upset she'd kept secrets.

I found I didn't mind his attention. He had a deep voice that worked to soothe, and he spoke more than any of us, including Jake, who'd been nudged up front, right next to the thief. She scowled at him whenever he attempted to open his mouth.

On the third day after encountering Jude and Liam, Finn told me the story of how he met Emelia.

"She was supposed to cut my finger off," he said with a dreamy smile, staring farther up the path where the Fox led us. "I'd broken into her office and she caught me trying to steal some silly bauble that wasn't worth the fuss, and instead of taking my finger like she was lawfully permitted, she slapped me on the back and said, 'Your lockpicking skills could use some work.' She laughed in my face before ordering me to take a seat."

"She doesn't seem to be the forgiving type."

"Ah, that she is not," he assented. "But only if you screw her twice. The Fox may be a notorious criminal rumored to lack a heart, but that woman has a soft spot for strays, and before I knew it, I was part of her pack. Though, if I had known she was *Raina's* daughter, I might not have tried to steal from her in the first place."

Finn barked out a laugh but carried on speaking of their ensuing adventures.

The robbery of the Parin armory in the south. The Conchetta ruby ring, which was supposedly crafted over a thousand years ago. The time they snuck into Lord Delonor's fortress and stole the man's golden timepiece right from his pocket, just for the hells of it.

Many of these tales began with boredom, the thief not easily kept still.

Only once did Emelia curve in her saddle and return his smile, brief as it was.

Like every evening since we reunited, Jude settled down as far from me as possible, facing the trees, giving me his back. I watched over the flames while everyone slept, unable to sleep until his breathing evened out.

Not once did he ever turn back.

"He's trying to protect you," Jake said the following day, nudging me with his knee as we sat beside the fire after everyone had gone to bed.

Another ten hours of travel had passed, and we were all worn to the bone.

"Same old story, then," I huffed, crossing my arms and giving Jake a knowing look.

"I'll kill him myself if he hurts you." Liam plopped beside us, his pale blue eyes venomous. Jake's lips curled up as he assessed the newest arrival, his eyes glittering.

"You used to be so very peaceful, Liam," I said, shaking my head. "Did you really miss me that much?"

He scoffed. "You still have the largest ego I've ever known."

"And yet you didn't deny you missed me." I slung an arm around my brother's shoulder, tugging him close. He felt like a piece of home.

My other arm reached out and snagged Jake's cloak, and I yanked him to my side. Whereas Liam groused, poking me in the ribs to free himself, Jake tightened his fingers and laughed, the sound deep and comforting and so pure, it nearly broke my heart.

Tomorrow we'd reach the temple, and I couldn't fathom what we'd find.

Even as I studied Jude's sleeping form, curled alone and away from the others beneath a low-hanging branch, I couldn't shake the feeling that there'd be no happy ending for me.

I had always been a warrior, and warriors were born to die.

CHAPTER TWENTY-TWO

JUDE

Beware the temples of the gods. While places of worship,
below the altars lie cavernous chambers filled with traps and
deadly puzzles.

EXCERPT FROM ASIDIAN LORE: A TALE OF THE GODS

I rose before the rest of the camp—all except the Fox, who'd
taken the last watch.

She didn't say a word, but she dipped her chin to me in a
poor attempt at welcome. I ignored it. Too little, too late.

Across the fire, Kiara slept, flanked by her brother and Jake.

My blood heated at the mere sight of her. The moonlight
swept across her sharp cheekbones, making her appear even
more feline, more threatening, and eerily stunning.

If life was kind, I would've woken up beside her this
morning, my arms snaked around her middle, her back pressed
to my chest.

We'd only just reunited, and I couldn't even touch her.
Couldn't brush my calloused fingers down her soft cheek, graze
her full bottom lip. Lips I yearned to taste.

These past days had been unbearable, excruciating to the
point where I forced myself to swallow some of Finn's foul-

tasting liquor. After the incident in the clearing, he'd handed me his metal flask, his eyes widening in surprise when I returned it empty.

Finn didn't press, which I appreciated, but I noticed how his gaze often strayed my way, deep lines creasing his forehead. He had every right to worry. I was in a sorry state, and that made me dangerous. Uncontrollable.

For just a few weeks, I'd started to believe I was worth something beyond my role in this divine power struggle. That I was someone who could be loved, even the corrupted and ugly parts. I had *hoped*, and that wasn't something I'd ever done.

And how quickly I had learned to harness such an emotion, only for it to be crushed.

I should've known better.

Dimitri plopped down beside me, lifting his hands to the fire to warm them. The woods pressed in on either side of our camp, spindly branches poking out like pointed spears.

It was always cold in Asidia, though this time of year was worse, and soon, snow would fall. We called it the Dark Winter, because even the snow was a shade of gray.

I tugged my cloak tighter, but I didn't need the warmth—my body continued to burn, warming fingers and toes that surely would've been half frozen had my magic not thrived.

Dimitri whistled the same tune over and over, his knee bumping mine.

I had to hold myself back from punching him square in the face and putting an end to the grating sound. I despised whistling. Or tapping. Jostling. Loud breathing.

Isiah had often tapped his foot when impatient, and it drove me damn near to the edge. He knew it, too, the bastard, and would see how far he could get before I barked at him to stop. He'd smirk in return.

"My daughter used to like it," Dimitri said without preamble, pausing his whistling and bringing me to the present. He wore a twisted smile that spoke of buried heartache. "Tell me to stop if it bothers you."

Gods above, I wanted nothing more, but his eyes shone with a desperateness I couldn't spurn.

"It's fine." It wasn't, but I took a sip from my canteen before I spoke the truth.

The dried meats the Fox packed were dispersed, though I hardly touched my rations. I probably should eat to maintain strength, but the offensive amount of salt she used might kill all of my remaining taste buds.

"My daughter died with her mother years ago."

I went rigid. Something told me that whatever Dimitri was about to tell me might end with me growing to care. Attachment had plagued me like a virus as of late…but for some reason, I found I *wanted* to know the man's secrets. Why his smile was weighed with sadness.

"She wasn't even eight," he said, swallowing thickly. "She was a spirited thing, and only when I whistled this tune did she settle." His somber smile fell, and I tracked his gaze across the fire to where Kiara was doing her best to inch away from Finn.

The bodyguard appeared to be telling some raucous tale, his hands moving excitedly, nearly smacking her in the face a few times. She shoved a few pieces of jerky into her mouth with a grimace.

Since our encounter in the clearing, Finn had lost his scowl, looking almost relaxed. It probably helped that Emelia had gradually grown less tense—the pair seemed to feed off each other.

"Don't you ever let go," Dimitri said, tilting his head toward the pair. "I learned the hard way that a heart can break over and over again when its missing half is taken. I promise you, boy. It'll never be the same again. No matter how hard you try to replace them, to carve out a new life. A love like that comes only once in a lifetime, and it can ruin you when it's gone." I watched as he lifted to his feet and wandered to where his mistress tended to the horses. The Fox's features softened at the sight of him, and she cocked her head in welcome.

I returned to the fire, contemplating his admission.

My heart had never been something I thought could break, merely because I didn't count myself lucky enough to one day fall in love. Dimitri was right, though...my love *would* be my ruin.

Deciding to torture myself, I sought the object of my thoughts. As if she felt my eyes on her, Kiara lifted her head and stared back at me, her eyes all but burning into my flesh. I felt like I was suffocating, the warmth in my chest radiating outward, the heat engulfing me until my lungs ached.

Loving Kiara was dangerous. But I was forever a glutton for punishment.

I held her gaze, silently relaying my apologies, my wishes, my heartache. My cowardice. Praying that she understood why we sat on different ends of the camp, why I didn't give in to my baser instincts. The slight tilt of her chin told me she did, but there was another emotion swimming in her eyes. Almost like... confusion.

Where is that confusion directed? I wondered. At our mission? Or *me*?

I bit into my lip hard enough that blood coated my tongue. I prayed it was the mission, but a nagging voice inside of my head taunted it was the latter. Maybe it was for the best, her slowly pushing me away. It would make everything easier in the end, right?

Even I couldn't convince myself of that.

Kiara was the first to turn away, her brother murmuring something in her ear. Liam hadn't left her side, and neither had

Jake. Liam smiled more in her presence, and whenever Jake shot him a lopsided grin, he blushed deeply, color stretching down his neck.

Thus far, I hadn't seen the two share a private conversation. Kiara always remained between them, a buffer. I caught Jake staring at Liam more times than I could count, but Liam was either too aloof or shy to meet his eye.

I was gathering my courage to walk over and ask what troubled her when Finn barked out an order.

"Time to head out! Evidently, we have a realm to save." He marched over to Dimitri and slapped him on the back none too gently. His comrade gave him the middle finger in reply, and Finn merely let out a rumbling chuckle with a childish glee I hadn't expected.

The Fox lingered on Finn as he mounted his horse, her hardened stare turning tender before she climbed into her saddle.

I'd studied her for hours on end during our travels. Sometimes I'd catch her staring at me, but she'd always shift her attention elsewhere when our gazes met.

Why she looked at me like that in the first place was a mystery. She hadn't attempted to speak with me in private. Not truly. Emelia had no right to steal glances at the son she left behind.

"The temple is beyond those hills," Finn said once everyone had saddled and mounted their mares minutes later. He pointed east, to where the land rose high into the sky, the black trees seeming to kiss the glimmering stars that shined above. "We are nothing but travelers wishing to bestow an offering, so keep your hoods up and knives concealed. But if you believe you've earned a soldier's attention, turn back. We'll formulate another plan." He stared a beat too long at Emelia, a silent conversation passing between them. As if they'd reached an agreement, she finally gave him a weary smile, one he returned.

My horse made no fuss as I guided her to the trail. Her lack of complaint had me missing Starlight, but the mare was with Kiara, and that eased the sting.

I'd insisted she ride her, even though the horse bestowed me with a look I'd characterize as "irritated." Her agitation had to be for show, because she nuzzled Kiara each time she mounted her and whinnied excitedly when she ran her hands through her forever-tangled mane.

"You ready for the big day, sunshine?" Dimitri asked as he steered himself my way. He'd taken to assuming the role of my shadow. I wasn't sure why he bothered.

"My name's Jude," I said, his little nickname for me like nails on glass.

Dimitri scoffed, rubbing at his short scruff. "I call you sunshine because you're so warm and fuzzy." When I rolled my eyes, he laughed. "You know, I've actually been to the temple before, but the second I tried to inspect the place, I was *kindly* escorted out. It probably didn't help that I was drunk off my ass, and I might not have been as stealthy as I'd believed."

"Shocking," I replied, focusing ahead, or more specifically, on the back of a certain redhead. Her hair was wild and free of her usual braid. I wanted to run my fingers through it.

"You won't have to worry about that happening again," Dimitri promised. "The Mistress helped me get my shit together, and I haven't touched a drink in years."

"At least she helped someone," I grumbled. My mother seemed to take in a lot of strays, caring for them as her own. Bitterness soured my mouth, even as I thought of all Dimitri had lost. I'd have taken to the bottle as well, had the roles been reversed.

The world was a brutal place. The closer we ventured to the temple where we'd meet our destiny, the more I decided upon one single notion—

I wouldn't allow the one beautiful thing in my life to be taken from me. Fate would have to pry Kiara from my cold, dead hands, and it should expect a fight.

· · ·

There were more people than we anticipated loitering on the outskirts of the temple.

That was favorable for us. Blending in with the crowd bestowed the perfect cover.

Dismounting our steeds, we steered them along a path leading to a stable packed with horses. A young boy no more than fourteen accepted our coins and led our horses away. Starlight flashed me her signature glower before she vanished into her pen. I suspected she was sick and tired of being caged.

The earth was worn from too many footprints, making the route heading to the temple easy to follow, though a few torches were lit every fifty feet. With our hoods pulled low, we took on the personas of weary travelers seeking the Moon God's grace.

Even Emelia dropped her chin and raised her hands as if in prayer, but her jaw was clenched so tightly, I heard her teeth grind. Finn sidled close to her, always close, and hunched his shoulders, trying to make himself appear smaller and less of a threat.

The final three in our group transformed before my eyes. Adorning a mask of naivety and pure childlike wonder, my girl lost that fire in her gaze, turning her smile timid and soft. And at her side, Jake's trademark swagger became almost bashful, his head lowered demurely.

Liam, on the other hand, didn't have to fake his innocence.

The temple was constructed of marble, the palest shade

of moonstone. A gold crescent moon hung from its apex, the metal glowing as if it were a beacon. It towered over a field of Midnight Blooms, the flowers swaying gently in the breeze, a spot of color among so much pale white.

A handful of moon priests and priestesses wearing silken ivory robes stood guard at the bottom of a formidable staircase leading up to the main entry. I squinted, noting several more of the cloaked individuals manning their stations at the top. Shivers raced down my arms. None moved, not even an inch.

They reminded me of statues—their deadened eyes unblinking.

I dipped my chin, looking anywhere but at the *faithful*. Still, those watchful eyes seared my flesh, the intensity causing the hair on my arms to rise in warning.

Our group paused at the steps where a handful of travelers conversed in hushed tones, their arms laden with offerings. I tilted my head, taking in the arching stairs winding high into the never-ending night.

A soft snort sounded to my left.

Kiara hadn't been strong enough to hide her annoyance at the promise of cardio, and my lips tugged up against my will. Climbing this monstrosity would certainly get her heart racing. As if she knew I thought of her, Kiara's head whipped my way, and our eyes locked.

She mouthed, "*Cardio*," before scowling. *Just as I thought.*

While I maintained the distance between us, I found myself lifting a brow, eyeing her in a way I used to when I was merely her commander.

My body could be reduced to ash, and yet I'd still be drawn to her, whatever pieces that remained of me lifting on the winds and demanding to circle her orbit. Her fearlessness never ceased to amaze me.

"Take your time climbing," she instructed Liam. To everyone

else, she threatened, "Go slow or I'll incinerate you."

Grabbing her brother's hand, she set the pace, and I watched from the back, my scar throbbing in tune with my heartbeat. That throbbing transformed into a sharp stinging the farther we journeyed, and I gritted my teeth, knowing my body reacted to the sacred ground where we stood.

It did not welcome me or my magic, and I sensed my power recoil.

It took us over twenty minutes to reach the top at our relaxed pace. Liam's exhales held a slight rasp, but he appeared otherwise in good health, and I attributed his vigor to my mother's medicine.

I scanned the temple, noting the arch the size of ten men outlining the entrance. A dozen or more priests and priestesses lined its sides, all frozen until approached by a traveler.

"Welcome." A priestess with jet-black hair jerked mechanically to life, waving me forward. The others flanking her remained stoically in place.

Instinctively, my hand went to my sheath. This priestess's eyes were too bright, her pupils too dilated. Silver-painted nails caught my focus, the tips as sharp as a blade. No trace of warmth radiated off her.

"We come to offer tribute," Emelia announced, making an exaggerated show of bowing.

The priestess smiled with all her teeth, though it had the opposite effect of calming. "I'll be happy to deliver you to the offering chamber," she said, her long nails clicking against one another as she cocked her head. When her gaze fell on Kiara, I reined in my urge to growl. I didn't like how she studied her, like she was a fly caught in a web.

My mother muttered some more magnanimous bullshit before the priestess ushered us through the archway. Metal sculptures framed another set of stairs in the center of the space, sinister winged beasts suspended in mid-flight. I couldn't help but wonder if they were modeled after the very same creature Kiara had fought off a decade before.

Tension saturated the air, and sweat trickled down my spine, the sense of foreboding weighing on my every exhale. That same heat expanded down my back, and the feeling of eyes burning into the back of my skull grew. I glanced over my shoulder.

This time, I regarded a hooded priest who trained his eyes dutifully on the marble as he climbed the last step. There was a familiarity about the confident way he moved—I longed to shove aside his hood and glimpse his face for myself.

"Through here," the priestess commanded, forcing my attention away from the curious priest. She ushered us past a twenty-foot-tall statue of the Moon God that had been erected at the top of the stairs, the center of the dome open to the night sky.

No two depictions of the god were the same, but they were all beautiful. It was said he transformed as often as the phases of the moon.

This particular sculpture painted the god slightly older than the others, his hair masked by his hood. Round eyes peered at us, slight creases lining the sides. A tingling scraped down my spine.

"Jude."

I tore away from the statue and fixed my attention on the woman who'd called my name. Kiara had shucked her innocent act, if only briefly, her stare hard when she assessed me. "Everything all right?" she asked, brazenly moving closer. Too close.

I held out a hand, my throat constricting. "Please. No further."

Kiara didn't listen. It shouldn't have shocked me.

"I won't touch you," she promised, less than three feet away. Jake lifted his head, observing her from the corner of his eye with tangible worry.

"I feel off here," she admitted, her gloved hand motioning to the temple floor. "It's unnerving." Her eyes lost their edge, turning glassy and unfocused. "Wherever the talisman is, I sense its power, and whoever dares cross us—Moon God or not—should be frightened when we have it in our grasp."

Her voice was a rasp. Nothing about her posture or words felt *right*, and I started to reach for her before cursing and dropping my arm. Fuck, I wanted to touch her. To grab her hand, her waist, to caress her chin, lower my head to her lips and taste her.

It was maddening.

"Soon," she murmured, a frustrated grumble leaving her. Kiara's stare roamed my form, straying on my arms and torso before lifting back to my face. Her admiration made me want to lunge for her, danger be damned.

Thankfully, Kiara moved out of my reach before I could do anything stupid. She stood beside Liam, as tense as I'd ever seen her. I wondered if she had similar thoughts.

"Almost there." The priestess spun on a heel, her robes waving about her lithe form. She moved like air, guiding us down a hall boasting dozens of offering rooms. With each step, my thoughts blurred, my need for Kiara overshadowed by a surge of warning.

Something was coming. My newfound power buzzed in my veins, and with every blink, tiny pinpricks of light danced across my eyes.

A door off the main chamber creaked open with a single wave of the priestess's hand. "Come inside," she intoned, her attention once again aimed solely at Kiara.

I didn't like that one bit.

Kiara grabbed Liam tighter, gifting the woman a tight smile as she led the way.

I came up last, right after Dimitri, who grinned like this was some joyous sightseeing trip. I was thankful he wasn't whistling.

"Each of you can offer your blood to the God of the Moon. The merciful god who watches over us all and commands the night." The priestess nodded her chin toward a platform where a bronze bowl rested atop a velvet-lined table. A simple blade sat beside it, the serrated edges clean. "He might grant your prayers, should they be worthy enough."

We'd planned on scoping the temple out once alone in an offering room, and Emelia had promised she'd be able to help locate an entry to what lay below, to where the *real* entrance hid.

From what I understood, the faithful were left to their prayers during the ritual, but the priestess didn't retreat. Her unwavering stare targeted Kiara before veering to me. When she lingered on my face, her nose wrinkled.

"Well, go on," she pressed, nodding to Kiara first, her grin shrewd. "Will you be the first, child?"

Kiara shifted on her feet, her cool mask slipping. I could nearly make out the thudding pulse point on her neck. "I—"

"I wish to go first," Liam interjected, stepping up to the dais, much to the priestess's dismay. Her grin faltered, her canines poking into her thin bottom lip.

Kiara began to protest, but Jake whispered something in her ear, silencing her.

While the chamber was dimly lit with torchlight, I made out how Liam's hands shook, his posture slumping. It didn't stop him from taking the blade in his hand and slicing it clean through his palm.

Thick blood bubbled up, and when he made a fist and squeezed, it dripped into the bowl. The droplets pinged ominously as they fell one by one. Gray steam rose from the basin's edges, and the scent of the dense wood and fresh snow wafted to my nostrils.

Liam stumbled back a step, his still-bleeding palm leaving a trail of red on the floor. Beside him, Jake's jaw clenched, his deadly stare focused on the open wound.

"Ah. You didn't send out a prayer, dear boy," the priestess warned, her voice sounding tinny and far away. The whites of her eyes nearly eclipsed her pupils. "Give yourself to him and he will grant you something in return. He grants us all peace, if only we devote ourselves to him."

It couldn't have been merely *peace* that turned the priests into these fanatical shells.

Liam stuttered, trying and failing to form a coherent thought, every word coming out garbled. He grasped the edges of the table with both hands, swaying. The steam rose from the offering dish, spiraling into the air where it curled around his face like claws.

"That's it," the priestess praised, taking a step closer. "Inhale."

Liam coughed, his eyes watering from whatever poison he breathed in. Kiara curled her fists, the leather of her gloves squelching.

She lunged at the same moment shouts rang out from the hall.

Kiara dove for Liam and wrenched him back, away from that cursed bowl. With him safely in her arms, her focus aimed for the door, where more screams sounded from beyond, the walls practically shaking from their force.

"What in the hells..." Jake flanked her, dagger drawn and ready, and Emelia and her men straightened and whipped out their blades.

"One moment." The priestess hissed in annoyance before sauntering toward the door and whipping it open, exposing the unfolding chaos.

The pristine white hall was packed with soldiers clad in red, the men shouting over the screams of the patrons. Grasping each traveler, the King's Guard lifted hoods and removed scarves, shoving people to their knees as they exposed faces. Like a plague, they spread across the hall, searching...

Undoubtedly searching for *us*.

"Screw this." The Fox sprinted to the door. "Thanks for the help, but we'll take it from here," she said, just before shoving against the priestess's back. With a yelp, the woman stumbled out into the hall. The Fox slammed the door in her face and grabbed a nearby chair to prop it against the handle, locking us inside.

"We need to find the entry!" Finn shouted, jerking his stubbled chin in the direction of the dais. "Didn't you say all these rooms had a way below?"

"Not all—"

A body thudded against the door, interrupting her. Before any of us could jump to secure it in place, the wooden chair propped against it went flying across the room. The door splintered and shattered, revealing a muscled figure. Instantly, my blood boiled when I took in his face.

Harlow. He entered the room, his cold eyes bottomless pits of apathy. Even the Fox stumbled out of his way in shock, staring at him as if he were a ghost. And by all accounts, he should've been.

Was Harlow the "priest" who'd trailed me? The eyes I felt on my skin?

Thick bandages poked out from his cloak, and he had a slight limp from where the jaguar had dug his teeth into his leg. Yet he still rolled his shoulders back and appraised us all like unworthy opponents.

"How..." Jake trailed off, asking the question we all thought.

Harlow grimaced. "The beast was easy to wound once arrogance blinded it," he said, much to our shock. He raised his weapon, but his grip wasn't firm. Brax had done more damage than he showed.

I felt no pity.

"All I've done was protect you, and now you've entered the one place you should've steered clear of. You've all but welcomed him to destroy you."

He claimed he was there to protect us, yet he'd allowed me to be tortured. A *friend* didn't let that happen.

"Oh, lieutenant," Kiara snarled, stepping into the light. "Your first mistake was threatening Jude. Your second was coming in here alone."

CHAPTER TWENTY-THREE

KIARA

The legend of Aloria, Protector of the South, is one of profound loss. Heartbroken after the death of her lover on the battlefield, her grief turned to flames, setting her body alight. A creature of sorrow and rage, she raced into a surge of enemy soldiers. They say she fought, even as she burned, and only when the last assailant fell did she crumble to ash.

EXCERPT FROM ASIDIAN LORE: A TALE OF THE GODS

The instant that Harlow set his sights on Jude, I'd reached my limit.

Hells, I'd already been teetering on the edge before he'd shown up and flaunted his blade, spouting lies.

If anyone was to blame for the pandemonium that was about to unfold, it was him.

My shadows burst free—thick coils of smoke lashing out from my shoulders, my torso, and my chest. They sliced through the air like whips before crashing onto the ground, leaving smoke steaming up from the stones.

There were shouts and pleas and the sound of my name.

I ignored them all.

My ears were ringing, my magic reacting to my rage,

feeding off it.

The darkness flared like sparking flames, streaming up my back and taking on the shape of twisted wings. They unfurled with a resounding snap, curving about my frame protectively.

Being here, in the temple, bolstered my strength, and the ground I stood upon shuddered as if in reverence.

My attention returned to Harlow, my power a storm of beautiful chaos. I was fear itself, and the thought of watching the light in his eyes die sent a thrill down my spine.

All but one of the sparse torches bracketing the walls fluttered out, the breeze forged by my wrath now casting us in a near cloak of darkness. Or casting the *others* in darkness.

I, on the other hand, could see quite well. My vision was a thing of distorted yellow, the temple's chamber highlighted with the same shimmering gold I'd come to know and now cherish.

My anger drove me. My frustration, my pain.

Years of abuse spun in brutal circles around my head, the memories seeming to squeeze until I could focus on nothing more. I wanted to hurt everyone who'd hurt me. Who'd called me cruel names and bowed their heads, unwilling to meet my gaze. Like I was some feral beast rather than a lonely girl with misery in her heart and wasted hope in her soul.

Copper washed across my tongue, and I smiled, swallowing the flavor of the night with a grin. If this was evil, why did it feel so damned *right*?

Jude stood immobile. He didn't move closer, but he didn't need to. Once his eyes landed on me, my racing adrenaline seemed to pause, to take a deep breath, and listen.

"Kiara," he whispered calmly, "you're letting it rule you. Not the other way around."

Didn't he realize darkness ruled us *all*? It had for the last five decades.

"It feels right," I protested, but the words were hollow.

Jude shook his head as the Fox and her men scrambled back, pressing themselves against the chamber's walls and far from me and my shadows.

Only when Jake snatched Liam, shoving him behind his frame, did my magic truly waver with indecision.

Liam. His eyes were squeezed shut as he bowed his head, which rested against Jake's shoulder. Fear seeped from his pores and all but scented the air.

He was afraid. Of *me.*

"Come back to me," Jude ordered from far away. "I won't lose you."

I abandoned Liam and gazed upon the commander. He'd taken a step forward, the only one who dared approach.

I bit into my bottom lip so hard, more blood trickled forth, the sting clearing some of the haze. He spoke my name again, and I closed my eyes, lulled by the sound.

"Center yourself," he coaxed gently, and I swam in the echo of his command. There was a note of awe mixed in with his fear, his tone soft but firm.

The rage that fueled me simmered, almost screaming as I shoved it down.

I homed in on his voice as he continued to whisper words of encouragement, and slowly, I grew strong enough to open my eyes and cease the violent trembling that racked my body.

"Watch out!"

I jerked to the side on instinct, seconds before Harlow lunged for me, a blade glinting in the dim light of the single torch.

My frail calm vanished.

Thrusting my arms up into the air, I focused my weapons of night on the impending threat. My magic hissed as I wielded it, not yet used to being tamed. It buzzed, waiting for my direction.

Harlow swayed feet away, his mouth pressed in a thin line.

"She's too dangerous," he muttered before he raised his blade defensively. The weapon he carried hung by his side, and I knew he debated striking again. He shook his head as if disappointed. In *what*, I wasn't sure.

My nostrils flared as fierce golden light blazed at my back. I spun in place, the air stolen from my lungs at what I found.

Jude's eyes glowed like pits of pure fire, just like the night he'd healed and saved me from the threshold of death's sweet abyss.

Against my wishes, my power reacted, recoiling as if sensing an enemy. One who wore Jude's face.

"Kiara," Jude repeated once more, though this time, he garnered my entire focus, Harlow and the others blurring. He lifted his palms as he took another bold step. "Control it. I know you can." His eyes tracked to where the others cowered. "Do not kill him when his intentions are not yet clear. You'll never forgive yourself." His tone held an ethereal quality to it, tiny bells resonating after each syllable. My shadows swayed as if caught in a gentle breeze, bespelled by his voice, his light.

"But he threatened you! Let you be tortured!" I protested, even as my demons calmed, even as my magic cooled. A man such as Harlow didn't deserve to live, and he'd obviously chosen Cirian's side. He wore his insignia. His colors.

A flash of gray whipped out from my body and struck the ground inches from Harlow's boots. Surprisingly, he remained unfazed. His shoulders were rolled back, his chin lifted. Ice snaked around my neck and tightened.

The shadow beast warred with my will, and I feared it was winning.

"Don't!" Jude warned as a foul wind whooshed into the chambers, causing the ceremonial bowl to go flying against the wall. It shattered upon impact, the shards of porcelain picked up by my wind and becoming a part of my arsenal. Harlow stumbled as my power advanced his way, his arrogant sneer wiped clean.

My body flickered in and out of focus as it had done before, and I raised my arms high before me. I was the only weapon I'd ever need.

Jude stood behind me. I could feel him, could sense his presence and the mere inches separating us. He held me back, making me falter.

"Let me finish this," I snapped, focusing on a single rope of ash, the shadow closest to the lieutenant. It rose, inching for Harlow's neck —

Jude grabbed my arm, and a searing spasm worked down my spine, forcing me to my knees. I fell, crumbling to the hard floor. As did my shadows.

Where Jude touched, it burned, his heat battling with the chill of my night, fighting to maintain the upper hand, even when he loosened his grip. The sliver of Raina I possessed awoke, like it was a slumbering dragon forced to peel open its eyes.

"Please," Jude rasped. "You're so much stronger than this, and killing Harlow won't fix anything."

"He wants to hurt you!" I shouted, feeling delirious, feverish, and unhinged. Warmth trickled from my nose, slipping between my frozen lips. *Blood*.

Jude's hand twitched around mine, but he didn't let go. "You once brought me back from the brink, and I plan to do the same for you. You fall and I catch you."

The twin scars connecting us gleamed, shining a hesitant gold.

My chin dropped, and I drank in the ethereal vision of my scar glowing through my shirt, its effulgent light mingling with the shadows emanating from my torso.

My name was a desperate whisper in my ear, hot breath tickling the outer shell. Jude pressed his lips to my skin, moving down my jaw, my neck, then back again. He released my arm, only to grasp my chin and angle my head, compelling me to soak in depthless yellow eyes.

I drowned in them. I drowned even as burning pain slithered down my body, blood gushing from my nose. It had to be his touch, his closeness, that was destroying me. But at that moment, I hardly cared. I'd missed his touch so very much.

"Let go, Kiara."

A rush of panic engulfed me, and the ice in my blood warmed. The thought of killing Harlow didn't feel as appealing as it had seconds before, not with Jude's glassy eyes on me, his lips at my ear, whispering dulcet promises. He emboldened the divinity I contained, and it was winning out against my baser instincts.

I let go.

"Then catch me, Commander."

The room shook as I screamed, my magic rushing back into my mortal body. The flashes of silver ceased to strike, and that vile wind stopped blowing. Nausea threatened as I stole more of my power back, the darkness restless and unwilling to be restrained.

I fought. I fought because Jude didn't look at me as though I was a beast; he never had. Even now, at my worst, when I'd lost all restraint and turned into the monster I always feared, his features were soft and warm and hopeful. Jude guided me home.

When I fell, the last piece of the shadow beast vanishing from the room, Jude kept his promise.

He caught me.

"Shhh," he murmured in my ear. "I got you." The blood trickling down my nose continued to flow, and Jude cursed, screaming out for Jake.

The commander's otherworldly eyes brightened the space enough for my friend to see, and he bounded to our side a heartbeat later. Gently, Jude transferred me into Jake's arms, the act causing his lips to thin and his brows to furrow. A deep rumble shook his chest, and he gritted his teeth when my hand fell from his skin.

The bleeding stopped almost immediately, but my ribs ached as my scar pulsated, matching the beating of my heart. Matching Jude's.

Without the whooshing of my power, thunderous clamoring sounded from the hall beyond, and I made out the telltale shouts of soldiers. There was an ambush occurring, and I'd already wasted so much time.

"Go!" Harlow shocked me by speaking, his gravelly voice ringing in the dim chamber. He made no more moves to attack, his shoulders slumped in defeat.

Emelia didn't waste time. Using the faint light shining from Jude, she rushed to the altar, her movements sure as she searched beneath its smooth surface.

"There should be a lever here," she said, fumbling for a crease in the marble.

I gazed at Harlow as she sought out our exit, analyzing him for a flicker of emotion. He displayed nothing, not anger or relief. And it had me questioning if he was telling us to go because he couldn't beat me, or if he actually was on our side as he claimed.

"Hurry, you fools! Before the damned guards find you!" Harlow ordered, followed by a spark of light to his left. Finn lit a handheld torch, the weak flames barely reaching me. He hovered above Emelia, aiding her quest.

"I told you I had your best interests in mind," Harlow spoke to Jude as he clutched his wounded shoulder, his chest rising unevenly. His focus swayed to me. "Before Kiara tried to kill me, I was attempting to warn you. You may love her, but she has the power to destroy you in the end. Destroy us all. If you didn't have a death wish, you'd have already carved out the missing piece. As you should have weeks ago."

With those parting words, the man I'd attempted to kill rushed for the threshold, kicking away pieces of the ruined door. He stood guard, his back toward us as he awaited advancing guards.

Maybe he wasn't on *my* side, after all. Rather, he was on Jude's.

"I got it!" A gear clicked into place, drawing my attention from the lieutenant. Emelia had managed to lift the top of the altar with Finn's assistance. "Hurry! The soldiers will be here any second now."

Jake and Liam each took one of my arms, hoisting me to my feet.

Everything ached, just as it had after Jude and I kissed, right before he set fire to the woods. Touching him pained me, and yet it was all I wanted to do. I wasn't usually an affectionate person, but I craved him like no other. I both hated and loved that he had such an effect on me—

Because I didn't know if what I felt was genuine or magic. A connection forced upon me.

Arlo's warning continued to ring in my head, and no matter how much I argued, the doubt lingered.

I was frightened, and not of gods or monsters.

The Fox placed the thin wood of the torch's handle between her teeth and gracefully hoisted herself over the sides of the now open passage. She felt around until her boot clanged against metal. A ladder.

Another loud crash rang out in the hall, and Emelia hastily descended into the unknown, Finn and Dimitri trailing after. Jude ushered Jake, Liam, and me in front. His ethereal eyes maintained their glow, although they had faded ever so slightly.

"Her first," he ordered. I met his stare, and something fragile within me broke. If only he knew my traitorous thoughts.

Liam helped me climb onto the side of the altar, and I followed Emelia's example, swinging my legs over and into the void.

When my foot clanged against the first rung of the ladder, I nodded at Liam and he reluctantly released me, leaving me free to descend.

My arms ached and my muscles burned from the effort, but I numbly grasped the rungs and pressed ahead, knowing I had to move fast so the others had time to escape.

The damage I caused was done, even if my insides churned and my magic hissed. I had to be stronger. I couldn't risk everyone I cared for again.

When we were all inside, clinging to the ladder, Jude swung the top of the altar shut, the resounding crash stinging my eardrums.

There was no returning. Not until we completed the mission.

Chapter Twenty-Four

Jude

Your mother kept her secret for a reason. She'd been broken beyond all belief, and spent the rest of her life making sure her daughter was safe from that same misery. She might've gone about it the wrong way, but it was all done out of love. Sometimes even gods are painfully human.

Letter from Aurora Adair sent to The Sly Fox Tavern, year 32 of the curse

I wasn't sure how far we'd traveled, but every time I peered over my shoulder, the abyss continued on forever, an endless shadow stretching beneath my boots.

Something had transpired in that chamber. My eyes were too hot. My sight was changing with every blink. I could see through the veil of black, and I caught the sight of a stony bottom. An *end*.

Wherever my gaze traveled, a soft yellow light followed—from the metal rungs of the ladder, down to the tops of my companions' heads. It wasn't strong, this light, but my right eye picked up details I hadn't been able to detect in over a decade. The abrupt change sent my world askew.

Below, Liam let out a grunt, his boot clashing against metal.

Like the rest, he struggled from exertion and waning adrenaline, and the climb down was by no means easy. Hands shook, sweat glistened on brows, and curses were loud and raspy.

Kiara's movements, on the other hand, were far too stiff. Too mechanical. She didn't exude her usual grace, and I suspected she was ruminating over what transpired in the offering chamber.

Too close. Kiara had nearly lost herself, hardly putting up a fight until I intervened. Gods, I hadn't wanted to touch her, to cause any pain, but if she'd killed Harlow, I knew her well enough that she wouldn't forgive herself.

We both had to learn how to maintain our powers, lest they control us. And at this point, it was becoming more and more difficult.

A few more minutes passed before I made out a small circular room below our feet.

Emelia dropped first, commanding us to wait while she adjusted her handheld torch. Carefully, she inspected the enclosure. When she gave the go-ahead, more boots struck stone. The last to dismount, I landed in a circle of bodies, the space not large enough to house everyone comfortably. The close proximity between myself and Kiara set my body abuzz with apprehension.

I was grateful when Liam slipped between me and the woman I couldn't touch without ruining. She'd been a frenzied storm of lightning and shadows minutes before, but now, her chin was tucked low, and her shoulders slumped in what I took as shame.

Kiara had shown the horrors she could be capable of when she faced Harlow, her shadows itching to wrap around his neck and squeeze the life out of him. But such a terrifying display hadn't frightened me—I'd felt nothing other than the need to protect.

How we'd switched roles over the course of a few days. She

had held me once, her ungloved fingertips pressed to my cheeks, insisting that my past deeds didn't define me. She helped me release a little of the weight I'd carried for years, and now, I'd do the same for her.

I meant what I'd said up there—I would forever catch her.

"Anyone else lose sensation in their hands?" Liam complained, stretching out his lean fingers. With my eyes on him, the boy shined a pale yellow. He lifted his head and wrinkled his nose at my light, his stare turning into a squint.

"Gods, Sunshine. Keep those things pointed out of our eyes," Dimitri quipped, teasing in his voice.

Fucking nickname.

I quickly looked at the floor. My body temperature was hotter than normal, and my cheeks were blazing. Willing my breathing to even, to release the lingering emotions fueling my magic, I set my mind on the task. *Only* the task—survive and find the talisman. Gradually, the brightness of my gaze mercifully lessened.

Jake smacked Liam on the shoulder, causing the boy to jump with a squeak. "You did good. I half expected you to fall to your death."

Liam quickly regained his composure, looking down his nose at Jake like a noble. "Only half expected? Such confidence in me. You'd be surprised what I'm capable of," he said, whirling away, but I caught the smirk he tried to hide. I also happened to notice Jake's ensuing grin.

"Enough with this." The Fox motioned to the boys in exasperation, both of whom had the decent sense to bow their heads. "We're all here, alive. Safe. Well, *relatively*." She locked eyes with me while Finn touched her arm, sliding a comforting hand up to her shoulder. "We got lucky up there with Scarlet." Kiara grumbled at the name, and I had to bite back my own grin—now I wasn't the only one with an unwanted nickname.

"But you almost lost control and killed us all, so you better keep that shit under control going forward."

"Yes, so easy to do," Kiara volleyed back. "I'll just flip an invisible switch. Poof, gone." She smacked her hands together for emphasis.

"Tone down the attitude," Emelia ordered. "Let's go before those thick-skulled guards find a way down here and give chase. That's the last thing we need."

Kiara rolled her eyes. Watching her spar with my mother was...odd.

Finn reached for his pocket watch. "We have a few hours left until we should rest. We don't want to be stuck down here longer than necessary."

Liam hastily mumbled in agreement.

"At least our friend here is still glowing and *not* starting fires," Finn added, slapping me on the back. I choked on an inhale, the smack harder than I'd expected. Finn didn't notice.

Emelia's eyes flickered up and down my form, narrowing when she reached my face. She lingered there for more than was comfortable. "Jude's getting stronger. Kiara is, too. Though I suspect her strength comes from these sacred grounds."

I *did* feel stronger, my magic easier to access. While my sight rippled with white sparks, the bursts causing my eyes to prickle, it reminded me of staring into a fire for too long. The Fox was right about another thing—I wasn't the only one whose magic grew stronger.

"Jude." Kiara stepped from behind Jake. Playing with the hem of her gloves, she tilted her chin and feigned a confidence I knew she didn't feel. "I'll take up the back this time," she asserted, squaring her shoulders and putting on a brave face. "The light in your eyes will help lead the way, and Emelia should stay in the middle with her torch."

"Oh, wait." Dimitri smacked his forehead. "I forgot."

My brows pressed together when he dug around in his satchel and brought out a sunfire. He struck it a few times before it lit up with a sputter.

"You had that the *whole* time?" Emelia snarled. "You could've mentioned it when our last few died out on the road!"

"Sorry, I was a little distracted!" Dimitri retorted. "And you're welcome." He waved toward a narrow doorway barely large enough to fit a grown man and resumed that dastardly whistling.

"If he whistles the entire time, I'm gonna kill him," Finn said, reading my mind.

"Children, all of you," the Fox chastised. She sauntered through the slim archway, her men bumping shoulders as they tailed her. Jake and Liam walked side by side, the former's hand accidentally brushing the back of Liam's. Jake didn't pull away.

Kiara stayed where she was, watching her friend and brother before her eyes found mine. Our connection brought forth my powers, my magic illuminating her face, tracing her features with reverence. Her lips curled hesitantly, and the flames within my chest ignited.

"I'm sorry about earlier," she said, low enough so only I could hear. "I didn't mean to lose control."

"It's new to all of us," I said. "Think of it like a weapon you've yet to learn." Her eyes grew less clouded at that—weapons she knew well. "You just need to hone your skills."

She paused, the furrow in her brow telling me something heavy weighed on her mind.

Just like that, her demeanor shifted, and her left eye twitched, a sign she was doubting something. My heart plummeted in my chest when all she said was, "Better get to the front and lead the way, Commander."

I did as she asked, entering a long and winding corridor and making my way to the front beside the Fox.

I wondered what had put that questioning look on Kiara's face...but deep down, I already knew the answer.

Me.

. . .

We strode through a tunnel etched with constellations and rudimentary depictions of the moon and stars. The engraved walls were eroded and damp, in stark contrast to the beauty of the veiny white stone we stepped upon.

"Does anyone know what these markings mean?" Kiara inquired from the back. "I've never seen symbols like these before."

I frowned. "The constellations?"

"No. The circles. They remind me of your tattoo but with more detail." I peered behind me, finding Kiara running her hand across a piece of blank stone. There were no drawings there.

"I don't see any circles," Jake voiced my thoughts, lines denting his brow. Liam nodded solemnly, eyeing his sister with uncertainty. He hadn't been given time to adjust to her changes, but he tried to hide his fear. I saw it clearly enough.

"None of you see them?" Kiara shouldered her way to the front, careful to maintain her distance from me. My fists curled at my sides to keep from reaching for her. Cocking her head to the nearest slab, she said, "The other etchings are black, but these"—she trailed a fingertip down a symbol only she appeared to see—"are blue and white. They almost...shimmer."

Emelia slipped between us, forcing Kiara to take a step back. "Seeing as she's part...*beast*," the Fox hissed, "we should take her warnings seriously. I suspect those symbols are warnings." My hackles rose at the term *beast*. Emelia hurried to add, "I only mean she's imbued with dark magic"—she took a step back—"and we should get out of this tunnel that's obviously not meant for *us.*"

Us, being humans.

Those who didn't emit shadows and spark lightning. But this woman would be a fool to believe I wasn't a beast, either.

When I continued to glower, she huffed, walking backward in hopes I'd follow. On her fifth step, something *clicked.*

"Emelia—" Finn's scream was cut off by a whooshing sound.

I turned too late, my sight showing the blur of a feathered arrow soaring through the air. Time slowed to a crawl and my scream lodged in my throat and—

Shadows fired out from behind me, flying before Emelia, curving around her body.

The arrow shattered against a wall of moving ash, splintering into a dozen pieces. I brought my hands to my face, fragments piercing my skin, digging into my knuckles, arms, and biceps.

I opened my eyes, expecting to see blood, or maybe an unmoving body crumpled on the floor, but there was only the Fox, her eyes wide and full of relief.

Kiara's shadows surrounded my mother, the sentient wisps swirling in the air before returning to their master, leaving the potent scent of smoke and burned wood in their wake.

Kiara shuddered as she inhaled them, her entire body vibrating with raw energy.

She'd saved my mother.

Visibly shaking, Finn dropped into a crouch, one hand reaching for Emelia, the other hovering above the ground.

"This piece of marble is discolored," he whispered, peering up at the Fox. "Your weight triggered the arrow."

Emelia swallowed thickly, her nostrils flaring. She looked at Kiara, but she didn't say, "Thank you." Not that I expected her to.

Finn continued, "If you look closely enough, there are seams here. It's not one solid piece at all."

"Pressurized traps," Dimitri noted. "How delightful."

Kiara pushed to the front and eyed the stone Emelia had triggered. She sank to her knees and placed a hand over the rock, forcing Finn to step aside. It didn't escape my notice how the Fox angled her body around his, or how his hand reached for her waist, tugging her close.

"The same marking as before," Kiara murmured, wrinkling her nose.

The ones only she could see.

"*You* need to lead us," I argued, as much as I didn't want that to be true. I'd planned to be the one at the front, taking the first hit or strike. Not her. But there were no other options.

Kiara nodded, not able to meet my eyes. It was how she avoided me while at the same time shifting her body toward me that cemented what I so clearly felt—fate had decreed we separate, but the invisible tether tying us together couldn't easily be severed.

Sucking in a breath through her teeth, she scanned the ground. "Well, looks like you're all following me, then."

Occasionally, she'd halt, motioning to us which areas to avoid. Left and right, we zigzagged down the corridor, Kiara cautiously guiding us to safety.

We did this uneasy dance for another half hour—no one keen on speaking—until a looming wall towered in the distance.

A circle of pure onyx stone glittered, taller than me, and equally as wide. With my eyes trained on the stone, and with Emelia's torch, its facets captured the light and sparkled, sending glimmering stars dancing across our skin.

Kiara lifted a hand. "Wait," she intoned, shifting around the imposing gem. She bent to her knees, her face inches away from the luminous rock.

"The suspense is killing me, Ki," Jake said after some time. Kiara ignored him, continuing her exploration with a steady concentration I admired.

"There are more than a dozen different symbols on this thing, and none of them match the ones from the corridor. So excuse me if I'm taking too long, but if you'd like to try to figure it out, be my guest." She smiled a sickly-sweet smile at her friend, whose own grin fell. "That's what I thought."

"It would be best not to argue," Liam whispered to Jake. "She gets cranky when she's hungry."

"I noticed that, too!"

Liam beamed. "That's why I usually keep snacks on me at all times…" The pair carried on, but I tuned them out. My focus homed in on the subject of their conversation.

Kiara gave the rock her attention again, mumbling to herself as she worked. Shadows floated off her frame like steam, vibrating as they wavered in place.

"It's some sort of riddle," she whispered, and her magic swelled, winglike creations sprouting from her back before slithering around her head like an eerie halo. Cautiously, Kiara grazed her index finger across a serrated edge. "Each symbol is a story."

"Go on," Finn pressured. "Let's hear it."

"The first line shows the moon, the constellation of Aloria, a sword, and what I think is a teardrop?"

"Isn't Aloria the ancient fighter who supposedly set herself on fire after her lover was killed in battle?" Liam asked, though, by his confident tone, I imagined he already knew the answer.

"Yes." Kiara dipped lower. "And then there are three symbols below. A skull, a dagger, and a…a heart split in two."

All of them could relate to the warrior's story. How she ended her life because her grief drowned her. "Are you sure we can only push one? Or are they switches at all?" I asked.

"Maybe it isn't a riddle."

Liam stepped up to his sister. "It's not a riddle, Ki," he agreed, bending to his knees beside her, even if he couldn't see the symbols for himself.

"Each one is part of the full story, and look here..." He traveled to the side of the circle, to the roughened edges.

I followed where his eyes aimed, and my heart skipped several beats.

It looked like a single needle jutting out from the rock.

Liam stood. "Blood," he said, his voice echoing in the corridor. "Aloria's tale is one of great loss and heartache. In the myth, her lover's blood was drained on the battlefield by his enemies, and his remains were thrown from the top of the Argondale Mountains. After Aloria learned of his fate, her grief became a blaze, and she ignited in flames before rushing into the enemy camp, killing any she could until none were left. Arlo, so stirred by her sorrow, shed a tear, and a field of Midnight Blossoms rose from the dirt where her lover had fallen. Rebirth after such devastation."

"It requires blood, then," Kiara said, already moving to shuck off her gloves. But Liam grasped her wrist, stopping her.

"Not yours." He shook his head. "Aloria was heartbroken and destroyed. A woman who'd lost the love of her life forever. You"—Liam's eyes hesitantly rose to mine—"have not yet lost yours."

Silence.

I didn't miss his choice of words. *Yet.*

Kiara avoided me, her attention on the symbols. She hadn't said those three tender words. I'd opened my soul to her and she'd merely planted her lips to mine. I dug my nails into the flesh of my palm, loathing how my doubts morphed into a blade aimed for my chest.

Death was at our heels, and I feared I may never hear the

declaration I craved. I felt like a lovesick fool.

Liam hummed in thought. "This requires the blood of someone with a broken heart." He glanced around the group, a question in his eyes.

My mother opened and closed her mouth but made no move forward, and Finn let out a frustrated scowl, indicating he wasn't our man. That left us—

Dimitri shoved past the others.

"What are you doing?" Finn gawked at his comrade.

"The boy said it needs the blood of the heartbroken, right?" He shrugged, emotionless. "That would obviously be me."

Emelia nodded to Finn to step down. "If Liam is right about this, then Dimitri's blood will work."

Aloria's heartbreak was legendary, and few understood that kind of immense pain. The kind that literally set her mortal body aflame.

Some romances didn't conclude with a happily-ever-after. Sometimes, they were fleeting and lasted a heartbeat, although their end didn't make the love any less profound.

Tearing my gaze from Kiara, I drank in Dimitri, whose eyes had creased at the sides in a way they hadn't before.

"My wife and daughter," he whispered, lifting his finger and aiming for the jagged edge of the needle. "They were murdered years ago." His finger poised above the tip, his hand trembling. "I...I was beaten down and knocked unconscious. When I woke, it was just long enough to watch as Cirian's soldiers sliced their throats. They laughed as I screamed. As I tried to crawl to them. But they kicked me back, holding me in place. Making me watch as my daughter's blood spilled across our kitchen floor. Her last words were her screaming for her father."

A single tear fell down his tanned skin. He didn't bother brushing it off. "I was left there, alive, when all I wanted to do was join them. Apparently the soldiers had come to the wrong house. Killed the wrong family. It was our neighbor they'd wanted, and after they realized their mistake, they simply left and kicked down his door, spilling more blood."

My throat grew tight. *I* had been a faithful soldier of Cirian's, committing unspeakable acts. Killing innocents. While I'd never slaughtered a child, shame weighed on my shoulders, knowing I'd worked alongside such evil.

Carefully, Dimitri pressed his finger to the stone's sharpened tip and pushed down, hissing when it pierced his skin. "I lived like a dead man until Emelia found me. And by that time there wasn't much soul left in me. There still isn't."

My attention darted to the Fox, stunned when a tear of her own slipped free. She hurriedly swiped at the evidence.

"Danielle and Tilly," Dimitri whispered. Their names hung thick in the air, almost solid, almost real.

Something clicked into place. A gear.

Dimitri jolted back. The glimmering stone creaked and shifted, the edges vibrating as the wall behind it quaked.

"Keep back!" Kiara warned, lunging forward, dagger raised in one hand, her other lifted, palm out. She remained by my side as I also readied for the worst.

Dimitri shifted to the Fox, ignoring Finn's pitying look. He shoved the hand with his bloodied finger inside his pocket. I didn't need to see the red on his finger to know he bled on the inside. I suddenly realized how quickly I'd judged him.

Everyone hid their pain. Dimitri only showed his with a lullaby. A song meant for a little girl whom he'd hopefully see again one day.

A thunderous crash sounded, forcing my attention from the thief. The circular gem began to roll, sliding across the stone until it collided with the wall. A gap had been created, broad enough to fit two men.

I faced Kiara.

The unspoken word passed between us. We were more than capable of defending ourselves, and in a much better position than the others. If anything attacked, we'd be the first line of defense.

"*Together*," she mouthed, and I nodded.

We walked through the doorway, side by side—

And fell.

Chapter Twenty-Five

Kiara

To take a leap of faith is knowing you may likely fall and doing so anyway.

Asidian proverb

There was no floor beneath us.

Literally. No. Damned. Floor.

We plummeted for an eternity, the ground never rising up to end our ceaseless dive into the bowels of the underworld.

The grisly tale of Aloria and her lover briefly crossed my mind, of how the soldiers had tossed him over the side of the Argondale Mountains. And we'd all but leapt off a cliff without so much as looking. I should've paid more attention.

I cursed my recklessness a thousand times in my head. Not that cursing helped slow my speed.

Air rushed up on either side, whipping at my cheeks, hair, and clothes. Desperately, I reached out, trying to grab hold of something, anything. I was met with useless open air.

Just as I said my final farewells, preparing for the unforgiving solidness of the earth, the infinite darkness detonated.

Pure, scorching light erupted from what appeared to be a shooting star at my side. But of course, it wasn't a star, it was the commander, whose magic illuminated the tunnel. I couldn't decide which was worse—seeing how narrow the passageway was, or knowing there was no escape.

Down, down, down, we fell, until Jude's incandescent form vanished with a splash.

I struck water a second later.

Pins and needles stabbed at my exposed skin, the impact jarring, my vision blackening.

The water was merciless, surging into my mouth and lungs, suffocating me each time I opened my lips to scream.

Hands grabbed around my middle, fingers digging into my skin through my thin shirt. I was being yanked, pulled to gods knew where. Unconsciousness called like a siren in a gale, and my eyes were already shutting.

I broke through the surface, a gust of icy air striking my cheeks. The water I'd swallowed flowed from my lips, and I sputtered helplessly. With the black spots winning, I couldn't see clearly as my body met hard earth.

There was pressure on my chest, hands shoving against my body, urging the water up and out.

"You're making me touch you again." Jude's voice drifted to my ears. "I better not be fucking hurting you more." Frustration cracked his voice, *almost* masking the sheer panic beneath. "Come on, Kiara," he pressed, continuing to push. "Wake the hells up."

I wanted to tell him I was already awake, but he kept going, the radiance of his magic blazing behind my closed lids as his fear powered him. After what felt like a lifetime, my body convulsed, and I jerked to the side, retching, water spilling free and onto rough stone. Jude patted my back, cursing and praying at the same time.

"There you go," he murmured, rubbing soothing circles on my back. I greedily sucked in fresh air, shivering from both cold and lingering terror.

If I hadn't hated heights before, I sure did now.

I anxiously took in our surroundings. With Jude's glow brightening most of the space, I nearly didn't notice the faint blue light coming through cracks in the stone walls. It wasn't caused by Jude—it came from the temple itself.

We were sitting on a circular stone, enfolded in eerie light, the pool of crystal water washing gently against the rounded banks. For some reason, *this* felt like the true entrance to the temple.

I angled toward the commander, my temperature settling back to normal. In fact, I was beginning to grow warm from his touch, and the longer I stayed close, the hotter I became. It wasn't unpleasant. Not as before, *above*.

Jude, as if just realizing how his fingers grazed my skin, shoved away with a frustrated grunt. "Did I hurt you?" He rose to his feet, continuing to place distance between us.

"I'm...fine," I said, stunned. No nosebleeds. No searing agony racing through my veins. *Nothing*.

Jude looked to his hands as if he also considered why his touch hadn't hurt me.

"It seems as if you've saved me yet again," I remarked to break up the silence, rolling onto my back, exhausted. "Next time, it'll be my turn to rescue you. You're making me look bad."

I tried to laugh, but only a wheezing huff sounded pathetically. I hadn't lied though. His hands had done nothing to hurt me, which had me questioning *why*. Judging by the amount of space Jude put between us, he wasn't willing to try out my growing theory—that in this temple of the Moon God, we were finally on equal footing.

With a groan, I lifted to my elbows, careful to avoid the edge of the pool.

The surface twinkled with shimmering orbs that blinked in

and out of existence, reminding me of the night sky. If we hadn't almost died, I'd have found it beautiful.

"Did the others fall?" I was too busy drowning to notice if anyone else came plummeting down after me.

Jude ambled to the edge of the water, his back to me while he caught his breath. He shook his head. "No, it was just us."

"Good."

I prayed they had enough sense to watch us tumble into nothing and take one giant step backward. Although I imagined Jake had to be physically restrained from lunging after.

Craning my neck, I looked up into the heavy blackness. When I shouted for Liam, nothing came back in reply. We'd fallen much too far for our words to carry.

Jude scanned the area, analyzing the many glowing cracks and crevices, likely plotting our escape. The glow emanating from his body had simmered out, but his eyes remained luminous. They darted back and forth until he bolted to his feet, an eager expression causing his lips to slightly part.

"What is it?"

He moved to a wall of stone, his hands gliding along the uneven edges. He said nothing, forcing me to my feet and to his side.

"These cracks," he eventually ground out. He pushed at the stone. His eyes shined while he struggled, the space bright enough where my own magic didn't rise to the surface.

A rock crumbled beneath his exertion, exposing more soft blue light.

A way out.

I shoved against the wall with my hands, clawing and pulling at the loose stones.

We both groaned from the effort, and sweat quickly seeped from my pores and slipped down the nape of my neck. Together we worked to free ourselves from this rocky prison, and when dirt and grime covered my hands, the wall finally gave way.

Jude and I stumbled into an opening and onto our hands and knees as the stones crumbled and fell. Dust rushed into my nose, eyes, and lungs, and I barely caught myself from landing on my face.

"Can't there just be a normal entrance?" I grumbled, thrusting upright, my arms probably riddled with scrapes from taking the brunt of the fall. Bending at the waist, I hacked my lungs out.

A white fog coated everything, and I felt as if we'd stepped inside a cloud—nothing above us, and nothing I could see below. Jude panted beside me, waiting for the rubble to settle.

He let out a rumbling cough before saying, "I think there's another door."

Great. More doors.

Jude snatched the corner of my cloak, guiding me. It was like being inside a blizzard, or maybe more accurately, a sandstorm. Bits of rock struck my exposed skin as the dust swirled chaotically around our frames, the slight resistance it gave seeming to urge us away. Yet there was no direction but forward, the veiny blue lights we'd seen earlier coaxing us onward.

"Look," Jude coaxed, tugging at my cloak.

A silver door came into focus ahead.

"That better not be another one-way ticket to death by drowning," I grumbled.

Jude released me and approached slowly, like the door itself might be a predator set to lunge. He peered over his shoulder, making sure I followed. "Stand back," he instructed before reaching for the curved handle and pushing down.

It creaked open like a weary sigh, icy air rushing out in a gust. The force of it nearly sent me back a few steps.

Rubbing at my eyes, I willed my vision to clear as the newest scene slowly took shape.

An impressive slab of stone jutted out to touch crystal waters, the surface so still, it appeared like glass. Tumbling through the threshold, I tilted my head, powerless but to admire the space.

A bronze tunnel with an open roof had been crafted inside an infinite cavern, the night sky showcasing millions of glittering stars. They were three times their normal size, and not a single cloud tarnished their shine. I paused upon a full moon ringed in blue, unable to squash the notion that it stared back, its glow highlighting the cavern as far as the eye could see.

Luxurious boats swayed nearby, all painted in silver, their edges decorated by the phases of the moon that watched from overhead. All around me, the air glimmered, the luster of the bronze reflecting the light upon the top of the still water. There was no end to the magnificent pillars that formed the airy passageway, their design reminiscent of coiling vines.

"Where are we?" I walked closer to the edge of the stone slab, my hands poised over one of the swaying boats. The stars' reflections dazzled in the bluest water I'd ever seen, the surface masked by a sheen of purple and iridescent glaze.

We might as well have walked into another realm entirely. Squinting, I made out a shooting comet, rushing by so quickly, it vanished in a blink.

"The night sky," Jude whispered reverently. Even he was helpless to admire the beauty. "I've never seen it so clear and bright. So *close*."

I dipped into a crouch. Cupping my hands, I immersed them in the water, scooping out a cup of magic.

If I didn't know any better, I'd have said actual stars floated across my palms.

"Careful," Jude warned, suddenly a foot away.

I peered up, finding his eyes burning. They flared brighter when they fixed on me. Him being so near made me weak in the knees, and I debated acting out on impulse, on seeing if my hopeful thoughts were correct. I hesitated, though, fearful of another disappointment.

My insides didn't churn with magic, not seeming to sense impending danger, but I couldn't shake the buzz of disbelief and intoxicating adrenaline from falling from one world into the next, into an in-between dimension. I didn't feel the same, my body almost weightless, every inch of skin tingling. I experienced everything and too much of it.

Looking at the commander and his unusual eyes, I lost my bearings, the reality of our situation crushing in on all sides like a toppling house of cards.

We were in the temple. One step closer to death or triumph.

My heart sank—my mind had already decided which one I believed we'd find. Harlow had gotten into my head, his words echoing like falling rain. With each loop of doubt, I worried that I'd choose cowardice when the time came, when the hard decision needed to be made.

I'd never realized how exhausting it was to be *good*. To do the right thing.

Jude made a deep rumbling sound in the back of his throat. "I swear to all the gods, Kiara. You better not be getting in your head. That's my job." He coerced his lips to lift into a smile, but it was strained.

Him beside me, my friends and brother not far behind…it was my fault. What if we couldn't make our way out? There was a chance we'd die. A large chance, and—

"Whatever happens, I regret nothing," Jude cut into my rambling thoughts. "Something tells me we were always meant to come here, and I refuse to believe it was just for us to die."

My eyes met his. "Did you just read my mind? Because if so, I didn't approve of that new power."

He laughed. "No, but I didn't need to read your mind. Just

your expressions. Your eye sometimes twitches when you're hurt or doubting." He dared a step closer. "Your nose wrinkles ever so slightly right before you begin a fight. When you're tired, you tap out this tune with your index finger. I don't even think you realize you're doing it, but I've spent ages trying to figure out the song, though I've come to the conclusion it's yours alone." Another step. "But mostly, you blush the prettiest pink whenever I get near you, which I quite enjoy, by the way."

His lips were so close.

One. Step.

The corner of my mouth tugged up, my pulse racing. Arlo and his poisonous warning vanished from my head, my doubts dissolving like the dust we just parted.

A shock of awareness jolted through me.

I didn't want Jude because of the power he wielded. The magic may lie in my soul, but it didn't control my heart. It had been my own long before the shadows touched it, before the sun goddess' light awoke.

Arlo hadn't known love, and therefore, he'd assumed the worst.

But I wasn't him, nor was I lacking love. I just needed to be brave enough to accept it.

The commander assessed me in that clinical way of his, and to anyone else, it might appear cold, but I knew better. The intensity in his stare was for me alone, and surrounded by such magic, after nearly drowning, I decided to give in, for just a moment.

"You've made me wonder about so many new things. Things I never considered possible before," Jude continued, his eyes not on the mystical temple but on me. "Mostly, I wonder if you have the faintest idea how much power you wield over me. How you could easily destroy me with just one smile."

My lips curled up in the smile he spoke of, the one reserved only for him. His words...no one had ever spoken to me in such a way. I couldn't imagine wanting anyone but him speaking directly to my heart.

When his entire face lit up, I reached out and fisted his cloak. With a yank, I pressed against him. I needed to taste the lips that formed such pretty words.

When our lips met, the world didn't turn to night, and blood didn't gush from my nose. Only bliss so heady, I grew dizzy.

Jude groaned, his fingers threading through my hair, holding me in place, even though there was nowhere I'd rather be.

He tasted like freedom and sin, and I craved his kind of rush.

"How?" he asked as he reluctantly drew away.

Arlo had said Jude's magic overwhelmed mine in the mortal world, but here in the darkness of a sacred temple, my magic flourished, matching his.

"Eh, magic or some other nonsense that I don't care about right now," I said. "Now, come back."

I didn't wait for him. I pressed against him once more, and he easily conceded to my demand, meeting my eager kisses with ones of his own.

Destiny or a pretty lie, I didn't care. Whatever called me to him was mine, and I owned it like I owned him.

Chapter Twenty-Six

Jude

The temples of the gods are seen as their own realm. Built with magic and prayers, the rules of the mortal plane do not apply. In fact, no rules apply except death. Death is just as final.

Excerpt from Asidian Lore: a Tale of the Gods

"I-I can touch you," I said. I kissed the corner of her mouth, moving to her jaw. She was soft and pliable in my hold, and I couldn't resist the temptation.

Days before, my touch had been poisonous. While I knew I should restrain, I simply couldn't...not when she smiled at me like that as my fingers grazed her cheek, her jaw, her lips.

"I think it's because of where we are." She tilted her chin, taking in the luminous passageway and ethereal stars. "I think we're somewhere where my darkness and your light can...just *be*. Where they don't feel the need to battle."

We stood in a place made by a god. I hadn't a doubt the same rules didn't apply, as the world we witnessed now came from the pages of a myth.

I swiped my thumb against her full lower lip, my other hand working to her nape. "I've never been more grateful to be in a place of danger than I am right now."

Kiara lifted onto her tiptoes and flicked my nose playfully. "You'd be happy to risk your life for a kiss, Jude Maddox? I had no idea you were so easy to persuade."

I frowned. "Technically, it would be *your* life we risked," I said, starting to shift away.

Kiara grabbed my hands and held them in place on her hips. "Oh, I don't think so, Commander."

My lips formed a thin line meant to warn, but she was far from dissuaded. Instead, she brought her lips to my neck, kissing up and down the column of my throat. I groaned.

"Not fair," I ground out.

"I've never played fair."

Kiara worked her way to my stubbled jaw, leaving a devilish trail up to my cheekbones, to my scars. She lingered there, worshiping me, the marks I'd once considered monstrous. To her, they were merely a part of me, and she showed me exactly how she felt.

A shooting star flashed to our right.

Reluctantly, I drew away, just enough to study the bronze tunnel ahead. I wasn't sure what I'd expected after plummeting through the void, but this realm of light and stars and shimmering water was not anywhere close.

Without a doubt, there was a catch.

"What is it?" Kiara asked.

"You're distracting me. Again." We had to at least explore our new surroundings. Make sure there weren't any surprises waiting. Namely, surprises carrying daggers.

Kiara sighed. "We should rest for a bit and wait to see if the others make their way down by less terrifying means. I'm sure the Fox has a coil of rope and some climbing gear in her satchel. I've heard she collects all sorts of gadgets."

I still hadn't released her. It was difficult to remind myself of the mission. All I desired to do was touch her, everywhere and anywhere. To make her moan my name...

"You're looking at me as if you want to eat me alive," she teased, though her eyes had turned hooded, her voice a rasp of a thing.

"And what if I do?" I asked, slipping my fingers through her hair, reveling in the silky texture. I tilted her head back with a gentle pull. I'd suddenly convinced myself no monsters were waiting. There was no danger. Though I wasn't exactly using my head.

"What if I've been dreaming of tasting you for weeks, and you've only taunted me every single day of every moment," I said. "Each time you strode into a room as if you owned it, it stole my breath and demanded my attention, and every brash word you've spoken only heated my blood until I feared you'd destroy me."

Kiara was speechless, staring at me with wide eyes and parted lips.

My heart beat too loudly in my ears, my cheeks growing too hot.

That's when I noticed the subtle light filtering through the linen of her cloak. Frowning, I tugged aside the material. Kiara gasped, her hand reaching to graze the spot above my own.

Our matching scars were gleaming, pulsating in rhythm with each other's. I lowered my hand and she did the same, bringing hers to my chest. The light flared brilliantly before waning, but the glow never went away completely.

I didn't care that the others were likely on their way to us now or that we faced a path that would bring us deeper into the pits of the Moon God's lair.

Fate had stolen too much from me already, but it wouldn't steal this night.

"Jude," Kiara started, a shyness in her tone that was unlike her. "Do you think we only feel this way, because..." She pointed to our scars, the question spelled out. "Arlo said—"

"I don't give a damn what he said." I didn't mean to snap, but the mere thought he suggested such a thing had fire boiling my blood. "Nothing like this has ever happened in our history, and I think the old god cares about you, as much as he knows how. I feel something more powerful than magic when I'm around you, greater than what's inside of me. So while I believe I might've been *drawn* to you due to our fates, I don't think it has anything to do with my heart."

I was an open book, exposing everything for her to tear apart if she so wished it. It was as terrifying as it was exhilarating. Mostly terrifying with how she stared at me, unspeaking. Gods, I needed her to say *something*.

But then her scar flared brighter, nearly as luminous as her smile.

"Good," she said simply, smirking. "Although a part of me has to think it's magic for you to be speaking this way. So uninhibited. So...idealistic."

I refrained from rolling my eyes. "What can I say? You're a terrible influence."

Kiara's teasing smirk fell. Whatever she glimpsed on my face had her clutching me. Seizing me like a lifeline. I hoped she saw my truth as clearly as I did hers.

Slowly, she brought her fingers to my shirt, pulling it down to expose my blazing scar.

Her lips descended, grazing my skin, sending shivers racing across my body. Kiara kissed every inch of my wound, taking her time, torturing me. With every brush of her mouth, my need grew, and almost in reply, her movements became impatient.

No more doubts. No more fears.

She placed one final kiss over my thudding heart and then lifted her head. There was another question in her eyes, and one I knew how to answer.

Chapter Twenty-Seven

Kiara

The binds that tie two hearts together cannot be easily severed. Once fashioned, such a silent oath is just as potent as any magic, if not more so.

Cerys, God of Love

"Kiara," Jude breathed, his voice deeper than usual. It was a plea, a prayer, and I was all too keen to answer it.

My skin vibrated with raw awareness, Raina's magic practically reaching out for him, as impatient as I was to touch and mark him as my own.

His eyes burned, his stare piercing, seeing beyond my barriers and walls. I gazed right back, past his doubts and insecurities, past the mask he wore for everyone but me. The raw truth of him was perfect, made for me, and my pulse danced with anticipation.

I wanted him. More than anything. I craved being as close to him as one could physically be, the need almost painful.

We collided, our power, our lips, our bodies, and Jude swept me into his arms, never once abandoning my mouth. His kisses were feverish, frantic, and behind my closed eyes, our combined light became golden flames.

My shadow beast opened an eye, a hint of ice mingling with the fire coiling around its phantom form. Jude pulled away to lay me on the stone ledge, the polished marble cool underneath me. He glanced over my body, at the wisps of shadows peeking out. He smiled then, his leisurely perusal causing me to blush.

"Kiara." He said my name with such care, like he was savoring each syllable. "Look at yourself. You're magnificent."

I'd been too focused on him to notice what I'd become.

I peered down.

My skin was the shade of the moon when cradled by shrouds of onyx clouds, my shadows shimmering as they danced about in his gold. When it touched Jude, he shivered, letting out a deep rumble. His body flickered with magic, each flash matching his thumping heartbeat.

The adoration in his eyes was a puncture wound, a blow to the chest that both slayed and restarted my heart. He looked at me like I was something heavenly, a star out of reach, a wish he dared dream.

A lifetime of scorn and lies and hatred was shredded by Jude's faith in the span of a stuttering breath. And a new pathway opened up, leading to a future where my life was what I could make of it—

And gods, I wanted it to be beautiful.

My fingers were in Jude's hair and my lips were on his before he could take in his next breath. Instantly, his arms were around me, pulling me forward, his mouth moving with mine in equal fervor. This was home, my safety.

"I missed you," he spoke against me. "I told myself I'd give anything to embrace you again, but this"—he pressed a chaste kiss to my lips—"this is a gift I'll never be deserving of."

I shook my head. I tightened my fingers in his hair, pulling his head back so he was forced to look at me. He groaned, seemingly upset with the fact that I kept him from my lips. My grin was wicked.

"You, Jude Maddox, are absolutely infuriating." Confusion furrowed his brows. "I want you for purely selfish reasons. You make me feel invincible. You make me feel strong and capable and powerful—without magic. You, Jude, simply make me *feel*."

He traced his fingers down the side of my face, down my neck, my shoulders, my arms. When he met my gloved hand, he lifted his eyes, a question burning in them.

"Then don't hide from me, Kiara," he said. "I fell in love with all of you."

My shadows wavered at his words. They caressed his skin, speaking for me when my voice failed.

I felt his declaration well beyond flesh and bone. Well beyond fate and destiny and gods.

Jude held my eyes, his fingers on my glove, waiting for permission. I awarded him with a subtle nod. Gently, he removed it, taking his time, holding my stare. Fresh air kissed my skin, and I shivered again, though it had everything to do with Jude and not the magic in our veins.

He moved for the other one, peeling it off and placing it beside its twin.

I was free.

"There she is," he murmured, laying a kiss on my temple. The tender act broke me further.

I slid my bare hands into his hair and brought my mouth to his scars, kissing them lightly. He shut his eyes as I worshiped them with all the tenderness in my soul.

His entire body shook with restrained control as he held himself aloft over me, waiting for me to make the first move. Always the gentleman.

My very own moral assassin.

"They could arrive at any moment now," he groaned, eyes darting to the silver archway we passed through.

"It'll be a long, *long* climb," I said with a pointed grin, earning a smirk from him.

Jude inhaled sharply before he grasped my hips and rolled over, hauling me into his lap. I relished how firmly he clutched me.

"That's more like it." I grabbed onto his shoulders, steadying myself, my thighs resting on either side of his.

Jude tilted his head, his throat exposed, his eyes barely open. This close, an ache built deep within me, insistent and erratic and entirely electrifying.

"I do enjoy your demanding side," he nearly growled, lifting his arms, his hands moving leisurely up and down my spine. Even fully clothed, I could feel him—his heat, his desire—and my knees trembled in anticipation.

We were heart to heart, pain meeting hope and finding a tender compromise of love.

Jude's hands found my backside, and he let out a deep noise from his chest, the sound of torment. As if by merely touching me, his body shattered and broke.

I loved that sound. I would make it my life's mission to hear more of it.

His touch turned teasing, and he took his time exploring me, my hips, my waist, my curves, driving me closer to the edge. I wanted more of it. I was greedy for it all.

I tugged at his shirt, yanking it up and off. My ungloved fingers explored the hard planes of his chest, the sinewy muscles that comprised his glorious body. Jude snaked a hand in my hair, fisting the strands, watching me as I hungrily drank him in. When I lowered my exploration, moving down, down, down, he groaned.

"Gods," he rasped, "you're killing me."

"Good. Now please, return the favor."

The instant the words left me, his hands worked to remove

my shirt, his fingers undoing the buttons with graceful dexterity. Soon, cool air caressed my upper body, and when he connected with my bare flesh, I became delirious, so very drunk from the power of his touch.

His lips never ceased tasting me, coasting along my jaw, gliding down my neck, paving a delicious trail to my chest. He was everywhere all at once, and I wanted more.

Jude swept a reverent hand across my ribs before moving up to skim the curves of my breasts, his body quivering with need.

When he pulled back, stealing his warmth, I let out a sound of protest.

"I want you, Kiara. I want your mind. Your body. Your strength. Your innate stubbornness." He was smiling brilliantly, so uninhibited, that I tried to memorize the shape of it.

I captured his face, cupping his jaw. "You make me feel like no one has ever truly seen me before you." I placed a gentle kiss on his temple, and he shut his eyes, a shiver running through his frame. "I want you," I whispered against him. Our lips were an inch apart.

So close. Too far.

Still, Jude drew away, hesitation in his eyes, a silent question. His breathing was labored, his doubts laid upon his chest like stones.

"Please," I begged, knowing exactly what I wanted. "*Please*, Jude."

His golden eyes darkened. One moment I was straddling his hips, and the next, he placed me gently on my back. I stared up at the boy who had thoroughly ruined me in the best way, my heart thumping wildly against my ribs.

Its beating became erratic as Jude lowered himself down my body, his fingers toying with the band of my trousers. He smiled, savoring his decadent torment, his hot breath fanning across my stomach, igniting every nerve.

"Let me enjoy myself, Kiara," he chided, smirking triumphantly.

"Enjoy yourself faster," I mumbled.

He laughed, deep and low, the noise going straight to my core. Slowly, *too* damn slowly, he pulled off my boots and then my trousers, treating me as if I were a delicate creature made of glass. Like I was his greatest treasure.

Jude disappeared for a second, but it was to free himself from his remaining clothing. In his hands, he held an unopened black packet. My cheeks reddened when I realized what it was. "Dimitri uh…he gave this to me in the woods," he said by way of explanation, his cheeks flushed.

"I've never been as grateful for Dimitri as I am at this moment."

Jude *tsk*ed. "Let's not think about him too much."

My eyes tracked Jude's form.

"I don't think that will be a problem," I said.

Hells, he was so remarkably beautiful, and I couldn't help but drink in every stunning inch of his exposed and battle-worn flesh. I couldn't believe he was mine.

He caught me admiring him as he prepared himself with the protection, a devilish smirk on his lips. Suddenly, my mouth was too dry.

Jude knelt and brought his muscled arms to rest on either side of me, his head moving to meet mine. But he didn't kiss me, not yet.

He stared at me for many long moments, and I swore I could hear his heartbeat hammering out of his chest.

"My beautiful goddess." He moved his hips, and I gasped at the feel of him, his weight.

And then Jude didn't hold back.

A moan slipped out and I lifted my hips in reply, greedy for more. More of Jude making me his. *Completely*.

I'd hidden behind so many barriers and walls and excuses. Sarcasm and steel. I pretended death never frightened me or that I was never just a girl searching for acceptance and a place in this world. Jude burst through my walls with such ease, planting flowers where bricks and stone used to be.

I lost myself to him, to his kisses, his rhythm, the way the world of night shifted with our every ragged exhale. The way he moved had me seeing stars. I called out his name, and Jude replied by taking my bottom lip between his teeth. He gently bit down, slowly releasing me only to lower his head to my chest. I arched my back as he kissed and teased, turning me into a mess of desire. We fit together so well. Light and dark. Anger and hope. Complete opposites that couldn't help but fall in love with the other's missing pieces.

Bliss filled me completely, and I let out a strangled moan, the noise causing Jude to unravel entirely. He spoke my name, murmuring it over and over again until it might be the only word he knew how to speak.

I was soaring and drowning and alive and destroyed all at the same time, and I'd never been happier. My arms were around his neck, in his hair, my lips on his, and everything in this rotten and cruel world, for just a fluttering heartbeat, became right.

Jude's mouth found my ear, and he said three words, three tiny words that shattered me.

Tears of joy dripped down my face, and he kissed away each one, his lips devouring my glimmering drops of happiness.

The monsters and nightmares that lay ahead would have to wait. Tonight was ours.

• • •

I dreamed I was a bird soaring into the stars, racing to catch them like raindrops.

Someone called my name, whether it was the night or Jude or even myself. All I knew was that I had to fly, to spread invisible wings of the darkest magic.

Higher, the night whispered, and I obliged. But before I touched the edges of the expanding universe, I peered down into the tunnel with its silver boats, Jude sleeping soundly on a rocky bank. I hesitated, wishing to return to his arms, but the night was insistent.

There was something I had to do, an important thing, but I was dreaming, and as it often happened in dreams, I delved into the story, eagerly awaiting where it would take me. What it would reveal.

Yet with every blink, I grew more and more wary. That feeling of *something* missing pulsated within me like a beating heart, and I ignored the now-screaming night and glided down, away from the vastness of the open sky.

A spiraling palace of smooth, snow-white rock twisted up from the clouds. It reminded me of a fairy tale and a nightmare all at the same time, and as I landed on an arching bridge before a towering wall of smooth marble, fatigue swept me away, forcing my eyes to close.

I plummeted from one dream to the next, until the chilled dampness of the floor froze my human bones, and I realized it hadn't been a dream after all.

Chapter Twenty-Eight

Jude

In the western lands, there is a myth about the Wailing Woman of Livian Lake. It is said she rises beneath the moon with a scream so sharp, her prey is rendered immobile. She drags them below the surface and makes a garden out of their bones.

Excerpt from Asidian Lore: Legends and Myths of the Realm

I rolled over with a contented sigh, my body still tingling from her touch, my heart still racing from how her fingernails dug into my back while she melted in my arms.

I was so far gone for this woman, I doubted she realized how much power she truly held.

Kiara's name formed on my lips with ease, like they'd shaped it for a thousand lifetimes. My eyes were heavy from the paltry few hours of sleep, though my body ached exquisitely. I whispered her name again, but when she didn't reply, I reached out, frowning at the fact she'd rolled so far from me in her slumber.

Cold stones greeted my hand. My eyes flicked open with a start.

She wasn't there.

"Kiara?" I scanned the tunnel, the silver boats rocking against the shore, the twinkling water lapping at the rock I lay on. *Nothing.* No one was there.

Had she taken one of the boats, abandoning me so she could journey ahead and possibly play the role of willing sacrifice...

No. There were the same number of vessels as yesterday— four. Which meant...which meant what, exactly?

Hurt and alarm sent my pulse beating wildly against my neck. Beside me, where Kiara should have been, laid a single feather. I flinched at how it swayed, tendrils of soft black undulating in the subtle breeze.

I held my breath while I brushed a finger along the spine.

The feather wavered, fluttering like wings, the shadows dispersing, floating away and out of reach.

Before I could rue my mistake, it was gone. The veiny marble floor shone brighter where the feather had been, like its magic still graced the ground.

A thud echoed in the quiet, and I lurched to my feet, facing the silver doorway we'd entered. I froze in anticipation, praying Kiara would walk through and dispel all worry.

"Gods above. I never want to do any sort of physical activity again." Jake sauntered across the threshold, his hair slicked back with sweat, dirt streaked across his cheeks.

He stopped short when he saw me in nothing but my trousers, my chest bare. His eyes went wide, and then he searched the shore, looking for the woman who'd drifted off like a dream in the night.

Disappointment filled me.

Before he could question Kiara's whereabouts, the remaining crew eased past.

"Where is she?" Liam demanded, his brown curls damp, his face as grimy as Jake's, no doubt from climbing down the tunnel.

Ropes wound about his waist, and I realized the others had similar gear fastened to them as well.

Dimitri tossed a pickaxe to the ground and replaced it with a blade, a wary expression contorting his usually serene face. Emelia and Finn stood with their arms crossed, matching somber expressions on their faces.

"She…" I met Liam's pleading gaze. "She disappeared. She's not here."

I sounded a bumbling fool, and perhaps I was. All I recalled was drifting to sleep with her securely in my arms, her head on my chest, dark copper hair tickling my chin. I'd fallen asleep with a smile so wide, my jaw still ached.

"What the hells do you mean she's gone?" Liam pressed, scrambling along the thin strip of solid ground. "She was with you after you fell?"

I nodded, but my voice didn't work. The heat of Raina's magic slithered farther away, as if it, too, grieved its missing piece.

"Maybe she took a boat?" Jake questioned, stepping around Liam and laying a hand on his shoulder. His eyes offered compassion and hope and all the things I never thought I'd feel but now felt too much.

The idea that something nefarious occurred sent me spiraling, and nausea churned in my stomach. I peered at her brother, wishing I had an answer, but his face was screwed up in fierce determination, his mind latching on to Jake's paltry explanation.

"Then we find her," Liam said with more confidence than I'd ever heard him use. "There must've been another boat you didn't see, and she probably took it thinking she could save us the trouble." He sounded so certain, and if I hadn't awoken to that feather and the sense of loss, I'd have agreed.

I simply didn't believe that was what had occurred.

Kiara wouldn't have left me. Not like I'd left her.

"Obviously she's not here," the Fox said. "I'd gamble on what Liam said. She had to have taken a boat you missed. I'm sure you were…distracted." Her eyes tapered into thin slits as she appraised my undone state.

Unwanted heat burned my cheeks.

Jake and Liam each made an effort *not* to comment, averting their gazes and looking at anything but my naked torso.

Of course, they knew what transpired.

What was worse was my *mother* bearing witness to the aftermath.

Mercifully, Emelia flicked her attention to her men, motioning for Finn and Dimitri to head to the boats. She was just as filthy as her crew, but the hard edge to her eyes made the dirt streaking her features appear like war paint. "We can rest once we locate her, and she couldn't have made it all that far, but we should leave. Now."

"Sounds like you almost care." The words slipped out, anger and fear taking over my mouth.

She didn't justify that with a response, though her jaw perceptively clenched. Emelia stalked past me without meeting my eyes and heaved her bag onto the flat bottom of a boat. Close to the rippling water, she paused, her lips parting at whatever she saw swirling across the iridescent surface. I would've said she experienced awe, but she quickly wiped the emotion from her face.

The others followed suit, not bothering to hide their reactions to the beauty of the tunnel, while I reached for my shirt and cloak, tugging both on mechanically. I felt numb.

"We'll find her, Commander," Jake said sternly, clapping me on the back. He jumped on the ship, which swayed slightly under his weight. "You *know* she would do something like this. If anything, I would've been surprised if she hadn't."

I didn't say a word. I *didn't* think she would. Not after what we shared. Unless she had doubts...

She'd mentioned what Arlo suspected, that we were only drawn to each other romantically because of our power. But I thought I'd ridden such an absurd notion from her mind.

Finn, Dimitri, and the Fox took up one vessel, Jake, Liam, and I the other. The bottoms were wide and flat, constructed to minimize rocking while we assumed our positions. Two of us held a long oar, standing atop the opposite ends of the boat, while the third person rested in the center.

The oar sliced through the twinkling water with ease, my arms moving rhythmically, matching Jake's pace where he commanded the front.

The others were speaking, Liam arguing about taking a turn with the oar, Jake shutting him down, protesting that Liam needed to rest. The Fox and her men whispered about the treasures they'd find, and I...

I blocked them all out.

Something horrible *had* to have occurred, and no one else appeared fazed. Or maybe I was overreacting.

Above, the moon illuminated our path, the open ceiling bearing the universe and all its spectacular divine glory.

The temple of the Moon God was a shrine to the exquisitely dark splendor of night. The bronze columns rose from the watery depths, the twisting metal crafted with an expert hand. Every now and again, I glimpsed my grim expression upon their polished surface, my reflection unrecognizable from the one I'd known most of my life.

I felt as if I coasted through space, sandwiched between the stars in the water and those in the sky. Planets glittered in reds and blues, larger than should be possible. Utterly breathtaking.

It was a shame I hardly cared.

Raina's magic finally opened its eye, heat winding around

my torso the farther we traveled, seeming to sense my distress. Warmth spread to my toes, to the tips of my fingers. It caressed my cheeks, banishing the chill of the otherworldly breeze.

It sought to comfort me when unease held me in its clutches, and I accepted its efforts, if only to clear my head and prepare for the inevitable battle.

For now, I'd pretend she'd done as Liam suggested—taken a boat I hadn't seen and tried to play hero. Although, I'd been vigilant to take stock of the scene we'd stepped into and had only tallied four boats, but—I could be wrong. *I had to be.*

Over and over, I repeated this. Trying to make it true.

So consumed with doubts, I didn't see the hand that burst free from the water and seized Liam's ankle until it was too late. A shrieking wail shook the quiet, replacing it with a weighted sense of terror.

Liam's scream died beneath the water a moment later.

Chapter Twenty-Nine

Kiara

Even when Raina had become Rae, she maintained faith. That, I think, is why she made connections with sun priests across the realm. One day, her successor would call for help, and she prayed her followers would be there to answer.

Entry in Aurora Adair's Diary, year 20 of the curse

I woke on a bridge of marble and glass.

Shards of clear gems and glass were embedded in the stone, capturing the focus of the moon. They shone like frozen stars, the fractured pieces stretching the length of the bridge.

My shirt was unbuttoned, my pants unlaced, and my hair tangled in my face. Swiping it aside, I rubbed my eyes, certain I still dreamed, that my physical body waited for me in Jude's arms, where I was safe and untouchable.

The more I rubbed, the more I realized that wasn't the case.

This was my reality. I was alone. On a bridge leading to a lofty palace surrounded by marble walls. And to my left was a storm of lightning and fog that reminded me of the Mist. I shivered.

Jude was gone. My friends were lost.

A wave of dizziness had me staggering as I lurched to my

feet. My hand flung out, seeking purchase, grabbing on to the walled edge of the bridge. It came up to my chest, not quite tall enough to hide the star-speckled waters about a hundred feet beneath my feet.

My fingertips smarted as the shards of glass pricked them, and I tore my hand away with a curse. Blood welled up on my index and middle fingers, and I wiped them on the abrasive linen of my pants.

My gloves were absent, no doubt left behind from where I'd shared the evening with Jude. I imagined what he thought when he woke and found me gone. Would he believe I ran off as he'd done in the Mist?

A choked laugh left me. I was more worried about his reaction than about *why* I was here in the first place.

Come closer, a voice whispered across my mind. It was deep and seductive, a rumble of a command. *Look over the ledge.*

I went stiff, my muscles straining.

The voice from my dreams. From last night, the one that led me here —

The night itself.

Like a fool, I listened, my fingers biting into the bridge's ledge once more. I didn't care when the glass sliced me. I was instantly swept away by the vision below.

The waters that had swirled with a thousand stars now churned, black shadows grazing the surface, twirling around and around in a never-ending loop. I fixated upon the clear center, my body tingling with anticipation.

A form took shape.

My brother's face, diluted and blurred, greeted me. Cold sweat trickled down my forehead, down the back of my neck. Liam waved, his mouth forming my name, and in my precarious state, I almost waved back.

Not real, not real, not real.

"Jump in!" he ordered playfully.

I shook my head, my knuckles turning a sickly white. The moon grew in size, spreading its pale light across the bridge, over the roiling waters, and the eerie vision of my brother.

"Kiara," he chided. "I thought you were more fun than this." Liam made a show of splashing, swimming around in the circle of shadows, his grin contagious.

I went rigid.

Liam never called me *Kiara*. Meaning, it wasn't merely my subconscious playing tricks. *Someone* was controlling this. None of it was real, but it wasn't some hallucination my mind had brought about.

It was the same someone that must have brought me here, pulling my strings as if I were a puppet to control.

Unease clawed at my insides, my pulse racing. I tried to release the ledge, but my hands wouldn't allow me an inch of freedom. My fingers gripped the stone like they had a mind of their own. Or as if someone held them down.

Shadows appeared, ones that didn't belong to me. Rather than the black and gray I'd become accustomed to, their shade was a stark white. They circled my wrists like manacles, forcing me to take in the shifting scene.

Fine. We'll do it the hard way, the voice whispered across my mind.

Who are you? Show your face! I screamed inside my head, trying to yank free. All to no avail.

Silence.

In the waters, my brother's face morphed from one of joy to rage. His canines extended, becoming fanged, pointed, and like those of the masked men from the Mist. The whites of his eyes eclipsed his pupils, and his soft brown curls were caked in mud and black blood.

I screamed until my throat became raw.

"Let go!" I shouted to the unseen entity imprisoning me, infiltrating my mind. The snow-white shadows binding me to the bridge merely tightened in reply.

Liam snapped his jaw, his grin wicked. My shadow beast slunk into the recesses of my soul, offering no help...but another entity rose to my aid.

Raina's magic spread across my chest, and golden rays washed over the horrific scene of an undead Liam. I called out to Raina, like the faithful, repeating her name like a prayer.

Channeling her warmth, I worked to pry my hands free. I envisioned the orb I'd seen in my dream when my grandmother visited me in the Mist. Its image eased the pressure surrounding my wrists, chasing away the cruel vision of Liam. With my darker magic restrained, I allowed the golden magic control.

Flames ignited where the white shadows grazed my sensitive flesh, roaring to life and sparking. My shackles fizzled to nothing, and the flames of a goddess flared before extinguishing entirely.

I reared back, the abrupt action sending me stumbling and falling onto my bottom.

Dreams and nightmares. Shadows and flames.

I was well and truly in the realm of a god, and as if to confirm, a cloak of blue fog shrouded the moon, which pulsated like a heartbeat.

To my right, the bridge led to the walled palace, which I took in with greater scrutiny.

The white walls were veined in blue, reminding me of the scars covering my hands. It was a jagged, stunning creation, the construction intricate yet effortless, as if the architect followed the natural direction of the stones. Well over ten stories high, three towers rose, the middle higher, its roof a pointed half of a diamond.

I forced my attention on the other bank.

To my left, in the distance, was that storm of silver, black, and glittering dust. It blocked my view of what lay beyond, and no matter how many times I attempted to summon my heightened sight, I perceived nothing but terror and beautiful destruction.

I had two choices—

Both promised the start of a ruinous nightmare.

There was only one reason I'd been brought here—to separate me from my friends, from Jude. I'd fallen under the spell of my shadows and soared away easily, without an ounce of fight.

The night had coaxed me with little to no effort. How very weak I felt.

My temper flared.

Raina's warmth battled with the ice infiltrating my veins, but it raged to the forefront, urging my steps into the gale of swirling gloom and fierce lightning.

Do your worst, I thought to the watching night. Above, the moon and all its many stars trembled in reply.

I took my first step into the darkness.

CHAPTER THIRTY

JUDE

Our nightmares are merely reflections of our true selves.

ASIDIAN PROVERB

The creature's ungodly screech rang through the tunnel.
Acute bolts of pain stabbed at my temples, and try as I might to muffle the noise—my hands pressed firmly against my ears—it was no use. The discordant sound scraped along the insides of my skull like a rusty blade.

Liam struggled to free himself from its clutches, and when he thrust an elbow into the beast's face, he was afforded a few precious gulps of air. The creature let out a withering cry, thrashing its too-long arms, attempting to seize Liam once more.

Hair the color of snow draped around its body like tangled seaweed. Its wide eyes were all silver, and its mouth…it didn't possess one—just smooth, unblemished skin.

I'd never seen such a monster.

Before Liam could gain ground and grasp the boat, he was yanked down by spindly hands, three long, clawed fingers holding him tight.

The creature had the ability to be heard even out of sight, and warmth trickled from both ears, the heat of blood bringing forth the heady scent of copper. My eardrums were bursting, the sharp stabbing nearly causing me to double over.

The Fox dumped out her bag and brought forth an odd contraption shaped like a crossbow and no larger than my dagger. Trembling hands notched an arrow in its slot, her features contorted in concentration. She pressed a button on the device and the entire bow ignited, glowing like a lethal sunfire gem.

The silver tip was a promise of death, as beautiful as it was deadly. Aiming the device over the side of the boat, she released the shaft, sending the arrow driving out of sight and below the thick waters.

As it sliced through the dense blue, its glimmer never wavered, and I caught a flash of white hair and a glimpse of a sickly pale, naked body.

Emelia cursed at her miss, notching another arrow.

My mother aimed, though she missed once more, the glowing bolt doing nothing but illuminating the waters.

I was grateful Liam wasn't being taken easily. He fought his way to the surface, bringing forth a wave that crashed against my chest.

Compelling myself into motion, I fought the instinct to curl up and block my ears with my hands. Gripping the boat's wooden edge, I ignored my bleeding ears and the agony splitting my skull and peered over the side.

It began as it had before—the rush of raw energy invading my body—but it happened in the blink of an eye.

My knuckles were white from squeezing the wood, the onslaught of adrenaline and magic wreaking havoc on my system.

I was incandescent, my vision in my left eye sharp, the right blanketed in gold. With Liam's life on the line, I didn't have the time to ponder why I felt more at home in this otherworldly state, like I'd shucked off a heavy wool coat.

Instead, I dove in.

I arced through the water, the wailing unbearable. I was certain more blood pooled from my ears, my head growing fuzzy. But I was accustomed to pain, and once it made a home in my skull, an odd sort of calmness settled over me.

There.

Its frail arms clung to its prey, the light I radiated washing over its scalelike skin. Liam's fight was dwindling. He ceased to claw at his captor, his eyes shuttering closed.

The creature dug its clawed fingers deeper into Liam's torso. As Liam opened his mouth in a silent scream, tinges of red escaped the shallow puncture wounds.

With the power of the sun beating against my skin, begging to be liberated, I set my sights on its face, directly between its deadened eyes.

The second I'd found him in that tavern in Lis, I felt the urge to protect him like my kin. I admired his bravery, the light in his eyes, the need to fight, even in the face of probable defeat.

Liam would not die today.

All of my suppressed magic burst free in a ruinous tide of bright yellow and orange flames, the water doing nothing to diminish its force as my power rushed toward the creature's exposed back.

Bubbles escaped from between my lips and I gritted my teeth in determination, hoping my aim was true.

The waters trembled at the impact.

Fire cleaved its skull in two, cutting off the creature's torturous cries. Its smooth, slick back withered and burned, charring like lit parchment. It contorted and shrieked, twisting until its mouthless face turned my way, vicious flames eating away at its eyes.

Liam finally came into view as it released its grip on the

boy, its decaying body sinking. In seconds, all that remained of my assault was the bottom half of its torso and its too-long legs, which continued to twitch as if trying to kick to the surface.

Liam didn't move. His hands were raised above his head, his eyes shut tight. He looked a sickly shade of pale blue.

Kicking forward, I raged against the thick waters, battling toward his listless body. Tiny lights sparkled as I swam, reappearing now that the creature had vanished. It was like swimming in the heavens, in a black sky filled with stars.

With my energy waning, I ground my teeth and kicked, finally able to grab hold of one of his hands. Yanking him up, I wrapped an arm around his waist and shot for the surface, too fearful to check if he still lived.

Lights rippled overhead, teasing me. We were so close…but black spots were dancing across my sight, my oxygen-deprived lungs burning. Liam was limp in my hold.

So close—

I broke free with a gasp. Liam made no sound at all.

Frantically, I spun around, finding the twin boats twenty feet away. But while I'd been down fighting a beast, chaos had broken out above.

Nightmares were everywhere, in all forms, all engaged with a member of our crew.

Emelia currently clashed with a hooded figure of similar stature, a blade in her hand as she swiped for its throat, uncharacteristic tears dripping down her face.

Finn stood with his eyes shut while a snake curled around his bicep, quickly moving to his neck. Its pink tongue licked his skin as it worked toward his face, its soulless black eyes seeming to sparkle in anticipation.

Dimitri hovered over the body of a King's Guard clothed in a torn crimson tunic.

He clutched a dagger, his face screwed with rage as he

brought the weapon down over and over again, aiming for the man's already ruined face. He shouted two names I'd only recently learned, repeating them like a mantra as blood streamed over the side of the rocking vessel, coating the water in vicious red.

I whirled to Jake, alone in his own craft. He held the focus of a snarling coyote. Its teeth bared, its furry hind legs taut.

Impossible beasts battled with the crew, and Liam was either unconscious or dead in my arms.

"Help!" Finn begged, and Dimitri leapt off the bloodied King's Guard with a brutal scowl. Crimson had splattered his weathered face and stained his tunic. With the same blade he'd used to end the soldier's life, Dimitri sliced the snake encircling Finn in half, its fangs an inch from his throat. It dropped to the bottom of the boat with a thud.

With both men able to assist Emelia, who'd earned a nasty cut across her forearm, I swam to the nearest boat, Liam in tow.

Jake hardly appeared aware of anything but the coyote yelping and nipping at the air, its serrated fangs snapping close to where he held his weapon, his hand shaking violently.

"Not again," Jake panted, eyeing the coyote. It kicked its back leg and leaned into a crouch, set to pounce. He briefly closed his eyes as if willing it away.

"Recruit!" I snapped, but Jake was lost to some cruel memory.

I needed to call more magic, but my body was nearly depleted.

Come on, I roared, screaming inside my head, struggling with no one but myself. *Help him!*

My hands were numb, pins and needles working their way to my calves. Any second now, I'd collapse and drown along with Liam. But I recognized the subtle humming, a sliver of magic left over from destroying the water beast.

Reaching in with invisible hands, I dragged that minuscule

shard of magic forth, aiming it directly at the snapping coyote.

Heat expanded in my chest, and flames erupted, set on the animal. When my power scorched its matted gray fur, it howled, the flames licking at its legs and soft underbelly.

Jake yelled before he lunged, tears wetting his cheeks as he drove his blade into the coyote's head. Blood sprayed across the recruit's face when he yanked it free, and a wild look overtook his features when he kicked the dead creature over the side of the boat.

Finally, his attention landed on me, sweat and gore slicking his brow.

"Help me get Liam up!" I commanded, grasping the edge of the craft. The black dots had returned, the pins and needles numbing my arms and legs almost entirely.

My very bones were heavy, my movements sluggish as Jake fumbled to reach me. He hoisted Liam over the side before coming back for me, and it took all his strength to pull me to safety. We both landed in a heap.

"Help him," I sputtered, and Jake rushed to Liam.

He felt for a pulse, fear widening his eyes.

"He's not breathing!" Jake pressed against Liam's chest while I willed my sight to clear.

I could feel my hands again, if only barely.

Across the way, Emelia had taken down her attacker with a gash to their chest. The thick linen hood shrouded their identity save for strands of short black hair that fell free, the same deep dark color as Emelia's. Finn kicked the injured assailant overboard with a guttural cry, Dimitri holding the Fox back from lunging in after.

"We need help!" My shout roused the Fox from her spell, but it was Finn who tossed the bag carrying medicine over to our vessel. Jake continued to revive Liam, his movements rough, likely to leave bruises.

I all but crawled to the bag. Rifling through the contents, I found dozens of vials, all unlabeled, and I couldn't recall what the thief used to save Liam in the clearing. He hadn't suffered an attack, but I wanted it on hand if—*when*—he woke.

This wasn't the end. I'd made a vow—to myself and to Liam.

"Come on," Jake hissed, pressing hard on Liam's chest. "Wake up!" He was relentless in his attempts.

Liam's eyes bolted open.

Jake heaved him onto his side as water flooded from his mouth, pouring out in a wave. He sputtered and coughed, his skin sickly in its paleness, his lips tinged in blue.

Jake patted him on the back, helping him get the water out of his lungs. "There you go," he soothed. "Get it all out." He rubbed at Liam's back, his hands shaking.

My mother rowed close enough to vault from her ship to ours. She whipped open the bag Finn had tossed and unearthed the proper medicine.

Uncorking the top, she forced the vial's contents down Liam's throat. His head lay in Jake's lap, his eyes blood red and his body weak, but he drank, and Jake's frantic breathing returned to a normal rhythm.

He still clutched Liam tightly, his arms banded around the boy's torso.

Jake shifted Liam until he rested against his chest, and he smoothed wayward curls from his eyes.

Liam was alive. We all were. And with the nightmares vanquished, I faced Emelia.

"Who were you fighting?" I had a feeling I already knew.

"A ghost," she answered curtly. Emelia averted her gaze and shoved her hands into her cloak before anyone else could see the slight quiver that ran through them.

The Fox had battled *herself*. Of that I was certain. I wasn't sure how I felt about that, but I did grasp what it symbolized, and a pang of unwanted pity struck me.

"Fucking snakes." Finn shivered in disgust before moving to wrap his arms around the Fox. She surprisingly allowed it, even permitting him to tuck a stray lock of hair behind her ear and run his palm across her cheek. Her eyes had grown lifeless, the spark in them absent.

I noted Liam and Jake both stealing glances at the pair, the former's eyes narrowed in confusion at their display of affection. I also hadn't expected my mother to be so open with her emotions, even after such a battle.

"Are you all right?" I finally asked Jake. He stiffened, but he didn't release Liam, who rested his head in the crook of Jake's neck.

Coyotes. I'd have assumed his nightmares would have come from our time in the Mist.

"Nic saved me from one years ago," he murmured, almost to himself. "I was hungry and half-starved already when I went hunting for game in the woods. He shot an arrow through its skull, and then he brought me to his house and fed me for the first time in days." Jake sucked in a stuttering breath. "I was seven."

I'd forgotten just how much Nic had meant to Jake. I'd carry the weight of shame for the rest of my days because he died on *my* watch.

Jake slid a gentle finger down Liam's cheek. "What was that thing that attacked you?" he asked softly, his finger pausing when it reached Liam's jaw.

"I b-blame my grandmother," Liam choked out. Color was slowly returning to his cheeks. While the medicine appeared to have prevented an attack, I watched as he settled in the former recruit's arms, clutching Jake like an anchor to this realm.

"My grandma always told me horror stories of the wailing woman in the l-lake." He nearly smiled at the memory.

"Supposedly she stole small children if they ventured too far from the dock. Kiara would l-laugh at me, saying she wasn't real, but I never went swimming because of that story."

When Liam tried to sit up, he was immediately shoved back in place. "Don't be stubborn," Jake chastised. "You need to rest. I think I'd miss you if you died."

"Such sweet words," Liam said, though he bestowed him with a half smile.

"Jake's right. You do need to rest," Emelia added, and Liam gave her a halfhearted roll of his eyes. Still, he made no effort to free himself again.

I surveyed the daring few who'd traveled with me to the Moon God's temple, risking their lives to return the sun. Or, in the case of the Fox and her men, risking their lives for coin. I hadn't the foolish notion she'd done it for *me*.

Unlike the Mist, where our fears played tricks on our eyes, our nightmares were composed of flesh and blood here, brought to life by magic and terror.

"We have to get off the water," I blurted out, assuming command. Agony ripped across my muscles as I strained them, rising to peer into the distance. My pulse leapt as I made out the hint of a dark gray shore. Shadows curled around its edge, growing with each passing second. It appeared as if a storm was brewing.

"Agreed," Liam said, and Jake unwound his arms. He eased him into the center of the vessel, slipping off his jacket to wrap around Liam's shoulders.

No one dared speak when we readied ourselves, oars in hand, my mother and her men back in their boat. I realized I hadn't fought off a creature of my own imagination. Or maybe I hadn't needed to. I was already living my worst nightmare.

Kiara was gone. Again.

An eerie chuckle floated to my ears, hardly above a whisper.

It tickled the hairs on the back of my neck, prompting me to glance over my shoulder. I found nothing but stagnant waters, those eerie lights resuming their infuriating twinkling.

Yet I couldn't shake the familiarity of that laugh...like I'd heard it many times before.

CHAPTER THIRTY-ONE

KIARA

*While I pray the sun returns, I fear for people of the realm.
Peace may reign for a time, but war will inevitably break out.
It is simply human nature to find a new foe to fight, and in the
light of day, they will turn on one another.*

FOUND IN THE DIARY OF JUNIPER MARCHANT, SUN PRIESTESS

The storm raged, lashing out at my face with furious winds.
I could hardly see a few feet in front of me, the fog thick
and the air suffused with grit, but my friends were on the other
side. There would be no turning back.

I'd been alone for most of my life, save for Liam. The
journey through the Mist had taught me I was stronger with
support, and I'd brave any storm or obstacle to get to Jude and
my friends now.

Pins and needles tickled my palms. The black and blue scars
slowly came to life, a soft glow pulsating in the dim. They were
reacting to this place. *Welcoming* it.

Which could only mean I was in trouble.

My body grew heavy, invisible hands pressing on my
shoulders, a weight settling in my chest. And while weakened,
my scars dazzled, wisps of night seeping from my pores, winding

up my exposed arms.

My steps wavered as regret soured my thoughts. The winds were too harsh, the air too dense, and the dark clouds disoriented me to the point where I couldn't recall from which direction I'd entered.

Minutes passed, and yet I'd only made it ten more steps. I crumbled to my knees when I attempted another.

Get up, I urged. *You're stronger than this.*

But I didn't feel so strong or confident now, not when the air turned foul and I swore I heard the distant ringing of laughter.

All I could focus on was moving, and I failed at even that. My arms were frozen in place, my fingertips numb as though they'd been dipped in ice.

The shadow beast inside of me surged forth, the darkness invading me, taking control. It shuddered as a gust of wind tossed me to the side, my head cracking against the ground. My vision swam.

This was a trap. Maybe the night *had* wanted me to choose the storm after all.

Stinging pain shot across both hands. In horror, I watched as my scars grew, the black stretching up to my forearms like voracious weeds.

No, no, no, no…

I didn't want to die here, suffocating in the cruel breeze. Each inhale felt poisonous.

Something approached. Movement from my periphery.

I lifted my head with a groan.

The same panic I'd experienced when I was eight years old and alone in the Pastoria Forest resurfaced.

Before me hovered the very creature that haunted my nightmares.

It's back. It came back to finish the job.

A shadow beast.

Cocking its head, its empty eyes assessed me like a snack. Swirls of black clouds churned where its mouth should've been, but I imagined it was smiling at its trapped prey.

It wasn't my darkness holding me back. Not the monster imprisoned inside my flesh. No. It was *me*. I'd been reminded of that time all those years ago when I'd felt small and helpless.

Terrified.

Suddenly, staring up at the faceless creature of quivering smoke, I yearned for Arlo. His steady presence. How he could dispel my fears by showing me a new trick with a sword or dagger. He'd been the one to tell me I was capable of greatness should I want it badly enough.

He never held me or coddled, but his harsh but bolstering words... Gods, I needed them now.

I found my voice, the only thing I seemed to be able to control.

"Isn't it rude to play with your food?" I said with shocking calm. I wouldn't quiver before it.

The beast went utterly still, and even the shadows that curled around its form paused.

It hadn't expected me to fight back, for my voice to remain steady. I'd taken it by surprise, and because of this, I grinned.

Never again. I wasn't that same little girl crying for her mother and father, bloody and screaming in the woods. The monster in front of me wasn't the same creature who'd left its mark. It was just another foe I had to take down.

And that was something I'd done countless times before.

"Come on, what are you waiting for?" I goaded, the numbness in my fingers lessening.

My fear was still there, but battling it was my will to survive. I had so much to live for. So much to become. I wouldn't allow this beast to ruin my future as it had stained my past.

Yes. Remember who you are. Fight. I could practically hear

Arlo whisper the words across my mind, his stern voice hacking away at the panic holding me down.

I met the vacant stare of the monster that lived in the corners of my mind.

I won't go down easily.

The shadow beast lunged toward me, and then my body split apart.

Chapter Thirty-Two

Jude

I hope to meet with you and explain in person. Rae...she's far different from what even I initially suspected. While her past is now clear, something besides her divinity was taken. She's mortal, and yet she doesn't possess the very thing that makes us human. I do not believe she has a heart.

<small>Letter from Aurora Adair to Juniper Marchant, year 30 of the curse</small>

Our boats nudged the shore a second before we heard a scream.

It didn't sound like the shriek of the wailing woman that attacked Liam. It sounded human.

"Kiara!" Jake called out in alarm, reading my thoughts.

He and I charged for the stony bank, running side by side in the face of a growing storm. Those shadows I'd glimpsed along the nearing shore flourished, shrouding everything in black silt and clogging the air with a sickly-sweet smell that churned my stomach.

The magic of the sun goddess strained, weakened by the nightmarish hellscape we walked through. I gritted my teeth and pressed on, willing my eyes to light the way. It was weak in this place, in the middle of this storm.

A second scream, this one muffled, came from my right, and I lurched into the bedlam without thought.

Kiara's pleas for help enlivened my power, gifting me with pure, heady adrenaline.

I fought to move, fought to continue—for her.

My eyes sparked and glowed, rays of light navigating the tumultuous winds.

A cluster of shadows formed ten feet away, gradually taking the shape of a man. It towered well over eight feet, its spindly arms lifted, coils of black curling around its elongated fingers.

Could it be…

A shadow beast.

That was the only explanation. And when I spotted a prone figure curled up at its feet, I pumped my legs even harder. Toward the monster. The legend and nightmare.

Luminous red strands flashed, a head tilting up, glaring at the beast with narrowed eyes.

Kiara.

It wouldn't have mattered if I had divine power or merely the aching will of a mortal man in love. I would've found my way to her, crawled my way to her. Cut or bleeding or on the cusp of death, nothing could've held me back.

Power thrummed in tune with each beat of my heart, heat invading my every inch. It didn't burn or harm. This magic was a part of me, and the more I accepted it, the more it felt *right*.

I finally embraced who I was.

Lightning crashed somewhere nearby, but the thunder that followed was nothing compared to the roar I released. "Get the fuck away from her."

The shadow beast was a failed creation of the Moon God. Rumored to have been a concept of good intent turned wicked—a being that hunted the darkest of nightmares and destroyed them—they had become the realm's most feared monster.

I, too, had been a soul born in darkness, and I could be just as wicked.

Flames climbed my back, rising into the air like the wings of night Kiara commanded.

Though, instead of black, my wings were limned in brilliant oranges and yellows. They illuminated the creature lurking over Kiara, the shadow beast's full attention landing on me. It let out a snarling hiss.

Good. I wanted it to watch me as I ended its life.

Inhaling sharply, I aimed all my power at the beast, my body curling inward as magic blasted free.

The shadow beast screamed when my fire scorched its back, and it teetered to the side, stunned. Kiara scrambled back, her ungloved hands rising to her face, protecting herself from the heat of my flames.

I recalled her story, how terrified she'd been as a child when she was attacked. Now, she'd been thrust back into that horrid reality all over again.

And yet she held her head high.

That's my girl.

I ducked to the right as black shadows limned in silver wafted from its reedy form, its poisonous magic shooting toward my face. The strike missed by an inch.

Before I could regain my bearings, it delivered another bolt, the shadows slashing my thigh and forming a shallow gash. It burned unlike anything I'd ever experienced, and the sheer torment of it would've made me stumble had it not been for Kiara gazing at me now, her hands lowered, eyes trusting.

She needed me now as I'd needed her so many times before. I refused to disappoint.

My flames spiraled out as phantom shackles fell and

clattered to pieces, destroying the manacles I'd placed on myself—the lies I told insisting this wasn't my destiny. That I would find a way out of this mess.

I was Raina's descendant, and her power called to me, begging I rid the world of this blasphemous creature.

My stare locked with Kiara's, and an entire lifetime seemed to pass in the span of a blink. Adventures and shared secrets. Laughter and long nights before a fire. Her showing me the meaning of what it was like to truly *live*.

A blast sent me off my feet, the beast taking me by surprise.

I tumbled through the air, flailing, reaching for anything solid to salvage control.

There was nothing.

Icy hands encircled my throat, squeezing, a resounding roar of triumph coming from the mouth of the beast.

Something tore inside of me, and pain greater than any whip raced down my neck and to my chest. The next scream I heard belonged to me.

Spots coated the gold of my sight, my lungs deprived of oxygen. I feebly swatted at the beast with my hands, but it only worked to infuriate it, and its hold on me tightened.

My eyes fluttered shut, yet I continued to struggle, not willing to surrender.

If only I could concentrate, summon my magic—

Something detonated, a blazing light erupted.

I opened my eyes, expecting to see flames like the ones I possessed engulfing the beast, but instead, I saw Kiara, drenched in a fire of both yellow and black, a shimmering gold weaving through her combined powers.

Fear shone in her eyes, but she didn't falter. She was a vengeful goddess as she directed her magic into the creature, sending it staggering back, a squelching noise sounding before something splintered.

Her teeth were bared as she strode its way, her peculiar fire striking it again and again without mercy. Sweat glistened on her brow, but she didn't appear fatigued. Just enraged. Furious in a way that I'd not seen before, not even when Harlow had threatened me.

"Do. Not. Touch. Him."

Each word was followed by an assault of black fire, her darkness working with the fragment of golden light she carried. Yet it was more than that—

The driving force was *her*.

The creature shriveled in on itself, its incorporeal skin eaten away by the flames. A cruel smile tilted her lips, and I watched, stunned, as Kiara tore her personal nightmare apart piece by piece.

"Never again," she screamed.

I knew exactly what her words meant. Tears stained her face, but they were beautiful in the flashes of light that exploded around us, the wet tracks turning into brilliant streaks of victory.

She would never be vulnerable to the beast again. Its victim. Kiara stared her greatest fear in the eyes and she fucking smiled.

Because this time, she could win. She *would* win.

Its body shriveled in on itself, the shadows comprising its long form wavering, growing weak. Kiara didn't relent, didn't hesitate. She didn't cease her assault until only ash remained at her feet, and even that was swept away by a fierce gust of wind.

Drenched in glistening sweat, she panted, her fists clenched. Her scars...

They'd grown. Swirls of black-and-blue vines reached below the cuff of her rolled-up shirt, the new marks gifted by the touch of the beast she'd just destroyed.

Kiara whirled to me, eyes aglow with amber, her body cloaked in power, and my heart ceased to beat for an entirely new reason.

I'd never seen anything more stunning, more frightening, or more devastating than her as she closed the distance. Her black-and-gold fire fizzled out, and she dropped to her knees before me. Reaching for my face, her scarred hand traced the curve of my jaw as if making sure I was real—alive and in front of her now.

I swallowed her body in my arms, clutching her to my chest. She let out a noise that sounded like a relieved sob, and then she dug her fingers into my back, refusing to let go.

Together we breathed; together we sat still in the middle of a merciless storm of dark magic.

Together, we found the strength to calm our pounding hearts until they matched, both seeking the steady song of their partner.

We didn't move until someone grabbed my arm.

Kiara was whipped out of my embrace, another figure clasping her wrist. Jake.

Behind me was Liam, his fingers a vise on my bicep. He hauled me to my feet.

Then Jake shouted one word that even the violent winds couldn't drown out.

"Run!"

Chapter Thirty-Three

Kiara

No entity is entirely good or evil. The gods are the same. They can be cruel and vicious, just as the realms and emotions they rule.

Excerpt from Asidian Lore: a Tale of the Gods

I was yanked forward by both my brother and Jake, my aching body forced into a run.

"Go!" Jude commanded, hot on our heels. "Get across the bridge!"

"Wait! What about the others?" I peered over my shoulder, too weakened to break out of their hold. Thankfully, Finn's hulking frame appeared, Dimitri and Emelia flanking him. They struggled to catch up, but the ruthless winds were making it difficult.

"Hurry, Ki," Liam cried out, his voice raspy, like he'd been shouting for hours. It had me wondering what they'd endured when I'd been stranded on the other side of this storm.

Winds whipped at my hair, the strands stinging my cheeks. They were angrier now that we'd escaped, powerful gusts barreling into us from all sides. I felt as if the night watched from above, and my stomach knotted as a rumbling growl of displeasure echoed in my head.

I couldn't help but feel as if the shadow beast's appearance hadn't been a coincidence. That somehow, it had been sent to me by the entity that ruled this temple.

If any opponent had the ability to steal my courage, it was the creature that had robbed me of my childhood.

Only when the beast had leveled its sights on the commander did my fear morph into a rage I could use and wield. I saw myself in Jude's place as the venomous shadows knocked him off his feet. He was *me* then, that child screaming in the woods, and I was going to save him. Save *myself*.

I'd get my revenge against the beast who'd tried to take and take and take from me until nothing remained. My spirit, while exhausted, was triumphant. Weary and bloodied but blazing with purpose.

"Come on!" Liam shouted, jerking me free of the past. We were surrounded by nothing, our path to the palace unclear, and for the life of me, I couldn't recall which direction I'd entered from.

A hint of warmth remained burning in the hearth of my heart, right beside my darkness.

Raina's power had been with me as well—her divine light a force that worked alongside my shadows to save Jude and me.

Her spirit stood beside me now as if she were flesh and bone, and I swore I felt her heated touch on my back, driving me to safety.

"The dust in this storm is affecting Liam," Jake yelled, peering to his left, at my brother.

His eyes were shut, his steps uneven. I hadn't even thought about his condition even though I *should* have. I was grateful for Jake then, knowing he trained his watchful gaze on Liam.

Liam's health wasn't the only reason we needed to hurry.

"A shadow beast attacked us," I said. "I'd bet there's more."

"We saw you kill it," Liam wheezed, and I threaded my fingers more securely through his.

"We should be out of this storm soon!" I promised. I didn't recall wandering for too long after I'd entered, so we *had* to be close.

Squinting, I searched for the bridge, grit and dust flying into my eyes and mouth. Just when I thought we had turned ourselves around, I saw it. Unmoving lines of luminous white.

I almost smiled at the sight.

Making sure Jude trailed behind, I steered Liam and Jake, both following without pause. I couldn't even hear my own thoughts, and communicating was becoming impossible.

While Liam and Jake coughed and sputtered, aching for fresh air, I began to breathe easier. I picked up the pace, propelling us out on the other side of the storm's end.

A final angry breeze struck my face with a force equaling a closed fist. We all stumbled, holding on to one another, our knees weak. Liam nearly collapsed, but Jake hastily grabbed him, angling around my body to wind his arm around Liam's waist. The bastard all but dropped me.

I was beginning to see who his new favorite was.

Seconds later, Jude and the others emerged, Dimitri crashing to his knees as he gulped in the brisk air. Finn released Emelia's hand and moved to his friend, pushing Jude gently out of the way. He grasped Dimitri under both arms and hauled him to his feet. They embraced, Finn patting Dimitri on the back forcefully, Emelia looking on in stark relief.

With the others safe, I ran toward the commander. If he hadn't shown up when he had—

My arms were around him in the span of a heartbeat, and Jude let out a stunned grunt. He caught me easily enough, though.

I didn't need his support with how very tightly my thighs

wrapped around his lean frame.

"You scared the shit out of me!" I scolded, even though he'd helped save my life.

"Then try to not get yourself killed," he said firmly. Jude fisted the back of my shirt, clutching me tighter, pressing me against his chest.

"You're touching," Jake observed, garnering suspicious looks from the rest of our companions. They pretended not to be keenly listening.

"We...we can touch here, it seems," I answered without looking at him—my eyes were reserved for one person alone. "I think it has to do with this place being built by a god. I can practically taste the magic in the air." The normal rules of the mortal realm didn't apply. Perhaps because we no longer walked that world. Then again, we knew so very little of the truth.

"If you start to feel dizzy, or if there's pain..." Jake trailed off, but I understood his meaning.

"Don't worry, I'll let you know," I promised over my shoulder.

With Jude standing alongside me, facing my greatest fear, I'd been reminded of who I truly was. A fighter.

"I'm ecstatic you can touch, and while you two lovebirds are sickeningly adorable, we really shouldn't waste time with all the cuddling," Jake said loudly.

Jude pressed his lips to my brow before he drew back with a disappointed frown. Reluctantly, I dropped to the ground and peered at Jake, skewering him with a half-hearted glower.

I'd stay glued to Jude all day, if possible—preferably far, *far* away from Jake and my brother—but Jake was right. We had to move before any more creatures discovered us.

"Holy shit." Emelia whistled, bravely stepping onto the bridge. Bits of gray dust churned under her heavy boots, a tinge of gleaming silver flecks catching the light of the overbright moon. The Fox crouched, brushing a hand across the veiny blue threads marking the stone, tracing them with her index finger. The dark colors grew vibrant beneath her touch.

She shot up with a start, her eyes falling to my scars, lingering on how far they'd traveled. Self-consciously, I pulled down my rolled sleeves, covering the evidence. Emelia arched a perfect dark brow.

"Well then." She adjusted her satchel. "We've already had enough shit thrown our way, and I'd prefer not to linger." She appeared a warrior set for battle, and her confident demeanor—even after the horror we'd walked through—was inspiring.

"What happened when I was gone?" I asked Jude as we trailed Emelia across the bridge.

His eyes darkened. "Nightmares. We all experienced a form of our worst fears when we sailed through the tunnel. Thankfully, there were no injuries."

I threaded my hand through his. I dreaded to think of what he envisioned.

"I was the only one not affected," he said softly, reading my mind. "I was already living my worst fear." He squeezed my hand to make his point.

Us separated. Again.

My heart fluttered as I tightened my grip on his hand, both of us hustling to keep pace with the others, who'd begun to slip away. At our backs, the unnatural wind howled as if it screamed for us not to go. I didn't look back.

Five minutes later, Emelia stopped so suddenly, Jake collided with her back. She whirled on him, and he tripped over his feet to place distance between him and her virulent scowl.

I found the thief was growing on me. I'd be taking notes on her particularly potent glares.

"Did any of you hear anything?" she asked, turning from Jake, her gaze landing on the path to the fortress. It was but a blur in the distance.

My ears perked. Only a prickling sensation tickled my palms, but other than that, I sensed nothing.

"No, just the wind," Finn assured, but Dimitri didn't appear as relaxed. His bushy brows were scrunched, and he slowly swiveled his head, his eyes narrowed while he assessed the bridge.

The air surrounding the temple, the palace, the fortress—whatever it was to the Moon God—began to ripple, the haze engulfing its imposing, seamless walls gradually easing. Its sharp edges became clearer with each blink, revealing a grand doorway, a set of steep stairs leading at its feet. But to get to those stairs, we needed to get past that wall.

Emelia studied it with a feline focus, her nose wrinkling. She appeared apprehensive, which didn't bode well.

"That's going to be a long climb to the top," Jake whispered to my left, cocking his head Liam's way.

"I heard that," my brother replied, rolling his eyes. "I'm perfectly capable of climbing—"

"I never said you weren't, I just…" Jake trailed off, unable to find the right words for once.

"I'd do anything for her," Liam argued, face etched in stone. His resolve was palpable, the look he delivered Jake potent.

"I would, too." Jake dipped his chin, something akin to deference replacing his worry.

The pair shared a look, a silent conversation passing that was clearly not meant for me to know.

As they bonded over their love for me—for which I could hardly blame them—I eased to Emelia's side where she was fumbling around in her bag. I peered inside, trying to ignore the bundles of meat. While far too salty, my mouth watered at the sight of food, and I nearly groaned when she pushed it aside. Instead, I took stock of all types of devices and foreign contraptions.

"What are you looking for?" I asked, my curiosity getting the best of me.

She huffed, not deigning to glance my way. "See that wall, Scarlet?" I bristled at the name. "There isn't a door in case you haven't noticed. And unless you can fly on command, we're going to have to be creative."

Walls of marble, almost three stories tall, encircled the structure. Worst of all, now that the thrill of seeing the temple had passed, I couldn't find a seam in the wall, no trace of a doorway in which to enter.

Emelia pulled out a circular gadget fashioned of copper. She retrieved a belted harness a second later, using hooks to attach it to the odd contraption.

"I've never seen anything like that before," I said reverently when we started walking again. She maintained a ruthless pace.

It was beautiful, the piece she carried, circular and polished. Tiny gears and levers blended seamlessly into the copper, and I itched to toy with it, though I suspected she'd smack me on the head should I try.

"Perks of being a thief. And knowing the best inventors in Asidia." Emelia turned, appraising me in a way that hardly appeared friendly. "Oh, and I've been meaning to speak with you about something…"

"What's that?" I asked, the hairs on my nape rising. She was giving me *that* stare. I was pinned and helpless beneath it.

She leaned in until her warm breath fanned against my ear. "Hurt him and I'll slit your throat." The Fox took off without another word, leaving me speechless.

Well. It seemed Emelia cared for her son far more than she was willing to let on. Not that I hadn't suspected as much.

"What did she say to you?" Jude appeared at my side. We stared after his mother, allowing the others ahead.

"She threatened to slit my throat if I hurt you," I said with a smile. "I like her."

Jude sighed, but he wound his arm around my waist, his fingers tightening on my hip. I decided I rather enjoyed this side of him. Apparently all it took for him to give in to his selfish desire was for me to nearly die. Multiple times.

"Be careful around her, Kiara. She's a criminal." Along with the warning in his tone, there was also...sorrow. Jude wanted what anyone in his position would—to imagine Emelia had a reason for her coldness. For why she left him.

I leaned deeper into him.

"Technically, *we* are wanted fugitives as well. Abandoning the Knights is highly frowned upon," I teased. While I stared ahead, I could practically feel Jude roll his eyes. His hold on my waist loosened, and I sensed a question perched on the tip of his tongue.

"Come on, Jude," I coaxed. "What's really on your mind?"

He swallowed thickly, his jaw feathering. "So. Last night. You vanished right after..." He trailed off, and I turned in time to see a rosy pink glow spread across his cheeks.

He'd nearly died minutes before, and yet he was concerned I regretted our night together.

As if I ever could.

I grinned wickedly. "Well, apparently I shouldn't fall asleep, because when I dreamed I was flying, I *actually* flew."

He fumbled a step. "What do you mean, *flew*? I didn't want to pry about why you left. Or rather, I didn't want to assume it wasn't because—"

"It's not because of what happened," I said sternly, saving him from his uncharacteristic rambling—even though I immensely enjoyed it. "I fell asleep and dreamed. But it felt too real to be a dream. My body was weightless and my mind somewhat clear. I was soaring through the skies like a starwing when I heard this voice in my head. It was directing me somewhere, and I didn't even hesitate to follow. Something similar happened back in the woods before we reunited," I admitted. "I'd seen the enemy's camp from above. Jake said I was practically transparent, and it had taken several attempts to rouse me."

Jude was silent for a bit, absorbing my confession. Finally, he spoke, but relief filled his voice. "That explains the shadowy feather I found when I woke." I frowned as he continued. "But I find an odd comfort knowing magic was at play rather than... disappointment," he said, trying and failing to sound playful. His cheeks became an even darker pink, and I laughed, much to his surprise. The *fearsome* commander blushing—what a sight.

Snuggling closer into his side, I said, "Oh, our night together was very satisfactory, Commander." I used my most serious voice. "I suggest we practice, just to make sure you have the hang of it."

His throat visibly bobbed, and he appeared not to be breathing.

"So easily riled." I flicked his nose, and it wrinkled. It didn't stop him from clutching me as if I'd float away again if he relaxed his grip.

For all I knew, I would.

• • •

The wall was higher than I'd anticipated.

"We climb here," Emelia instructed, appraising the wall as one would a puzzle. She ran her hands across her daggers lovingly, making sure they were secured, a glint sparking in her eyes at the challenge.

I wasn't as easily thrilled. And I wasn't the only one.

Jake cursed, grumbling something about how mortals weren't meant to be so high in the sky.

"If we were meant to be that high, then we'd be birds," Liam whispered, earning a nod of approval from Jake.

"Exactly," Jake replied, waving his hands about. "And don't even get me started on small spaces. I'm not a damned mole."

Emelia shook her head in annoyance and retrieved the copper device from earlier.

Whatever Liam was about to say to Jake died on the tip of his tongue. He ran to the thief's side, his eyes wide with excitement over the multiple gears, levers, and pea-sized buttons.

I shuddered to think of how it worked. It appeared far too small to hold any of our weight. "You're going first, Scarlet," Emelia said without turning. She thrust a thin leather harness in my general direction, only slightly managing to punch me in the gut.

"And *that*" — I eyed the device skeptically — "is going to hold me?"

"It supports up to four hundred pounds," she replied proudly, running a reverent finger over its smooth side. "The best craftsmanship in the realm."

When she thrust it toward me once more, I didn't take it. "Liam goes first," I said, my tone leaving no room for argument.

"Seriously," Liam groused. "Stop mothering me."

Jake ruffled his curls, earning a dour look. "I'd have thought you'd know better by now. Remember, it's less of a hassle to just agree with her."

My brother's glare became coy, and now I decidedly *did not* appreciate their unspoken stares. If they ganged up on me, I'd be outnumbered.

Emelia grabbed my elbow and swung me away from the boys and their teasing. "Now, what you want to do is attach the harness, connect the clips, and hit this button — "

A rock crumbled from the right side of the bridge. The tiny stone pattered across the smooth surface, rolling to a stop. We all froze.

A resounding crack split the air. I watched in horror as jagged lines surged across the marble surface like veins, stretching to reach for our feet.

More rocks toppled free from the sides of the bridge. It was breaking apart, the cracks forming too quickly to take stock of. My body swayed as the ground tilted, tiny rivulets spider-webbing from the points of my boots.

Emelia screamed for us to run, motioning toward the wall. It loomed a hundred feet away, four scrawled words marking its side.

Halfway there, I could make out their meaning.

The Night Will Reign.

What a lovely message, I thought bitterly, as nervous sweat soaked the material of my shirt. The literal ground beneath me was falling apart, and the Moon God goaded us with a threat.

"Faster!" Jake urged Liam, who was surprisingly keeping a decent pace.

Jude cursed, his long legs a whirl beside me. His eyes were glued to the warning ahead, and his mismatched irises darkened with malice.

More creaking sounded, the bridge swaying, tilting precariously to one side. We must've triggered something when we walked across. I should've been paying closer attention, but I'd been too distracted by the commander and how we all were alive and whole.

Ironic, given our current circumstances.

Rocks the size of raindrops sliced at my skin as they soared through the air, the walls shattering. There was no order to the destruction, no safety to be found.

All I could do was run, ignoring the bite of stone that struck me from all sides.

Liam smacked a hand right above the word *Night* as he leaned forward, panting and trying to compose himself from the unexpected sprint.

The harness Emelia had gifted me would be better suited for my brother. Grabbing for him, I slipped the harness in place, much to his annoyance. I was too quick, and the clips were fastened before he could curse me.

Screaming for Emelia, I waited with bated breath as she tossed me the gadget linked to the harness, locking it around my brother's wrist. The metal top enfolded around Liam's knuckles, two buttons in pressing distance of his thumb.

"Lift your arm and press the green button!" Emelia instructed Liam. "And hurry the hells up before we all die."

That warning propelled Liam into action. He lifted his arm and pushed the button, his eyes closed. Before I could yell at him to open them, something clicked, and a silver coil attached to the device went shooting in the air.

The sound of metal striking stone echoed a moment later, the end of the rope affixed to a clawlike apparatus embedded in the stone.

"Now wh—"

Liam whirled upward, airborne and screaming. His body tore into the skies, his arms flailing wildly for purchase. He struck the top of the wall with a distressed groan.

I snuck a look behind us.

The fissures were growing in size, sprouting like twisted roots. The sides of the bridge were all but demolished, fracturing slowly.

"Drop it back down!" Emelia ordered Liam, who heeded her command. I wanted to make some snarky comment about why she'd only brought *one*, but that probably wasn't helpful.

After Liam detached the harness and device, he tossed it down. A minute later, Jake went flying, a high-pitched scream reaching my ears. That scream died when his stomach collided against the top, replaced with a painful groan.

Fingers tightened on my wrist, and I whirled around.

"You need to go," Jude insisted, his stare hard and unyielding.

I shook my head. *Ah*, he should know me better by now.

The middle of the bridge finally split, rocks tumbling into the waters below with resounding splashes. Jude tried to push me forward, toward his mother, but I shoved Dimitri ahead of me.

Jude's frustration was palpable, but Dimitri ascended effortlessly and tossed the harness and device back to the Fox with ease. When she called for Jude, he shook his head, unbending as he all but thrust me into his mother's arms.

"Her first," he demanded, and I didn't have time to argue before he secured the harness with deft fingers. A click sounded, and I went barreling into space, a choked scream rumbling up my throat.

The impact stole a rough sound from my throat, the stone brutally digging into my flesh. Liam helped me up, already working on unclipping me while I fought a wave of dizziness.

He chucked both pieces down, and Emelia caught them while more rocks plummeted into the depths, swallowed by the water holding a universe of stars. Our only way back was vanishing before our eyes, leaving us no choice but to go forward.

Perhaps that was the entire point. The realization twisted my gut.

"Jude next!" I screamed, throwing down the equipment.

Thankfully, Emelia nodded in agreement or I would've murdered her myself.

Granted, Jude argued with her until I shouted his name—along with a very detailed threat—and then he reluctantly pulled the harness over his broad shoulders. His landing was far more graceful than mine, but he shot me a withering scowl before tossing down the gear.

I smiled. He could sulk all he wanted.

Emelia went next, Finn the last to make the ascent. The cracks had just reached his feet when he aimed for the ledge, the grapple flying through the air.

The device latched onto the wall...just as the ground beneath Finn vanished. He went soaring, and when he landed, he hit the ledge harder than us all, not only because of his sheer size but due to the position he'd shot the device.

Jude's mouth fell open as the mother he'd never known lunged for Finn and wrapped him in her arms. She didn't cry, but her body shook, and Finn clutched her against his brawny chest.

"You gave me a heart attack, you big fool," she snapped, her voice muffled against him.

He let out a deep rumble. "You can't get rid of me that easily, little fox," he cooed, and she drew away to deliver a light smack to his arm.

Jude and I caught each other's eyes. With every member of our group accounted for, and with no option of retreat, the time had come to face what lay ahead.

As one, the commander and I twisted around to face what rested on the other side. I almost wished we hadn't.

"Well, fuck me." I massaged the nape of my neck. "Can we not catch a break?"

Chapter Thirty-Four

JUDE

> The boy needs work. He feels too much emotion, which is a problem, and I worry it will get in the way. I'll start him on a stricter regimen come Monday. He is the key, and I can't allow him to wander from his role.
>
> Notes from Lieutenant Harlow's personal journal, year 46 of the curse

"That bad?" Jake grimaced at Kiara's words, before he spun around and joined the rest of the crew.

"Ah. The girl was right with her initial assessment." Dimitri swept a hand through his bright reddish orange hair, grime and grease causing the ends to stick up. They shook, his hands, and my right eye picked up the golden ripples of movement. He hid his nerves by shoving them into his jacket pocket, forcing sarcasm to line his words. "That screams death by a thousand ways to me. None of them pleasant."

He wasn't wrong. The scene below had been born of nightmares.

A damned maze.

Not only was it exceptionally large, complicated, and exceedingly high, but from this vantage point, I made out cryptic symbols. *Everywhere.* If those marks and whorls were anything like those from the tunnel we entered, I had a feeling the whole labyrinth was a giant death trap. One misstep and someone would meet the wrong end of an arrow.

The palace rose like a taunt, clearly within view from this high up, yet inaccessible. The design was truly remarkable. How it flowed seamlessly with the natural rock.

The three towers were of varying heights, the roofs of the outer two fashioned of some translucent gem, hundreds of facets glimmering in welcome. The middle tower had no roof, left open to the unknown elements of the realm of the Moon God.

A slight tingle of apprehension ghosted across each of my vertebrae, a phantom hand dragging its nails down my spine.

"This is why I never wanted to go on adventures with you, Ki," Liam said, still trying to manage his erratic breathing.

Jake chortled. "Finally. Someone who understands." He tilted his head Liam's way, a boyish grin on his face. "I have absolutely no idea how you survived her for so long. She's almost killed me fifteen times over."

Liam let out a snort of amusement. "Believe me, it hasn't been easy," he agreed dramatically, much to Jake's delight. "It's not like her sparkling personality helps at all."

Kiara let out a grumble. Undoubtedly, she was regretting their introduction.

"Plan?" Finn asked Emelia, giving the boys a stern glare.

Emelia stayed silent, scanning the walls, the grooves, the deceptively safe passageways. Her eyes were shrewd, calculated.

"Kiara," the Fox barked, and she nearly jumped out of her skin. "Yes?"

"Any more secret symbols I can't see?"

Kiara scoffed. "Most definitely."

"Then you and I are leading the way," Emelia asserted. "I can see the proper path, and your...ability will help us keep our heads attached to our necks."

I'd heard my mother was clever, but to have already figured out the maze?

"How did you manage that? You've hardly been looking for more than a minute," I asked, hating that my curiosity compelled me to speak to her in the first place.

"How do you think I became the thief I am today?" she volleyed back with a smirk, though her tone was laced with bitterness.

"She's got a mind unlike any other," Finn chimed in. "One look at any map or maze or vault, and she's got it figured out. I swear there's never been anyone like her before. Beauty and a brilliant mind," he added, smiling proudly. "Couldn't have asked for more."

"Oh, shut it," she warned, but one corner of her mouth quirked.

I turned away and unscrewed my canteen, taking a long drink.

I did so mostly to avoid my mother and whatever nauseating compliments Finn spewed.

We didn't have much water left to spare, and I drank more than I should have. I needed something to do with my hands, an excuse to appear unbothered.

"We'll rest once we get over the wall." Emelia made for the edge, already setting her contraption down and locking it in place on the stone.

Kiara laughed, the raspy sound easing the tension in my shoulders. "As if rest is possible in a place like this."

· · ·

I lowered myself to the other side of the wall, joining the others. My boots hit the ground hard. Bolts of pain ricocheted up and down my limbs, the muscles already sore from so much activity with little rest.

Hiding my wince from Kiara's keen gaze, I took in our surroundings.

The overlarge moon exuded pure, brilliant light. It lanced off the white stone walls, illuminating every inch, the brilliance of the veined marble uncomfortably bright.

Unlike the Mist, the temple held no shadows, not a trace of a darkened corner.

I might have believed we'd stepped into the day had it not been for the colorful planets and stars twinkling overhead. They hovered closer now that we neared the temple's entrance as if they were eager to spy on the trespassers who dared steal from their master.

Liam sniffed the air with distaste, breathing in the sickly-sweet floral scent that saturated the breeze.

My legs trembled, the ground swaying. I glanced at the others, noting that they also peered at their boots, sensing the slight shift. While perceptible, it wasn't enough to knock us all off our feet.

One thing to be grateful for.

"There are marks everywhere," Kiara observed with a frown. "Some are glowing, almost a light blue." She traced her finger across a pristine white wall, mapping out a shape I couldn't perceive.

"Scarlet?" Emelia prodded her shoulder. "What do you see?"

Kiara's gaze tapered as she pressed closer, her nose nearly touching the stone. "I'm not sure if these are warnings or — "

Gears ground together, the pitch of metal on metal forcing my attention to the left. No one dared to breathe, to run, to do any of the things we ought to. We were stuck, immobilized, all while the sound of something large and heavy and dangerous *rolled*.

Shit.

"Definitely a warning!" Kiara screeched, shoving the Fox forward. Jake snatched Liam's hand and pulled him into a run,

Finn and Dimitri close on their heels while I took up the rear.

"Step to the left! As close to the wall as you can," Kiara shouted, tugging Emelia away from a pressurized stone. I would've missed the trap entirely. As I passed, I noted how the floor panel was raised a few centimeters higher, thin lines carving its edges.

"It's moving faster," Liam screamed, accompanied by a gravelly rattle.

"There should be a passage coming up on the left!" Emelia said, her voice rising above our ragged panting. Her boot connected with what appeared to be a skull. It shattered against the wall with a sick crunch.

"You certain?" I demanded.

"Yes," she replied confidently. As if I'd question her now.

I wasn't keen on Kiara being the first to rush into this unknown world—if she missed a marking and fell into a trap, I'd never forgive myself. But as it was, I remained at the back, ensuring the others caught up.

"There it is," Dimitri cried.

I twisted, watching in horror as a spiked ball the size of five men barreled toward us.

Our welcome gift had arrived.

Fear thrust my power to the surface. I lifted my hands at the precise moment fire and magic flared from my palms, from my chest. The flames blasted into the spiked ball, bouncing harmlessly off its jagged points.

I hadn't even made a dent.

"That definitely should've done *something*, right?" Jake screeched after my explosion prompted him to turn mid sprint.

"Left!" Kiara shouted, wrenching Jake to the side. She cried out a few more orders—left, right, middle—guiding us through the carnage like a general leading an army into battle. We avoided five pressurized stones and five near deaths, though, judging by the brittle abundance of human bones littering the ground, not many had been as lucky.

"There it is. Tunnel approaching on the left!" Emelia quickened her pace, practically shoving Kiara and Jake into the widening passage. She made sure she snagged Liam's cloak as she dove for safety.

Finn leapt headfirst into the channel, his massive body colliding with the ground with an audible thump. He lurched to his feet just as Emelia screamed for Dimitri, who was lagging, his breathing hard.

I'd all but forgotten him.

Whirling back, I grabbed him by the waist and tossed him over my shoulders. He was heavier than I anticipated, and the ball was less than twenty feet away—

We weren't going to make it.

Emelia must've known this, too. She hurtled out of the passage and into the line of fire. With the grace of a hawk, she lifted her arm and pressed a green button on the underside of the device we used to scale the wall. A silver grapple embedded into the stone, and when she aimed and struck once more, another grapple rooted into the wall opposite. A horizontal line of coiled metal rope hung across the passageway.

"Duck!" Emelia warned, and I grunted while shifting Dimitri, lowering us below the rope.

There was a snapping sound, the spiked sphere catching on the metal coil blocking its path. It broke through seconds later, but they were seconds we needed. I dove for the enclosure, Dimitri on my back, both of us tumbling to the dirty stones.

The ball rolled past, continuing on its destructive path.

We all gasped for air, everyone a shade paler. We'd been so close to death that I could practically feel its icy hand on my shoulder.

Kiara sat propped against the opposite wall, her chest rising and falling with strain, her scarred hands clenched into fists at her side.

To everyone else, she might simply appear fatigued, but I saw more than that. She may wrinkle her nose before a fight and occasionally bite the inside of her cheek when she was nervous... but when Kiara Frey was scared, truly scared, she shut down.

Completely.

Her eyes were empty, her face slack.

Speaking only to her, I said, "We're alive. We're whole."

I loathed that look on her face. That emptiness.

She flinched slightly, seeming to jolt back into herself. I sensed she needed the reminder, and I repeated it once more until life reignited her dulled features, bringing back the fighter I adored.

When she wrinkled her nose, I smiled.

Kiara brought her attention to her hands, flexing them as light whispered along the dark black-and-blue vines. They shone from under her shirt, up to her elbows, and even with the sleeves pulled down, there was no masking them. Something had happened when the shadow beast attacked, and she wasn't eager to share. As much as I wanted to push, I respected her wishes.

My mother, however, did not.

The Fox scooted over, creases forming across her brow. She leaned close to Kiara's scars, fascinated. "Hmm. A little darker than I imagined. I pictured them being a little less...pretty, as well."

"Pretty? They're grotesque." Kiara twisted her wrists, showing off the reedy lines decorating her palms. She hastily shoved them into her pockets, her eyes downcast.

The Fox laughed softly, the kind of laugh that was dark and brimming with trapped bitterness. "If you think that's bad, you've never seen the true marks of war." Her gaze flickered to

Finn briefly before she lowered it to her boots. "The scars that are made by hatred are the truly grotesque ones, ones you feel beyond the skin."

Finn cleared his throat uncomfortably. "What's the plan?" he asked, wiping away the sweat dripping from his shaved head. Squinting, I noted the gleaming of a few shimmering scars along the curve of his right ear. Somehow, I didn't think those were the wounds Emelia had implied.

My mother bristled at him. "We'll head down this tunnel, make a right, another right, and then we'll find a long, narrow passage we'll travel down for some time. There, we'll take a left. The gates should be at the end of that hall."

"Damn. She's good," Liam whispered. "I'm unabashedly jealous."

"You would be," Kiara teased, but her voice lacked its usual lilt. "If you had such a gift, you'd be extra annoying. You'd probably recite *all* the details of your excruciatingly boring books."

"Hey. Intelligence is sexy," Liam snapped, but he wore a gentle smile.

"Don't say *sexy* around me, please." She rolled her eyes, more of her armor sliding into place.

"Oh, grow up." Liam scoffed. "I have to watch you and Commander-Broods-A-Lot all day shooting each other longing glances, and—"

"If you don't shut up now, I'll personally do it for you," Emelia threatened, a slight tinge of pink on her cheeks.

She waved at Kiara, back to business. "We're gonna eat and rest a few hours, but after, I expect you to do your job and watch out for any concealed threats."

"More of that disgusting dried meat. I can't wait," Kiara mumbled, ignoring my mother's order. "What poor animal did you kill to create that atrocity?"

The Fox grinned broadly, a playful glint in her eyes. "Who said it was an animal?"

The look Kiara shared with my mother was nothing short of sly, and for some reason, my magic responded even while resentment warmed my blood.

Why had I thought it wise to seek the Fox in the first place? Her involvement could only bring trouble, and introducing her to Kiara? Disastrous.

If Isiah were here, he'd probably say something sensible and intuitive, like I had run to my mother seeking comfort when I was lost or some other sort of introspective bullshit. And he might be right. But the more time I spent in Emelia's company and in that of the men who followed and adored her, the more the seeds of my anger took root.

She'd taken in Finn and Dimitri—two lost souls in search of a home—yet she'd abandoned me, her own son. When I first saw her back in Fortuna, there'd been pure apathy. I'd considered only Kiara and her safety, along with the curse we had to break in order to free us all from the shackles of Patrick's treachery.

Now? Now I had time to think, and I didn't particularly care for any of my thoughts.

Jake handed Liam a pack of loose granola and plopped down next to him. They shared the bag, murmuring in each other's ears, sometimes smiling.

Finn tore into his meal with exaggerated gusto, while Dimitri stared blankly ahead.

The story he'd shared continued to haunt me. I marveled at how he could even get up in the morning after what he'd lost, a wife and daughter, both taken so horrifically.

If I ever had a family—

No. I shouldn't even entertain the idea. Not now. It was dangerous to hope and think of the future.

Deep down, beneath the feigned optimism I conjured, I

didn't actually believe I would make it out of this ordeal alive.

There.

That was the truth.

Kiara rose to her feet only to move closer to me, sliding down the wall at my side. Leaning her head on my shoulder, she asked, "Rancid meat?"

I accepted when she thrust the bundle closer, though when I placed a bite on my tongue, I barely tasted anything at all.

My eyes drifted to her sheath. The Godslayer blade.

If things went wrong, I had my answer. I was going to make sure Kiara walked out of this temple. Even if I didn't.

. . .

"Sleeping on me, boy?"

My lids opened with a start. Emelia hovered before me, one hip cocked to the side, a shrewd look causing her harsh features to turn even more severe. I must've drifted off because Kiara was gone, speaking in hushed murmurs with her brother and Jake. I hadn't even felt her leave.

"I was trying to until you interrupted." I shut my eyes again, hoping she'd go away and leave me in peace. When the rustling of clothing reached my ears, I knew she'd taken a seat next to me.

Figures she wouldn't listen.

"You're going to have to talk to me at some point."

"I certainly do not. Unless it pertains to the mission, I have nothing to say."

More silence ensued. More awkwardness.

"I would've ruined you, you know," Emelia said, so softly I thought I'd misheard her. "Even my mother believed I was... *wrong*. She never smiled at me a day in my life, and the single occasion she expressed any genuine emotion was when she held you for the first time."

I opened my eyes at that.

"We'd been on the run for so long, never staying in one place long enough to form attachments. She was paranoid, continuously claiming someone was after us. When I was younger, I believed her, but as I grew up, I assumed she was unwell." Emelia let out a harsh scoff. "Only at the end did she tell me the truth about our family, right before taking her last breath."

I didn't have words, and I didn't attempt to find them. Raina might as well have been nothing more than a legend. I couldn't wrap my head around her being *family*. A part of me still didn't accept it.

"Was it easy for you?" I shocked myself by asking. My tone was coarse and unapologetically glacial.

I heard her swallow. She understood exactly what I meant.

"L-leaving you felt easy at the time," she confessed, and something inside of me shattered. "But only because I thought I'd done the decent thing and that you'd have a chance to grow up in a safe place without the burden of our family."

I laughed, the noise unhinged. "You left me with a sadistic asshole. You ruined my life. And you did that because you didn't want a child to take care of. Simple as that."

Silence.

Why was there always silence when I least wanted it?

"Nothing to say?" I pressed, daring to angle my head and take her in. She froze, her eyes widening, her lower lip trembling.

"I—I thought..." she stumbled, scrambling for the right words when there were none. "I'm not *good*, Jude. I didn't think your father would be worse. I wouldn't have left you if I'd known what he'd do, and when I found out, I wanted to kill him. Flay his skin and—"

"Then why didn't you?" I jumped to my feet, uncaring that

my voice had risen in pitch. I sensed Kiara's heated gaze, yet she didn't intervene. "Why didn't you come back after you'd learned how cruel he was?"

My eyes burned, and it had nothing to do with magic.

"Because—"

"Because why?" I screamed, startling the others. They stood, their boots thudding too loudly in my head. I could hear too much, feel too much, and it was drowning me.

"Because I was afraid!" Emilia scrambled back. She pressed both hands against the wall, her lips parting like she wanted to say more. Which she didn't.

Coward.

The declaration hung in the air between us like smoke, and I inhaled its poison.

"I'm a selfish person, Jude, always have been. But regardless of my many flaws, I can leave this earth knowing that even though I abandoned you, even though I was never the mother you deserved, I left the best part of myself in you. Doesn't mean I'm not sorry. I'll always be sorry."

Emelia didn't wait for me to respond. She shot to her feet and all but sprinted as far from me as possible.

The word was useless. Hollow.

Sorry did nothing to ease the pain of my childhood. *Sorry* didn't erase her selfish choice, regardless of her wrapping it up in the guise of kindness.

Finn took up the space she'd occupied as I seethed. I wanted to be alone, and his presence was the furthest thing from what I desired.

"She's not warm and fuzzy, that's for certain. Gods know, I've learned that the hard way over the years." He released a brittle laugh. "People like her who've had to fight their entire lives, every second of every day, they don't know how to accept the *good* when it comes. I think that's what happened with you, boy. And while you don't have to forgive her, know that every year on the coldest day of winter, she leaves the city. I never know where she goes or what she does, but when she returns, she always carries the same scrap of blue fabric."

I froze. When I'd been left on my father's doorstep in the dead of winter, Emelia had placed her book of lore and her compass beside me. But I'd also been wrapped in a thick, blue woven blanket that was frayed on one side, almost as if a piece had been torn off.

Finn patted me on the back. *Hard.*

"It's easy to hold on to that hatred, son. But she holds a lot of hatred for herself, too."

He walked away, leaving me reeling, on completely uneven ground.

Hatred was safe, but forgiveness? Forgiveness was departing the home you'd constructed of thorns and steel and venturing out into the trees, into the unknown. Forgiveness could mean opening yourself up again and pretending as if you didn't fear the ones you loved twisting the knife into your back for a second time.

More than that, forgiveness also meant the chance to find peace. And that wasn't something I was familiar with. That frightened me more than the possibility of betrayal.

I sought refuge at the other end of the wall. Kiara allowed me to pass, perhaps believing I needed space.

When I settled as far from the group as I dared, I realized I'd been wrong.

A shy coil of ash and night snuck up to graze my arm. It caressed me, winding around my frame like a hug.

Turning my head, I followed the length of the shadow, spotting a glistening tear fall down Kiara's cheek. She hurriedly brushed it away and fixed her face into stone, but her shadows tightened, refusing to let go until I remembered I wasn't alone.

Chapter Thirty-Five

Kiara

It has often been argued whether shadow beasts have the potential to become their namesake. If they can slip between the cracks of reality and travel the planes of the world with freedom. Of course, that is a mystery that will never be solved.

Excerpt from Asidian Lore: Legends and Myths of the Realm

We'd been walking for hours.

Surprisingly, there were no more symbols or pressurized stones, though several decayed bodies decorated the floor, the skeletons mostly intact. I surmised they'd died from dehydration or injuries sustained from one of the earlier traps.

We journeyed on like this for some time, each tunnel a replica of the one before. The Fox navigated them with remarkable ease, stiffly pointing me in the proper direction as I led us all.

Jude had avoided his mother after their confrontation, and while I gave him space, my shadows couldn't help but sneak out and touch him every so often as we traveled.

I felt him now, lingering at the back of our group, his tension causing my shadows to flicker.

Perhaps leaving him to his thoughts wasn't such a good idea—

I froze as soft vibrations worked their way up my legs.

"The ground…" I crouched, placing my palm upon the cold stone. "It's trembling. You feel it?"

Emelia shot me a concerned look.

This place was alive, as alive as any creature in the mortal world above our heads. It had a pulse as if the god himself had given his life over to his shrine.

Jude crept forward, his eyes aglow. When I held up a hand to stop him, he jerked to a halt. His own hands were balled into fists, his frame practically shaking with the need to assume command—the only way he believed he could protect me.

We'd have to work on those misguided notions.

My shadows unfurled from my skin, peeling away to slip along the stones. They caressed the ground until the sound of a single gear clicked.

The Fox jumped backward as the floor gave out where my shadows had touched, the ground now a gaping void of black. The eleventh trap so far.

"Good call." Finn slapped me on the back and then offered me a hand. "I could get used to this one, Emelia." He crooked a thumb my way. "Between her and the smooth-talking sidekick over there, we'd make a fortune."

Jake pouted. "Hey, I'm not a side—"

"No," Emelia said tightly, cutting him off. "We work alone."

As if I were eager to join her band of thieves. Jake, on the other hand, looked more annoyed by the idea that he wasn't invited.

"Stubborn lass," Finn teased, reaching for a flask that certainly wasn't filled with water. "Can't even admit the truth when it's staring you in the face."

My focus landed on Jude. His nostrils flared whenever

Emelia glanced in his general direction. Their talk had gone disastrously, and she didn't seem eager for a repeat.

All I could offer was support, and he would have that from me in spades.

My back prickled as shadows unfurled, swirling around my periphery. I swallowed a gasp when I peered over my shoulder.

They looked like wings, although they were more batlike in appearance, the almost translucent ends pointed and jagged, the shimmering silver specks gleaming from the subtle breeze.

Jude's eyes landed on the rippling black wings jutting out from my back, and the tension in his jaw lessened. I found myself relaxing beneath his reverent stare.

He didn't smile, but his eyes brightened, causing my heart to skip several beats. I cursed myself as my mind wandered to the other night when it was just the two of us, alone. Heat scorched my cheeks, and I had to glance away before the others took note, though seconds later, a deep chuckle sounded from behind. Jude missed nothing.

It took all my strength to continue, my steps leaden, my pulse hammering at my throat.

Life-or-death situation, Ki, I scolded, even as the heat worked its way down my neck. I swore I felt him smile.

Thankfully, I kept my lustful thoughts under control as we avoided a slew of arrows in the next passage, which boasted a swinging ax. By the sixth turn, my shadows triggered a gaping pit filled with razor-sharp blades. Easily avoided.

That was the problem. It felt too damned easy.

When Jude announced it was nearly ten in the evening, Emelia called out for us to rest. "We're almost to the end," she said while Finn passed out bundles of food.

I sensed she, too, was on edge, wary of the ease with which we'd infiltrated the temple. I caught her rubbing at her chin, Jude grasping his at the same time, both in thought while they ignored their too-salty meat.

Dimitri took the opportunity to whistle his lullaby as I gulped down the precious remains of my canteen. The tune had become a steadying constant, and my eyes flickered shut as it washed over me.

It didn't take long for snores to fill the open hall.

The glow of the blue-tinged moon blazed brightly enough that I couldn't find sleep, Jude appearing to have the same problem. He pressed his body closer to mine, and I rested my cheek on his shoulder. Both our heads tilted up toward the sky, soaking in the breathtaking enchantment of the endless universe. Such splendor was unexpected in a place of death.

Jake assumed the first watch and was currently busying himself with a piece of rope, tying intricate knots.

When I met his stare and cocked my head to Jude with a knowing wink, Jake groaned and rolled his eyes. He knew exactly what I was asking.

"Come on," I whispered to the commander, easing up from his arms. He made a deep sound of protest, but he must've understood my intention well enough when I impatiently pulled him to his feet and guided him down the next hall. Then he followed without a struggle.

Far enough from the others, I cast my shadows out, the slithering black wisps forming a wall, blocking off the rest of the world. It came easily, calling them, and being *here* where I felt my strongest, I found a beauty in my power.

It could be used to kill, to maim, to destroy, but now, I reveled in the grace with which the threads of shimmering night moved, carefully secluding us in a realm belonging to two.

Iridescent light radiated from under Jude's shirt, his magic pulsing, his glow a steady heartbeat. And while my own light emanated, I didn't need to look down to see that my scar reacted the same way. I felt it.

"Trying to get me alone?" Jude asked, shooting me with his oh-so-stern commander look of disapproval. Tease.

But yes. He was very much correct.

After seeing him earlier, after his confrontation with his mother, all I'd desired was to speak with him, to help carry the burden of his fear. But I couldn't very well do that in front of our crew.

"What if I did want to get you all to myself?" I wound my arms around his neck and held him close.

"So inappropriate." He leaned down, his lips an inch away. My breath hitched.

"Propriety was never really my thing." It hardly mattered where we were—reality slipped away whenever the commander looked at me with such fierce intensity.

I'd never experienced something this strong. This unbreakable. I wanted to make him feel the same way.

"Are you all right?" I asked, bracing for his reaction.

His face was stone, his lips pressed into a thin line. Just when I'd assumed he wouldn't answer, Jude stunned me into silence.

"Why is it that we care so much for those who often care so little about us?"

I flinched at the rawness of his voice, at how it cracked at the end. I tightened my grip around his neck, not allowing him an escape. He didn't fight the cage I'd made.

"I think we can't help it," I answered truthfully. "We want to pretend we're not torn apart by their apathy, but deep down, all we ever want is their approval. Maybe it's fucked up and we want it more *because* they shunned us so easily. Or it's simply because their lack of approval reinforces our disappointment in ourselves."

Jude glanced away from me, and I immediately hated that.

"I thought I'd gotten over it, but it looks like I was wrong," he murmured, jaw tight. "There are so many others I could've sought for answers, but at the first opportunity, I went running to her, begging."

Drawn to him, to the sorrow that eclipsed his features, my shadows curled protectively around his frame.

"For years I was numb under Cirian's command," Jude said. "It wasn't until the Mist, until *you*, that I began to feel again, and it's been both a gift and a curse ever since. Now I can't *stop* thinking. About the past and my mother. About my father. About you and what we're going to lose—"

"Enough." I grabbed his chin and made him face me. He could mourn his past—that was understandable—but the future was ours. And I'd be damned if I let him think nineteen years made up an entire life.

"You are unbelievably frustrating sometimes, you know that?" I laughed, shaking my head. "I mean, one second you look at me like we have nothing but time, and the next, you're acting as though we've already lost. We haven't lost anything yet, so you're gonna come to terms with the fact that you may very well be stuck with me at the end of all this. I'm not leaving you. I'm not running. And possibly for the first time in my life, I'm not afraid. You wanna know why?"

Jude inhaled sharply. I wasn't sure he dared exhale.

"I'm sick and tired of everything being decided for me all because Raina fell from the skies and we lost the light. We've spent our lives buried beneath the threat of death, and that's no way to live. I'm not done with this life yet, and I sure as hells am not done with your brooding ass."

Jude's lips twitched, just one corner lifting, but the sight of it was like a drink of ale on a snowy night, warmth trickling into your belly, your head growing exquisitely fuzzy.

"You know I blame you for this." He motioned between us, and I frowned. "You gave me a taste of hope, and now I'm a mess at the idea of losing it. Gods, Isiah would have laughed at the sight of me now. Talking about my emotions."

"He would've been thrilled," I said, grinning. "From what you told me, he was always telling you to live a little. To let loose. I saw the love he radiated when he looked at you."

Isiah. Jude's only real family. Dead in the Mist.

My heart gave an excruciating tug at the memory of those final moments, Isiah covered in blood, his eyes shutting forever.

I'd been falling for Jude then, so much so that I'd have given anything to bring back his friend. I still would.

Jude swallowed thickly. "Eh, Isiah might've been happy. But I wouldn't have heard the end of his teasing." He tugged me closer until my head rested over his erratically beating heart. "I could tell Isiah liked you. Even if he told me to stay as far away from you as possible. He knew you were trouble."

I made a sound of mock disgust. "I take back all the nice things I said about him."

A hesitant chuckle shook his chest, and I sighed, enjoying how he embraced me, both of us needing the contact. I wondered if anyone had ever dared hold him like this.

"Thank you, Kiara," Jude said, breaking the peaceful silence.

I craned my neck, shooting him a confused look. "For what?"

Jude's fingers went to my chin, drawing me back so he could place a tender kiss on my temple. "Just...thank you for always finding me. Whether I like it or not." His grin was charmingly lopsided.

My lips hovered above his, not quite kissing him, but close enough to feel his warmth. My skin tingled, heat rushing across my face, down my neck, and to my chest.

"You'll never be alone in the dark again," I whispered. His eyes shut, a tremor working down his body. "But if you do somehow slip and fall, I'll be right behind you."

Saying the words aloud cemented my faith, and while that frightened me to no end, I savored the sense of belonging. I hated myself for ever thinking that my feelings for Jude were due to our shared power.

I wouldn't doubt us again.

Slipping my hand from Jude's neck, I brought it to his cheek, my fingertips grazing his coarse stubble. He leaned into me, eyes flickering shut, a sigh leaving him.

"Promise me you won't do anything foolish if we fail." *Like steal the Godslayer from my sheath and carve out the missing pieces for me to accept.* He'd do it, too, without hesitation.

Jude blinked in surprise. The golden sheen masking his eyes dimmed, morphing back to the ones I'd gotten to know and love. One brown and flecked with gold, the other chaotic and full of mystery. While I adored the golden light he radiated every so often, I preferred him like this. Wholly himself.

"I can't make you that promise," he whispered, and my heart plummeted. "But I can promise to do everything in my power to find another way first. I'd give anything to wake up beside you. To watch the rays of dawn slide over your face, welcoming you to the new day. That would be the ending I'd prefer. Should I get to choose."

Imagining waking up next to Jude—our limbs tangled together under silken sheets, the early sun casting light upon his naked torso—drove my pulse to dangerous levels.

"I can't picture a better ending, either," I said, my voice low and raspy. I wanted to curse his ability to render me nothing but a girl whose heart had been stolen. "Now, you better kiss me before—"

Jude's lips silenced me. He held me like I was something fragile, his fingers in my hair, his hold firm yet soft. Every brush of his tongue sent shivers down my spine, and each of my exhales, he captured for himself.

"If we don't have much time"—Jude drew back, panting— "then I best show you all the many, *many* wicked ways you've utterly ruined me."

My mouth parted as his lips left mine, leisurely descending to graze my jaw, the column of my neck. A gasp left me when he reached my chest, leaving featherlight kisses in his wake.

With every caress, every reverent touch, Jude spoke his adoration, his devotion. I greedily unbuttoned my shirt, wanting more. Always more with him.

Once I was free of my tattered shirt, the gold in his eyes eclipsed all else. He made a deep rumbling sound before worshiping my body, savoring me as he reached the band of my trousers. When he halted on the button, he grinned, his single dimple appearing utterly devilish.

"Would you like me to show you another place I've been dying to kiss you, Kiara Frey?"

Shit. If he kept saying words like that my heart would give out.

I shook my head up and down so hard, I strained a muscle.

"Then lie back." Jude languidly unbuttoned my pants, his calloused hands nimble as they slid over my hips. His eyes never left mine. "Let me worship you properly."

I did as he asked, and I didn't speak when his mouth touched my sensitive flesh, but I bit my lip to keep from calling out his name loud enough for it to reach the mortal world and all the stars shining upon us.

Chapter Thirty-Six

Jude

The boy is a thorn in my side…and yet I cannot help but respect him. I often equate him to a little brother, although our relationship is, at most times, strained. I want him to succeed. Maddox is a worthy soul. If only he'd realize that, too.

Unmailed letter from the capital of Sciona to unknown recipient, year unknown

It was well into the next day when we reached an impasse. This particular tunnel was unlike all the others, filled with jutting levers and odd hooks, the passage considerably narrower than the ones before.

The walls were veined in red, the glaring streaks marring the white marble. Crushed bones were scattered throughout, the only trace of the explorers that had ventured this far and failed. The farther we went, the fewer remains we had found.

It wasn't a good sign.

"I say we send Ki and her shadows in first," Jake said, earning a glower from Liam.

"How kind of you, Jake," Kiara said with a sigh. "I so adore being used as the battering ram."

I interrupted before Jake could open his mouth and damn

himself further. "Something is off about this one." My insides warmed, seeming to confirm my hesitation. "I...I have a feeling her shadows aren't going to cut it."

"Could it be a puzzle?" Liam scanned the route with keen interest.

"You and your puzzles." Kiara ruffled her brother's hair, Liam swatting at her hands. "But no. I think this is the final section before we reach the palace, and I doubt the Moon God would play fair and provide rules."

From what I'd pieced together, the placement of the various levers didn't have any rhyme or reason. There were no obvious crevices in the stone, and everything flowed seamlessly together.

"Standing here is wasting time we don't have." Kiara traveled forward, making it three steps before Emelia huffed and trailed after.

A line formed, all of us placing our feet exactly where Kiara stepped, mindful of any creaking sounds or shift in the air. Not even a wind blustered.

Kiara's darkness soared ahead, caressing the stones, pressing at the levers with care. Nothing fired at her or sliced off her head, but that didn't mean I wasn't gritting my teeth and clenching my fists.

She can handle her own, I reminded myself, but it took considerable effort to keep the protests from leaving my lips. Caring about someone would be the death of me. Not gods or magic or sinister temples. Just a girl who'd bewitched me. What a way to die.

Halfway through, Kiara twisted around, smiling as though she'd been gifted a fresh cup of coffee. She waved about the passage and said, "See, nothing is happening—"

The floor shifted. Moved.

Lifted.

Liam shrieked as the patch of ground he stood upon

launched straight into the air, faster than a hawk in flight. His cries echoed as the three-foot slab climbed higher and higher, and the flailing lad did everything he could to stay balanced, to keep from teetering off the precarious ledge.

At the back of our procession, I could only watch as Kiara rushed in his direction. I screamed her name a second before the ground in front of her *dropped*.

Time froze as the marble split and a cloud of snowy dust choked my lungs. Kiara dove to the right, grasping at the smooth wall and narrowly avoiding slipping into the growing crevice.

Suffocating fear made a home amidst my heating magic. That had been far too close, and I immediately regretted allowing her to lead, however insolent that made me.

Every muscle ached to move. To do anything but stand still, watching uselessly.

Observe, then act.

It was what Isiah ingrained in me, but fuck if I didn't want to dive headfirst for Kiara and damn the consequences. I had to remind myself I'd be no good to her if I triggered another snare and fell to my death.

As I inched toward Kiara, the earth beneath Finn and Emelia rumbled. Dimitri wrapped his arms around the pair, holding on tight as the slab of stone they stood on lifted, rising higher than Liam's platform.

"Stay where you are!" I shouted, seeking a way out of this mess. Again, I couldn't discern any grooves or seams on the ground and the walls—

Wait.

I made out nearly imperceptible holes, no larger than the size of a pea. And of course, every member of our group was stationed before one.

"Update?" Emelia barked from her position above. She gripped Finn's torso for dear life, Dimitri practically a human band of steel around them.

They had about three feet to work with, and Finn was a large man. It wouldn't be long before one of them went plummeting off the side.

"There are sensors in the wall," I said calmly, more so than I actually felt. I donned the role I'd grown familiar with, shoving down the panic battling to break free.

Poring over the slats for signs of additional hidden triggers, I gingerly crept forward. "I'm not sure how they work, but they don't seem to be triggered by Kiara's shadows."

"That's not very helpful," Jake groused. "Any *good* news, Commander? Or are we all just winging it here? Because as someone who typically enjoys winging it, I can say with all confidence I'd prefer not to at the moment."

"I second that!" Liam shouted.

Kiara had gone rigid, but her eyes...they were wide and shifting in every direction.

I recognized that look. It both thrilled and terrified me.

"I have an idea," she shouted, a spark of cunning igniting her gaze.

"Hurry!" Liam griped. "You know I hate heights."

She gave him a pointed look. "You're like six feet off the ground—"

"Not the point."

She studied the rest of the corridor as her shadows rolled off her shoulders in black waves. Her magic slithered ahead, lingering before each sensor, endeavoring to activate the next trap. When nothing happened, she squeezed her lids tight in concentration, her nose wrinkling. I watched with pride as her shadows spun with a golden sheen. A soft heat entered the space, and I recognized Raina's gift working alongside her darkness.

With my enchanted sight, I noted how her breathing turned erratic, her pulse point thumping wildly.

An ominous click sounded. The floor below her outstretched magic collapsed, a gaping abyss at least five feet in width blocking the path to the temple.

"I think it's activated by warmth. Body heat!" She grinned, the gold in her shadows flaring in triumph.

Gods, my girl is brilliant.

"Yay." Jake groaned, his body trembling against the wall he leaned on. I made my way to him, *slowly*, and peered over the rift. There didn't appear to be a bottom…or not one I could make out.

Kiara's combined magic snaked out and through the hall, each burning tendril swaying from side to side as she concentrated on using the foreign fire of a goddess. Her arms trembled with exertion, all of her attention aimed at commanding her newfound abilities. It truly was a sight to behold, and the scar across my chest fluttered pleasantly.

An arrow whooshed into the air.

It flew through her black and gilded clouds and struck the stone with a resounding ping. Three more arrows blasted free, all clanging harmlessly against the opposite wall. The next sensor she triggered shook the entire cavern, and I realized too late what was happening.

"No!" she screamed, her head twisting my way.

The walls were *closing in*. Moving to crush us. We wouldn't have time to trip all the sensors safely. We didn't have time to be careful.

We had to move. *Now*.

No longer hesitating, I sprinted to Liam's swaying platform and offered him my hand. Jake cautiously peeled away from the wall he leaned against, and ran to Emelia and her men, his movements jerky and panicked.

Together, we worked as one unit, communicating only with our eyes. Fear had united us, but it would not lead to our defeat.

I opened my arms wide and allowed my thrashing magic to take the reins.

It did so eagerly.

A shimmering light bled from my skin, my entire frame glowing like my mind was sharpening with painful focus. Every muscle burned as energy tore through me, and the more it saturated my blood, the brighter the passage became, my body emanating light like a star in the night sky.

Whatever we'd soon face, I would be ready.

Jake's eyes flashed to me, the blue of his stare sparkling under the blanket of my power.

His lips parted, but his hands never faltered, steadying Emelia as she descended from the platform. Finn came next, trailed by Dimitri, who required the encouragement of all three in order to take their hands and make the leap.

It was chaos. The marble walls fractured as they slid closer together, stealing the precious space we'd need to make a run for the next corridor and to safety. From what I could see, the walls were solidly in place, only this hall working as a trap.

With Kiara on the other side of the gap, I was the closest to Liam, and his only chance of survival. My muscles burned as I ran toward him. I threw out a hand when I was near enough, ignoring how his hesitation upset me.

"Take it!" I commanded, struggling to snatch his shaking hand. His platform never ceased trembling, and it rocked uneasily back and forth, making it impossible for him to gain secure footing.

"I can't!" He squeezed his eyes as if he might shut out the world. "I'm going to fall. I—"

"You'll die if you don't move," I said roughly. My body pulsated in time with my heartbeat, time dangerously ticking by.

Strength infused me, a rush of adrenaline I used to shove at the wall closest to me. It halted, even moving back an inch or so.

Gritting my teeth, I said, "Either jump or be crushed to death. But decide now."

Immediately, Liam lowered to a crouch on weak knees. Letting go of the wall, I took my shot, leaping to snatch his wrist. With a hard yank, I brought him down. Before we collided with the stone, I propelled us into a roll, using my body to take the brunt of the fall as I cradled him. Liam landed on my chest with a muffled grunt.

"The walls are getting closer!" Kiara urged, her shadows spiraling out from her back, her face twisted with anxiety. She stood across the splintered rock, waving us on, shouting for her brother and me to run.

The passage was tapering, closing in at a much faster pace, leaving but a few feet on either side. Footsteps pounded at my back, the others running to catch up. With Liam's hand in mine, I navigated the traps that had already been set off.

When the chasm lay before us, I brought Liam to a stuttering halt. Even with my added light, I couldn't make out the bottom.

"You better jump with me this time," I threatened, and Liam made a distressed sound of protest.

I squeezed his clammy hand in mine and took the leap, compelling him to follow. His echoing scream pierced my eardrums, his grip painful.

We landed gracelessly on the other side, both of us tumbling, scrambling for purchase. I heaved him to his feet as the walls groaned, taunting us with those final inches of life. Another foot had been lost.

Emelia nimbly bounded across the gap, and Dimitri and Finn joined her, though Dimitri lost his balance, sending himself careening into Jake. I heard a distant crack.

"After me!" Kiara was sprinting, her shadows leading by only a couple of feet. More arrows flew as the end neared. We were almost safe, nearly out of harm's way—

Arrow after arrow fired in front of Kiara. Each glistening point whirled by mere inches from her face, and I swore I died every time.

All I could do was hold on to Liam. He fought with me, braving his fear and struggling to reach his sister as he neared the corridor. But he wasn't fast enough.

When he stumbled, I leaned down and dug my shoulder into his stomach. Heaving him up and over my back, I continued racing against time.

Three feet of room remained, the walls once again picking up speed. After lunging into the connecting hall, I gently lowered Liam and whipped around. My light washed across Emelia as she dove forward, safe.

The walls scraped at Finn's broad shoulders as he wriggled to safety. His linen-clad arms grew dark with blood, the smell of copper potent.

"Dimitri!" Finn called out from the protection of the adjoining tunnel. He screamed into the darkness. "Where are you, mate?"

He should've been here by now. Had he tripped? Did a rogue arrow hit him?

With my blazing sight brightening the dim tunnel, I finally spotted a slim form limping through a cloud of dust, his foot dragging behind his body.

Shit. I thought I had heard the sound of a bone snap a minute before.

"Dimitri's injured," I said numbly, rushing to the closing walls and attempting to pry them open, just as I'd shoved the wall back when rescuing Liam. This time, my magic waned, the power running low. Sweat slid down my forehead as I grunted with effort, but the stone refused to stop. If anything it felt like they were moving faster.

Without warning, Dimitri *stopped*.

He stopped running, and...stood there, staring straight ahead, straight at me, the remains of my magic casting his gaunt face in an eerie glow. Chills raced down my spine when he began to whistle a familiar tune, the sound broken. Two tears dripped down his stubbled cheeks. Two tears for two souls lost.

He wasn't giving up. He was *accepting* his fate. Dimitri wouldn't have made it, even if he tried.

Kiara screamed as Dimitri was crushed, his eyes still upward, his lips forming names I couldn't hear but knew. Bones crunched and blood sprayed, a macabre burst of red that would paint these walls for eternity. He never lowered his head.

With a heartbreaking thud, the passageway closed, sealed together without a crease.

The Fox collapsed to her knees, a soft keening sound leaving her. Finn grasped her shoulder, wetness in his eyes.

I prayed the man had returned to his lost family. Praying was all I could do.

The temple had finally taken a life, and I couldn't help but sense it was hungry for more.

Chapter Thirty-Seven

Kiara

We live two lives: one where we are made of flesh and bone, and the other where we are made of memories.

Asidian proverb

I rose on unsteady limbs, unable to meet Jude's eye. Wrapping my arms tightly around myself, I worked to find my center, to ground myself when I felt as if I were standing on the edge of a cliff in a storm.

Not one of us had the nerve to speak.

I'd seen death in the short time I'd been with the Knights, but Dimitri's death…gods. The mere thought of it had bile rising.

While I hadn't known the man for long, I sensed his loss. Could feel the absence of him like a missing blade in my arsenal. But my pain was nothing compared to Finn's or Emelia's.

Finn rubbed at his face, his eyes glassy and red, tear tracks staining his cheeks. He and Dimitri had been close.

Jude's gaze locked on him, his body swaying as he raised a hand, silently debating reaching out for the man. I wondered if he thought of Isiah then. How he'd lost his friend in a similarly horrific way.

Before Jude could act on his impulses, Emelia slipped into

Finn's arms, her hands gripping fistfuls of his shirt.

"He's with them," she said somberly, voice cracking. "He's with his family again."

Finn swallowed thickly. "But *we* were his family, too," he choked out. A tear slipped down his cheek. "I… He just *stopped*. Why did he stop? He could have—"

"No." Emelia grasped Finn's chin. "He wouldn't have made it, and he knew this. Dimitri understood the risks when he accepted this mission. He chose to come." She sighed, resting her head on Finn's chest. He clutched her tightly, both arms wrapped like a band around her waist. His body shook with sobs.

Jake and Liam bowed their heads, Liam uttering a soft prayer. I, however, glared at the space where the tunnel had been, anger seeping from my pores.

It wasn't fair. Not that I expected the world to be kind; it wasn't in its nature. What destroyed me was how the world seemed to keep knocking down those who'd experienced more than their share of pain.

Jude cleared his throat, his stare hardening as the commander in him assumed control.

"We have to keep going," he said, grimacing at the callous words. There should've been more time to mourn, but that wasn't our reality—time wasn't our friend.

His jaw feathered, and he glared at the wall, his hands curling into fists. He'd tried to stop it, tried holding the walls from colliding, but in the end, he failed.

I knew a part of him blamed himself.

"Come on, Finn," Emelia coaxed, keeping an arm around his torso. Finn nodded curtly, mechanically. He wiped away his tears, though his cheeks remained damp. While her face betrayed nothing, I grasped that she needed his support as much as he did hers.

I nodded my agreement, dazedly moving to the front. My

anger continued to burn like an eternal flame.

Jake ushered Liam after me, sparing Jude a glance to make sure he didn't lag.

Jude's glow from earlier was diminishing, leaving only his eyes alight. His power had erupted, become something bright and fierce…but without the third piece of divinity, he couldn't maintain his strength. He looked beyond exhausted.

My throat tightened, my eyes prickling. Before a tear fell, glimmering strands of onyx fluttered around my periphery, my shadows caressing me, petting my cheeks and hair. They were gentle, timid almost in their effort to soothe the tension tightening every muscle. I needed every ounce of confidence for what came next.

"Be alert," I warned, my voice stiff. "There are no symbols I can see." My steps were forceful, each impact sending harsh vibrations up my legs.

I couldn't bend now. I had to remain strong for the others. To pretend that Dimitri's death wasn't ripping me apart from the inside out.

When the final bend approached and we rounded the next corridor, all air in my lungs heaved out in a rush. I couldn't stop the slight tremble that racked my frame.

The palace.

We'd made it to the gates.

Chapter Thirty-Eight

Jude

I've spent my entire life seeking invaluable artifacts and treasures, hoping to fill a hole that can never be filled, and I've gone and screwed up the one thing I actually gave a damn about.

Note found in the desk of the notorious Fox, City of Fortuna

Beyond the looming gates was a set of double doors the size of ten men.

The smooth, silver sides were trimmed with diamonds, each striking gem perfect in cut and clarity. A copper moon hung over the apex where the doors joined, the metal hammered, the tiny dips and grooves reminiscent of crumpled parchment that had been unfurled.

"Who wants to go first?" Jake inquired, clearly not offering to do it himself.

Covered in blood and riddled with scrapes, we were all ragged and exhausted and in no mood to open a door that was guaranteed to lead to more misfortune.

Unsurprisingly, there weren't any eager hands being raised.

The talisman we needed had to be hidden somewhere in

this palace, the key to our salvation tauntingly within reach. We'd summon the god and be done with this. Whatever way it eventually ended.

No point in delaying fate.

I kicked open the doors with my boot.

Glittering white dust descended from above like falling snow. Bells chimed from somewhere deeper in the heart of the palace, a harp and lute joining together to form a disquieting melody.

I grasped Kiara's wrist as she stepped forward to enter, and I shook my head. After I failed to save Dimitri, there'd be no argument that I was going in first. Still, I felt her glare burn the side of my face.

The luminous powder continued to fall, coating my entire body as I stepped through.

I saw nothing at all for horrifying seconds, my limbs numb as a whispering voice danced across my mind. It was muffled and tinny, but it sounded strangely familiar.

When the dust settled, so did the voice.

I'd entered a grand foyer, larger than the one in Sciona's palace. Velvet loungers and fine chairs were dispersed without order, positioned beside tables covered in trinkets or dishes burdened with flaky pastries. The crystal glasses were filled with amber liquid, bubbles rising to the top with a soft hiss.

I craned my neck, taking in the carved walls, depictions of the stars and the constellations etched by an artist's hand. Not one inch of the space had been left untouched. Yet even the walls couldn't compete with the focal point of the room—the grand marble staircase.

Twisting metal vines formed a delicate banister winding up to the second-floor landing. I couldn't make out much, a thick fog twirling playfully at the top of the steps, shielding my view of what lay ahead.

Moonlight touched my skin, prompting me to look up past

the grandeur of the foyer. There was no roof to shield the open sky, the star-laden heavens clear and gleaming.

While stunning, a nearly perceptible air of dread smothered its beauty. I could taste it on the tip of my tongue, its bitterness a warning.

I reached for my blade...only to notice my clothing was not my own.

Luminous black boots rose to my calves, and my trousers were spun of the softest black fabric. A silver belt wound about my waist, and a crisp white shirt with mother-of-pearl buttons climbed to my throat. My weapons, along with all I'd brought with me into the temple, were on my person, but the sheath that carried my blade was a fine leather.

Footsteps pounded, the sound of others entering the palace causing eerie echoes to fill the cavernous space.

I spun around. Like mine, my companions' filthy attire had been replaced, their faces wiped clean of grime. Yet the only one I noticed was Kiara. Everyone else blended into the background.

Her bright red hair shined, and intricate braids crowned her head. Kohl lined her eyes, bringing out the amber in them, her lips painted a deep plum.

My mouth parted when I took in her clothing. Silk trousers clung to her hips, showing off every curve perfectly. Her top was cinched, a seamless corset with a *V* neckline. A black ribbon was tied around her neck, securing a gauzy train that drifted behind her, the gentle wind picking up its ends. Her sheath shifted locations to her thigh, the Godslayer blade on proud display.

In the span of a second, I'd forgotten our mission, forgotten what I'd done these last weeks, and entirely failed to recall even my own name.

"Gods," I breathed, entranced. "You look—"

"Ridiculous," she huffed, her face scrunched in annoyance. I walked up to her and pressed my finger against her wrinkling nose.

"No, you look like a heartbreak waiting to happen."

I traced her lower lip with my thumb, the plum shade garnering my entire focus. Her lips parted, warmth tickling my skin. She swallowed thickly, and my gaze fell to the delicate column of her throat.

"I think I look lovely, as well!"

I flinched at the sound of Jake's voice. He shouldered between us, flashing his silver jacket, white threads spun decadently along the hem. His dark hair had been pushed back and styled, and a hint of kohl lined his lower lids, bringing out the intense blue of his irises.

"You would be prancing around and admiring your clothing at a time like this," Kiara scolded, even as a gentle laugh escaped.

Liam walked into the center of the room, standing uncomfortably beside his sister, itching at the stiff material of his clothing. He wore something similar to Jake, although the top buttons of his shirt had been undone, his curls still effortlessly careless and grazing the collar's high back. It lent him a roguish look that Jake seemed to appreciate. He couldn't look away, and when Kiara groaned, shoving him closer to her brother, he happily obliged.

"If you insist," Jake called over his shoulder.

Emelia and Finn came last, my mother wearing loose-fitting trousers and a white tunic, her short hair appearing wet, styled out of her face to expose all her sharp angles.

"As if this couldn't get any worse," she mumbled, brushing at her new clothing with a lethal scowl. That scowl deepened as she surveyed the luxurious foyer, her painted lips thinning. She clutched her bag, which had transformed into the color of midnight, the material a matching silk. Ripping it open, she rifled through, relaxing when she discovered all her possessions remained.

"What's that?" Kiara rushed past, aiming for a glass side table positioned next to an elaborate lounger large enough to fit three. She picked up a single folded piece of parchment.

"You've made it this far. Dine and drink before we change the world," she read aloud. "What does that mean?"

On cue, the music I'd heard when I first entered played a song too ethereal and airy to have been performed by mere mortals. The despondent chords of a harp descended from the second story, a lute soon joining in, both instruments creating a melody that reminded me of the sensation of free-falling.

Lovely. A welcome party to our own funeral.

"It's obviously a trap," Liam remarked drily. "I've read enough books to know a trap when I see it. The haunting music is a nice touch, though."

Kiara made a face. "I thought you stuck to reading science and math texts?"

Liam's brow furrowed. "I'd have thought you would've discovered my secret stash of adventure and romance books. I'm disappointed."

The music swelled, compelling us toward the stairs and all the mysteries we sought. My heart pounded, my feet itching to move, to give in and feel the vibrations of the song.

"We left a world of ugly nightmares for one with beautiful lies." Emelia shook her head. Her eyes were clouded, the same as the others. "I don't see any choice but to head up, but be on your guard. This place has to be enchanted." She frowned, looking at her fine clothing. "Well, obviously it's enchanted. But more than that, it's…"

"It makes me want to dance," Kiara supplied with a grimace. "And drink and dine and *smile*." She shuddered.

Jake's expression sobered. "Definitely not good, then."

Kiara glided to the stairs, her gauzy train rippling and moving with each step. She grasped the silver banister, her hands aglow with magic, light reaching out to brush against her onyx and navy scars. Peering over her shoulder, she asked, "Well, are you coming?"

Chapter Thirty-Nine

Kiara

Not much is known about the Moon God, but he is notorious for his love of dreams, where mortals may experience just a touch of a god's power.

Excerpt from Asidian Lore: a Tale of the Gods

This wasn't a temple or a palace.

It was a dream.

I all but floated up the steps, the music luring me closer, urging my pace to quicken.

The longer the ethereal song played, the more weightless I became. I watched myself move forward as if I were hovering above my body, my silk trousers gleaming beneath the radiance of the overbright moon. It was so brilliant and welcoming, demanding my devotion—

Someone hooked their elbow through mine, tugging me into a solid chest. I smelled a familiar earthen scent, and it invaded my mind until it transported me to a memory. A dream of a memory trapped in a blanket of mist.

"Kiara?" I whirled around, finding Jude's face scrunched in concern. "What's wrong?"

"Nothing," I said too quickly. *Just that I'm being seduced by the damn moon.*

I could tell he didn't believe me.

Jude's hand returned to my waist, his grip firm, his steadying touch grounding me in reality. He didn't let go as we allowed Emelia to take charge, guiding us up the grand stairway.

Everything felt wrong. *I* felt wrong. And the worst part was knowing things were about to get worse.

The higher we climbed, the more my pulse hammered in my throat, right beside the delicate ribbon tied there. Cold sweat banded my brow, and I slipped my finger under the satin and gave it a jerky tug. The damned thing was choking me, forcing me to focus on every nervous swallow.

Jude paused and noted where I fought to free myself. He pulled out his blade and gently glided it beneath the fabric. The sharpened tip sliced through, and the gauzy train and black ribbon fell from my shoulders. It slipped down the steps, rippling like water.

I exhaled, swallowing thickly as I clutched my bare throat.

"There," he murmured, sheathing his blade. "Now you won't be hindered when you go on a murdering spree." The corners of his lips quirked, and that heavy feeling in my gut lessened. He was putting on an act for me. One I appreciated.

"There's something up here!" Emelia shouted, a level above us.

We sprinted up the stairs after her, only to stumble to a halt when our boots struck the seventh-floor landing. It had been demolished, the stairs blocked by rubble mixed with glittering amethyst stones the size of my head. The thief dipped down and swiped a finger across one of them.

"This was recent," she mused. "Not all the dust has even settled yet."

"*He* knows we're here, and he may be watching us already." We had to find the talisman and trap him. If only we knew what it looked like.

Without a path around the debris, we had no choice but to return to the sixth floor.

Our boots thudded and echoed in the circular tower, no one making an effort to maintain stealth. Time was moving quicker than sand in an hourglass. Hells, it was more like *water* in an hourglass.

We burst beyond the sixth landing and into an antechamber of dazzling copper. It made up the walls, the ornaments, the flooring. The moon's light didn't reach this room, and sconces were lit throughout, though they barely cast a steady glow. Darker furnishings decorated the space, though they weren't polished like the ones on the first floor, a thin coating of dust dulling their shine. I peered around, shivering when I noticed dozens of portraits, all depictions of a man wearing different faces but possessing the same eyes.

Gray irises so light and piercing, I shivered.

Some of the renderings portrayed him in a somber daylight, others cast him in a sheen of moonlight, his face a masterpiece of joy and unattainable perfection.

I noted how his smile lifted more with every illustration as if he had a secret he was finally preparing to share with the world.

Jude lingered by one, a painting of the hooded god, only his eyes visible. He lifted his finger and traced the gray eyes with a frown.

He said nothing as I gripped his hand and pushed on, though he glanced over his shoulder once more. I wondered what he saw that had given him pause. But save for Liam's ragged breaths, all was silent as we strolled through the gallery, and I was too on edge to break the hush.

I felt watched. Every painting we passed possessed eyes that appeared to follow us, the subject trapped within the frame unnervingly lifelike.

Relief swept through me as we turned a corner into a new hall, this one thankfully devoid of unnerving portraits. Numerous closed doors were erected on either side, all adorned with a silver crescent moon for a handle. Embedded diamonds shined from the metal, their clear radiance in stark contrast with the deep warmth of the copper walls.

The voice of caution I so often ignored urged me not to open any of them, no matter how my curiosity begged. They felt…sacred. And dangerous.

My dark magic lifted in my chest whenever we passed one, like it craved whatever lay on the other side. Another reason I held back.

Frost trickled down my spine and I shuddered. I craned my neck, half expecting someone to be standing behind me. There was no one.

Jude gently nudged me, a question in his eyes.

"Be careful," I warned, shaking off the sensation of that glacial touch. "I feel like something is in here with us. Watching."

My words were hardly above a whisper, but Jude nodded and tightened his fingers around mine.

A door lay at the end of the grand hall, and this time, I wasn't strong enough to ignore its influence. This one lured me with the promise of a new tomorrow.

The knob was reminiscent of a full moon, tiny pieces of opal flecking the otherworldly white stone. The surface itself glowed from within, the chipped gems radiating tiny pinpricks of light across the walls. It reminded me of hundreds of twinkling stars.

My body vibrated with raw energy—we were so close to the Moon God's inner sanctum, I could practically taste the ancient power of his magic saturating the air.

My shadows flickered at my fingers as if in confirmation.

Undoubtedly, it was a trap, but it didn't matter. We'd made it this far, and there was no other way but forward.

Jude maneuvered in front of me protectively, earning an eye roll that he couldn't see. His body was tense, and even through his fine jacket, I perceived how his muscles strained. "Stand back," he said. Advice that I entirely ignored.

Placing his hand on the knob, he rotated his wrist. Gradually, it creaked open, an ominous screech that had the tiny hairs on my arms rising to attention.

Nothing happened. No demon or monster tumbled out to grab us, no pointed teeth aimed at our throats. Just spine-chilling silence.

I tugged on Jude's hand. The stubborn man resisted, trying and failing to angle his body before mine. He let out a deep groan of frustration when I sidled next to him. He knew he'd lost.

A hundred heartbeats passed until we walked through.

Purple light the color of the softest Midnight Blooms swathed the enclosure, coming from everywhere and nowhere all at once. There were no moon or stars above, the domed roof made of lustrous steel blocking our view.

Rather than loungers and elegant tables and chairs, there were piles of silver coins. Among the mortal riches dispersed about were weapons, books, and figurines.

I spotted a bow and a quiver of arrows with Maliah's crest nearly hidden under a pile of lush fur pelts, the body of the arrows framed by a circlet of the richest red. The pelts themselves were free of symbols, though I couldn't help but sense a divine quality to them, the luscious brown shifting to russet and back with each new blink.

Arlo's sigil was branded across some of the nearby books, three stalks of grain sprouting from the underside of a deep *V*. I could imagine his anger if he'd discovered them here. Arlo had always been protective of his weapons, and books were weapons by themselves.

The Moon God...he'd stolen the sacred tools of his fellow

gods. But why?

I spun around to voice my suspicions just as the door slammed shut behind us—

Vanishing entirely into smooth stone as if it were never there at all.

Fuck.

"Don't just stand there!" Emelia shouted, rushing into action. "Look for another way out!" She flung aside priceless treasures like they meant nothing, and even Finn grimaced when she knocked over a glass sculpture that would've gathered a respectable amount of coin.

"Help me," she snapped, and I'd never seen Liam move as quickly as he did when she cast her trenchant stare his way.

A whirring noise that sounded like pattering rain drowned out my thudding heartbeat.

"Sand," Jake yelled, pointing a trembling finger to a statue of Silas, the Water God, his wizened face and muscled body framed by stone waves. Behind it, sand trickled out from a hidden spout, the color unusual in the way it shifted shades, from gray to blue to lilac. A lever clicked somewhere out of sight, and more of the sand rushed out and into the space from the other side, knocking over a pile of Arlo's books in the process.

"We need to get higher up," I said calmly, even if calm was the farthest emotion from my grasp. Arlo had taught me that showing fear could bring it about in others, and sometimes, a good leader had to be strong for the men they led. Even if it felt damn near impossible.

Twenty feet away, a stack of coins formed a massive mountain of wealth. I motioned in its direction, screaming at my friends to climb. We could figure out a way to get out of here, but not if we suffocated under this sea of sand first.

Jake's eyes bulged in his head. I practically dragged him over, and even with a not-so-gentle shove onto the pile of coins, he still hesitated to climb.

Jude snatched my hand and forced me higher, his other hand gripping Liam. Whenever my brother stumbled and coins skittered out from beneath his boots, Jude caught him and eased him back into place with a care that would've warmed my heart had it not been beating erratically.

"There's something up here."

I tilted my head, discovering Emelia already past us all. Damn, she was quick. She'd nearly made it to the top of the pile and was pointing wildly at the ceiling.

I focused my attention on where she directed, finding the oddest sight.

There was a handle fashioned like a crooked star in the very center of the dome above our heads. Surrounding it were crisp seams, the lines forming a rectangular shape.

A *door*.

Emelia jumped, fruitlessly aiming for the handle, attempting to wrench open the portal.

She huffed each time she missed. Coins flew every time she landed, a couple smacking me in the face.

Below, the sand had thoroughly coated the chamber's floor, rising steadily, making its way up. At the rate it had poured into the room, we wouldn't have much longer before it buried us.

Jude and I reached the summit just as Finn hauled himself up, his footing tremulous due to his weight and the ever-shifting coins. He leapt for the handle, and as he was over a foot and a half taller than Emelia, he managed to open the door on his third try.

Finn eased Emelia onto his shoulders, and she grasped the edges of the frame, pure darkness welcoming her from above.

With a grunt, she thrust up and through the entry. I held my breath, terrified we'd made a mistake and that the door led to nowhere. Or worse.

A hand lowered down through the opening.

"Come on!" Emelia called, waving her arm around. "Someone grab hold!"

The walls violently shook, the ground rocking back and forth. Fissures formed and stones plummeted, the entire room set to erupt.

I watched in relief as Emelia took my brother's hand, Jake keeping him steady as they assisted him. I released my breath when he vanished. He called out for Jake a second later.

Finn supported Jake's weight, guiding him to the others, but Finn's muscled arms shook, his exhaustion evident.

"Go, Kiara," Jude commanded. Heat emanated from his skin, his magic awakening.

"You better be right behind me."

"Always," he rasped, his eyes molten.

The bodyguard whirled on me, his deep brown skin covered in sweat. He held out his arm, waiting for me to take it. I peeked at Jude, wavering, not trusting that he wouldn't do something heroic and foolish if I went before him.

"I'm not leaving you," Jude said, his voice weighted with conviction. His nostrils flared as his words penetrated my doubts. "We finish this together."

I would've grinned had we not been in yet another life-or-death situation. Maybe I'd gotten through to the stubborn boy after all.

Finn grasped my outstretched hand as the chamber hissed and moaned, and something ominous creaked. As I was flung up and into the air, I heard another groan followed by a whoosh. A new spout must have opened.

"Hurry the hells up, child!" Emelia cried, swinging her arm about. I had no choice but to close the gap and snatch it. Her lean fingers locked around mine, and with surprising strength, she hauled me over.

I landed in a circular room, my divine vision awarding me sight. But I didn't linger on the new room or the peculiar door that stood at its center. I twisted back, readying to assist Jude. Emelia extended her hand, and the commander hastily glanced between us.

Sand gradually rose, now mere feet from grazing the bottom of Finn and Jude's boots. He gritted his teeth and lunged without Finn's aid, snagging both our hands and squeezing tight. Liam grabbed my waist to steady me, Jake doing the same for Emelia.

"I got you!" Emelia promised her son. I could see her muscles strain beneath her silken clothes, but a fire not born of magic brightened her eyes. She shrieked as she yanked herself back.

He tumbled to the ground at my side, his power surging, lighting the space around us in a warm gold.

But we weren't safe. Not yet.

"Finn!" The Fox hovered above the open door, and Jude replaced me to offer his hand to the bodyguard. Finn was sweating profusely, his chest heaving. The sands were less than a foot away and rising swiftly.

"Come on, you fool, jump!" Emelia was panting, wetness lining her eyes. "We've been through worse, and I can't lose..." She stopped there, biting her lip. Instead, she screamed, "Take my hand!"

Finn groaned as he reached up, but he missed her flailing fingers by less than an inch.

He tried again. Once more. On the third attempt, he made contact. Jude grasped his other wrist, and I held on to his forearm. Jude shouldered all of Finn's weight, but his mother wouldn't relinquish her hold.

Together, they gradually eased him up, and in a minute he'd—

The sand touched the bottom of his boot.

I'd seen a lot of grisly things in the past few weeks, but never before had I seen a man's foot crumble to dust.

Finn's screech was heard in the depths of my soul, his grip on Emelia and Jude loosening, his face turning a sickly shade of gray. As the sand climbed, it ate away at his heel, the polished leather of his shoe dissolving to dust.

There was no blood, no dripping red to emphasize the absence of his foot. It was as though the sand cauterized the wound while it greedily consumed his body.

"No!" Emelia lurched backward, moving him inches higher. The sand had passed his ankle, and Finn's eyes shuttered, his throaty screams a thing of nightmares.

"Not you!" Emelia cried, tears freely dripping down her sharp cheeks. "I can't lose you, too!"

Finn's eyes were closed, the man likely passing out due to the pain.

"Mother! You need to let go!" Jude screamed. He'd never called her mother with such sincerity before, and if she heard the endearment, she didn't let on. She couldn't look away from Finn, and her hand refused to release his.

Her love for Finn was a tangible thing, and it bolstered my strength, inciting my shadows to unfurl as I moved into place between Jude and Emelia. Night rushed from my shoulders and surged from my palms, fully enveloping Finn.

In all the chaos, I remembered something Arlo had told me years ago, back when he'd pretended to be my uncle. *"Panic is a weakness you can't afford,"* he grunted one day during practice. *"The only way to overcome your doubt is to center yourself. If your mind is off-balance, your body will be, too."*

I might feel anger toward the earth god for his deceit, but his teachings taught me how to be strong. And strong, I'd be now.

As my magic gripped Finn—holding his heavy weight—I shut out Emelia's cries and the whooshing noise of the poisonous sand. I pictured a glen that belonged to me and my brooding commander. In that very place, I'd exposed my deepest self and found a peace I hadn't believed possible.

From somewhere in the background, Jude whispered my name. Even with my mind working to command my magic and pull Finn to safety, I could feel his warm exhales fan across my cheek.

A great tug jerked me forward, but hands were once more around my middle, keeping me centered. My brother without a doubt.

"Kiara!"

I opened my eyes. A gust of wind and night sent me barreling back, the glen torn from my thoughts. I tumbled onto my hands and knees, struggling to glance up, hoping I hadn't failed another person.

Emelia's shout reached me.

Finn lay in her arms, unconscious and still except for the subtle lift and fall of his chest. Liam shoved the door closed with a grunt, his breaths agonizing wheezes.

"He's alive," Emelia sobbed, hugging Finn's head to rest over her heart. "He's—he's breathing."

Jude hovered above his mother, watching as she clung to Finn. An indiscernible look passed across his features before his focus landed on me.

I'd done it. I used my shadows and bent them to my will.

My darkness hadn't killed. It *saved*.

CHAPTER FORTY

JUDE

I left my heart on a doorstep in Mena nineteen years ago. I miss it with every passing day, and I wish I'd been brave enough to realize I could have been enough for you.

<small>UNMAILED LETTER FROM THE FOX, YEAR 45 OF THE CURSE</small>

My mother was crying.

It struck me as such a peculiar sight that I didn't react right away.

Kiara did.

She worked her arms around Emelia—who still hadn't released Finn—and pushed herself against my mother's chest, the silk of her corset absorbing the overflowing tears. They'd run rampant, unrestrained as they trickled down from her kohl-smudged eyes. Kiara shooshed into Emelia's ear, running her scarred hand up and down her cheek.

I hadn't moved since we'd bolted the door. Neither had Jake or Liam. They bowed their heads, unable to look upon the wounded bodyguard.

As I watched the mother I'd never known cry over the man she'd loved, another thought struck me: she'd given up so much for this mission, prepared to lose *everything*. Emelia had enlisted those closest to her knowing how treacherous this endeavor would be.

And she'd done it for *me*.

In that raw moment where streaks of misery and relief wet her ruddy cheeks, I saw her for the first time.

Broken. Flawed. *Human.*

Somewhere along the way, whether it was before Raina delivered her the truth or after, my mother had been shattered.

Hells, I'd been broken, but I also had support in Isiah, and now, Kiara. Finn was hers. I'd been wrong to assume that my mother was an unfeeling wench. A woman without remorse.

She'd left me because she was frightened, and I suspected being the daughter of a fallen goddess hadn't been easy. Moving from town to town to avoid suspicion. Never knowing who or *what* you were. And a mother who likely thought her distance would protect her child.

It must've been incredibly lonely.

I hadn't realized I'd moved until I stood before her.

Tentatively, I reached around Emelia's waist, easing her to my chest, my hands drifting up her back. She must've sensed it was me, because she melted in my arms, her grip on my shirt fierce as she fisted the material. She whispered my name and repeated the same word over and over again until it echoed like a grief-riddled mantra.

Sorry.

Neither Jake nor Liam interrupted, the boys delving deeper into the recesses of the dimly lit room. I detected no imminent danger, so I indulged, allowing myself to hold the woman that gave me life, a slowly rousing Finn resting between us.

Emelia continued to repeat the lone word, and the final time she murmured it, I responded.

"I...I understand," I sighed, meaning it. I didn't forgive her, not yet—I wasn't a saint—but I *understood.* "It's all right." I shushed her as Kiara had done, and she sobbed harder after my admission.

The minutes slipped by, one joining the other, time a distant, flimsy thing. Only when Emelia sniffled and drew away did I allow my arms to fall. Coldness greeted me, replacing her warmth, and the lost child in me wanted to run back into her embrace.

Emelia brought her red-streaked stare to me, the subtle glow of my eyes shedding light upon every fallen and smothered tear.

We didn't say another word to each other. Nothing cliche or sentimental. And that was all right. Instead, she took one of my hands in hers and squeezed.

Such a simple thing, and yet years of hatred and blame and *anger* slipped from me like forlorn sighs.

"It seems like the sand cauterized Finn's wound," Kiara observed, stepping into view, her luminous strands catching the golden rays of the lingering magic seeping from my skin. Her braided hair had come nearly undone, loose tendrils falling into her eyes, the ends slipping down to graze her stained top. I imagined the pristine silk would soon be marked with blood.

"Jude, maybe you and Emelia can help transport him," she suggested. Kiara scanned the small room, doubt causing her to chew her bottom lip. "I don't know what else is in store for us if we remain here."

Jake reached into Finn's discarded satchel and produced a box of matches. He walked over to where two sconces were bracketed to the wall and lit a spark, holding the match until the flames caught on the wick. The meager light glanced off a metal doorway encased in shadows.

The next door, and hopefully, the final room.

"I'll help carry him," Emelia said stiffly, her familiar mask sliding into place. I wouldn't have known she had been crying if not for the redness of her eyes or the wetness still drying on her rosy cheeks. She clenched her jaw and tilted her head to the doorway.

Kiara gave us room as I shifted a groaning Finn from my mother's arms. He was heavy and barely cognizant, but with Emelia on his other side, we managed to carry him with greater ease.

My girl had drifted toward the dim, beyond the light of the flames.

"This door feels different," Kiara said, apprehension darkening her words.

I cast my gaze forward, the subtle light I exuded allowing the others to take in the finer details. Several moons were etched onto its unblemished silver surface, tiny inlaid gems of blue and purple sparkling like vibrant stars. The metal lit up brilliantly.

Kiara released a sudden gasp.

"What is it?" I asked, my adrenaline spiking. In my grasp, Finn jerked, his pulse growing stronger.

"It's...guarded. I can practically taste the magic coming off of it," she explained. I frowned. I didn't perceive the enchantment she spoke of, and that worried me.

Liam crouched next to his sister. The pair of them worked together, each gripping their chins in thought. They had similar mannerisms, and I even caught sight of Liam's nostrils flaring at the same moment as hers.

"Hmm." Liam leaned forward to inspect a larger piece of gemstone. Lifting his hand, he aimed for the twinkling stone—

A brilliant flare erupted the instant his finger connected, forcing us all to shield our eyes against the onslaught of blazing light.

Kiara's shadows whirled from her shoulders, enfolding her brother.

The light went out as quickly as it appeared.

Finn grunted as if in pain, and Emelia immediately whispered in his ear, calming him as his eyes fluttered halfway open.

"What the hells was that?" Kiara yelled, grabbing for her brother's hand. He winced. "Your finger is fucking *blue*, Liam."

Liam's finger, the one he'd used to touch the door, was indeed blue. He grimaced when she flipped it around to examine the unusual wound. It reminded me of frostbite. A few of my soldiers had lost their fingers and toes when we'd ventured to the far north during the Dark Winter a few years back, hoping to squash a rebel uprising.

"And it hurts, so there's that," Liam said with a strained smile. He tried to yank his hand back, but his sister wouldn't allow it.

"Emelia, do you have anything you could use to wrap it up?" she asked tightly, her worry bleeding into her voice. Before the Fox could answer, Jake jumped into motion, searching the contents of her satchel. He came away with a roll of fresh linen.

Kiara hovered like a mother hen as Jake assumed control, and only when he scowled at her did she give them room.

"Let me know if it's too tight," Jake said gently to Liam, his tone not one I'd heard before. Cautiously, he wound the linen around Liam's finger, taking great efforts to be careful. When he finished, I watched in shock as Jake leaned down to press a kiss to Liam's injury. He held on to him long after the job was finished.

Jake had grown attached, his usual swagger absent when Liam faced any sort of danger. I wondered if it was new for him—the intense concern.

"I got him, Ki. Go on." Jake motioned to the door. She lingered on her brother, but finally, she tore herself away, knowing he would be safe in Jake's arms.

She stared upon the portal's surface for far too long for my comfort before whirling around. "Fuck," she cursed harshly, frustration evident in her eyes.

"Was that a good fuck, or a bad fuck?" Jake asked with another furtive peek at Liam.

"Take a lucky guess," she mumbled as she caught my gaze. "I'm the only one that can enter."

Hells no. "And why's that?" I grated out, my muscles instantly tensing. Before she could reply, a howling wind swept through, blowing our hair and whipping at our fine clothes. It came from nowhere and everywhere, and Kiara's lips parted in alarm.

"Can you hear them?" Kiara canted her head, moving frighteningly close to the door. "There are so many…"

"So many what?"

"They sound like…like *prayers*," she mused, blinking rapidly as if in a trance. "Not all of them belong here. Some are calling out for Lorian or Silas. To the other gods and goddesses."

That made no sense. We were in the Moon God's temple. Only his prayers should be heard.

"Maliah…" Jake began softly, his brow scrunched. "Back in the Pastoria Forest, she told us she didn't have the same power as before, the same abilities. I wonder if—"

"He's stealing prayers." Everyone turned to Kiara. "The God of the Moon, he has to be stealing them to weaken the others. Prayers hold power, and without them…" She trailed off, not needing to finish her thought. We all knew.

If the Moon God was robbing the deities of their prayers, then he'd be unstoppable, and it would explain why they hadn't banded together to take him down.

Emelia, who'd been silent until now, said, "The conniving bastard." She shook her head in disgust. "The prayers directed to the other gods haven't been answered in many years. At least, I don't hear about the miracles like I used to. That's why most people pray to the Moon God. Why they feel as if the rest of the immortals abandoned their people."

Kiara nodded. "And this door...it's enchanted. Sealed so only the Moon God or his...creations can enter." She bit the inside of her cheek. "It reminds me of the forest when I was little. Of the—"

"The shadow beast," Liam finished for her. His sister squeezed her eyes in reply. She'd already faced her greatest fear, and I understood how much it had wrecked her.

But she was right. As much as I despised it, Liam's injury was the proof.

"That's why it has to be you," I said, hating every word.

Wetness glistened in her eyes, and when she gazed upon me, it felt final.

She held my stare. "If any of you enter, you'll die."

CHAPTER FORTY-ONE

KIARA

The treasures of the gods are disguised as everyday objects.
They hold immense power, infused with magic by the deities
themselves. While impressive, none are as remarkable or as
elusive as Arlo's looking glasses, mirrors crafted during the
birth of the world. They display the owner's greatest fears
and most ambitious desires. Too late is it discovered that they
expose nothing but lies.

EXCERPT FROM ASIDIAN LORE: A TALE OF THE GODS

Jude's searing gaze burned into me.

I looked anywhere but at him. Truth was, looking at Jude
now, knowing what could happen—

I was terrified I'd walk through that portal and never come
back. That *this*—here in this cursed tomb—would be the final
time I'd see his hauntingly handsome face.

Liam was arguing with me, his voice a distant screeching in
the background. Only my heartbeat thudded clearly, pounding
away in my ears, fraying my already unraveled nerves.

Jake joined in on the yelling, but my attention stayed locked
on the door that would either lead me to salvation or damn me
to the underworld.

I was a creature of both light and dark…and only I could do this.

Through all my inner turmoil, the steady throbbing of my scar remained constant, reminding me that Jude was *right there*. At my side. Waiting.

Look at him, I scolded. *This might be the last time.*

As much as I didn't wish to think that way, I had to. If I *did* die, then what would happen to the sliver of power inside of me?

Sounds came rushing back as reality settled in like an intolerable itch.

The blade.

Reaching down, I slipped my fingers around its hilt and retrieved the one tool that could slay a god.

I looked at Jude.

Hardly any emotion showed in his expression, and his ethereal glow diminished until I could make out the traces of gold dotting his brown iris. Even his left eye had returned to its cloudy blue-white haze.

The pain scrunching his features froze me in place.

This next step was bigger than us—we stood on the precipice of salvation. Our realm finally being brought back into the light. Children with full bellies and fields thriving with healthy crops.

If I didn't make it…Jude needed the Godslayer. He wouldn't rest until our enemies were struck down. He'd find a way to save our people from vengeful gods.

We locked eyes as I offered him the blade I'd kept secure throughout our little journey, the onyx metal vibrating. He hesitated, like I knew he would, his lips twisting. He understood why I presented him with the cursed weapon now.

I let out a relieved sigh when Jude grasped the handle. He tucked the weapon into his jacket, his eyes searing into mine.

I never expected to find Jude on the day of the Calling. Never expected to journey into the Mist with him and fall for the sensitive and caring man behind the mask of death.

And how could I not?

I glanced at his old scars, the ones he'd received before his magic awoke. He hated them, the red slashes given to him by his father. He was just a boy when he'd been injured, and he had to look in the mirror every single day and be reminded of the man who called him worthless.

While Jude beheld a monster, I saw a man who rose above pain and brutality, who stepped into the flames and fought his way to the other side. He may believe it was his trauma that marked him, but I saw only his strength. His beauty.

"Do you trust me?" I asked, lifting onto my toes to touch my temple to his. His arms were around me, the action instinctive.

"Always," he replied, his voice cracking.

"*When* I return with what we need, we'll finish this together," I said. "We'll figure a way to save us both, and then, we'll have that ending you're so fond of."

I felt his lips quirk into a smile, and I melted, shutting my eyes.

A pleasant warmth flared in my chest, and in my mind, it was just us and the rising sun, and all the possibilities laid out, ours for the taking.

In this dream, I wore armor that gleamed gold, and Jude… he was radiant in a tunic of ivory with gilded threads. A warrior and a god.

I let myself envision the future I desperately desired, and in return, my scar seared bright and unapologetic. It didn't hurt, but it overwhelmed in a way that reminded me of how love felt.

Jude drew back, his finger moving to my chin so he could hold me captive with his trenchant gaze. "I trust in you, I do, but I swear to all the gods, Kiara, if you don't come back through that door, I will raze this entire realm to the ground."

"So bossy."

Jude shook his head, strands of black hair falling low over

his temples.

"I love you, Kiara Frey," he whispered, barely loud enough for me to hear. "You have years of ruining me to do yet."

It wasn't a demand so much as a plea, and it knocked down the final wall barricading my heart.

"I...I love you, Jude Maddox," I said, *finally* releasing the words that had been trapped. I should've spoken them aloud a hundred times, and yet they'd always failed to form on my tongue, even though my actions relayed what my voice could not.

Perhaps I hadn't considered myself worthy or maybe I'd been too fearful of what would happen should I make this *real*. Terrified it would be taken the second I put my love into the universe. But I said those three words now, and a great relief whispered through my soul. My heart felt light.

His face went slack, a breath whooshing from his lungs. I glimpsed a matching relief spreading across his harsh features, his eyes wide with yearning, with a happiness that would surely vanish the moment I gave him my back.

Before Jude could form a response, I severed contact, looking to the others, who watched on quietly. Liam swallowed thickly, trying his best to smile. Jake, holding my brother in his arms, his eyes gleaming with unshed tears. And the Fox, who held Finn steady, dipped her chin in encouragement.

My body felt too hot, the sudden flush causing my hands to shake. I brushed it aside as nerves, knowing deep down, it was a lie.

Something had shifted when I told Jude I loved him, and while the curse didn't break and the world wasn't cast in light— not that we could see it from inside the temple—it felt like the start of a great change.

Not that it mattered. I still had to finish this by myself.

I sucked in a deep breath and pressed against the handle, and then I walked through.

Chapter Forty-Two

Kiara

The moon is seen as a beacon of hope, yet it rises at a time devoted to nightmares and brutal truths. And the sun, while it provides a sense of safety, shines a light on the humans when they're at their most cruel.

Excerpt from Asidian Lore: a Tale of the Gods

The world was white and bleached of all color.

Fog swirled around my boots, around my silk-clad trousers. I took a step, peering at the ground, trying to discern what I stood on, but I might as well have been walking on a cloud.

I could see nothing but the white glow surrounding me, and the only sounds were the whispering of prayers, the words too light and airy to make out.

Five more steps and I saw a staircase. The steps led up, higher than I could see, so steep it might as well have been a ladder. Wind whistled in my ears, the lilting melody a taunt of Dimitri's lullaby. I began the climb, feeling adrift and numb.

Whatever this place was, it robbed me of a clear head.

I rose, higher and higher into nothing. I had to make it to the top, to the end of this stairway. To the possibility of saving Jude and myself.

Kiara. My name was whispered on a breeze of cloying blooms, rising above the gentle prayers, the thousands of voices all morphing into one lyrical song.

Gradually, the dense fog cleared.

A landing opened to a wall of purple stones, all crushed and glimmering, sparkling like vivid flames. It was stunning, otherworldly, but my focus lay on what hung before me.

An intricate silver mirror was affixed upon a wall, reflecting my wonder. Reedy vines and thorns wound around its frame, all twisting together seamlessly in an endless loop.

My breath caught. I looked…different. Not myself.

While stained, the silk corset and matching trousers hugged my frame, the material tailored specifically to my figure. My face belonged to that of a stranger, all made up and smokey, seductive almost. The girl in the glass smiled, seeming to like what she saw.

Yet I *knew* I frowned. Could feel the tug of my lips.

Enchanted, I thought. It had to be spelled, and I trusted nothing but my own magic.

On either side of the oval mirror hung two smaller replicas.

The one on the left appeared older, the material tarnished and the surface mottled. On the right, the looking glass shined too brightly for me to see clearly. My eyes straining the longer I stared. I had to look away lest it blind me.

My name sounded again, and I spun around. No one was there. Just the fog.

As if drawn by an invisible thread, I wandered to the mirror on the left, craving to look upon its faded surface, to peek beyond the speckled silver, and discover what truths it hid.

Before my eyes, a scene played out, wisps of smoke slithering around a lone hooded figure in the night. Atop a cliff, he stared out over a modest village, his back to me.

The moon was his sole companion, even the stars not

deigning to come out and play. I couldn't help but feel his melancholy as I looked at him, steadfast in his watch, like he aimed to protect the people sleeping soundly at his feet.

The image shuddered and blinked out, replaced by a new one, of the same broad-shouldered man. He must've waited until dawn, because when the orb I knew to be the sun rose in the sky, his shoulders slumped, and he tilted his chin down, away from the village.

A whirl of smiling faces flashed, leaving the man and his lone watch behind. I witnessed people from all over Asidia, their eyes twinkling as they mouthed Raina's name. They loved the sun and felt safe below its welcoming presence.

The next scene was the man once more, his features still obscured, night cloaking the realm and drowning it in darkness. He clenched his hands into tight fists, and I recognized the power emanating from him, shadows curling up and along his back. They formed the prettiest wings I'd ever seen—glittering black that quivered and swayed, a metallic sheen giving them a dreamlike quality.

Silver and purple light seeped from his form, trickling down into the slumbering town, through windows and under the cracks of doors. Instead of bright faces, I saw sleeping forms, soft smiles on their lips whenever a spark of the man's power graced them, soaking into their skin.

Dreams. He was granting them dreams.

Night transformed to day, and the sun appeared, the people shucking off sleep and rising to praise the sun once more. They bowed to statues of Raina, praying to her, lending their devotion.

This cycle repeated, and it felt like years until the man returned and despondency shrouded his entire frame, his wings drooping and dull.

I sensed his grief deep in my bones, his loneliness. He wasn't appreciated for the comfort he provided. The dreams he gifted.

The man was overlooked, every night, and still, he sought to bring the people peace once their eyes had fluttered shut.

The image on the mirror's surface fell away, and now only my face stared back at me.

The God of the Moon was misunderstood. From what I'd seen, he cared deeply for the people, only to get nothing in return. Over the centuries, he had grown bitter, and a part of me didn't blame him.

I traveled to the mirror on the far right, yet no images played out like before, the glare it cast too bright. It forced me to return to the center.

Coils of black shadows circled behind my back, my face growing into a distorted blur.

Squinting, I stepped closer still, nearly nose-to-nose with the glass. Something was taking shape alongside me...or rather, *someone*.

I jolted backward. The hooded man had replaced me, his imposing figure taking up the entire frame of the mirror. He wore a cloak of satin, soft blue threads decorating the hems. I ached to see his face, but he never turned, just stared out into a growing sea of night, and while I sensed triumph radiating from his every pore, there was also a sense of fear. His neck tilted back as he gazed up at the sky, but it wasn't the moon he sought...

Whispers belonging to a thousand voices—nearly identical to the ones flooding the temple now—all spoke at once, and the man raised his arms high, embracing them all. He captured them—even the ones speaking the names of the other gods—the incandescent luster he radiated growing more and more potent.

"He's stealing prayers," I murmured, confirming what we already knew. Seeing it before my eyes was another thing entirely.

And yet, he didn't feel evil. Not in the way that Patrick had once he revealed his true self.

This enchanted mirror bestowed emotions, not merely images, and this enigmatic god emanated a true sense of purpose and love.

I tore my focus from the mirror's surface. The Moon God wasn't set on harming us. He thought he was going to save us all, and in the process, he would finally be loved.

Something glimmered just out of sight.

A single black gem. It stood out among all the purple stones and glass embedded in the wall. Without thought, my fingers traced its smooth facets, and a shudder worked its way through me, the hairs on my nape rising.

The scars spider-webbing my hands and arms matched the otherworldly gem, and my blackened fingertips flashed with an iridescent hue as I dug my nails around the edges, trying to pry it from its rocky prison.

Powdery dust flew, and I inhaled a lungful of silt, but I pressed on, cursing until I yanked it free.

I held the peculiar stone that called to me in the most frightening of ways.

"I was wondering when you'd show up."

Shoving the stone into my pocket, I whirled around, adrenaline freezing my blood.

The King of Asidia stood five feet away, his silken white robes lending him an air of false purity. The notorious silver mask curved about his face, his pointed chin and thin lips the only visible features aside from his dull, clouded eyes.

I stifled a gasp, my pulse hammering at my throat.

Cirian may have been a pawn of the Moon God, but I hadn't expected him to be *here*. In the god's innermost chambers, hundreds of feet beneath the temple.

"King Cirian," I snarled, his name like poison. "What are you doing here?"

His presence sharpened my thoughts, my true mission returning to me in a rush—this man aimed to kill me. To kill Asidia's hope.

The king took a languid step in my direction, his narrowed eyes drifting to my pocket, the black gem concealed within. He *tsk*ed.

"That doesn't belong to you," he said, his voice colder than steel. "And here I thought you'd have died long before you reached this point. A shame, really."

I advanced, my blade out and at his throat in the blink of an eye.

A twisted smile prospered on his lips.

"So quick to anger," he chided. His voice sounded muffled now, as if he spoke from a distance. "What would your dear grandmother say if she saw you now? Aurora, I believe it was? Such a duplicitous traitor. If only I had gotten ahold of her before death took her soul."

I flinched, but my grip didn't waver. My grandmother hid many things from me, but I had to believe she'd done so for a reason. That she was fighting for the right side.

"What are you?" I didn't need to clarify; we both knew what I meant. He could try and distract me with my grandmother's name, but I wasn't that naive.

"Are you asking if I am *him*?" Cirian canted his head, dark hair tumbling over the silver of his mask. "I thought you already knew the truth."

His arrogance made me want to carve out his larynx.

"Tell me the truth, then," I seethed, my temper rising, my shadows slithering across my hands, winding around the fingers guiding the knife at his throat.

Whoever he was, this man had tortured and tormented Jude, and for that, he deserved an excruciatingly slow death.

I would deliver it. *After* I got answers.

"I am everyone and no one at all," he replied. "I am a product of a dream."

When his cackle rent the air, I lost the little control I had. My blade slipped, nicking the fragile top layer of skin. But he didn't appear to care.

Or bleed.

"Don't speak in riddles," I snapped, eyeing where blood *should* be trickling free. "We're well beyond games."

Cirian made a thoughtful noise, a humming deep in his throat. My blade shifted deeper. Still, no blood rose.

"You know, it's better this way," he said, glancing around the room as if seeking an invisible audience. "He actually listens to the prayers and has answered more than any other immortal. Since Raina fell, he's risen to the challenge, though all his hard work has hardly been appreciated. I hope that given time, the people will embrace the night as they should have ages ago. They'll see all its beauty and the peace it could bring."

"Peace?" I asked, my hand beginning to tremble. The sense of wrongness seized every muscle as his words settled over me. Cirian admitted my fears—he *was* a pawn. Just like me.

For some ridiculous reason, battling him felt safer. Easier than an unknown face hiding in the shadows.

"There hasn't been a single war in decades," Cirian continued. "Since he took control, the people have settled. The sun brought the humans delusions of power, whereas he brings them calm."

How absolutely deranged. "It's been peaceful because we've all been working to bring back the sun."

Cirian sighed. "If that's what you wish to believe."

I shoved the blade farther, the skin beginning to flay at the edges of the incision. I pressed until black rot oozed, the viscous liquid trickling from the cut and bringing with it the aroma of death.

Flashbacks from the Mist and the masked men flooded my

mind, my knees growing weak.

"R-raise your mask." My command echoed…as did his ensuing laughter. "I said, raise your damn mask!"

When Cirian's bitter laughter grew shrill, I made the decision for him, thrusting the gaudy silver from his face.

A scream ripped free from my throat as my nightmares became my reality. He had *no face.*

A black void of swirling ash churned where the mask had lain, the rest of his skin cracked and fractured. He was like a clay pot in an oven, the temperature too high. He chuckled still, as bits of himself fell to the ground, crumbling to even tinier pieces.

"I'm only the beginning," he warned, his voice hollow.

He laughed while his torso splintered in half, one side sliding to the right. Black rot dripped to the floor, a squelching noise filling the air as his arms split off at the elbows.

His lean fingers creaked as they snapped off one by one, the sickening popping noises causing nausea to churn in my belly.

It was as if the mask was enchanted to keep alive the illusion of a living man. Now that I'd removed it, the twisted spell holding him together had been broken.

I watched in disgust as the King of Asidia disintegrated into a cloud of dust and brittle bones. Only foul-smelling black smeared the ground, covering the gray splinters of bone, the blood as foul and pungent as the masked men from the Mist.

A flare of searing hot light flashed behind me.

Spinning around, expecting another foe, I found only my own reflection. I stared into the largest mirror, my features stretched in horror. The silken clothes clinging to my body were drenched with black blood. It trickled down my cheeks. Slipped from my eyes. My ears. The corner of my mouth.

A soundless scream parted my lips. The girl wearing my face was a nightmare.

It's not real, I thought. *It's not real.*

The amber of my irises evolved into silver. Blood oozed from the corners of each eye, rivulets of black glancing down my cheeks.

It's all in your imagination. You aren't that thing.

I couldn't turn away. My limbs were frozen, my stare held in place, unable to leave the polished surface and liberate myself.

The prayers I'd heard earlier came back in a nauseating rush, the cacophony of voices prompting me to thrust my palms to my ears, where that viscous blood flowed. The louder the voices became, the more my body trembled, and I fell, plummeting as an ear-shattering scream pierced the air.

I drowned in an overwhelming wave of prayers, and soon, I couldn't separate one voice from the other. I suffocated in the thousands of pleas sent to the gods who couldn't hear them even if they wanted to—

Because they'd been delivered *here*, to the Moon God's temple.

People didn't realize how precious a simple prayer could be. The unspoken words cast to the skies in times of need were born of pure and raw human emotion. They came from a part of a person's very soul, and in that way, they maintained a life all their own.

Right then, staring into this mirror, it felt like I was peeking into a side of my soul that frightened me. And yet *I* couldn't seem to gather the strength to muster a prayer myself.

A dull ache throbbed in my ribs, my chest, up to my shoulders. Night cloaked everything, and soon I was falling deeper into an abyss where my shadows lived and breathed.

Chapter Forty-Three

Jude

I have my suspicions about who the Moon God is... I cannot
meet with you in person, as he watches me closely. Please
tread carefully and keep the girl safe.

Letter from unknown sender to Aurora Adair, year 49 of
the curse

My insides were being torn to shreds by the weapon of
fear. Of not knowing. Each inhale was a slash across
my chest, a phantom blade bleeding me dry.

"I love you, Jude Maddox."

No one had ever spoken those words aloud to me.

Seconds before she left me. Possibly forever.

"She's taking too long," Emelia muttered, the corners of her
eyes creased. She ran a hand through her straight black hair, her
fingers giving a slight quiver. She began to pace.

"I didn't think you cared," Jake retorted, his anxiety igniting
his temper. "You only did this for *him*." He gave me a look that
was neither kind nor malicious. "Don't act as if you give a flying
shit about anyone else."

My mother faced me, her brown eyes sparkling. "My son
cares about her, that much is obvious, and therefore, so do I."

Such a simple statement, but as it was delivered by the notorious Fox, I knew it meant more than most would understand. Gripped in a chokehold of heartache and trepidation, all I could do was nod.

Maybe, in this monstrous situation, I'd form the connection I had sought with my mother, after all. The irony hadn't gone unnoticed.

Emelia ceased her pacing to rest a featherlight hand on my shoulder before letting it slide down and back to her side. A mollifying sort of acceptance worked its way into my heart, nipping away at the years of hatred I held for her.

A start.

"Jake, can you check the time—"

Coldness unlike I'd ever known swarmed across my upper body, curving around my midsection. My scar pulsed, a hint of gold shining through my shirt.

Frowning, I undid the top buttons, expecting to see the familiar veins of black-and-blue vines. But they weren't black or blue anymore.

They were *silver*...and pulsating.

Worry crept into my chest, alarm bells resonating in my ears. More ice trickled from the top of my skull, pooling down my spine like the spindly fingers of death's hand.

"Something's wrong," I blurted, itching to reach for the door. It had injured Liam with a mere touch...and Kiara insisted she was the only one capable of entering due to her contact with one of the Moon God's creatures, but—

So had I.

Kiara's brand. The one *she* had left on me.

"I'm going in," I stated, my tone brooking no room for argument. My mother grasped my arm, her grip biting.

"You can't!" she protested, tugging me back. "You saw what happened to her brother!"

A sharp stabbing sensation pulsated over my scar, the ice in my blood gradually heating.

I didn't have time to argue. This was a sign of danger, Kiara's way of calling out for me, and I promised I would always be there to catch her when she fell.

I tore off my fine jacket and flung it to the ground. Tugging down the collar of my shirt, I exposed the twisting vine-like scars to Emelia. "Kiara left a piece of herself with me, whether she realized it or not. I'll be able to enter."

Ignoring the protests from Jake and Liam, and yanking my arm free from Emelia, I lifted my palm and pressed forward, connecting with the cool surface of the door.

A flash of white blinded me, and the air in my lungs froze over, but it lasted but a heartbeat.

I stepped onto a cloud, into a realm of dreams and numbing fog.

"Kiara!" I shouted, racing forward, unable to see where I stepped. I didn't care. "Where are you?"

I ran until a steep staircase took shape, rising into clouds. Terror was my faithful companion as I raced up the steps, higher into the nothingness, losing myself to the magic of the Moon God.

My breaths were uneven when I made it to the top, a wall of crushed amethysts and white stone showcasing three intricate mirrors. I didn't have time to inspect them, because below their imposing surfaces lay a curled-up figure on the ground.

Kiara.

Calling her name, I dropped to the ground and grasped her shoulder. Her amber eyes were open and glazed. Unresponsive.

Retracting my hand, I cursed, hastily glancing around. My panic made the world hazy, a buzzing noise droning in my ears.

I scanned the space until I saw it.

There. Five feet from where she'd collapsed lay an object I knew all too well.

I lunged for the King of Asidia's mask, and my fingers wrapped around its dense, cool metal. How on earth had this gotten here? I twisted it back and forth, finding no evidence of blood, just an odd smear of black grime. There was no body.

"That silly thing no longer matters."

I dropped the mask, and it clattered to the ground, its jarring clang echoing painfully in the stifling hush.

No. I hadn't heard that voice since—

Kiara let out a groan at my side, and I chanced a peek in her direction. She lay unmoving, but she blinked, and for a sliver of a second, I swore I glimpsed a flicker of panic captured inside her eyes.

Footsteps pounded, heavy boots striking the stone with cruel purpose.

I couldn't look. If I did, I would confirm my worst nightmare. I'd break even further, and if I lost Kiara, too...

Fuck.

"I've missed you, Jude."

Ice careened down my spine as I faced the man who I had once considered my kin. My brother. My family.

"Isiah." His name on my lips was both a curse and a twisted gift.

It wasn't possible, it shouldn't have been, but there he stood, tall and as striking as ever, a broad and almost warm smile stretching his lips. Underneath silken robes, he wore a simple white tunic and matching trousers, the intricate threads woven along the hems a luminous silver. His dark hair, which had always been slicked back, was now wild and loose, granting him an air of innocence.

He looked like my friend, *sounded* like my friend, and yet something was horribly *off*. How he cocked his head to the side in a way that was more cunning than playful. The way his cold gray eyes grew brighter.

I had to believe he was a ghost. A monster born from the temple's cruel imagination.

"Jude?" Isiah questioned, and I swore he sounded hurt. "Why won't you talk to me?"

"You're d-dead." The Godslayer dagger thrummed to life inside my jacket pocket. "I *saw* you die."

I blinked, and that vile day came back to me: his tunic drenched in blood, his eyes wide and pleading. He'd fought against the masked monsters until they'd stolen him from me, and even then, just before he shut his eyes, I'd felt his love for me deep in my soul.

Isiah ran a hand over his face, a tinge of hurt pulling at his features. "You thought you left me for dead, all alone in the Mist. Bleeding out on the forest floor." Now his pain was evident. "But I suppose I had to pretend in order for you to retrieve the blade. Things have to play out a certain way or else the future you intend changes."

I wanted to scream, to rage against this man and his lies. Because this *couldn't* be my brother. Yet...how he looked at me now, his familiar eyes brimming with pity, was exactly how my old friend stared at me every time I came back from a mission. Every time I was hurting and alone.

It was Isiah. Whether the truth tore me in two or not.

Isiah glanced to the mirror hanging on the right, the intense light shining from its surface making it impossible to look into the glass. I followed his every movement as he readied himself to speak, and even then, I was broken by the sound of his voice.

"I wasn't planning on revealing myself this way, but the girl found the one thing that could summon me. *Trap* me like a beast. The very first moonstone," he said with a sigh. "I'd hoped it had lost its power on me when it changed to black decades ago, but it appears as if I was wrong." His attention flitted to her form and then to the wall of mirrors. But it wasn't the mirrors he homed in on—it was a crude dimple in the otherwise smooth rock. As if something had been embedded there...

That had to be where Kiara found the moonstone. The dent and the pile of crumbled dust was out of place in such a pristine room.

Isiah tore his gaze from the mirrors and peered at his feet, his Adam's apple bobbing. "Maybe it would've made me a coward, but things would be so much easier if you hadn't seen my face. I suppose I hadn't prepared myself for this moment."

I recalled how Kiara had paused at his body back in the Mist. She'd said she saw his chest rise and fall, and at the time, I'd dismissed her, my grief clouding my judgment.

"You." It was the only word I could conjure. My throat was drier than sand.

Isiah scrubbed at his jaw in frustration. "Yes, *me*. It's always the ones closest to you that you should watch out for. I told you that once, I believe."

The Moon God. The whole time, Isiah had been my only friend and greatest enemy.

"Why?" I appeared capable of only one-word responses.

"I'm sorry it had to be this way, truly, I am." He squeezed his eyes shut. "I care about you, and maybe if you'll let me explain, you will come to see why I refuse to bring the sun back." He started to pace, his hands twitching at his sides. He was nervous, hardly able to look at me.

"I don't want to hear anything from you. Not anymore," I said through my teeth, anger and betrayal coursing through my heating blood.

He didn't listen. Then again, Isiah was often stubborn. "The night has brought about so many good things! Can't you see?" he shouted, his voice cracking. "There are no more wars, fewer deaths. More *dreams*! Dreams carry so much power, Jude, allowing people to see what matters most in their lives. And *I* deliver them, and the moon watches over them as they sleep."

He faced me, sincerity masking his features, which were stricken with tangible regret.

"The sun casts too much truth upon the world, and in the stark light of day, the mortals allowed their baser instincts control. They acted on their schemes. Their ambitions of greed and corruption. I aim to stop them before they ruin themselves. I've always watched out for them, even when they shunned me, and I always will."

He actually believed what he spoke. That was the truly sickening part. I clutched at my chest absently, seeking the heat of my throbbing scar, needing its warmth as a reminder of why I couldn't succumb to my pain.

None of it had been real. It had all been a game—and I'd lost.

"I've hunted you all for years," Isiah said, finally meeting my stare. "The three vessels carrying Raina's magic. Patrick, I'd known about for ages, but you came into my life unexpectedly, a joyous surprise nonetheless." Isiah's eyes sparkled, the tender grin breaking across his lips one of affection.

Bile seared my throat.

"And Kiara…" he began slowly, taking his time. My upper lip curled. "She was the final missing piece. I knew when rumors of her spread that fate worked in my favor. A sign from the universe that it would finally be *my* time to reign."

I looked at the mask, which lay discarded like rubbish. My head grew heavy with all the unanswered questions.

"Was it always you behind the mask, then? Controlling the undead king with enchantment?" I asked with bated breath. I knew his answer, yet I had to hear the words.

My old friend scoffed. "Cirian was a horrid creation of mine, but necessary. I'd planned to do away with him once I accomplished my mission."

"A creation?"

"He's what you refer to as a masked man. One of the creatures from the Mist. Which was not my doing, you should know. After Raina fell and the Mist rose, the mortals who roamed those lands were plagued by the curse, changing them into monsters. I simply learned how to train them and use them to my advantage. If people were too fearful to venture beyond the borders, then they wouldn't leave Asidia. They wouldn't leave *me.*"

A cruel thought struck me then, one that should have occurred to me minutes before.

Isiah controlled the king. Cirian had made the Calling mandatory, and he knew me well enough to know I'd select her, which also meant... "You were the one sending me on my nightly missions." Betrayal needled my insides like tiny thorns on a wilted rose. And afterward, like the sick bastard he was, Isiah would *comfort* me, bringing me food, cleaning me up, telling me everything would be all right. I trusted him. *Loved* him.

Isiah glanced to the corner, his cheeks reddening. "I followed the path I needed to in order to make you strong. You wouldn't have lasted in this world without me, and we had to wait until Kiara showed herself."

I stumbled back a step, his confession like a physical blow. "Fuck. You," I said, uncaring of the consequences. I wanted him to feel my wrath, to know I despised him well before I ended his life, once and for all.

"I know you're angry, but I did what I had to do. To make sure you were hardened enough to live in this world. To make certain you'd be the warrior I needed you to be." Isiah's nostrils flared. "You would have died ages ago if I hadn't intervened, and every mission, every strike you were dealt, allowed you to live that much longer. I only wish you'd be here at the end of all of this. That you'd be by my side. Of every mortal I've ever known, *you*, Jude, are truly one of the most deserving."

My magic thrashed against the confines of my body. It wanted to wrap around his neck and squeeze. To burn him until nothing remained.

Before I allowed my power to be released, Kiara's body shifted below me, just the barest hint of a shiver. My magic calmed instantly, outweighed by my fear.

"What did you do to her?" He hadn't killed her, not yet, but he would.

Isiah's jaw clenched when my attention wandered from him. "These mirrors show the past, present, and future, although the final mirror never allowed me to see much. I'm assuming she stared into one of them far too long and lost herself to the onslaught of prayers I keep inside. Only a powerful god, one with *full* divinity, is immune to their pull. She likely fell *into* herself and into her own darkness."

Every muscle locked in place.

Thinking of her frightened and lost in the dark ignited a spark deep within, well beyond my magic. I inhaled slowly, trying to think without emotion, to think like a commander.

I had to do it for *her*, even if I was breaking, piece by piece.

Kiara must've found the tool to summon him here now. But why wasn't he trapped? Had she not had the chance before she was struck down? I did a quick scan of the room, finding nothing of note. Maybe she hid the talisman somewhere on her person, but I couldn't search her and rouse Isiah's suspicions.

"Isiah," I started, and his entire face brightened. "You don't have to do this. Our realm is dying. Crops are finally failing entirely, people are starved, and without the sun, they've lost a part of themselves they cannot get back. There needs to be balance."

I lifted Kiara, easing her head against my chest, her ear pressed over my thudding heart. My hand reached for her pocket. She could've shoved it inside when he appeared—

The ground trembled as Isiah closed the final few feet separating us. I retracted my hand and wrapped it around Kiara's waist.

"You have no idea what it's like to forever be the last thought. The god people cursed. I am the cool blanket of night, the shining moon, the faraway stars. But I am also every shadow and nightmare that frightens the hearts of mortals. They all but shunned me, deeming me evil and twisted. But you…you understood me, didn't you, Jude? You were my friend, and maybe I should have told you sooner, but I'm still hopeful enough that you'll come around now."

My scar panged as Kiara twitched in my arms. I peered down, taking in every delicate line, every smooth facet of her striking features. She almost looked peaceful. I knew that to be a lie.

"You're living up to their expectations by doing this," I said, trying a different approach. "Help us restore the sun without killing one another, and you'll be a hero. They'll worship *you* for your heroism."

He'd been lonely. That was the root of it all. It was an emotion I was all too familiar with.

Isiah barked out a laugh, though his eyes grew wet with unshed tears. "She truly has changed you, hasn't she? It's funny because for years I'd tried to get you to lighten up. Looks like all it took was a pretty face."

A low growl rumbled in my chest. I wasn't getting anywhere with him. He wasn't going to change his plans, not even for me.

The fractures in my heart that *he* had repaired over the years suddenly cracked open once more.

Memories of Isiah tending to my wounds flickered across

my mind. Nights when he hovered over my bedside and talked my ear off, knowing I hungered for comfort so I could escape my mind. He'd been my family, my *everything*, and for so long, he was all I had in this world.

I couldn't fucking breathe.

He'd been the *cause* of so much of my sorrow.

"I meant what I said," he whispered as if reading my thoughts. "At first you were a mission, a means to an end, but over time, I grew to care for you. I saw myself in you, a boy discarded, thought weak by others. Someone whose potential had been overlooked all because of how he was perceived by the ignorant. Yet as hard as this all will be, you *must* die. I'd only prefer if you'd sacrifice yourself willingly."

"Willingly?" I rasped, stunned. "You claim to know me, but you realize I'd never help you with this!"

Isiah's nostrils flared, and he presented me his back, his long white cloak picked up by a breeze.

I wouldn't let him get off that easily. Besides, another thought plagued me. "Why not take us all when we were in that field? Why wait until now?"

He had us exactly where he wanted us. It didn't make sense.

Isiah spun around, his face pinched, lacking all traces of warmth. "Lorian wasn't thrilled by the prospect of me killing Raina's kin. He *distracted* me while you all escaped."

That's why Lorian had vanished so quickly.

In my arms, Kiara shook, her lips forming nonsensical words.

She blinked rapidly, her face twitching, muscles spasming. She looked to be in pain, and my blood boiled as a reddish gold spread across my vision. The scar on my chest heated, the agony only bearable because of the beast rearing its head beneath my flesh.

When Kiara cried out again, a soft whimper, I nearly lost my mind.

I was all fire and wrath, not a man, not even a half-formed god. I was the embodiment of rage, and I couldn't control my actions even if I tried.

Isiah's lips parted, his eyes widening—

The entire room exploded with my fury, golden rays igniting every nook and cranny, brightening the space until I could take in each minuscule feature on my enemy's familiar face.

Horror. I witnessed horror wash across his features.

I smiled, my girl cradled in my arm as my power erupted, heat sweeping across the temple floor.

"Come back to me, Kiara," I whispered, my eyes prickling. "I can't lose you." *I won't.*

Isiah held up his palm, but my light broke through. It afforded me just enough time.

With one hand resting on her scar, I lifted to my feet and rushed to the mirror that had stolen Kiara away. Without hesitation, I stared into its surface, one hand reaching for the glass.

Annihilating night swallowed my world.

Chapter Forty-Four

Kiara

The lost will not always be this way
just as the broken can mend;
But those who have been neither
lost nor broken cannot understand
what it is to heal

Asidian proverb

The night stretched endlessly. I was enveloped in stars, wrapped in darkness, below, above, *inside*.

I was the night covering the realm and the quiet peace of cool nothingness. I stepped forward, my body a shadow, a wisp of black. The stars below my boots glimmered, winking, causing pleasant tingles of awareness to creep down my spine.

I'd entirely forgotten everything that had occurred until this moment—down to who I was. I felt weightless and free and utterly intoxicated by the beauty I witnessed.

Below, Asidia spread out like the veins of a leaf, the large cities, the foreboding capital of Sciona, the many villages littering the countryside. It all shined for me, the light emanating from the towns battling against the radiance of the stars and a shy moon.

I glided, floated, and soared over the scene, unable to do

anything but worship the darkness, how it embraced us all, blanketing our skin and kissing our sight.

Peaceful. So peaceful.

I might've flown for hours or days or years, time didn't matter, but eventually, the sky rippled, gusts of wind whooshing forward to tickle my cheeks.

Squinting, I watched as silhouettes exited the gaping chasm in the clouds, the universe seeming to rip open. Claws and teeth glimmered. Red eyes sparkled. Gravelly roars drowned the soothing winds.

Before my eyes, nightmares stole the spotlight, cascading down upon the sleeping realm like a plague. Worry tensed my phantom shoulders. My body was growing too heavy, unable to float.

I sank. Lower and lower I plummeted, dropping like the nightmares that were blocking the heavens. Through it all, fear remained absent, like I recognized the haunting forms fluttering to earth and found no imminent danger. At least, not to myself.

Nightmares were the price of the dark, and nothing beautiful ever came without consequences.

Yet I knew I'd missed something vital, that I was forgetting pieces of myself. A memory teetered on the edge of my subconscious, taunting me. A face, all angles and crowned in raven locks, hovered in front of me, though the details remained obscured.

Down I fell, the earth ready to swallow me up, the tops of the black trees rising to meet me. Fear trickled into the place it had once been missing, gradually filling the crevices. The closer I got to the world of men, the more that fear grew like a ravenous weed…or perhaps it wasn't simply fear, but a mixture of anticipation and adrenaline.

I collided harshly with the soil, though I experienced neither pain nor much of anything else. And that face…it loomed above me now, in a meadow of Midnight Blooms and charred trees.

All my missing memories rushed back in a crushing wave. Jude.

He stood before me, seemingly solid, not some horrid illusion sent to destroy me.

Jude drew closer, his brown eye glazed in gold, his right one a storm of ivory and blues, two jagged lines of red slashing across. I breathed him in, my body shaking with every step he took.

"Kiara." He rasped the name like a plea, his deep timbre sending goose bumps down my arms. He was feet away, gliding toward me on a breeze. "You went too deep. You're lost inside yourself." Frustration caused the crack in his voice, his eyes lined in wetness.

"Are you real?" I had to ask, had to make certain. I lifted a trembling hand, too afraid to graze his skin.

"You can feel me now, can't you, Kiara? You know I'm real. That I'd follow you into the dark and catch you if you fell." Jude reached for his chest, touching his scar. Light radiated from underneath his palm.

I slipped my own hand to my chest, right above my heart, its beat matching Jude's pulsating glow.

He was inches away in my next breath, his hands winding around my waist, the solidness of his touch grounding me in this realm of shadows and nightmares.

"I'm here," he murmured, almost to himself. "And I refuse to let you fall alone."

I was awash with relief and fear, the combination causing my knees to buckle. Jude tightened his grip, holding me up.

"How—how did I get here?"

"Shhh." Jude cupped my cheek, his thumb wiping at the wetness dampening my cheeks. "You got lost. Just as we've all been before."

And he'd found me. The question was *where*?

I tilted my chin and peered around the obscure woods we stood in. I didn't recognize a thing, and panic caused my chest to expand unevenly. I'd been...I'd been in a void of fog, brilliant white light highlighting three mirrors. Cirian had appeared, his mask had fallen, and then I'd stared at my reflection in a mirror surrounded by silver vines and thorns.

"But *where* are we?" I finally asked, gathering the strength to form the words. Each one burned my throat. We weren't on earth, not in the true sense, and I had the suspicion Jude following me to this place was nothing short of miraculous.

"You shouldn't have looked into that final mirror, Kiara. It's too powerful for any other being besides a god." Jude lowered his head, his brow touching mine. "You were enchanted by it, and fell into *yourself*, into your darkness."

My darkness was Asidia's darkness, its loss of faith.

I peered around Jude, looking over the land that I'd known my whole life. A place of both misery and desperate hope. But it was home, and I couldn't squash the desire to protect it. To protect myself. However *dark* I may be.

Jude grasped my chin, tilting my eyes back to his. "We don't have much time. I stunned Isiah with my magic to follow you through the mirror, but he could be ready to cut our throats as we speak."

"Wait..." I pushed at his chest, staring up at him in alarm. "Did you say *Isiah* was there?" That wasn't possible. I watched him die.

But then I went still.

I'd seen his body shudder with an inhale before we left him in the Mist. I'd assumed exhaustion had been the cause of my misplaced hope, but...

Jude squeezed his eyes, a tormented noise rumbling in his chest. "Yes, I saw him, but I don't know what's real at this point. If he's the Moon God or if it's another twisted illusion. I didn't deem it possible, but…"

I made a point of scanning our surroundings. "But nothing is impossible anymore, right?"

We were stranded in an in-between world where nothing felt solid and nothing certainly felt *real*. Our physical bodies were somewhere else, likely still beneath the temple and under the watchful eye of his duplicitous brother.

"We need to leave," I said quickly, my magic flaring in my chest. I wasn't sure how time worked in this place, if it slowed or froze entirely, but Isiah wouldn't hesitate to kill us if we were laid out before him, defenseless in his temple.

Jude nodded, opening his mouth as if to reply. But I perched on my tiptoes and silenced him with a tender kiss. In that press of our lips, I experienced a lifetime of dreams that would never pass.

Us waking up every morning, limbs tangled, and the sun shining through the curtains. Jude and I on horseback, traveling the continent—farther, even—discovering new lands and peoples and adventure. Us settling down each night, sitting comfortably before a fire in one another's silences, feasting upon the precious moments in between that most people overlook. Seeing and feeling and adoring the truths of each other with simple touches and embraces. Smiles and laughter.

Knowing we both had found home.

I realized that my magic was growing too strong, too potent to be kept inside my flesh.

With Jude in my arms and the taste of him on my tongue, my love for him flowed through me, rivaling the power of the Moon God and the dark beast I possessed. No. It was *greater*.

We were *soul to soul*.

There was a way out of this.

For one of us.

My power could be used to Travel—proven when I'd transformed into shadows and ventured into Jude's cell, into the very skies. *Maybe* there was *just* enough dark magic in me to give to Jude. To get him out of the temple and away from Isiah.

If I could gift him *both* of my powers—the dark and the missing light from Raina—he could escape. Be strong enough to save the realm and everyone we'd ever cared about. I could do this, relinquish myself. *All* of me.

A warrior was born to die, after all.

I drew back slightly, my lips a centimeter from his. "I love you, Jude Maddox. With everything I am and all that I ever could've hoped to be."

It was different from when I said it before.

This time, there was no hesitation. No physical barriers. No fear.

The sky erupted, an odd sort of tingling causing my body to grow heavy, too heavy. But Jude...he wavered in front of me, lighter than air, as weightless as the shadows I commanded.

The sun priestesses and their prophecy were right—the sun would return to the skies when the darkness fell for the light. And Jude had fallen into the darkness to save me. To *love* me. True love was nothing if not sacrifice, and I had just paid the ultimate cost.

Jude didn't have the time to protest, but the fear in his eyes relayed he understood exactly what I'd done.

The prophecy had been fulfilled. Except there'd be no happy ending for me.

Somewhere far away, I heard the shattering of a mirror, the flood of divinity breaking the ancient pools of enchanted silver. Prayers escaped, their frantic pleas shooting out across the world. Finally free.

Yet in the chaos, I garnered the energy to whisper those three little words one final time as Jude vanished entirely, slipping away into the dim, and taking the blazing sliver of the divine power I held...along with all of my darkness.

Chapter Forty-Five

Jude

Cerys, the God of Love, may not show themselves often, but they are there, working their magic and changing fates across the realm. All they ask in return is to cherish the gift they give.

It can be potent enough to alter the course of history.

Excerpt from Asidian Lore: a Tale of the Gods

I woke with a gasp, panting, reaching wildly for the woman who'd been in my arms seconds before.

They were empty. But my fingers...

Veiny scars branched from each tip, stretching to my elbows. A quivering exhale left me.

These were *her* scars. The mark of the dark creature that attacked her a decade ago. So why did they now decorate my skin?

When she touched me in that in-between realm, had she—

No. Impossible.

"Kiara!" I called out, my vision gradually settling, the golden light dissipating. Whirling in place, I found myself staring at a copse of trees.

Aboveground.

I couldn't Travel, not like Kiara could while using her

shadows. And I was alone, not a soul or building in sight. Reaching for the welcoming heat of my power, I allowed it to stream down my limbs and burst free from my skin. A yellowish light shone from my body, casting an ominous glow upon the dark woods.

I hadn't the faintest idea what would happen when I'd looked into that mirror, but I didn't believe I'd wake...not when Isiah would likely seize the opportunity to kill us both.

Unless Kiara had done what I feared most.

She'd given herself to me when our very souls had been connected. She offered me her heart, her magic, her very *life*. She gave them to me—to Asidia—freely, all while adoration brightened her face. No fear, no regret.

The day will be restored when the darkness falls for the light.

Kiara had bestowed the final sliver of divinity *without* the Godslayer. She'd given me her powers. And with them, she'd gifted me the ability to Travel—far from the temple.

Leaving her defenseless.

She could be—

I couldn't even think the word.

Everything closed in on me, and the night sky—which had brightened ever so slightly—seemed more like a roof set on collapsing. I'd failed, not just myself, not just Asidia and my brothers, but the person who mattered to me the most. Who'd fought for me until the very end.

Gods, even with all pieces of Raina's light united, it still felt like the end.

I hissed as power flooded my system, causing me to stagger forward beneath the immense weight of it all.

My body burned, a match having been struck, my flames spreading, out of control and unable to be extinguished.

Surging ahead, I wove through the woods, every leaf and branch highlighted by the full power of Raina's magic. *My* magic.

Magic that had possibly cost me my soul.

I was whole.

I was a *god*.

And I was about to set the world on fire before the new sun even had the chance to rise.

Chapter Forty-Six

Kiara

He's been deceiving them all with fallacious smiles. I feign ignorance, but as the years pass, I am certain he's aware of my ruse. I have no doubt he'll come for me soon. He already has the boy wrapped around his finger.

Letter from Lieutenant Harlow to Aurora Adair, year 48 of the curse

There'd been just enough energy inside of me to get Jude and his physical body to safety. Outside the temple. Away from Isiah.

The Moon God stood before me now, holding his hands over his face as if he'd been blocking an attack. Slowly, he lowered his arms, blinking rapidly as he searched the room, his body swaying.

I flinched from where I lay on the floor. His handsome face was nearly unrecognizable, and even though Jude had told me the truth of his treachery, my heart still sank at how cold he appeared.

There could be no denying it now. He'd deceived us all.

Isiah whirled to where the three enchanted mirrors had been, finding nothing but shards of glass. He cursed, scanning the room before he lowered his icy eyes to my curled-up form.

Confusion swam in those endless depths.

"He's gone," he spoke under his breath. "How? He was just here seconds ago, he just—" Isiah paused, his lips falling closed as annoyance darkened his eyes.

It appeared as though time had worked in our favor. *Once.*

I smiled at the god, my heart lifting. Jude should be far enough away, able to secure an advantageous location to strike. My banishment gave him time to come to terms with his brother's betrayal, and while my body ached and stabbing bolts seared across my temples, I had never felt better.

Jude would live, if only long enough for a fair battle.

"What did you do?" Isiah peered at the fractured glass, anger flushing his cheeks.

All three mirrors—past, present, and future—were broken as if someone had taken a sledgehammer to their surfaces, setting free all the stolen prayers.

Good. He couldn't use them ever again. Couldn't steal what wasn't rightfully his.

My smile broadened, even as my ribs ached, each inhale producing a searing twinge. There was no trace of magic kissing my insides, and the subtle buzzing I'd grown accustomed to was now gone. I felt only emptiness…and triumph. Isiah didn't have Jude in his clutches, and that meant I had won.

"He has the blade," I rasped, grinning wickedly. "And the next time he finds you, he'll kill you."

Isiah lunged. Grasping me by the collar, he yanked me up until my feet kicked open air. I fought, thrashing wildly as he brought his face close to mine.

"If he kills me, who will rule the moon and all it watches over? Without me, there's no rest, no stars, no tides. No *dreams.* I command the hours of darkness, and soon, I'll find Jude, even if he has your stolen powers." Isiah's gaze softened ever so slightly. "He should've understood. If anyone would have, it should've been him. You tainted him in some way. Ruined the man he was born to be." He looked away, losing focus, his stare glossy.

Isiah blamed me and that was fine. He could wring my neck and I'd die with a smile. It was worth it, seeing him lose this battle, even if I wouldn't be around to see him lose the war.

With a snarl, Isiah released me, and I crumpled to the floor.

He went on to pace, speaking aloud to himself. I imagined he wasn't used to things not going his way, and he'd played such a magnificent game thus far, all of us pawns. Until I'd gone and tossed the board.

I shoved to my elbows. The room was spinning. I couldn't overpower Isiah in my state, even if I had the Godslayer in my possession. Whatever I'd done in the depths of the mirror—a place where my soul and reality collided—had cost me dearly.

But I'd fucking done it.

I was alive...and the most impossible part of it all was that I'd given Jude the last piece of Raina's divinity. He'd found me in the depths of myself, and I'd eagerly offered him all that I was in a place where our souls could touch.

A violent cough rattled my lungs, causing me to lurch to the side, twisting onto my hands and knees. Isiah continued to murmur to himself, and the hint of the shadows whispering at his feet rippled forcefully. Copper filled my mouth and I spat onto the pristine white floor.

Red.

I should've known the consequences would catch up to me.

"It's a tragedy it came to this," Isiah said, a tear tracking down his cheek. He stilled in place, though his shadows persisted, vibrating, lifting higher and higher up his body like smoke. "Jude isn't the man I believed him to be, after all."

A swirl of black enveloped him, silver lights sparking as he vanished.

His magic delivered him somewhere I'd never reach, leaving

me alone to die in a room of endless white fog and shattered glass.

I was now a mortal who trespassed upon sacred ground, the trace of the Moon God's darkness no longer within me. It felt like I was being shredded from the inside out.

My eyes grew blurry. It wasn't just me left to rot in this place. Emelia, Finn, Jake, Liam—they also were trapped on the other side of the door in the palace.

I took little consolation knowing they'd die together while I'd die alone, in a puddle of my own blood.

Rolling onto my side, I faced the middle mirror, taking in the vortex of spinning black where the glass had once been. At least I'd done one thing to help—freeing the prayers of the realm. Maybe in time, it would make the other gods strong enough to fight Isiah, should Jude fail.

Which he better not.

Another brutal cough had me retching, the warm blood rising up my throat and searing my insides. What I wouldn't give for a hand to hold right about now. I'd heard tales of how the imminence of death could make someone yearn for comfort, even from an enemy. Hells, I'd settle for Arlo's hand.

I hope you can hear me now, old bastard, I mocked, staring at the largest mirror's frame, at the ominous emptiness of its center. *I wish you could help me out. It's not fun dying. Though if you were here, you'd probably yell at me for getting myself killed in the first place.*

I laughed at the thought. Or maybe I just imagined I did. He *would* scream at me for giving up the position of power. Arlo truly was a piece of work…but I missed him.

We couldn't choose our family in this life, and while he was far from perfect, Arlo had *stayed*. He protected me the only way a ruthless god knew how. He cared.

My body grew cold, much colder than it should have been.

It wouldn't be long before I'd exhale my last wheezing breath. I tried to conjure Jude and my friends. If I couldn't hold them, I wanted to be surrounded by their faces.

It was all I had, but my mind refused to preserve their images, and their faces faded, vanishing before I could reach out and grasp them.

Dying, thus far, was not recommended.

A great crash came from above. A splattering of grit fell across my closed lids, which were too heavy to open, and dirt slipped between my parted lips. I couldn't manage to cough, the dusty air slipping into my lungs, choking me.

Whatever was coming for me couldn't hurt me much more anyway.

Chapter Forty-Seven

Jude

There are no known cures for shadow beasts, although some
believe they can be saved when in their humanlike form.
These scholars claim that since they live and breathe like
mortals, they possess a soul. And souls, they say, can be healed
like any other ailment.

Excerpt from Asidian Lore: Legends and Myths of the
Realm

With outstretched arms, blazing wings sprouted behind
me—twin weapons of cruel beauty.

Magic streamed forth, gold erupting from my pores, my
eyes, my open mouth. I wasn't human at that moment, not even
slightly. I felt like a god. A vengeful one.

A humming sensation rattled my rib cage, an ancient heat
boiling my blood. Each exhale was a scorching flame, every
swallow raw. And while I'd become a raging inferno, there
was no discomfort, only weightlessness. It had my body flying
through spindly branches, arms shoving aside blackened leaves
and debris, racing back to the temple where this all would end.

For Kiara, for our friends, I'd push forward. She'd given me
a gift, and I would not squander her sacrifice. I prayed she still

breathed, *had* to believe it. My greatest fear was her below the earth, back in the Moon God's temple, with Isiah. Helpless, and waiting to be killed.

The traitor. My duplicitous brother.

If my initial strike hadn't wounded him, he'd kill her. If he hadn't done so already.

She could've saved herself, but the insufferable girl saved *me.*

Again.

A snarl ripped free from my throat as I pushed my muscles to the point of pain. There was no sign of life in the woods, and wherever Kiara had sent me was a decent way from the temple. Meaning time was of the essence.

Why did she have to choose me? Again and again?

I was hardly worthy of the life destined for me—I was selfish and irritable, and I despised most people and things. And I'd been fine with that reality for most of my life.

Kiara changed everything.

Soon, the sun would rise; I felt it, the nearness of its approach. When that time came, I planned to be standing over Isiah's remains. Though if he touched her, hurt her in any way—I'd prolong his torture. I would take my time with him and revel in his agony. The gruesome images might've sickened anyone else, but I had been raised by evil's guiding hand, and I feared what I would do should Kiara be gone.

I razed a forest when I wasn't able to *touch* Kiara. Gods knew what atrocities I'd perform if she was taken from me.

As the temple drew closer, the heat inside of me began to mutate, to bend and reshape into something new. *Whole.* All three pieces were reuniting, fusing together.

The proof rested in the way my pace quickened, how my exhaustion slipped from my body like a loose cloak. All three orbs seemed to sing as they fused into one single entity.

There was also something else swimming in the core of my power. A dark shard of magic. *Kiara's darkness.* And without her shadows or her scars, she was just a human, unable to travel, unfit to enter the Moon God's inner sanctum.

I squeezed my eyes and focused on her face, trying desperately to Travel as I had seconds before, but Raina's magic was too strong, and it overpowered all else. Only because of Kiara's guidance had I been delivered from danger. There was nothing I could do to command the shadows—at least not to the same extent.

I growled in frustration, the feral noise shaking the trees. They swayed when I sprinted by, their deadened branches curving into a mockery of a bow. The whole forest quivered, the ground my boots pressed upon softening like it was coming alive after a long, brutal winter.

Ahead, the pointed roof of the temple emerged, tall and proud, a prison of lies. I hungered to storm its gates and break it apart piece by piece. To ruin Isiah's temple before I ruined him, the Godslayer piercing his heart.

Yet as much as I hated to admit it, that final thought was a hollow one. Less of a triumph and more of a loss.

My relationship with Isiah had never been real to begin with, and I'd do whatever was necessary to defend myself and the others. The people that cared for me.

My boot landed on the temple's first step when a series of bone-chilling howls rented the air.

Tinny and high-pitched, the sound reminded me of the masked men. But that couldn't be possible. The borders were far from here, and—

"They're coming. I've called them because you can't see reason, and now that you're...*whole*, I can't take any chances."

Spiraling shadows parted, revealing Isiah, standing in all his glory beside his cursed temple. He strode with purpose, Midnight

Blooms crunching beneath his boots. The rest surrounding the temple began to wither, slowly turning to black.

Fire raged at my fingertips, aching to be set free. My eyes glowed, the scene in front of me cast in tints of red and yellow and orange. The power of the sun goddess was eager for carnage.

"What did you do?" I seethed as new screams and howls hailed from the trees. But selfishly, my focus wasn't on the undead creatures marching to Isiah's aid. "What did you do to Kiara?"

"I left her in the temple," he replied coolly. "She's free of the gift the shadow beast awarded her. Utterly mortal now." He cocked a disdainful brow as he glanced at my hands, to where Kiara's scars covered my fingers, my hands, and my arms. Her final gift.

Sizzling flames sparked across my brow like a vicious crown. I was going to end him. And I would take my damned time. I'd enjoy it.

Footsteps struck the earth. Whatever Isiah had released was nearly upon us.

"The masked men answer to me. And since you refuse to save your kingdom, I've invited them here, hoping they might… sway you to hand over the blade. You made this difficult, Jude. Not me." Isiah clenched his fists, his eyes glassy when he stared at my flames. "You were the closest thing I've ever had to a friend. What a disappointment you ended up being." The last part was a whisper, and I doubted he meant to say the words aloud.

"You *were* my friend," I said, my eyes prickling. "But friends don't manipulate each other for years! They don't pretend to care when they plan to sacrifice the other!"

"It's for *all* of us!" Isiah argued. "It's for all the people you could save. The entire realm. Your precious Kiara. I know you've always wanted to be a hero, a true hero, and now, I'm giving you the chance."

I couldn't believe this was the same man who held me that night when I made my first kill for the king. He shushed in my ears and brought me tea, rubbing my back until my lids grew heavy and sleep claimed me.

"Was it all a lie?" I questioned, mostly to myself. "It had to be, or maybe you're not even him."

Perhaps he'd stolen his face. No one could possibly keep up such an act for *years*. The Moon God was notorious for shifting appearances as often as it suited him—

"I am who I've always been. Regardless of how this has to end, I'll always care for you. But that's another testament to how far I'm willing to go to save the mortals from their own destruction. I'd sacrifice the most important person in my life. My brother."

A twinge pulsated over my chest, Kiara's scar awakening. Against all hope, I prayed it meant she still lived. I resisted reaching for it, knowing Isiah might see.

"You are not my brother," I said, bitterness lining every syllable.

Shadows curled from Isiah's shoulders and neck, rising into the air and forming wings. They were similar to those Kiara had grown, and yet, while hers glimmered with silver, his were horrifically heart-stopping in their size, the rugged wings devoid of any light.

My own flames whooshed from my back, rising high, the glow they emitted casting the field in gold. Even as the moon pulsated overhead—reacting to Isiah's magic—my power settled me, a physical reminder I wasn't the same helpless boy Isiah had manipulated for years.

We were facing each other, fire and darkness, the true kind, and my heart cleaved in two. Isiah had been the lone bright spot in my life for so, so long. Without him, I'd have broken long ago.

The irony wasn't lost on me.

"I see your reluctance, dear boy, your hesitation, and it warms my soul." Isiah's shadows settled, twisting around his neck as if nothing more than a pet snake. "If only you didn't need to die. But I promise I'll try to make it quick if you let me. I'll immortalize your name, and you'll live in my heart long after your body is gone. This I promise."

He struck so quickly, so suddenly, I didn't have time to react.

Blackness shot out from his hands, the blast sending me soaring across the clearing. I struck the ground hard, landing on my right arm painfully. I coughed, hacking up steam and spitting out a black, viscous liquid. It seeped from my lips and fell to the soil, turning to soot where it dropped.

I should've attacked when I had the chance, but like a sentimental fool, I wavered.

"Come on, Jude. You can do better than that! I taught you better! If you're not willing to accept your destiny, then at least *try* to fight me."

I shut my eyes, shoving his words out of my head. Instead, I focused on a striking face framed in gold. My scar ached as Kiara's ethereal picture became clearer, her features soft yet fierce. Lips I'd tasted and kissed, quirking into a coy, devious smile. Eyes that had always been reminiscent of the sun from my dreams.

Placing my hand over my aching scar, I rose. The fight hadn't left me yet.

Before Isiah could muster up some inane taunt, I flung out my power, fueled not by hurt or rage, but by what Kiara inspired. An emotion I cherished and wished to carry inside my heart until my final breath.

Fire licked over the earth, shooting toward the God of the Moon.

My flames advanced, striking him hard enough to knock

him onto his back. Not allowing him a chance to recover, they circled him, trapping him in a ring of unholy heat, his white cloak billowing about his tall, muscular frame.

His ensuing smile caused me to pause.

I realized why a second later.

Screams of the undead filtered through the trees and toward the temple. Glinting eyes of steel shone, all aimed at me, their intentioned prey.

"They've arrived," Isiah said, flicking his chin in the monsters' direction.

CHAPTER FORTY-EIGHT

KIARA

Arlo is a complicated being. While he delivered the Godslayer
to Raina's lover, it is said he journeyed to her empty temple
after her fall. There, he supposedly fell to his knees and
begged forgiveness. His envy caused devastation, but I
maintain that he is eager to fix the mistakes of his past. Even
gods are strikingly human at times, and that gives me hope.

FOUND IN THE DIARY OF JUNIPER MARCHANT, SUN PRIESTESS,
YEAR 5 OF THE CURSE

Arms of steel circled me, squeezing tight enough that I
stuttered for breath.

In my daze, I recognized the scent of the open woods, the
aroma bringing back a memory of clashing swords and hot
chocolates. Pouring rain and sweat. Standards I never had been
able to meet. The praise I so desperately sought.

"Hello, Kiara," Arlo's voice murmured in my ear. "Don't
worry. I'll yell at you as soon as I save you."

Arlo.

My desperate prayers reached him.

I stared for precious seconds I knew I didn't have. I gazed
upon his wizened face, my heart lifting at the concern marring

his brow. He'd come for me. He pulled me from the earth and was *holding* me, cradling my bruised body with all the gentleness he possessed.

My eyes filled with burning tears, blurring him further. He gripped me tighter at the sight.

We had to be somewhere outside. The air was fresh, and I heard the rustling of leaves nearby. Soft dirt filtered through my open palms as I steadied myself, attempting to rise. I failed.

"My friends," I croaked, melting in Arlo's hold. "They're trapped."

Arlo tutted. "For once, can you think about yourself? I doubt they're bleeding from the inside out at the moment." He moved my head to rest against his chest. "Have you forgotten everything I've taught you? Get yourself out of danger before helping others."

"Yeah, yeah," I said, hacking up another lungful of blood. "You're no use to anyone if you're dead." I deepened my tone, mocking him. On the verge of death, likely hallucinating my former *uncle*, I chose snark as my weapon of choice. It was fitting.

He bristled. "And to think I missed you."

"Your first mistake," I teased, although the confession made my heart flutter. I'd missed him, too, missed his commandeering presence and frowns. His growling voice and the way he snapped at me when he knew I could do better. I felt safe with him, oddly enough, and I supposed seeing him in my current state wasn't the worst thing to happen tonight.

Arlo sobered, releasing a profound sigh that shook my bones. "You're dying, girl," he whispered, his disappointed features coming in and out of focus. "When your shadows left, the temple rejected you, poisoning your blood. It won't be long before it reaches your mortal heart."

I might've been delusional due to the loss of blood, but I

could've sworn his icy hands grazed my cheek in a moment of tenderness.

"We all have to die sometime," I said quietly. And what a way to go. I would've smiled if I had the energy.

"Yes. You were always meant to die," Arlo muttered, low and soft. He rocked me back and forth. "So why is it that I'm having a hard time letting go?"

I stilled at his confession. The man I knew as Micah had never shown such emotion, never cradled me, and rubbed my cheeks, trying to usher life back into my features. He became more of a stranger now than when I discovered his true identity.

"Going soft on me, old man?" I grinned, my teeth likely slicked in blood. Copper was all I tasted.

People on the verge of death never were able to fully recount their experience. Now that I was there, it was surprisingly peaceful. My limbs were numb, my body cold, and an odd sort of acceptance had taken hold.

I'd leave this life having helped those I loved, and a little part of me would forever live on in Jude's heart. Selfishly, I prayed he'd feel me every now and again when he defeated Isiah and returned the sun to the skies. I hoped he took in that first glorious sunset and smiled, remembering me.

"No." The harshness of Arlo's tone jerked me from my reverie. "I feel you slipping, and...and I won't allow it. I've invested too much. It would be a waste for you to die so young after all my training and hard work."

I attempted a laugh, but nothing came out. I couldn't feel my face.

"You may not understand the importance of this, Kiara Frey, but know what I'm about to do shouldn't be taken lightly. Such an act can only be done once, and unlike Raina, I have faith you won't stab me in the heart."

What was he talking about? My lids were closing, the weight

of the welcoming void calling me home.

"When Raina made her lover an immortal, she tied her heart to his. And when he broke it, she never loved the same. Was physically unable to." Arlo's voice became muffled, and I strained to hear. Thoughts of Emelia came to mind, of how difficult it must've been to grow up with a mother incapable of feeling love, no matter how much she ached for the emotion. "But seeing as I don't have true love to offer you, or a heart that beats in sync with yours, I'll offer you the next best thing. Just don't make me regret it."

Of course he had to add that last bit. Arlo wasn't one for sentimental expressions.

"W-what—"

"Shush," he ordered harshly. "I can bind your life force so we're connected. We're stubborn, you and I, and while I've been tough on you for many years, know I've been...I've been proud. You're made of the same grit as I, and it appears our souls are connected in other ways."

I was being shifted and laid upon the hard earth, but it didn't matter. I could be lying on a bed of nails and not feel a thing. Arlo's deep timbre was a melody, a lullaby like Dimitri's. It soothed all my aches. I felt peace.

"Remember these nice words because it's the only time you'll hear them from me. You'll probably forget them anyway, which is preferred. I wouldn't want you to get any silly ideas of affection."

Before I lost consciousness, I glimpsed vines sprouting from the earth and wrapping around my limbs, holding me down. Unable to fight, I lay there, uncaring of what happened to my mortal body. My mind began to drift anyway.

"Now." Arlo stroked at his graying beard, his steel eyes narrowed. "This might hurt a bit."

I passed out the instant his hands pressed against my heart.

Chapter Forty-Nine

Jude

Below the false bravado, I see how lonely Kiara truly is, how much she yearns for acceptance. But some people aren't made to fit into this world—they're made to break it.

Entry in Aurora Adair's Diary, year 42 of the curse

The attack came from all sides.

People who'd long ago taken their last breath now stormed the field. Most wore linen wrapped around their decayed faces, the rot peeking out through the soiled cloth, but others went without, uncaring that pieces of themselves were missing or hanging on by a thin tendon set to snap.

They raised their rusted weapons high in the air as they sprinted down from the hill, escaping the refuge the woods provided. Their eyes were wide and inhuman—depthless pits that glowed whenever they captured me in their sights.

My magic and soul were one, and together, they reacted before my mind caught up.

Flames detonated from my body, licking at every inch of my skin until I was only heat and fire. A pleasant buzzing caused me to shudder, a humming that spoke to the divinity in my blood.

I was a force, not Jude Maddox, a mere mortal. I'd become

something far greater than flesh and blood.

I cast my flames into the horde of attackers, setting them ablaze in one sweep. Their shrill cries punctured the night, those without tongues or lips flailing wildly before succumbing to their final death.

They aren't alive, I reminded myself. It should've been easy to watch such monsters fall, but they'd been people once before, misfortunate enough to have been victims of the curse.

Isiah's chuckle followed me as I strode across the field, flames emanating from my core, my eyes, and my hands. It collided with some of the undead, but there were far too many to wipe out entirely.

Those who had evaded my fire were quick to attack.

One of the bastards lifted his sword while I struck down his ghastly companions, the dull blade aimed at my heart. Before I could dodge out of the way, he made contact.

The steel slipped into my chest, a searing ache shooting from the wound, and my vision momentarily darkened as black spots danced along the edges of my right eye. Blood seeped from the gash, but within seconds of ripping the knife free, my pain transformed into a manageable tingling—I'd experienced far worse by Isiah's hands. I watched in surprise as the flesh knitted together and the wound closed.

The undead man paused, cocking his head.

He didn't stand a chance.

A roar rumbled in my throat, and I set my sight on his chest, right where he'd driven in his blade. The creature shrieked, stumbling back as he erupted, bones and gray skin raining from the skies. There weren't even cinders when I finished him.

I grabbed at my chest, triumphant, all the while feeling Isiah's eyes upon me.

In his mind, I was already set to die, whether he cared for me or not. But he could send all the masked men he desired—

Only the Godslayer could kill me.

A weapon I had on my person.

Perhaps Isiah had been too stunned by my disappearance below his temple to recall I held it. Or maybe he merely didn't see me as a threat, planning to retrieve it once I was weakened from his beasts.

His hubris would be his downfall.

I'd see the dawn. I'd save my girl. And I would make my own fate.

Because. I. Was. Worthy.

The Mist crawled from the brush, licking at my enemies' boots, climbing up their legs and torsos. They were ravenous, their necks craning at impossible angles, their dull eyes searching for a fresh kill.

I released a wave of fire across the blackened field, my magic coming to me with ease.

Fire encircled the bodies of the undead, scorching their bones and permeating the air with foul smoke.

But then I heard screams from the distance—*human* screams.

They were likely swarming nearby homes and villages. Devouring the inhabitants and causing pandemonium.

"You're letting them murder the very people you claim to serve!" I shouted over a shoulder, sensing Isiah's stare boring into me. Out of breath, I slaughtered an incoming creature brandishing a rusted mace, its jaw hanging from its socket, rot and mold breeding across its nose and lips.

"I know it's heartbreaking, Jude, but sometimes the world has to burn in order to be reborn," Isiah said somberly. "We all will rise from the ashes, united and stronger. Besides, I see it as a little incentive for you to accept your fate. *Give in.*"

The friend I'd cared for had died in the Mist. I refused to believe the monster behind me shared his heart. His face remained blank, emotionless, and it chilled me to my core.

A howl shook the branches of the trees.

The hairs on my arms raised, and slowly, I turned toward the woods.

Blue eyes glinted, and haunting wails preceded the sound of paws hammering the ground. Something was coming. A *lot* of somethings.

What fresh hells is this?

A figure took shape at the edge of the clearing, their stature short and petite, long strands of hair billowing behind them. Those fierce blue eyes brightened upon their approach, and I prepared to release another blast of fire when the newcomer's face came into view.

"Ah. I see you've started the party without me." Maliah adjusted her belt of blades, dozens of weapons adorning her willowy frame. Her brown skin glimmered under the stars, her emerald eyes striking, even from such a distance. "And here I thought I was early."

She hadn't abandoned us after all. Elation flourished and fed my magic.

The Goddess of Revenge wasn't afraid to get her hands dirty.

Isiah, on the other hand, was far from pleased. He swiped a hand through his dark hair, scowling. "Stay out of this, Maliah, and I may just let you live."

She continued ahead with a coy grin, tossing daggers at the scrambling undead without so much as taking aim. Each blade struck true, black blood seeping from the centers of their foreheads. She didn't look back.

Prowling at her side was Brax—along with more of Lorian's jaguars. There had to be over ten of the giant beasts, all sprinting in various directions to rip out the enemies' throats.

Maliah was a blessed vision—a warrior fighting for her people.

"*I* may have been too weak to face you," she said, deceivingly calm. "But thankfully, I'm far from alone now."

My pulse skittered. I had a suspicion.

"Even with Jude at your side, I'll defeat you." Isiah lashed out, his shadows trained on the deity.

She laughed before lifting a tarnished shield slung across her back and thrusting it into the earth, kneeling behind it. The shadows hissed when they crashed into the metal, skittering off as though it stung.

"Just as you can't kill me," she retorted. "Besides, we never aimed to kill you. That's his job." She tilted her head my way.

"He would have if he wanted to," Isiah argued, voice cracking. He was trying to convince himself. *Still.*

Maliah lowered her voice. "I take it you found the moonstone?" I nodded, but dread settled in my stomach. Kiara last possessed the talisman. "Good." She turned back to Isiah, more confident than before. If such a thing was possible.

"You should know, Isiah, the God of Beasts is so very angry with you for stealing his powers and targeting Raina's kin. I'd prepare yourself. He doesn't tend to forgive."

As Isiah's lips parted and he anxiously searched the trees, Maliah laughed, the sound like bells. This was what she lived for, the battle, the game.

Maliah's smile widened. "Lorian has always been the sentimental type. Though he often shows his fondness by less… affectionate means."

On cue, Lorian emerged through the thicket, minus the same theatrics as his predecessor.

The hulking giant of a man sprinted to Maliah's left, his wolf pelt strung across his strong shoulders, his snow-white hair tied back with leather strings. He didn't speak, but his stare lingered on me, and he gave a nod so subtle I would've missed it had I not been focused entirely on his stoic face.

"Now." Maliah slapped her palms together. "Let's have some real fun."

Chapter Fifty

Kiara

Some of the earth and soil priestesses say Arlo is headed west.
If this is true, then he's surely on his way to you and the girl.
He better train her properly, or I'll attempt to kill him myself,
with or without an enchanted blade.

Letter from Lieutenant Harlow to Aurora Adair, year 40
of the curse

The pain finally stopped.

The second Arlo arranged his hands on my torso, the pleasant numbness of death had been shocked away, his fingertips emitting sparks of pure, unfiltered power.

I lay there, unable to do anything but accept the agony. It didn't burn like Jude's touch, and his power wasn't icy like my shadows. Arlo's magic was a devastating thing, a force that tore into my flesh, the sensation of phantom hands violently digging around my insides.

"Get it together," Arlo ordered from somewhere above me. "Our training sessions were more painful than this."

"A-asshole," I croaked, my vision gradually settling. The god studied me through narrowed eyes, his lips twisting into a frown.

"Asshole I might be, but I'm an asshole that's kept you alive this long." He reached around me with both hands, scooping me up and into the air. I barely regained my balance before he set me on the ground. When I swayed, he imparted me with a look of warning.

Slowly, I began to feel the tips of my fingers, pins and needles stinging my legs. I was reformed in a way I couldn't describe. Still human, but abuzz with power that hummed through my bones.

"I f-forgot how empathetic you w-were, *Uncle*." My sarcasm didn't hit quite as strongly as I intended given my trembling voice, so I attempted my best glower in its place. "What did you d-do to me? Twist m-my insides?"

He had the audacity to chuckle. "So dramatic. I only saved your life, you ungrateful child." Arlo's hand hovered beside my shoulder, prepared to steady me. "Pain is nothing if nothing is gained."

I groaned. "Always the philosopher."

"Always *right*," he corrected, finally inching back. He coughed awkwardly, then scanned the woods over my shoulder, avoiding my eyes.

I stretched my arms out, wiggling my fingers and my toes. There was an enduring ache in my limbs, but it was lessening with each stiff movement.

Peering down upon myself, I'd expected to be different in some way, having been tied to a god...but I was still me. Seemingly unchanged. My clothes were stained, my trousers ripped, the corset seeped in my blood. I looked half dead with the amount of red defiling the silk, yet Arlo's gift granted me energy. The will to fight.

All was in place except—

Except... My scars. My hands were free of the twisting vines, and my skin appeared smooth where scars had grown to graze my elbows.

"That happened when you presented your soul to that boy,"

he said, not hiding his sneer.

"I..." I didn't know what to feel. A part of me felt naked, and in a way, I missed them.

Arlo scoffed when I lowered my arms. He wouldn't understand anyway.

"You did the right thing. But now, you'll have nothing but yourself to rely on. Which should be enough, given all the time I spent on you. Certainly *should* be," Arlo grumbled. He jerked his chin to the side, to where my still ringing ears picked up the echoes of screams.

Jude.

A wave of panic engulfed me. "Where is he?" I asked, frantically patting for the Godslayer. Of course. I'd given it to Jude. I still carried my own blade in a sheath at my hip, however unimpressive it was in comparison.

If the mark of the shadow beast was gone, did that also mean...

I reached for the scar on my chest tying me to Jude and sighed with relief when my fingers grazed bumpy and raised skin an inch below my beating heart. It was still there.

Somehow, against all the odds, against being saved and practically reborn, I still retained the one scar I never wished to part with. I supposed some bonds couldn't be broken.

Arlo grasped my shoulders, forcing me to look into his stony eyes.

"People think power comes from magic, but that is far from the truth. As much as I take credit for your skill"—his nostrils flared as he paused—"it was you who worked to attain such strength. Achieve such competence. And without the aid of a single spark of divine influence."

I stilled. "Is that a *compliment*?"

Arlo shoved off me like I carried the plague. "Here," he barked, fumbling at his hip. He moved to his sheath, retrieving a sword that had me drooling. Sleek and commanding, the polished steel greeted a hilt of emerald green. Amber gems were embedded in the metal, surrounded by brass vines, and sharp thorns encircled the magnificent hilt.

"Take it before I change my mind." Arlo pushed it forward, still not looking at me. I noted how his hand held a slight tremble.

This was no simple gift.

My jaw dropped, but nevertheless, I reached out, unable to help myself. *Needing* to hold such striking craftsmanship in my hands more than my next breath.

"Hurry. Your commander needs you," Arlo reminded.

I grasped the mighty weapon, my limbs buzzing, my adrenaline picking up. The time to fight neared, but there was one thing left to do before I went into battle.

"My friends," I said weakly, thinking of where they were still imprisoned. "Can you help me reach them? They're stuck right outside the doorway that leads to the chamber with the mirrors."

Arlo growled again. He was more bear than man. Perhaps he'd have been better suited for Lorian's position. "You ask for too much of a weakened god, child. Especially after you broke *my* mirrors."

"The Moon God stole them in the first place," I mumbled, but he was already marching away, compelling me to follow. About thirty feet from where he saved me, a gaping chasm opened in the earth. This must've been where he pulled me out.

I peered down, spotting a hint of white smoke rising to the surface.

Arlo pressed on, walking farther into the trees. A minute later, he dipped into a crouch, placed his hands on the ground, and shut his eyes. The first tremor shook the soles of my boots, the earth shuddering. Vibrations danced up my calves as the quake increased in strength, and I teetered to the side, quickly knocked onto my back.

Arlo glowed a soft blue as he worked, his lids fluttering in concentration. Murderous screams came from beyond the trees.

The fight was well underway, but I had to save my companions, even if I was tempted to find Jude first. If he believed he was the cause of my death, he'd do something obnoxiously heroic.

Another violent shift cracked the earth, the land splitting as the chasm spread.

"What are you—"

I scrambled back before I fell into the pit. More voices rose from below, those not belonging to the battle taking place.

"I may not be capable of entering his inner chamber without my full power," Arlo hissed between his teeth, his brow creasing, "but I command the earth his temple sits upon, and I still have a few devoted followers who haven't abandoned me yet."

"So you could've helped us get outside the main vault this entire time?" I nearly screamed. We'd lost a life on this journey, and Finn was missing a foot. Unbelievable.

"I didn't have the power to help until the prayers were released. So I'd appreciate it if you ceased your whining and accepted the help I can offer you now."

I shook my head. He could hide behind the persona of heartless prick all he desired, but he'd shown his hand. Arlo cared far more than he let on.

Arlo's light slipped down into the split earth, and the voices I'd heard evolved into shrieks. "Your friends are resisting," he added, displeased.

Jake was likely swatting at Arlo's magic with his fists.

Sweat slicked Arlo's brow—the energy leaving him a pale shade of white. He grunted with exertion, already having expended too much when he saved my life.

A minute later, four bodies were hoisted from the depths of the rocky fissure, all flailing wildly, screaming curses—mainly Jake—and deposited at my side, soft blue winding around their torsos. The light flickered gently before sliding back and rushing into the god's body.

Arlo stumbled to his feet and wiped his hands down his robes. "I've done enough," he said to no one at all, though he carefully inspected my friends, who were just now thrusting to their feet, their eyes trained on him, unsure of whether or not to be thankful. To me, he said, "I'm drained and must recover, meaning you must go and do what I trained you for on your own. And don't you dare disappoint me."

A flash of blue, and Arlo vanished into thin air as if he didn't just save my life, make me immortal, and rescue my friends.

He knew how to make an exit.

"Everyone all right?" I asked quickly, scanning them.

Emelia had Finn propped up between her and Jake, the bodyguard's chin lowered, his face in a permanent grimace. And Jake...well, the bastard was smiling at me as though we weren't fighting for our lives.

"I can't say I appreciated the surprise of being yanked through the earth by a god, but I love the new sword, Ki." He whistled appreciatively, eyeing the weapon cradled in my hands. "But how about we put it to use? Those screams don't sound fun."

Indeed.

"Was that really Micah? Or Arlo, I mean?" Liam gasped out, squinting to where the god had disappeared. I nodded in reply. "I didn't believe Jude when he told me, but seeing him..."

Seeing him in all his divine glory was an entirely different story.

I faced Emelia. Her eyes were puffy and red, and she visibly trembled beneath Finn's weight, even with Jake's assistance. To her, I asked, "Can you take care of them while I help Jude?"

I may not have any powers, but Arlo was right. I never needed them.

The Fox nodded stiffly, though she added, "We'll be out of

sight but close by. I won't sit back and watch my son perish if I can do anything about it."

"Emelia," Finn rasped, his voice strained. "Leave me behind and fight for him yourself. I know how much you hate to miss out on a good bloodbath." He cupped her cheek, and she shut her eyes leaning into him. When she opened them, he gave her a knowing nod.

Her decision was made.

"It's decided," Jake said. "Finn and Liam stay behind. Emelia, Ki, and I are going in." I went to protest, but he cut me off. "I haven't left your side once, and I don't plan on doing so now." Jake shot me with a fierce stare, his eyes blazing with intensity, the blue in them shining clear, even in the soft moonlight.

I wouldn't be able to dissuade him.

"Fine. But let me do most of the heavy lifting," I conceded, and he mumbled some unintelligible curses in reply.

I started to walk off toward the sounds of battle when Liam grasped my arm. I had a difficult time looking at him.

"I need my sister," Liam said, his jaw tense, brows drawn together in concern. "Come back to me."

Swallowing thickly, I forced a nod. Liam was having none of it. He snatched me in his arms and wound himself around me tight, squeezing the life from my bones.

"Go out there and be nothing but Kiara Frey," he whispered into my ear. "You've always been enough."

"I love you, Liam." I swiped at the errant tear that had escaped, drawing back.

A furious neigh and the pounding of hooves severed our connection. I'd recognize that glorious sound anywhere, and my heart gave a hopeful lurch.

Starlight. She'd come for me.

Jake and I marched into the woods toward the furious neighs belonging to Starlight, two mortals with not an ounce of power and all the odds against us.

But one thing was certain—

We wouldn't be brought to our knees. We wouldn't surrender. And we'd go down swinging...taking as many monsters with us as we could.

Chapter Fifty-One

Jude

Lorian is a recluse, deigning to serve the beasts he cherishes from a distance. It is said only one entity owns his heart, though she refuses to accept that he also owns hers.

Excerpt from Asidian Lore: a Tale of the Gods

Lorian's jaguars were as deadly as the legends claimed. One of the bastards pounced, capturing an undead creature's throat between his giant maw, a sickening crunch following.

Lorian trailed Maliah, forever scowling, forever sneaking looks at the goddess. When he lingered too long on her, his features would soften just the slightest. I might've believed it to be a concern, but his attention swiftly fell back to Isiah, and he turned to stone once more.

Isiah released a burst of shadows with a roar, his magic snatching a jaguar and flinging it off its feet. When he forced it down to earth, the animal whimpered, the gruesome snapping of bones preceding the silence. The jaguar didn't move.

"You bastard!" Maliah screamed, flinging a dagger his way. His shadows shoved it aside with nothing but a flick of his wrist.

Lorian snagged her hand before she could send another

useless weapon Isiah's way. Her expression morphed from anger to sorrow and then back to rage, but she lowered her arm, glancing briefly at Lorian.

More jaguars surged into the clearing, snapping their jaws at our foes, their growls ringing in my ears. Murderous rage gleamed in their eyes.

Isiah squared off with the approaching gods, his demeanor calm, frighteningly so. Even as they stood together, he didn't fear them, and why would he? He'd stolen their power, their prayers, and he truly believed he would be the only immortal to walk off this field alive.

With his attention diverted, it should've been the perfect opportunity for me to test my new strengths. Yet as I spun his way, fully intent on discharging a blast of fire, I hesitated.

You're like the annoying little brother I never had, Isiah had once told me, right after we'd finished training in the yard. Harlow had been extra grueling that day, his mood sour. Isiah had ruffled my hair, and I'd smacked his arm. Little had he known that simple statement bolstered me for weeks.

The very thought of family had my chest aching, and at the time, I would've done anything to pretend we truly were brothers.

Lost in my memory of a lie, I didn't see the shadows coming until it was too late.

The blast Isiah sent knocked me onto my back. I sputtered for air, wispy black smoke billowing from my open mouth as I choked.

"Get up!" a familiar voice came from behind me, sharp and brimming with fire. "Jude!"

I struggled in earnest, my inner flames surging up my throat, battling with the acidic shadows. They were so cold, they burned.

While my body had taken a beating, I heard *her* voice calling out my name. That was all it took for my magic to flare, to reignite at the possibility of a brand-new tomorrow...a tomorrow with the woman who continued to scream for me from afar.

My girl was *alive*.

Isiah's shadows hissed as they skittered away. I coughed violently, working to release the darkness he'd thrust into my lungs.

Maliah sent a flaming arrow arching through the night sky. The tip lodged into Isiah's shoulder, the flames a blazing red. The god bared his teeth, his focus returning to Maliah and her impeccable aim while Lorian whipped free a blade of his own.

With Isiah cornered and distracted, I turned, finding Kiara atop Starlight, Jake behind her, encircling her waist.

She was more than a warrior then—she was a symbol, a myth captured in flesh. Atop her steed, she raced into a battle that would rock the world.

I couldn't love her more.

Starlight's muscles rippled beneath the brilliant mahogany coat, her eyes aglow with shimmering gold. Kiara patted her flank before she yanked on her reins and threw herself to the ground. She took off into a sprint, her eyes aimed solely on me.

When we collided, she leapt up my body and wrapped her legs around my torso. Kiara didn't shirk from the feel of my heated skin, her fingers tracing every inch she could grab. Her hands were in my hair, and she peered into my eyes, hers alight with precious adoration.

Jake chuckled from behind her, but my attention belonged to her, even as Maliah's curses and endless blades sliced the air. The goddess was laughing, asserting her ground as she made Isiah bleed, Lorian a shadow at her back. I didn't waste the opportunity.

"You're alive," Kiara whispered, just as a shriek sounded.

A jaguar had been struck down before it had the chance to latch onto Isiah's throat. He whirled for Lorian next, but he dodged to the right at a speed that shouldn't have been possible.

"You gave it all up." I reached around my neck to grasp one of her hands. Sure enough, her fingers were bare, mine now decorated with the veiny black designs she'd worn most of her life.

Kiara shook her head. "Between some power I never wanted or needed, and you?" She scoffed. "Not a single regret. Besides, it was the only way to get you out of there, and I'm not done torturing you yet."

I wanted to kiss and strangle her at the same time. "And here I thought *I* was the selfless hero."

She rested her brow against mine. "You were the only thing of value I could've lost."

I pressed a chaste kiss to her lips, my hands in her hair, my fingers tightening. Holding her to me. Knowing that she felt our bond as clearly as I did.

Kiara was my soul's home, the place where my hope lived. Where *I* lived.

She pulled away too soon and slipped to the ground. As she righted herself I noticed the magnificent sword she must've tossed to the ground. It lay next to us, in the dirt.

"You dropped your weapon for me." The words came out in an incredible whisper, and she scoffed, a somber smile curling the corners of her mouth.

"That's how you know I care, dear commander." Kiara lifted onto her tiptoes, twisted her fingers in my hair, and pulled me in for another kiss. She released me just as suddenly, and although I possessed all the power of an immortal, a rush of lightheadedness had me swaying.

My pulse roared in my ears.

I was so far gone for this woman.

"Now," Kiara said, leaning down to snatch the discarded weapon. She raised it before her, nodding to Jake, who'd graciously averted his attention, patting Starlight as she stomped the earth. "Let's go kill the dead."

Before she could dash away, I grabbed her arm.

"Wait." Reaching into my jacket pocket, I retrieved the Godslayer blade and hastily shoved it into her hands. "Take this, just in case." She tried to push it away, but I gave her a stern shake of my head. "Trust me. Do you have the moonstone?"

She patted her pocket where the gem resided, warring with herself, her eyes darkening, as she prepared for an argument.

"Don't make me regret this," she whispered, yanking her old blade from its sheath and replacing it with the onyx dagger.

Good. At least she listened to me. For once.

"Right." Kiara lingered on me for another exquisite heartbeat before she took off and climbed onto Starlight's back. She jerked the reins and sent her and Jake barreling into a mass of gray bodies, her weapon ready to be marked in their blood.

I smiled against my will.

She had that effect on me, even surrounded by enemies, death's hand firmly on my shoulder. But she'd lived, and at that moment, all was right.

Lorian stood his ground in the center of the field, still fighting to maintain the storm that Isiah had become. Maliah aided him, her jaguars and arrows making small cuts in Isiah's silken robes, which were riddled with bloodied stains.

And even though he was outnumbered, Isiah grinned at them like he'd already won. His magic rose from his shoulders, preparing to unleash another round of terror when I acted.

Fire curled around my form with a hiss, and then it went shooting directly for Isiah's heart.

He faltered when my flames struck his back, allowing Lorian the opportunity to stretch his arms, his massive body rippling as though he were fashioned from water, all fluid grace and might. I watched in awe as the God of Beasts grimaced, sweat beading his brow.

He was trying to shift…and failing.

All the legends claimed he could transform into one of the creatures he commanded, but it appeared as if years of missing prayers hindered the ability. He dropped his arms with an incensed sneer, only to emit a shrill whistle.

Isiah readied to finish the job when a pack of wolves bounded into the clearing, called forth by their master. They were the beasts we'd fought in the field when Patrick had deceived us. That felt like a lifetime ago.

"The same old tricks," Isiah muttered, sending wave after wave of glittery darkness toward Lorian. He evaded every intended strike, though his pace gradually slowed.

Meanwhile, Jake and Kiara stood back-to-back, dealing with the incoming pack of the undead. Starlight, not to be outdone, rushed into the horde, trampling their brittle bodies beneath her hooves. The mare attacked any who neared Kiara, and the ones she missed were easily stricken down by Kiara's new sword.

A different kind of heat filled me watching her slice clean through torsos and hack off limbs, her weapon slick with black gore. Her garments were drenched, and now there were only splatters of white remaining. With her hair braided in a crown across her head, she was the warrior goddess of my dreams.

As Kiara stood firm on her own, I strode toward the heart of the battle.

Isiah faced off with Lorian as Maliah sent forth a silver-tipped arrow, her face scrunched with anger. The way she looked at Lorian was not the way a soldier looked at another.

It was *more*.

Before the arrow struck between his eyes, Isiah lifted a hand and swiped it, an inch away from his skull. He snapped it in half.

"You bore me," Isiah said to Lorian. "Always so full of yourself. But I bet you're not feeling so mighty now that I have the power you coveted not too long ago. A power you squandered for selfish purposes!"

This time, when Isiah extended his hands, his shadows struck true. Black-and-silver fog encircled Lorian, trapping him in a prison of burning night.

"Lorian!" Maliah roared into the darkness, slinging her blades so quickly, the silver blurred into one line.

Isiah avoided all but one, its hilt protruding from his stomach. With bared teeth, he ripped it out. Maliah, so full of rage, nearly didn't react in time to save herself.

"R-run!" Lorian shouted, his voice cracking.

Maliah jerked away from Isiah's magic at the last possible second, sprinting into the chaos of the undead bodies. Soon she was hidden by the gray mass of masked men, and Lorian sagged with visible relief.

While Isiah's magic imprisoned the God of Beasts and Prey, my old friend sauntered in my direction, his every step full of arrogance. I prayed it would be his downfall.

"I haven't forgotten about you, Jude," Isiah said. Instantly, my magic simmered. "I know you have the blade. Good luck trying to keep it from me."

"Then come and get it."

Kiara had the blade, and now, Isiah's life would be hers to take.

I skimmed the field, focusing on where she'd last fought beside Jake, but she'd vanished. I didn't have time to search further. The wolves Lorian had summoned were nearly upon us.

Isiah cocked his head in their direction, launching a wave of magic that swarmed the field. His dark magic washed over the pack of wolves at the same time that Lorian unleashed an ear-shattering roar.

Bones splintered and snapped, spines breaking. The wolves whimpered as Isiah killed them in front of Lorian, who screamed until he grew hoarse. One by one, the magnificent animals dropped to the earth, their furry bodies unmoving.

"See what happens when I get angry?" Isiah asked me without emotion. "I really wanted to make your death quick, because I did care for you, but now you've gone and pissed me the fuck off."

His ensuing grin was twisted, wicked in a sense that had me shivering, even as my flames radiated from my torso, brightening the night.

I lifted my newly scarred arm on instinct as his magic fired from his body like an arrow. Heat licked at my skin, flames coming to life. Isiah's magic collided with mine — light and dark dancing for the briefest of moments...*my* dark. Kiara's dark.

Isiah hissed, his shadows not knowing what to do as Kiara's gifted power attacked alongside my fire. A few coils of magic withdrew, while others paused, seeming to sense its likeness and not recognizing an enemy.

I struck again. And again. I hit my old friend with everything I was and didn't know I could be. We fought, Isiah doing his best to block my assault, which had transformed into one of rage and sorrow. Sorrow he'd birthed.

Just when I believed I had him — the god shrinking beneath my force, his frame curling in on itself — Isiah *vanished*.

I heard my mother's scream a moment later.

Chapter Fifty-Two

Kiara

Magic itself is not power. Power comes from knowing your own heart and not fearing what you find.

As said by Cerys, the God of Love, on the day the first heart match was made

I'd left the undead to Jake as I raced across the field to where Isiah and Jude faced off. The Godslayer hummed in its sheath, ready to be used. All I had to do was aim—

A figure darted out from behind the Moon God. Emelia, so slight and dressed in all black, blended into the night. She brandished a weapon of her own, a useless steel dagger with a simple steel hilt. It would do nothing but aggravate Isiah, but she didn't seem to care...

Behind the thief, at the edge of the woods, Maliah reappeared, Isiah's attention mercifully elsewhere. Covered in black blood, she lifted her bow and sent an arrow shooting into the sky, her aim set for...*Emelia?*

Maliah didn't miss, meaning it was a warning shot, the sharpened tip slicing clean through Emelia's pant legs.

Emelia didn't even pause.

Maliah snarled in reproach, aiming now for our mutual

enemy. I thought she'd run off when Lorian was trapped by Isiah's shadows, but she hadn't abandoned us yet. Though even with her and Jude's power combined, it didn't feel like enough.

Her arrow shot across the field, the precision impeccable, her form flawless. It would've killed any mortal, but Isiah's shadows swatted the arrow like a pesky fly. The next arrow, however, pierced his palm, embedding itself deep in his immortal flesh. Maliah grinned in triumph as he ripped it free and smeared his palms down his robes, painting them in crimson as his skin stitched itself back up.

As Maliah distracted Isiah, Jude's flames had grown. They spread over his shoulders and rose above his head, forming two scorching wings of light. His eyes were aglow as he glared daggers at the Moon God.

Jude opened his palms—

Isiah lurched to the side as fire barreled his way. Jude's flames struck the trees behind the Moon God, the branches and leaves erupting in a ball of raging orange and yellow. Jude snarled in frustration, eyeing the tree line.

"Careful," Isiah seethed. He whirled around just as Emelia reached his back, her dagger raised and ready to plunge into his flesh. When he seized her wrist, she let out a sharp cry, the god's hold merciless. Her hand went limp and her blade fell to the grass.

Jude's attention landed on his mother, who was clawing at Isiah's arms. He paid her no attention, almost like she was some housecat who'd discovered claws.

I made out a rumbling cry, Emelia's name being called from the woods. *Finn.* It had to be Finn, stuck where Emelia had left him. My heart ached for him.

Isiah brought a hand to rest around the Fox's neck, and she let loose a string of curses before black fog encircled her throat, cutting off her air. The god lifted his gaze to Jude, a somber expression pulling at his features.

"Enough with the games," Isiah said, upper lip curling. "Give me the blade and let's be done with this. I'll even let your mother live. Even if she doesn't deserve such mercy after what she put you through."

Isiah tightened his grip on Emelia's neck, and Jude hesitated, a muscle in his jaw feathering. His hands trembled, the gold light he'd emitted diminishing with every ragged exhale. He couldn't do it…was physically unable to strike, even with the world hanging in the balance.

Emelia had left him on his father's doorstep as a babe. Yet Jude, a man who claimed he didn't possess a heart, contained one large enough to forgive.

Both had been robbed, both misled. It was a tragedy that had the rare chance of being given a new life. New breath. Hope.

Isiah's magic constricted, and Emelia gasped for air. It wouldn't be much longer. "Give it to me!" he ordered once more, his calm wiped away entirely.

"Let her go and I will," Jude said, though he lacked conviction. His gaze flickered my way briefly, but in that split second, so many things were relayed.

I had the blade. He did not. And judging by the subtle nod of his head, he knew there was little choice but for me to take action.

This was a decision that would forever haunt Jude Maddox and follow him for the remainder of his days. Even if we won, he'd lose a piece of his soul.

"K-kill h-him," Emelia sputtered, clawing at Isiah's arms. A tear slipped from Jude's eye, and he gently shook his head.

"I forgive you," he whispered to her, swallowing thickly. Wetness glazed across the gold in his eyes, muting its glorious sheen. "And I'm so, so sorry."

Emelia forced a smirk to her face, which was quickly turning a ghastly blue. "I l-love you." She sniffled, tears rolling down and past her strained smile. "Now make me p-proud."

Isiah, believing me powerless, weak, *mortal*, didn't consider me a threat as I neared. But I didn't need the powers of a shadow, not when I'd trained my entire life as Kiara Frey. I'd been taught by an immortal. Shunned by my village. I had brandished every weapon known to man and mastered them through hard work and sweat.

I was a warrior, and warriors saved their kingdoms—no matter if the cost would break me.

The Godslayer vibrated in my grasp, and when I sent it soaring through the air, it whistled, seeming to hum in delight. As Isiah's eyes narrowed, realization parting his lips, Emelia elbowed him in the ribs and shifted to the side. Isiah tried to position her body before his, much like a shield, but it was too late.

The dagger struck.

The entire clearing seemed to hold its breath as blood pooled around Isiah's chest, staining his already macabre robes. He let out a sound between a gasp and a sob, craning his neck to where the dagger's hilt protruded from his heart.

Seconds were hours, time frozen. Isiah sputtered and coughed, swaying before he plunged to his knees. The Fox slid out of his limp arms and rolled across the earth. She grabbed at her bruising neck and panted, heaving in fresh air.

Silver light radiated from the Moon God's chest, and an otherworldly humming compelled me to his side.

A single entity of light broke free from his flesh, gradually splitting into three delicate pieces.

Isiah's lips were moving, but no words escaped, his horror written plainly across his face. He watched helplessly as those orbs slipped away…turning him into a mortal.

There was a buzzing in my pocket, a high-pitched whining.

The closer I ventured to Isiah and his magic, the more potent the buzzing in my pocket became.

I grasped the god's shoulders, whose eyes were trained on Jude, a flicker of emotion darkening his eyes. In his screwed-up way, Isiah had cared for him, and while I'd been the one to deliver the fateful blow, Isiah believed it to be Jude's betrayal alone.

The first orb slipped free, a blazing circle of divinity, igniting the field full of dead bodies and ash, and casting away the blanket of darkness. The vibrations in my pocket grew fierce, and I seized the object causing such turmoil...

The stone I'd stolen from the temple.

Its black surface shimmered, and the first of the Moon God's orbs flickered as I lifted the stone before me.

It had summoned Isiah, but I hadn't finished the job and trapped him.

The first orb flickered before crashing into the gem, the force of its impact sending me back a step. Isiah sagged, falling onto his back.

Hovering above his body, I braced for the collision of the second orb, holding my ground when the stone caged it. My hands shook, and it took every ounce of energy to keep steady, to maintain my grip on the gem that now contained two pieces of a god.

The third and final piece escaped.

Dazzling light danced from Isiah's chest and to the gem, sending me reeling when the stone trapped its essence. I fell to my back, grasping all three pieces, the black facets of the stone now glimmering like the night sky.

"You've just d-doomed them all," Isiah choked out, blood slipping over his bottom lip. "You—"

Fire shot into his chest, cutting off his callous words. Jude strode close, his magic scorching Isiah from the inside out. The

Moon God had been transformed into a mortal, the same as Raina. Meaning he could now be killed.

"You're the only one to blame," Jude snarled, his jaw clenched as his eyes glazed with wetness. His fire spread to Isiah's torso, winding around him and traveling to his legs. It scorched his handsome face, devouring his slate-gray eyes until they saw no more. Jude didn't relent, and neither did his magic.

On his back, writhing in agony, Isiah was silent. And soon, he didn't breathe.

Jude's chest heaved as he glared upon the burned body, staring while the remaining flesh and bone smoldered to cinders. He watched until only gray dust stained the grass, his eyes dimming, the fierce gold in them softening. The tears he'd repressed slipped free, dropping to the pile of ash where they sizzled, steam rising into the air. Jude swiped at his eyes, his shoulders slumping as the tension left him.

It was over.

Isiah was defeated.

My chest squeezed as the breeze swept the pieces of him away, but my pain belonged only to Jude and everything he had lost.

"Kiara."

I must've shut my eyes, because when I opened them, Jude was crouched at my side, his hand on my shoulder. So stunned, I hadn't even heard him approach. His touch was too hot, but I hungered for the slight burn. It kept me grounded.

I couldn't believe we'd done it.

"Look at me," Jude pressed, enfolding me in his arms. He rested his chin atop my hair, his breathing uneven as he gripped me for dear life. I spun, clinging to him with equal ferocity.

He was the only thing that felt real, and if I let go, I feared I'd wake and it would all be a dream.

That I'd be a failure. That I had died back there inside the temple and lost him all over again.

Something shifted in the air. Perhaps it was simply the winds changing course, or maybe it was something far greater than I could possibly perceive.

Even snuggled against his shirt, light shone against my closed lids, stealing away the night, growing stronger with the passing seconds.

I drew back.

Soothing pink-and-yellow beams slipped over the tops of the trees, brushing the woods in a sheen of dawn. Jude let out a surprised gasp, his grip on my waist tight. It was pure and soft, almost hesitant, as if it were fighting to not flicker out entirely.

I knew what it was missing—Jude.

Emelia brought Finn from the trees to bear witness, and even as he limped, grimacing from the pain of losing his foot, his eyes were cast to the sky. Finn leaned down to whisper in Emelia's ear, and she drew away to grin at him, her smile full of newfound hope.

Dawn. I never thought I'd see it with my own eyes.

I almost laughed out loud when Jake released a joyous whoop and then proceeded to grab Liam's hand. Jake tugged him into a kiss, one hand slipping into Liam's curls. They were oblivious to us all, and while I didn't linger on Liam and my friend for long, I noticed the enormous grins spreading across both of their faces when they came up for air.

I knew it was inevitable. They hadn't exactly been discreet.

"You did it," Maliah said, her eyes flicking to the patch of scorched earth where Isiah's life ended.

Lorian—who'd been freed from his cage of shadows upon Isiah's death—now joined us. He tilted his unsmiling face to where the weak light fluttered into the sky, remaining close to Maliah, a silent protector at her back.

Surrounded by friends, family, and gods, I twisted to Jude.

He cupped both my cheeks, a single tear dripping from his shimmering, mismatched eyes. He tugged me even closer until we were heart to heart.

"Good thing you have exceptional aim, recruit."

I let out an exhausted exhale and flicked his nose. Elation bubbled through me.

"Now is not the time for jokes," I reprimanded, surprised the roles had been reversed. He merely grinned like the luckiest bastard in the realm. And maybe he was. We all were.

"You realize the sun is trying to rise as we speak," I whispered. Tears ran down my cheeks and slipped between my lips, salt exploding on my tongue. There was sorrow and hope and possibility happening all around us, and we only had eyes for each other.

Jude kissed my nose, his hands drifting to my face, his thumbs caressing my dirtied cheeks. "I'd rather look at you."

"Going sappy on me, Commander?" I asked, feeling how swiftly his heart beat against mine. They made their own music, celebrating the future we'd been dreaming of.

"For you, Kiara? Always."

I didn't dare take my focus off him. I simply desired to stare at the boy who'd robbed me of a heart. I'd happily relinquish it over and over again.

"You did good, child."

Jude shifted, freeing me from his arms as Arlo approached. The God of the Earth and Soil glided to our side, soft blue light emanating from his form. Color had returned to his cheeks. Isiah's demise had given him new life, had given all the gods new life.

When his attention shifted to my pocket, I went still, understanding causing my head to spin.

The stone.

"You have a choice, Kiara," Arlo said solemnly. "You are

worthy of this gift, but only you can make the decision. Accept the power of the night, or..."

Or remain on earth, still tied to Arlo's life, immortal but powerless.

I turned to Jude, Jake, Liam, Emelia, and Finn. I held all of their eyes.

A whole unexplored world beckoned, and I had always desired to travel it, to brandish my blade for good. To be the protector of those who couldn't defend themselves.

If I were to be a god and properly wield my power, I'd be dedicated to the skies, forced to roam only when the night reigned.

Raina had made the mistake of shirking her duties for her lover—spending her days and nights on earth—but I knew such a thing could not be done again.

The world deserved better.

And I did, too.

I regarded Jude, whose crinkled eyes told me he knew my answer before I spoke it and that he understood. A gentle smile tugged at his mouth.

"You were meant to be here, Kiara," he whispered, leaning to brush his lips against the shell of my ear. I shivered. "You were born to be this realm's savior." His voice cracked slightly. "There's so much more for you out there, and if you chose the life of a god, you'd be giving away pieces of yourself."

"Decide, child," Arlo reminded, his voice firm. Always so firm.

"Then, no. I do not want to accept the gift," I said firmly.

Lifting onto my tiptoes, I kissed Jude tenderly, enjoying how his mouth melded to mine.

Two pieces forming a whole. My entire body burned, now, almost *too* hot—

A sudden burst of ice raced down my frame and to my

fingertips, which were threading through his hair.

I drew back, slowly, so very slowly, and brought my hands to my face.

My scars. They were back.

I stared up at Jude, mouth parted, heart thudding. "How?" I asked, marveling at the blue-black veins that I once reviled. They were lighter, shining with iridescent hues of gold and silver each time I twisted my wrist.

Jude smiled, so warm and endearing I melted. He tucked a stray strand of hair behind my ears, leaning down to whisper so only I could hear.

"It never belonged to me, Kiara. I'm merely returning what you allowed me to borrow."

"But what if I hurt—"

"Being touched by darkness doesn't make you dark. You wielded the powers you were given to help others, and I will not be the cause of you giving up yet another piece of yourself."

I couldn't love this man more. He saw beyond the lies I told to hide myself away, and he worshiped the beautifully imperfect soul that would forever be tied to his.

"I love you, Jude Maddox. From now until my final dawn."

Jude pressed another kiss to my temple, lingering. His lips whispered against my brow as he said, "And I will spend every one of my nights loving you in return."

I smelled flowers in the air, a fragrance I wasn't familiar with. It was sweet and soothing, and it made a home in my lungs. The breeze that carried it whirled around the two of us, tickling my exposed skin, and while I shut my eyes and leaned into Jude, it grew more potent.

My arms pressed deeper, trying to tie him to me forever. But cool air replaced his heat, and when I opened my eyes, the boy who'd become a god was no longer in my hold.

I stumbled back, searching the field. Jude was...gone.

"He has to greet the new day," Arlo said, his steadying hand reaching for my shoulder. "It was what he was born to do, after all."

I wiped at my tears, which were once again flowing. I didn't care who witnessed them. For once, Arlo didn't chastise me, and when he wrapped his arms around me, I returned the embrace.

"Do not worry, child. Every day ends with the night."

Arlo stepped back, clearing his throat as though he'd never hugged before. Perhaps he hadn't.

I would see him when the day was done. I knew this in my bones. In my core. My soul. Hesitantly, I asked the question that had been on my mind from the moment I declined the gift of divinity. "What will happen to the stone?"

"We will need to seek a worthy vessel to carry such power," he said. "Until that someone is located, I will watch over the stone and the orbs it contains. I will make sure night and day remain in balance, but no ruler will reign until a soul is found. Though I suggest we find them as soon as we possibly can."

I nodded. "Then I will offer my services to find this vessel." We locked eyes, my mentor's softening until they became unrecognizable.

"And I shall accept."

"Hey!" Jake rushed into our fold. "You better not leave me after all this." Liam was hot on his heels. He grinned widely before dipping his chin my way.

Arlo released a frustrated noise from deep in his throat. "I accept all the help you can give, Kiara Frey. Bringer of Light. Warrior of Asidia." He looked at the sky, to where the light grew stronger now, the fluttering glow becoming clearer, brighter. The sphere that was both the sun and a boy blessed by fate was finally rising.

I shut my eyes and relished the tingling warmth spreading across my body. I imagined my grandmother smiling from wherever her soul rested.

A hand slipped into mine and my eyes opened. Another hand gripped my free one. Jake and Liam sandwiched me between them, and my heart panged.

"I knew you'd be an adventure," Jake whispered in my ear.

I nudged his shoulder. "Shut up, Jake, and watch the damned sunrise with me."

Light may be casting the world in gold, but I couldn't wait until the blanket of darkness cloaked me.

I had a god to find.

The world of Asidia was graced with its first sunrise in over five decades.

The people stumbled out into the streets, the rays of gold warming their upturned faces. There was a sense of quiet hope that grew louder the higher the sun climbed into the sky.

Days would pass, and a story that would one day become a legend spread across the realm, about a girl tainted by shadows and a mortal boy turned a god.

And while the boy guarded the light, the girl became a symbol of the future the people so desperately needed.

They called her Dawn's Champion.

EXCERPT FROM ASIDIAN LORE: THE LEGEND OF DAWN'S CHAMPION

EPILOGUE

JUDE

A long time ago, I'd dreamed of the sun.

It was this untouchable orb in the sky. A distant thing that would bring light and warmth but not much else. I lived so long in the darkness that the possibility of it meaning anything had been inconceivable.

Then the sun and what it represented changed one fateful day in a town called Cila.

I watched a young woman defend her brother in the square of her village, and a flood of life heated my blood. At that moment, I felt hope. The possibility of a new beginning.

That was what the sun was. What it represented.

It was a gift of a beginning.

My obligations had been filled for the day. I was exhausted, even as an immortal, but I knew I wouldn't get rest tonight.

My mother was getting married in a small ceremony overlooking the southern marshes.

Apparently, after our near-deaths, she'd finally accepted Finn's proposal. A proposal delivered five years ago.

Even Arlo had been invited.

The cranky god had become a permanent fixture in my life. During the very early days of my ascension, he'd been at my side, guiding my hand, easing the transformation.

He didn't offer smiles or kind words, but he'd been there when I needed him, even if he occasionally tested my temper. Arlo was many things, but cordial wasn't one of them.

The day I invited him to come to my mother's wedding, Arlo grumbled something about wasting his time with frivolity. Yet the following day, he asked if Emelia preferred white flowers or red.

Of course, she chose red.

Each new dawn I soared across the skies and guided the sun to its proper place in the heavens. And when I was gifted with the wishes of those who prayed, I answered the best way I could. It had taken months to learn how to focus the sun's energy on the areas requiring the direst of aid, the lands that needed its rays in order to yield food and fill empty bellies.

But the sun heeded my commands eagerly, its life essence connected to mine. All it took was a shared thought, and I was granted its strength.

Sometimes, I'd bring out the sun from behind the clouds on the whim of a child's wish. Other times, I hovered above the earth, observing the people who now thrived in the daylight, their faces etched in grins, faith restored to their souls.

That was the beautiful thing about light—it awarded people hope.

Nighttime could be stunning in its own right, but the sun? I found by simply basking in its heat, parts of myself I didn't realize needed mending could heal.

After I dragged the sun down to rest, my heart required a different kind of warmth only *she* could provide.

Gliding to earth on a cloud of wispy white, I landed on a

hillside at Montemore.

The region rested in the marshlands, home to a people in dire need of aid. Once Cirian had been pronounced dead, the realm rose in upheaval, no region knowing how to efficiently govern and some fighting for supremacy.

But that was a problem for another day.

My eyes found her form immediately. Kiara Frey, Leader of the 7th Legion of Asidia—or, as the people named them, the Dawn Chasers—gazed over the cliffs, tendrils of copper hair flying free from her loose braid.

Her scars were proudly displayed, no gloves in sight, and her sword, Echo, was slung across her back, ready to slay any who dared threaten her or those she loved.

And of course, her faithful steed stood watch. Starlight had fought alongside us on that field, and she'd been Kiara's devoted companion ever since.

I shouldn't continue to call her Starlight, though, as Thea was her true name, Raina's legendary steed. When we first spoke the name aloud, the mare kicked her hooves in the air and neighed so loudly, wolves howled in the distance. She looked at us as if to say, *Finally.*

"Took you long enough, Commander," Kiara muttered without turning. I smiled. She could always sense me as thoroughly as I could her.

I took my place beside her, reaching for her hand and pressing a kiss on her knuckles. Her scars shimmered a brilliant gold before settling to a luminous silvery-black.

"So impatient." I *tsk*ed. My eyes fell to the speckles of blood marking her skin. I froze. "Are you all right?"

She wound her arm around my waist and tugged me close. Resting her head over my chest, she listened to the beating heart caged inside.

"I'm fine," she admitted on a sigh. "It belongs to an enemy.

The lords battling for the throne are sending out more and more soldiers…and they're ruthless."

I relaxed, though I felt guilty for feeling joy at the death of another.

"Each day is a battle to be won." She tilted her chin, a hesitant smile blooming. Instantly my skin warmed and a subtle glow spread across my every inch. Kiara merely shook her head. "I see you've missed me. You're even glowing."

"Such an ego," I teased, kissing her brow. She flicked my nose.

"As if you don't have one also, almighty *god*," she returned, raising a brow. "I saw how brightly you burned today, like the show-off you've become."

"I was trying to impress you." I shrugged. "Seems it worked."

Silence fell, blissful quiet. I held her and she held me. Nights were ours, the darkness ours. We'd claimed it for ourselves long ago.

As much as I yearned to have Kiara at my side, always, I understood her well enough to realize she'd never be happy if kept away from the kingdom she wanted to protect. To the people, she was already a living legend, and to most, a symbol of rebirth.

I didn't mind sharing her in that respect, but once the moon rose, she was mine.

Except for tonight. I bit down my groan. I'd become greedy, and when nine struck, we were all to be gathered to witness my mother marry Finn. That time was swiftly approaching but we had a few more minutes to spare. I planned on taking advantage.

"Any news on the vessel?" I asked, running my fingers down the side of her arm. Goose bumps pebbled in my wake.

"Yes, actually," she said, sitting up straighter. I groaned when she pulled away, but my protests died upon seeing shimmering excitement grace her eyes. "There's a girl a few villages from here that Arlo believes has promise. We should find her soon. Liam has been utilizing his connections and mapping out a course."

Liam had eagerly taken to being Kiara's advisor.

While he didn't engage in battles, his place beside his sister was equally as vital, and he'd discovered he had a knack for diplomacy, an area in which Kiara *sometimes* could be found wanting. Jake, unsurprisingly, preferred the blade to Liam's pen.

"What is it?" Kiara asked when I remained silent, content to lose myself in her.

"I'm just thinking about how absolutely stunning you look tonight." I pressed a kiss to her full lips, nipping at the bottom one. Not a second went by when I wasn't grateful to be hers. Her choice.

Choice. So many had been stolen from me, but now, so many lay at my feet.

Our feet.

Kiara cupped the sides of my face and held me in place, her lips working a quick trail up my jaw, my cheeks, my nose. She leaned her brow against mine.

"When I first met you, I never would've believed you might be a romantic at heart," she murmured, her warm breath tickling my already heated skin. It flashed brighter, my reaction to her something I couldn't hide. Not that I wished to.

"I kept telling you that you've thoroughly ruined me. I meant it."

Kiara grinned widely, an impish smirk tilting her lips. "Well, Jude Maddox, be prepared to be ruined every night for the rest of our immortal lives."

My insides boiled and the scar on my chest twinged. It still retained her mark, her hauntingly beautiful vines, and whenever I missed her, all I had to do was look at it. Some bonds even magic couldn't wipe away.

Kiara's lips were once more on mine, and the cliffs became illuminated by my unearthly glow. By my pure *joy*.

In my life, I'd worn many faces, but none had been as true as the one I wore for her—a woman whose inner radiance was a wavering flame in a sea of night. And I believed the darkness itself couldn't help but fall in love with the way her brilliance made its shadows dance.

We fell to the cool grass, a tangle of hands and limbs and lips.

Our time together was a gift, and I'd spend every night selfishly kissing the woman who shattered the skies and brought light back to a realm that was only now relearning the magic of hope.

· · ·

Red flowers surrounded the mouth of a cave decorated with lush green vines. Arlo had outdone himself, the ill-tempered god smugly sitting in the corner. He didn't make an effort to speak to anyone besides Harlow.

The older knight returned for us after the battle, and he hadn't left us since. He claimed Kiara needed guidance... especially seeing as she'd suspected *him* of all people to be an enemy.

Now, he was a part of her legion, a few other warriors joining the ranks in the months following Isiah's downfall. Jake acted as her second, much to Harlow's dismay. The pair argued constantly.

Currently, the former lieutenant mirrored Arlo's pose, the two of them leaning against nearby trees, whispering among themselves. Probably complaining.

"Ki!" Jake tossed an arm over her shoulder. He tugged her into an exuberant hug, his face aglow from the effects of the wine being served. Liam appeared on his heels, shaking his head at his boyfriend. Apparently opposites did attract.

Before Jake could ruffle Kiara's hair as he was often prone to do, she returned to my side and gripped the fine red jacket I'd chosen for tonight, the style reminding me of Dimitri's old coat.

Kiara had to be forced out of her armor by none other than the bride herself. The Fox shocked us all by dictating the details of the celebration as if she commanded an army. Who would've thought she possessed a romantic side? Albeit a violent one.

Behind Jake, Kiara's parents glided into view. Her father stole her from my hold, pressing her against his brawny chest and wrapping his arms around her as if she'd float away. Tears slipped down his cheek, his pride evident. When he finally released her, her mother inched forward, her long brown hair billowing in the subtle breeze. She gripped both of Kiara's shoulders and looked her daughter over, her dark eyes glittering. They'd been reunited after we escaped, and while they had a lot of tense history to work through, I knew they were making an effort.

As her parents took their seats across the aisle, I turned to Kiara. My fingers grazed her hip, my hold firm and possessive. After I'd thoroughly ruined her up on the cliffs mere minutes before our arrival, she'd slipped into a gold dress that fell to her feet. Intricate ropes crisscrossed below her breasts, working their way up to her neck, where they were tied into a knot. Simple, yet something Emelia couldn't yell at her for.

On cue, a harp played, and I forced Kiara to follow me to our seats at the front of the aisle.

Jake and Liam sat beside us, the pair's hands intertwined. Liam had lost the top half of his finger after escaping the temple, but Jake assured him that it only made him look devastatingly roguish. Liam dropped his head on Jake's shoulder, prompting Jake to brush his fingers gently through his curls.

Jake had been wrong after all about not wishing to settle down. I wondered if Kiara and I were as nauseatingly affectionate. I suspected we were somehow worse.

I smiled at that.

"What is it?" Kiara asked, leaning over to whisper in my ear.

"I'm...happy," I said. It was such a silly thing to utter, but to say it and mean it? I never realized how rare that was.

The music swelled, joined by a lute, and I knew my mother would walk down the aisle any moment now. Finn slid into place with the aid of a finely carved crutch. Emelia had commissioned the piece herself, even adding the depictions of foxes along its length.

Finn yanked out a bright orange handkerchief, already dabbing below his eyes. The color was the same shade as Dimitri's coat, and I knew that Dimitri was smiling upon his old friend from the afterlife.

Kiara boldly tilted my head her way, our lips an inch apart.

"This is just the start," she said, and my stomach tied into knots. Her nearness often ruined me in all the best ways. Yet she was right; this was the beginning, for all of us.

I closed the distance and kissed her lips, savoring her for only a second before Jake got the chance to elbow me.

Not the time or place, I had to remind myself. *Later.*

Drawing away, I returned to the aisle, just in time for Emelia to emerge. She'd chosen to have her ceremony at night so I could attend, and she locked eyes with me immediately, a relieved look gracing her severe features.

Kiara's shadows swelled up, curling down the aisle to dance at the thief's feet, the shimmering wisps caressing the hem of her midnight blue dress. She rolled her eyes at Kiara but grinned, nonetheless. Her power highlighted Emelia's joy, which shone on her face in a way I'd not seen.

I beheld a now openly crying Finn, though he wasn't the

only one with tears shining in his eyes. Liam, Jake, and even Arlo and the stoic lieutenant were fighting their emotions. Behind us were the newest soldiers Kiara had recruited, and in them, I saw determination to mend our broken world.

Tomorrow was a new day. A new battle. A new obstacle—

But I found that surrounded by all those I loved, holding Kiara's hand—bolstered by her obstinate faith—I could do anything. *We* could do anything.

And together we could accomplish the impossible. Like set fire to the night.

ᴀCKNOWLEDGMENTS

Ever since I was young, I was enthralled by the moon, believing it was the closest thing to magic I'd ever get. I even started writing *under* the moon when life turned cruel, sneaking off from wherever I was, notebook and pen in hand, eager to escape. It became the light I used to craft my dreams, and it will always be a symbol of perseverance for me, of hope. And hope is what I pray is taken from this story.

I want to thank the people in my life who have lifted me up when I could barely stand. The people who held my hand when I told myself I wasn't good enough, strong enough, smart enough to be someone of value. My husband's faith never wavered. He's my best friend, my confidant, my own sun. He shines on all my darkness and refuses to let me hide. I've never loved a soul as I do his.

To my mother, who has never stopped believing in me. To Justine Bylo, who helped me write again after I'd lost my way, and to Jen Bouvier, who edited this beast of a novel three times. To my friend Ashley R. King, whose support is precious, and brilliant, and beautiful—I am lucky to have you in my life.

I want to thank the team at Entangled and profess my sincerest gratitude. Liz Pelletier for granting me this chance to write and rediscover my passion. To Stacy Abrams, Bree Archer, Heather Riccio, Brittany Zimmerman, Meredith Johnson, Adia

Wright, Brittany Marczak, and Curtis Svehlak. You all have made me believe in magic once again.

And to the readers...how can I thank you for reading this book? How can I thank you for reading a piece of my soul? You are the reason I craft stories and the reason I dream. Thank you for dreaming with me.

Let's be friends!

Instagram @EntangledTeen

Facebook @EntangledTeen

TikTok @EntangledTeen

bit.ly/TeenNewsletter

entangled teen

an imprint of Entangled Publishing LLC